"TANKA WAKAN

the recumbent hr... slowly, and you cannot break his heart, for you are not his children.

"You new ones must tell your elders: stay in the valley; he will endure you there. Tend your crops and your animals. But do not tear his flesh with machines, as the Quakers did in the beginning, and make only as many children as the valley can keep. And tell the ships of many humans not to come here, for if they come these humans will die, and you will die with them before your time; that is what will happen: they will come so far and die! It will be terrible for us and terrible for them, and in the end all of you will certainly be dead."

ISAAC ASIMOV PRESENTS

PENNTERRA

JUDITH MOFFETT

WORLDWIDE®

TORONTO · NEW YORK · LONDON · PARIS
AMSTERDAM · STOCKHOLM · HAMBURG
ATHENS · MILAN · TOKYO · SYDNEY

For Ted,
my Quaker-in-Residence

The author wishes to thank the National Endowment
for the Arts for a Creative Writing Fellowship Grant
that helped support the writing of this novel.

PENNTERRA

A Worldwide Library Book/October 1988

ISBN 0-373-30305-X

First published by Congdon & Weed, Inc.

Quotations from the poem "The Ghosts of the Buffaloes"
by Vachel Lindsay from *The Chinese Nightingale and Other Poems*
(Macmillan, 1917).

Quotations from the poem "Unicorn" by Judith Moffett from
Whinny Moor Crossing. Copyright © 1984 by Princeton University
Press. "Unicorn" reprinted with permission of Princeton University Press.

Quotations from the poem "Congo" by Vachel Lindsay from
The Congo and Other Poems (Macmillan, 1914).

Printed in U.S.A.

Nonviolence

by Isaac Asimov

Forty-five years ago, in the very first story of my *Foundation* series, I had my hero say, "Violence is the last refuge of the incompetent."

Not everyone thinks so, of course. Big men are often firm in the belief that violence is the correct way of deciding a dispute, especially if they are facing small men. People with guns are similarly firm in that belief, especially if facing unarmed people. And a mob believes in violence when facing an individual. In short, if violence seems as though it is on your side then you like it.

Of course, if big people, armed people, many people just happen to be on the side of the right, then violence becomes a way of ensuring justice, doesn't it? We watch an infinite number of movies and television plays in which right defeats wrong because it always happens that the "good guy" just happens to be bigger and stronger than the "bad guy"; the good guy just happens to be able to shoot faster and more accurately than the bad guy.

Sometimes it is clear that the good guy is more stupid than the bad guy, who is very often presented as the most intelligent person in the drama. However, the good guy is sometimes saved by the fact that he has a horse that is smarter than he is, and besides the faster gun beats the faster mind every time. And so we are taught not only that violence is the path to right and justice but intelligence is usually wicked.

My own feeling is that violence usually brings about the victory of the unjust and barbaric. As an example, the number of muggers who knife, shoot, or otherwise inflict violence on peaceful citizens is far greater than the number of muggers who are themselves beaten up by those same peaceful citizens.

The answer of the violence-lovers is: "Give all those peaceful citizens guns of their own."

Why not? In this way, we convert everyone to muggers of a sort and we have gunfights with each side claiming the other drew his weapon first. (My own bet, in this connection, is that the more experienced gun-toter—i.e., the greater ciminal—will win virtually every time.)

The situation of mugger-versus-mugger is nowhere truly to be found in any nation, but I am told that the nation which most nearly approaches it is the United States, for nowhere else is there such a tender love for guns and weapons.

If we want the real mugger-versus-mugger situation, however, we must consider the international situation. Every nation that is larger than a vest-pocket is armed. Every nation is convinced that in all disputes it is right and the other nation is wrong. Every nation seems to feel that it is thoroughly justified in using all possible force any time it gets mad.

So what do we have? Terrorism and the constant threat of nuclear war.

What a great world!

Isn't there any way of running the world without making violence the decisive way of judging between right and wrong? Says the lover of violence: "No way. We have always had wars. That's just the way things are. The answer is to make ourselves stronger than the other guy."

That is exactly what the other side says, too.

We consequently live in a world in which the Soviet Union disposes of enough weapons to kill everyone on Earth 50 times over, and feels insecure because the United States has enough to kill everyone 60 times over. Then, because we suspect that the Soviet Union really disposes of enough to kill everyone 70 times over, we feel insecure, too.

What a relief both sides would feel, if they could believe with all their heart and soul that the enemy, no matter how hard he tried could only kill everyone once—just once. We would all dance in the streets, wouldn't we?

Does this strike you as making sense, by the way? Does it sound like the action of competent people?

A reader once wrote: "If violence is the last refuge of the incompetent, why is there so much violence in the world?"

And I replied, "Because there is so much incompetence."

In any case, Judith Moffett's *Pennterra* takes up the matter of violence and nonviolence.

Part One SWARTHMORE: MEETINGS

...whenever Friends came together and sat down in stillness and quietness they came to find the benefit, advantage
and glory thereof in a wonderful and remarkable manner,
for they became all as one body...yea in silence and ceasing of all words they were inwardly refreshed, comforted,
quickened and strengthened through that communion and
communication of spirit and life of God...as from one upon
all, and from all upon one.

George Keith, 17th-century Quaker

Each individual will be acutely aware of his "oneness" with
life itself.... The goal of the meeting, that destiny to which
it is being called, is unity.

George H. Gorman,
The Amazing Fact of Quaker Worship

1 George and KliUrrh

When the stock alarm clanged, George Quinlan was on his knees in the hot sun, weeding sweet corn with a short-handled hoe. A very small part of his attention sufficed to direct the blade—a bite-shaped piece cut from a tractor panel—deftly round and between the bases of the stately plants and grub out whatever seedling invaders had sprouted in the weeks since the previous weeding. The rest of his mind was free to go on fretting about his forthcoming meeting with the officers of the *Down Plus Six*, the colony ship whose arrival would soon be the second most eventful occurrence in the six-year history of the settlement the Quakers had named Swarthmore.

George frowned and sighed unhappily as he weeded. He was forty-five years old, a superb geologist, a widower, a father, and a settlement leader, with a minor back malady that limited his field work assignments to hydroponics, aquaculture, light stock duty, and row crops—reaching across the wide raised vegetable beds put a lot of stress on a lower back. To his own surprise he had taken to peasant-style farming wholeheartedly and at once, and would ordinarily have "walked" along the rows on his knee pads entirely absorbed, keeping his back nice and straight, neatly extracting the slow-growing (but madly greedy) blue-green native "weeds" from the soil and taking a puzzling but profound satisfaction in performing this simple task well. Today his consciousness would not stay submerged in the work; he minded badly that this should be so.

When the triangle began to shout its pattern of five short whangs (for "stock alarm") followed by two long ones (for "sheep") he rose stiffly, groaning a little. All eleven other members of his work squad popped up too between the rows of corn, dropping hoes, shucking gloves, unstrapping knee pads, pelting off at the best speed they could muster through the settlement toward the sheep pastures on the other side of the river they

called the Delaware, a quarter of a mile away. Jogging behind the
field of sprinters, George could see other runners converging on
the pastures from several directions. None carried any kind of
weapon, for no native predator could eat a sheep with profit, and
in six years none had ever killed one, or even so much as chased
one, out of devilment—a trait the native wildlife seemed remarkably to lack. Almost certainly the devilment would turn out
to be of the flock's own making: they'd have broken out and
strayed, fallen into the river, hung themselves up in a snaggle of
rotten willow fence—

"—in the river meadows!" someone shouted hoarsely as the
runners pounded across the bridge, and they rushed in a pack
around the animal enclosures without slowing down, angling
upstream toward a broad handsome strip of alfalfa bordering the
river, into which George could now see flattened signs of the
sheep's untidy progress. Puffing hard—he was a swimmer, not
a runner—he scrambled down the bank and splashed through the
little pasture brook, ignoring the stepping stones farther along,
then fell belatedly into position in a wing of beaters yelling and
clapping as they edged through the strip and spread out along the
riverbank. The idea, obviously, was to chase the sheep back out
the way they'd come without damaging the precious hay themselves, and George whooped and yelled with the others. No car-
nivores but Quakers had been brought to Pennterra; the present
occasion was typical of a good many that had caused them all to
regret not having made an exception of some shelties to control
the sheep.

These now blundered witlessly about in the tall alfalfa, baaing
and trampling their winter fodder like the idiots they were. Finally, giving up, the beaters entered the meadow from the river
in a straight line. The sheep, giving up as well, plunged out the
other side into the lane, to be smartly seized and hauled back to
their proper pasture by an assortment of muscular young people, and moments later, with neither discussion nor the giving of
a single order, the incident was over.

George stood with the other drivers afterwards, laughing and
swabbing his forehead with a rag, and watched the two dozen
ewes and large late-summer lambs be manhandled away: black-
faced Suffolks, long-fleeced Herdwicks—not many of those
left—and the all-white Dorsets, which the breeders had been
concentrating on for the past year or so, since these had proved
best adapted to conditions in the valley. George was fonder,
himself, of the Herdwicks, a surefooted English mountain breed

able to withstand harsh weather and thrive on rough forage—
traits superfluous on Pennterra, where nothing growing in the
maroon-colored mountains northwest of the settlement, from
whence the Delaware descended, could nourish a sheep, nor so
much as a cockroach, brought from Earth. The Dorsets made
excellent mothers, superior wool, and abundant mutton; for
these reasons they also made better sense as homestead stock to
be kept on pasture.

Soon the Herdwicks might be phased out altogether—though
a decision to allow any Earth-born species to become extinct on
Pennterra must always be emotion-fraught and reluctantly taken.
Almost certainly, there would never again be Herdwicks here
when these were gone.

Gradually the groups began to break up and straggle back to
whatever they'd been doing when the alarm stuck. "Little Boy
Blue, come blow your horn," quoted handsome Andrew Bell
cheerfully, pausing to throw one bare sweaty arm around his
wife, Norah, in passing. "The sheep's in the meadow, the cow's
in the corn."

"Watch out who you're calling a cow," said Norah; but she
kissed Andrew—a gingerly kiss, for his whole face was sweat-
soaked—before trudging back toward the cornfield with George,
while Andrew went off with a few others to find and fix the break
in the fence. "Come fall," said Norah grimly, "that hurdle
fencing has got to be replaced. Not repaired, replaced—sooner
if possible, if anybody has a minute to spare before harvest.
Which I doubt," she said, "but if the goats get into the orchard
again we'll be in a bad way. That one little midnight raid of theirs
last spring is probably going to mean rationed apples and no
pears for adults this winter as it is. God, I wish I knew whether
the Sixers're bringing us some trees!"

A third corn-chopper, overhearing this, fell into step on the
other side of George. "If they haven't, won't we pretty much be
forced to ask KliUrrh about fencing with mountain hardwood
now, George? I know you're trying to tread carefully there, but
it's a pure waste of time to put this stuff up," waving vaguely at
the treelike shapes bent out over the river, "and nobody wants
to dip into the ship's stores again for fencing. That'll go for the
Down Plus Six as much as the *Woolman*, wouldn't you think?
We'd buy a little time that way, but we're going to be mending
fences for—well, effectively forever." The speaker had a hesi-
tant, flat, rather didactic way of speaking and hair as red as a
brick.

When George started to reply, Norah butted in tensely: "Oh, Bob, how can KliUrrh possibly say no? What are we supposed to do, tether every single sheep and goat to a mesh lead? And a stone fence would have to be *how* tall to keep a billy goat and a doe in season away from each other? He'll *have* to let us use hardwood, for a while anyway."

"We could make cement and forms from local stuff and stuff we brought," said the redhead, Bob Wellwood, "and a stone wall's zero maintenance; in the long run stone's our best bet. But a fence like that would take a couple of years to build; we still need something for the short run. And I don't think dry stone's worth the trouble, not for us—nobody, here's got the know-how, and it takes a lot of skill to do right. We'll *always* need fences," he repeated in his flat loud voice. "KliUrrh *knows* that. I think you ought to bring it up now, George—ask him to tide us over till we have time to build in stone." Then, finally, Bob and Norah both stopped talking and looked expectantly at George, who walked a few paces farther, head down, to be sure they were really done before speaking.

"We've been over this all before," he said finally, glancing sideways at Bob. "Nothing's changed. There'd be no objection at all to our using the deadfall from the mountain hardwoods however we liked, if there were any *flokh* trees or whatever growing below the falls, but the elders insist they don't want us wandering out of bounds for any reason, and they *mean* it—they really do mean it. KliUrrh himself might take a more flexible line, but he couldn't decide something like that on his own. There's just no point in asking, Bob. Maybe when our credibility's better."

"In about fifty years," said Bob, not bitterly; he was a dogged but pretty reasonable young man. "But still, would it *hurt* to ask? I know you know KliUrrh better than any of us, but mightn't you be guessing wrong on this one?"

"Oh, it wouldn't hurt, exactly, but it would reinforce his impression of us as dangerously childish characters, and I'd just as soon not. If we'd known when we chose this site that we'd be here forevermore, we'd have looked more carefully and picked someplace with hardwood and a swamp, a lot closer to the coast. But we didn't and there it is." The bridge, planks laid across cask pontoons, bobbed under them as they padded back across the river. From the small vantage of its height George looked about him at the sun-saturated landscape, at the cultivated fields on either side of the glancing stream, the bluegreen slopes of the valley beyond. "We didn't choose so badly, at that. Don't you ever forget what Earth was like, you two. I don't expect the Sixers have." He scowled suddenly, a scowl that looked peculiar on a face so pleasant. "There's *nobody* back home who wouldn't be glad to trade places with us. And even if we have to make do with hurdles for now—"

"You're going to say, 'Way will open,'" interrupted Norah, oblivious to the scowl and agitation evident in George's little outburst; Bob, though, was now looking at him oddly as Norah went on: "Way will open, way will open—how long did it take you to acquire the knack of looking ahead and planning without *worrying*? God!" Under the tone of complaint she sounded a little frantic. "Andrew's *just* as bad—just as good, I ought to say, but it's awful being so comparatively feeble! I'll get to stewing about, oh, what if the corn's wiped out by hail some summer—thinking about the kids, you know, and how narrow our margin is, how easily the odds could shift against us—lucky or not, George, and I know we are—I really do know it!—this is still a damn hard, uncertain life we're living. Anyway, Andrew will just say, very patiently, 'Well, we're here, which ought to be impossible, so we have to assume we're meant to survive here; if we're meant to, we will; if not, we won't, and it's as much as *I* can do to concentrate on every day as it comes along—the rest is up to Providence.' Now, I'm as clear about all that as—well, as you are yourself, George, but Andrew *feels* it the way you do. He's honestly content to work and wait upon the Lord. Me, I have to keep yanking myself up short. I wish I knew how you chaps do it. I'd give anything to be that free of plain old common-or-garden fretting about the future. It's not even *noble* fretting, about the future of the race, not anymore—just the future of the Bell family and the settlement, and quite a bit lately about how the Sixers are going to fit in. I don't deserve to be here, I suppose." She looked glum, and also resentful. "I admire the hell out of you and Andrew, and I envy you too, but I can't be like you to save my life."

"As a matter of fact, I wasn't going to say one word about way opening," said George, rather nettled. Norah's nervous neediness—because he had no help to offer—wore upon his own nerves; and it mortified him to be viewed as a figure of heroic serenity. "I was about to say that we might try growing hedges of native brush that the stock wouldn't even want to nibble. And that since the pasture windmills should be operational by the end of the year, we can easily spare enough power and parts to electrify the fences for a while." He took in the startled faces on either side and shook his head. "You overestimate me—yes you do, Norah. This past half-hour of sheep-doggery is the first half-hour since we raised the *Down Plus Six* that I haven't spent fretting about how to cope with what's coming when the Sixers land."

They had stopped walking; the other two stared in consternation at imperturbable George. "It'll be different once they're down and we're talking, but the *anticipation* of conflict gives me the galloping golliwicks. Always did. I lose sleep, fight my field work, growl at Danny, can't stay centered—Norah, you nitwit, I'm not one bit different from you! Andrew is the real thing if you like. Not me. Thank God they'll be landing tomorrow; another week of suspense and my self-esteem would be damaged beyond repair." He swept an arm around each of his companions, propelling them back into motion. "Just for the record, though, Andrew's perfectly right. Why should we be here, if not to mend our fences somehow, and act as a buffer between the Sixers and the hrossa? *And* survive? The Mormons had it worse, didn't they? And lived to populate a desert and a dozen space colonies? What would George Fox and Margaret Fell think of all this fussing and bitching, hmm? Not much!"

"Oh God, George," began Norah, stricken, but Bob broke in firmly: "We're going to have some silence. Now. Yes, right now." He braked the three of them to another halt and passed his free arm around Norah, closing the circle.

The rest of their work squad, filing back between the shoulder-high rows of corn, scarcely gave a passing glance to the little huddle; in general they understood perfectly what they were seeing, a usual sight about the settlement from its inception. An unknowing observer—had there been one such within millions of miles or light-years of that spot—would have seen what appeared to be three barefoot but particularly clean, attractive peasants dressed in short, loose, light-colored tunics tied at the waist with rope. Standing, they held one another toward a common center—eyes closed, heads lowered, faces graced with similar expressions of listening and of calm. Of the two men, both Caucasians, one was tall and lean, with beautiful gray-white hair; the other, thirtyish, was of middling height and build, his hair and short thick beard two violent shades of red; the third person was a young Asian woman, small and very pretty. They stood like that for nearly a quarter of an hour.

They looked, and labored, like peasants. But they were Quakers, starfarers, uniting in impromptu meeting for worship; and they and their fellow settlers, 312 souls in all, were the only human beings in all the world.

For one more day.

"How come *I* never thought of hedges?" Bob asked as they finally separated, and George replied in his old, nice voice: "Because you're a builder, I expect," and smiled. Norah gave him a quick apologetic hug before slipping between the rows.

AT THE BOTTOM of the lake the hross KliUrrh, an early elder, unlatched a lattice gate and began inviting several of the sluggish eel-shaped beings inside to swim from the cage into his basket. His four hindmost limbs swirled the water, holding his large, buoyant body in position; two stubby lower forelimbs held the basket open like a lopsided clamshell, while the longer two gently herded in the swillets that, cleaned and sectioned, would become the main course of his family's evening meal. The image of bowls of hollowed stone filled with bits of swillet rose in KliUrrh's mind and communicated itself to the little creatures, along with his feelings of anticipation and thankfulness, and they came willingly enough. He released the few that had yet to complete their lives by replication—*Not this time, cousin!*—judged he had taken enough, shooed back the others, and closed the basket's lid and the holding pen's hatch. *Feed and content yourselves till I come again.* His body turned and glided at once toward the surface, lifted by the kind clear water, all his arms clasping the basket full of stirring consciousness to his thorax.

He came up into a soft, dull afternoon, a pale gray sky above the pewter-gray water. Soothing the uneasy swillets, which never themselves swam so near the sunlight, he paddled toward a wide beach of blue-gray sand. Beyond, a cluster of dwellings rose humpily. Swimming thus, polar-bear fashion, he looked rather like a smallish, neckless sea monster; as he walked up out of the water on his four strong legs, the impression was rather that of an outsize frog that did not leap, a seal that did not waddle, but with twice too many limbs to be much like either. There was something of the centaur about him, and something of the dinosaur.

Before his domed house he found his family occupied quietly with domestic business, their personalities forming a composite aura like an odor of which he was scarcely conscious, yet that set his own lodge apart from every other in his village. KliUrrh set down the basket, now leaking a few droplets through its tight weave, with a ritual emotional "gesture" meaning roughly, "These are the kind ones who give up their lives to ours." Aloud he said (in effect)—the supple blowholes in his brow region forming the sound—"I'll see if I can grub up a few last hiding nuts to throw in with them, unless I'm needed for some other task."

No one looked up or replied, but the household aura became tinged pleasurably with encouragement and gratitude, and he turned back toward the water, first taking a small net, and a digging scoop carved from a piece of preserved wood, from hooks on a rack inside the door.

Hiding "nuts," a dietary staple of KliUrrh's people, grew plentifully in marshy places at that latitude on that world. The single blue-green frond, like a fan spread flat on the oozy ground, produced a husked starchy fruit on a stalk projecting from the underside of the frond. As the fruit matured, its own weight tended to bury it in the soft mud below, where it then anchored itself by putting out a mass of hairlike structures that sponged up nutrients from the semiliquid soil. The ripe nut was large, very nutritious, and strongly flavored, and kept well in underground pits or caves through the cold season. Raw, it was an ideal trail food; dried, pounded to flour, and mixed with other foods, it gave substance and piquancy to the dish.

KliUrrh reentered the lake, the net and scoop gripped in his lower arms. His sense of the village dwindled, blocked by the static interference formed of the lake's many small lives, of its muds and sands and the mass of water itself, much as the sound of wind and waves drowns out the noise of picnickers talking and singing on a beach for those in a sailboat headed out from shore. *Sound* is a feeble metaphor for this extra sense of KliUrrh's, not least because his people were equipped with excellent organs of hearing. Their awareness of the living world about and below them, and of one another, was literally the sixth of their senses and the most highly valued—a sensitivity they shared to varying degrees with all the life forms on their world, plant life as well as animal.

For this reason KliUrrh's kind were generally without meaningful postures or physical gestures, or anything corresponding to facial expression, as the lower forms generally lacked behaviors corresponding to rites of courtship or appeasement. Emotion being manifested not outwardly and symbolically but directly and empathically, such expressiveness had served no evolutionary function. Thus a hatchling gipgip made no signal to stimulate feeding behavior in its parent; thus had KliUrrh omitted to wave goodbye to his family.

In a while the hross's broad feet touched bottom. Emerging, he began to squelch through bogland, spiracles contracted against the gases released from decomposing vegetation by his passage. He was semiaware as he progressed of the needle-points of life that pierced his thick smooth hide and borrowed a little blood, but his senses were held on alert for the sensation of dumb bulbousness or the sight of a flat blue-green fan, either of which would signal the belated presence of hiding nuts. He saw plenty of withered fronds blackening into the ooze, but their nuts had been taken.

KliUrrh had nearly accepted failure when finally, pushing through a clump of large-celled water-filled stalks without breaking or bruising them and climbing a fallen trunk in the slow process of being preserved by chemicals in the ground water, he spotted not one but three fans spread on the ground; at the same instant he felt the triple throb that told him all three nuts were both present and infertile. He stood still in the muck and experienced his gratitude in the consciousness of TuwukhKawan, for the unseasonal bounty; then he slopped forward, deftly twisted and thrust the scoop in with one long arm, spread the net between his two short ones, snapped the stalks, and dropped the dark, muddy, hairy lumps in, one after another, with his fourth hand. The hands on his longer arms had two stubby opposable pairs of single-jointed digits and were fairly dexterous; the second pair were useful for holding, but their "hands" were little more than flat, padded paws.

Now they clasped the bulging net and the scoop again while KliUrrh's upper arms parted the canes and his four legs drove him forward, leaving tracks that the water rapidly filled. *First a swim to cleanse you, then you bless us.* It was late for fresh nuts. These heavy three would be tough but very sweet. They would delight SwikhKarrh, and delighting SwikhKarrh was a foremost pleasure of KliUrrh's existence.

Now that, reflected KliUrrh, that for example was a feeling the People and the Quakers could experience in common. KliUrrh had been present, and had picked up George Quinlan's buoyant pleasure in his own child's pride and delight, when Danny had at last become a strong enough swimmer to make the long reach clear across the lake on his own. Among many differences, sev-

eral deep and truly disturbing, it was good to feel where his own
kind and the aliens most resembled one another.

And in this too—this rejoicing in their alikeness, the excitement about their differences that had nothing to do with fear—
he and George Quinlan were kindred spirits; for unlike certain
others among both their peoples, neither of these two had any
inclination to be wary of the other.

Though thoroughly conscious of the mischief they might make
out of quarantine, and genuinely grieved at the death of the little valley the Quakers called Delaware, KliUrrh could not help
his gladness about the coming of the humans. He would not have
missed knowing George, or Danny or Katy, for the world. In a
long life full of pleasures, there was hardly anything he would
have traded for the fascinating taking-in of them.

2 George

Danny had tried to wait up for his father, but the meeting ran late
and he had had an exciting couple of days. When George finally
came in with Billy Purvis they found him asleep in his dhoti on
the sheepskin patchwork that covered half the metal floor of the
sitting room; but he got right up, groggily, and splashed water
from a plastic bucket onto his face and rubbed it hard with a
towel, asking even before he was fully awake, "How'd it go?
What happened? What'd they say?"

"I taped the whole thing for the archives," said Billy. "Play
it if you like, but there's a couple of hours' worth here, and I
want to file it in the morning."

He flipped the little disc to Danny, who teetered between
wanting to know what everyone had said in the meeting and
wanting to know what George and Billy were going to say in the
postmortem.

"It went about like we thought," said George. He had lost the
air of fretful unease that had clung about him for weeks, but
looked exhausted. He pulled his blue dress tunic over his head
and dropped onto some taut cushions arranged on the floor and
against the wall, automatically stuffing a little pillow behind the

small of his back. "They're bewildered and disappointed, and pretty angry. It looks like they'll draw the line at mass murder, thank God, but they don't much see why they shouldn't proceed according to the original plan and just pay no attention to what the hrossa want. They've only known for a couple of months what Pennterra's like, remember, after years of suspense, so it's just not possible yet for them to take us seriously when we say they have to tell the UN not to send any more ships." He yawned and stretched his arms over his head. "All in all, about what we figured for Round One."

"Also," Billy put in, "they can't for the life of 'em figure out why *we* went along with the restrictions." There was a padded metal chair with arms, bolted to the floor, and he settled into it, crossing his long legs straight out in front of him. "Most of them are struggling to be courteous and reserve judgment, but they're not Quakers, Danny, and at this point what we've done here makes sense to them only as a piece of pure Quaker foolishness." He made a rueful face at George. "It's been such a long while since I sat through a meeting with non-Quakers, I'd kind of forgot what it's like. Mm-*mmm*. This isn't going to be easy."

"Did you ever expect it to be? I didn't," said George. "Take that hot thing off before you melt, Billy. I'm going down cellar and draw us some cider."

Danny had *never* sat through a meeting with non-Quakers; before today he had never laid eyes on a non-Quaker in his whole life, that he could remember (though in fact, in infancy, he had). There were a lot of things he was dying to know; but he could read in the plain signs of weariness and gloom how poor was the outlook for a lively rehash of the evening's events between these two, and was grateful that he would not have to be bratty and pump them anyway. "I'll get it, Dad," he said. "You stay there. And then I guess I'll play the tape."

The way the two men drank, reflectively, respectfully, as if rehearsing the amazing facts behind the plastic mugs of brown brew they held in hands coarsened by grubbing in dirt—planting the specially selected seeds, watering, grafting, greenhousing, and pruning the little trees, transplanting them into the carefully conditioned soil of the orchard, years of anxious training, more pruning, propping, and finally the labor of harvest and the pressing—spoke volumes about their situation. So did the fact that Danny brought up no third mug for himself and would accept only one good-sized swig out of his father's. He went into the other room, taking the tape disc. "I'll keep the

volume down," he promised as George was opening his mouth
to tell him to. They had a player in the flat but no earpiece, and
the radio station was too far to go to borrow one this night.

Alone in the sitting room, Billy and George sipped at the cider slowly for some moments without speaking, for in their different ways both were depressed. Voices, gently muffled, soon
floated through the heavy curtain hung in the doorway and filled
the mutual silence. It was no trick to discern the note of politely
restrained incredulity that overtook one side of the discussion
almost at once, and after listening for a few minutes Billy shook
his head. "I tell you what, ol' George. This stuff upsets me worse
than I expected, *it brings it all back*. I listen to those arguments,
and I can remember arguing the very same points myself six years
back. We've insulated ourselves in practical problems, we gave
up the mission such a *long* time ago and just got on with learning how to farm, but remember how fired up we were at first to
make this planet into the Brave New World? And how infuriating—how goddamn *maddening* it was to be balked, when we finally really had to believe we just were not going to be sold or
given any more land at all, not *any*, not *ever*?"

"I remember all right." Tiredness settled over George, a web
of lead.

"And *then* remember how we argued and schemed, and how
hard we resisted being led to submit?" Billy shifted unhappily in
the stiff chair. "I mean to tell you, giving up that dream in full
view of achieving it was the hardest thing, bar none, I'll ever do
in my life. It's the hardest thing any of us will ever do—harder'n deciding to come in the first place! If you ask me, we're
going to need to meet a lot more than usual if we're going to keep
clear about ourselves and our decisions, as long as this tussling
with the Sixers goes on. Maybe every day."

"Maybe more than that." From the bedroom George could
now hear his own smudged voice echoing the sense of his friend's
lament: "...and though most of us here have come to admire and
respect the hrossa very much, please believe that our disappointment was as crushing in its time as yours is now. Every one
of us volunteered for this mission in the same hope and desire
that led every one of you to volunteer, and we were as reluctant
to give it up as you could possibly be. That we did give it up, despite our desire and our commitment, means simply that to us
there finally appeared to be no other moral choice."

Unexpectedly, to hear himself say these things discomfited
George intensely. What was he *pleading* with them for, for

Christ's sake? The merits of the case were their own defense. To appeal to the Sixers for understanding (and forgiveness?) for what his people had chosen to do was stupid; it was wrong.

I shouldn't have been set up to lead in this, he knew of a sudden with a flush of pure dismay. *Someone not in so deep with the hrossa could present the facts more honestly. No wonder I've been worried!* Everything he had told them was entirely true, yet now to his own ears his voice carried a clear taint of hypocrisy.

Three months after landfall, with construction in full swing, the hrossa had appeared one day out of the mountains northeast of the settlement. They had easily put across to the thunderstruck Quakers, who before this had observed not one hint of their existence, a demand that the building cease—that all activity cease, until a medium of communicating between the two peoples could be worked out.

The humans had rallied enough to put themselves at the disposal of the commanding, fantastical creatures whose emotional sendings invaded them as naturally as the brook's racket invaded their ears; and in mere weeks, in no time at all, the hrossa had acquired the means to tell the Quakers what they most needed them to know:

First, they could stay, and the capacity load of the *Down Plus Six*, more than three times as great as that of the *Woolman*, would be allowed to stay as well. They could rear their crops, and—as vacancies occurred through deaths—their families.

But three laws were to govern their activities completely. There must never be many more humans on Pennterra than the combined original number of humans, something on the order of 1,300. They were specifically forbidden to employ any but passive power sources—they must not use the rest of their expensively transported machinery for building or farming or anything else. And finally, all their enterprise, as well as their settlement or settlements, must be confined to the valley of the river called Delaware by the Quakers and [AhkKlahki] by themselves, where the ecology had already been disrupted; the humans were prohibited—forever?—from wandering the surface of the world at will. The valley, however beautiful and bountiful, would thus be a place of quarantine to them, a paradisal ghetto 120 kilometers long by several wide, bounded by a waterfall and a long lake to the north, the sea to the southeast, and the stony ridges of the hills to either side.

Our world (the hross elders had told them later, when they had learned more English) is ordered by imperatives that the hu-

mans may interfere with neither by accident nor by design. We
deeply sympathize with the plight of your people, we are moved
by the risks you took on their behalf, and by your safe arrival
here, but in our view your kind has broken faith with its own
world in a thousand ways. You are a danger to us. We cannot
allow you the freedom of ours.

George Quinlan had most heartily wished the rightful owners
of the planet Pennterra at the other end of the galaxy in those
days. He had yielded to their moral authority, when he heard
their terms and finally knew what it would mean for his own
people and his mission, with as poor a grace as any; and he too
could perfectly remember his own acute bitterness and frustration. The meeting, desiring earnestly to be led in the matter, had
been led to submit. And they had submitted; but how could they
have done so gladly? Yielding to the authority of the hrossa
seemed a hateful necessity to all of them, a personal defeat sustained but a whisker short of victory. Then.

For George, all that had changed long since.

I haven't had to face this before, he thought, *but I can't shirk
facing it any longer. It really feels to me, if I'm honest, as if my
whole life before knowing KliUrrh, even my part in the mission,
had been leading up to knowing him—as if he somehow completes me.*

And a peculiar thought struck him: *Would I feel this so
strongly if Susan were still alive? Is KliUrrh a kind of substitute
for the sort of intimacy I had with her and don't want again with
any woman?* It was like him to wonder this. He waited, trying to
puzzle out the answer honestly; he believed that he had been well
content in his marriage.

I really don't know, he finally had to admit. Such a lot would
have depended on how Susan felt about the hrossa. *They could
have brought us closer, as they've brought Danny and me. Or
come between us, as they've come between me and Norah Bell,
who used to be a better friend of mine, and who respects the
hrossa but feels nothing deeper for them.* And now his thoughts,
and his regard, rested on Billy Purvis, stretched out in the chair
scavenged from the lounge of the *John Woolman*—a biochem-
ist his own age, no particular hrossophile. Their friendship had
lasted twenty years, most of them stressful years, and after all
that time Billy was one of a number of friends who judged
George far less harshly than George was inclined to judge himself.

Billy had been watching him. "Sorry," said George. "I'm mighty poor company tonight.... I was just thinking the hrossa haven't made any difference between you and me."

"Um." Billy thought that over. "But between you and other people they have?"

"More than I'd realized, I suddenly seem to see. But mainly between me six years ago and me right now. A lot more difference than I've had to think about till this evening, as a matter of fact. Or cared to, either." He leaned forward, groaning softly, to unlatchet his shoes; he hadn't had on a pair of shoes for three months.

From the bedroom the voice of a male Sixer—was it the fat one?—now hinted that, as the Quakers had found themselves embarrassed by conflicting moral claims, and as they could hardly be comfortable sitting pretty in Paradise here while the people they felt unable to save went right on dying back on Earth, perhaps they ought to bend their efforts toward finding a way of getting back home again. George listened to his own brief response—that none of them had done much sitting since landfall, but that the questioner's point had, of course, occurred to them too—and then with deeper interest as Billy's light southern accent began to explain that refitting and resupplying the ship, to say nothing of refueling her, "just doesn't look possible without the construction of some fairly sizable machines that would have to be built *with* machines, on the planet's surface, whether the repair work's done on the surface or on the moon. And, as we've explained, the hross elders have proscribed machines." He pronounced the word "proscraaabed." ("Are you following this?" "Yep.") "They've made only one exception, for our two little electric whirligigs, so we can stay in close touch without having to build roads or their needing to use a radio. If any of your people have suggestions, I'd purely love to hear them."

"Here's where ol' Fussbudget McWhirter puts his oar in," said Billy, the broad dialect of his childhood asserting itself in unconscious reaction to the formality of his public speech. "I tell you what, I can speak to that of God in the rest of 'em just as nice as you please, but that fella's a right smart challenge for Friends as out of practice as we are at talkin' to people that aren't even *tryin'* to talk to us, you know?"

"Shush, I want to hear this." Several voices had been calling out "Mr. Chair!" together. One that aggressively identified itself as "Gerald McWhirter, Astrogation," now blurted, "Sorry,

Purvis, I just don't think that's good enough. 'Can't let anybody else come here because the natives say no, and can't go
home because the natives say no machines allowed.' How can
they stop you, man? If you really want to go home, go! If you
don't, I can't say I blame you, but why be a goddamned hypo-
crite about it?''

"Here it comes, you dragon slayer," said George's live voice
as Billy's recorded one spoke from the domicile bedroom: "Dr.
McWhirter, this is *their* world. They live here. They make the
rules, which we were led to obey. A number of us feel that, having failed to persuade the hrossa to take us in, and being unable
in conscience to force our people upon them against their will,
we ought in conscience to go back and share the common fate. I
repeat: if somebody aboard your vessel can show us how to do
what needs doing with surface equipment no more disturbing to
the environmental peace than, say, a small forge, we'll thank you
very kindly.''

There came a pause full of stirrings and mutterings; and then
Billy spoke again. "I don't believe you folks know very much
about the Quakers," he said pleasantly. "No reason you should;
their little time in the limelight was a long while back. But you
can take my word for it that their record for leaving very much
nicer, more comfortable situations than this one, voluntarily, to
go at God's behest into very much less comfortable ones, is pretty
hard to fault. I'm not a birthright Quaker, I can say this without immodesty. When God wanted the early Friends to go to
prison, or free their slaves and impoverish their families, or
found schools for orphans, or hospitals for the insane, he let
them know about it. And later on, when God wanted 111 Quaker
scientists to go live in a lab for nineteen months and not come out
without the ground-based defense that would guarantee the
Peace, he let them know about that, too. I don't doubt for a
minute that if he wants us to go home, way will open. When and
if that happens, those of us that are clear about going will go,
and we won't pussyfoot around about it when we do. But he
brought us here, and at least for the time being he seems to be
keeping us here.''

"Great stuff," said George above the voices softly clamoring
to speak. "No sooner do I get to wondering whether somebody
else mightn't do a more effective job with the Sixers than I realize somebody already did.''

"'Effective' is hardly the word *I'da* picked," said Billy,
glancing sharply at his friend. "You saw 'em all trying not to

look as fed up and disgusted as they felt. You can't even blame them all that much; it does sound like the baldest, most self-serving sophistry you ever heard in your life, even when you know durn well it's the truth."

"Eloquence *is* effective, deny it who will." George sighed. "Look—I'm as sorry as I can be, but I have to ask. I heard what you said before, and I don't ask lightly. But *would* you take over as chair at the next one? The same person really oughtn't to do it every time anyway, and the more I think about it, the clearer I am that I need to disqualify myself."

Billy peered at him, surprised, frowning a little. "Can you talk about why?"

"I'm not sure. Not too well. Not before the meeting yet. It just came over me tonight, just since we broke up, that—oh, put it like this: we've all been in a state of moral conflict here from the day we knew this planet wasn't ours for the claiming, right? But my position now is worse than that. I'm trapped between conflicting emotional claims too."

Billy's frown disappeared. "Because of KliUrrh."

George nodded. "Not just KliUrrh, but mainly him. I only just realized. It makes me feel like I'm hiding a guilty secret from the Sixers; there's something dishonest in the position, emotionally dishonest. I need to get out of this."

"I can see you do. We ought to have thought of it, actually." Billy made a sour face. "Oh, hell, running the meeting won't be any rougher on me than just being present would. So if nobody objects, I'll do it. Once, maybe twice—then somebody else can take a turn. You're right anyhow, it's a job that ought to be passed around."

"I'll tell the meeting myself, this Firstday. But nobody'll object, and you know it." Relief, spreading through him, lightened every part of his weary body.

"Not to me they won't. They'll wonder how come you asked to be let off so quick though; you were appointed unopposed, and not without good reason." He paused to think. "If you'd just as soon wait till things calm down some, I suppose it's enough for now to say you think the chair should rotate. But you'll need to tell people pretty soon."

"I suppose so." For the dozenth time that evening, anxiety tightened George's eloquent face. Billy gave him another sharp look, drained his cider mug, set it on the floor—a thin tap of plastic on metal—then stood and began to do up his uniform tunic. "Don't get up," he said, but as he moved to depart he creaked down on one knee and tightened his arm about George's chest in a firm half-hug, something he hadn't done in a couple of years. Surprised, George patted him automatically a time or two; then abruptly he put down his own mug and for a minute really held on to his old friend.

Billy let him go. "If I can help, say so." He padded to the door with his shoes under his arm, a tall, gray-haired figure, straight and lean, made on the whole remarkably like George Quinlan both inside and out. "Remind Danny to drop that tape by on his way to work, all right?"

Left by himself, George leaned back against the wall and closed his eyes. Billy's gesture had warmed him, as he had been warmed and steadied by Bob Wellwood's unlooked-for sensitivity to his condition on the day of the sheep chase. His relief was also great. What he seemed to have discovered about himself, however, had shaken him badly; it was like suddenly realizing that weeks or months ago, without suspecting a thing at the time, he must have fallen out of love.

From behind the curtain he now heard the muted voice of Maggie Smithson, a Sixer he had known nearly as long as he and Billy Purvis had known each other and a pretty ardent sort of friend for a while. He had been wholly surprised to see her. They had lost touch—forsworn it, really—some years before the data from the Voyager probe sent to Pennterra had reached Earth, before either could have imagined meeting again in the present circumstances, though yesterday the surprise had been all on George's side; Maggie, of course, had known when she shipped on the *Down Plus Six* that George had gone aboard the *Woolman*. "I would like to raise again an aspect of Jerry's question that I don't think got answered," she was saying. "Supposing we did drive a dozer out and start clearing forty acres of land outside the valley—what *could* they do about it, the—the hurrossa? How would they enforce the technology taboo if we simply set out to ignore it? I'm not suggesting we ought to, now, I'd just like to know what might happen if we did."

"They would experience deep distress, and that would distress us all," he heard himself reply, and the priggish earnestness that now seemed to taint his voice made George's heart sink dismally. Rolling off the cushions with a grunt, he lurched erect, thrust the curtain aside, and glowered into the bedroom. Danny lay sprawled across his father's bed on his stomach, sound asleep. The player sat on the floor. George resisted an impulse to stomp its twirling disc silent; he forced himself to listen. "...have to take our word for it for the time being, until you get to know the hrossa yourselves. I realize it's a lot to swallow. But I doubt that any of you, any more than we, would prefer sharing that distress to putting up with the difficulties—even if you were able to justify resettling, or using machinery, on moral grounds."

Here the ship's first officer interrupted to ask what he meant by *sharing*.

"Well, as we've told you, the hrossa are empathic to a fair degree, they can send as well as receive, weakly if you resist or aren't paying attention, quite powerfully if you invite them into your head." Here George detected a faint eagerness sneaking into his voice and ground his teeth. "That's why we communicate with one another as well as we do, despite the obvious biological incompatibilities. We've speculated that it's also why some of them have been able to learn fluent English while we haven't made much headway at all with their language, which is devilishly difficult to pronounce with the human vocal apparatus. Well, of course we've been too busy to give much time to it—"

"But would they, or could they, try to *stop* us by violent means, or make any resistance worth worrying about?" Maggie broke in.

George had hesitated, aware even in that moment that he had let himself stray from the point. "I'm inclined to think not, but I'm not entirely sure. The villages don't appear to fight among themselves. They don't seem to recognize tribes or clans, or any us-and-them relationships whatever, except parenthood and time of life—child, breeder, adult, elder…certainly they've never tried to impose their will on us by force, but then they've never had to try, since we've respected their feelings and their laws from the first." *Felt* their feelings, he remembered thinking. You haven't; that's why you don't understand.

"Then in fact they couldn't actually prevent us from taking over here, so far as you know?"

"Not so far as I know. Could the Aztecs stop Cortez? Practically speaking, you have the means to murder every last hross on the continent, if you could endure that much empathic anguish. You'd have to murder a lot of us first, though—this mission was never charged to proceed by way of genocide; but I'm going to assume your question was meant to be academic, Maggie. You're bound by the Hippocratic oath, you know."

Here George smiled slightly and let up on himself a little; that bit at least, buffered by the steady, pleasant tones in which he had spoken it, struck him as not half bad. The American analogy was, inevitably, in everybody's mind. Maggie had smiled also, and said, "I am indeed, and certainly it was."

But the astrogator now butted back into the fray. "Dr. Quinlan, with all due respect, I have to point out that what you've been describing sounds to me like a very *effective* means of control." (In the bedroom, observed by nobody, George permitted himself to make the terrible face he had itched to pull at McWhirter.) "In effect, you're saying they can cause you to feel pain when you hurt them and pleasure when you do what they want you to. Now, if they can really do that—I admit I find it hard to believe—it seems to me they have a very potent means of resisting our operations. You say they couldn't stop us developing the planet for human use by using force, but why use force when you've got thought control? Did you people *let* them hypnotize you, or can they put you under from a distance, or what? Either way, I don't agree at all that anything able to affect our feelings wouldn't be able to put up a very impressive resistance if it came to a showdown. If the Aztecs could have hypnotized the Spaniards just by thinking about it, things might have worked out a lot different."

By this means had McWhirter initiated the predictable next phase of the debate: the attempt to justify doing away with the hrossa by establishing that they were dangerous to humans and therefore evil. Though the Quakers had never entered the justification phase, they had expected that the Sixers would. It certainly hadn't taken them long. Moreover, since the Sixers had yet to meet the hrossa, it was a line of thought bound to strike them as plausible. It had been rather clever of the Quakers—whose invariable aim in meeting was consensus rather than domination through argument, whose persuasive strategy was to identify with the adversary, and who had lived in intimacy of a sort with the hrossa for six years—to anticipate and prepare for this turn of events.

"Mr. Chair?" Catherine Kendry spoke up promptly; this was her cue. George gave her the floor and she stood and addressed the inquisitor: "I understand why you'd think right away of hypnosis, Dr. McWhirter. I did myself, but that doesn't appear to come into it. I'm a psychologist, by the way—Katy Kendry. I did a series of EEG readings on our people while they were united with the hrossa on various occasions, during language lessons and so on, and they turned out to be virtually identical with readings taken in meeting for worship, or in meditation done by repeating a mantra, or self-hypnosis—I can show you the file if you like. It's a very light trance state, not nearly deep enough for loss of control. George has been referring to the effect an overwhelming disaster would have, or an act that would affront the hrossa as a whole people. One on one the effect is pretty mild, as you'll all have a chance to see for yourselves when you meet them. What it amounts to is that whatever they feel you feel, and vice versa. Distance quickly dilutes the force. To send to us here from the nearest village takes the concentrated efforts of that village plus a couple of others . . ."

Across the round room McWhirter's sour, untrusting face had not altered during Katy's speech; and at this point, standing in the bedroom, there flashed into George's mind a memory from the time before he knew the hrossa, when even in his own eyes they had lowered like freakish malevolent brutes between the advance team and the future of the human race. Pierced by the memory he crossed the floor and slapped the player still. Katy had spoken out of conviction born of her own experience, but the real truth was as he himself had stated it: not one of them knew what the hrossa could do if driven to defense, or to enforcing their laws upon alien invaders set on rearranging the world to suit themselves. The Quakers had yielded; the issue had never arisen. If the Sixers decided to resist they would all be in new territory, where nobody could say what would happen.

When the player fell silent, Danny drew a few deep breaths and turned on his side with George's pillow clasped in his arms. The pillow was a surrogate for the fuzzy stuffed stegosaurus named Stig they had brought from Earth. Danny had stopped taking Stig to bed with him years ago, but the habit of falling asleep while hugging something had persisted. He needed a bath, the soles of his feet were black. George straightened him round on the bed and puffed out the light. Wide awake himself, though dull with tiredness, he drew off the rest of his clothes in the warm dark, pulled a clean field tunic over his head, and let himself quietly out of the flat he shared with his boy.

He left the building by the back stairs, closing the metal door carefully and descending the metal treads on his tough bare feet. From the landing, halfway down, a splendid view of the valley done in black and silver fell away before him. Moonlight glinted in random flashes off the creek that twisted through the settlement, bisecting the scene on George's side of the river. Six long domicile buildings ranged along the creek, four on the downstream side of the Delaware, two on the upstream; most windows were dark, but the domicile serving as temporary quarters for the Sixer chiefs of staff was ablaze with lights. The community buildings—kitchen, bathhouse, dining hall, labs, greenhouses, and clothing shops—stood together on the river's upstream side; across the creek from these bulked the hexagonal meeting house that doubled as a school, the settlement's single most important structure, where Quakers and Sixers had met formally that evening for the first time.

Directly across the river from the bathhouse he could discern the large black rectangle of the dairy/sheepfold/barn. Another barn stood somewhere in the blackness behind him near the gristmill, straddling the creek where it flowed more swiftly down the valley's steeply sloping side. The henhouse-cum-rabbit hutch in one corner of the kitchen garden blocked George's view of the little hydroelectric plant at the mouth of the creek, which provided heat and light to bathhouse, kitchen, and dining hall, but not to the domiciles.

There were a few small trees among the buildings to break the straight prefabricated lines somewhat, but the settlement was bare enough of such softening touches. Yet for all their starkness the structures pulled together, they were cozily grouped and fitly proportioned in their placement if less so in themselves, in their own lines. It was obvious the place was somebody's home.

The Delaware ran shallow in all seasons and shallowest now in late summer, but at the outer edge of one of its meanders, behind the labs, it had scooped out a pool the size of a small farm pond that was deep enough for swimming. George crossed the creek, five strides over a long plank, and circled the width of bare open common space that normally served the settlement as playing field or picnic ground and that this night and for several others had become a small tent city for those whose domicile had been turned over to the Sixers. No one was abroad, and George was glad. Behind the hospital wing of the lab he dropped his single garment on the bank; and then—because swimming alone, especially at night, was contrary to the will of the meeting strictly speaking—compromised by not diving in. Instead he turned, grasped the tops of a light metal ladder, and backed down quickly into the tugging water.

Cold and pleasure shocked the doldrums clean out of him. He caught a great breath and shoved himself down to the gravelly bottom. Rising, he thrashed and kicked against the current, rather harder than necessary, right across the pool to the shallows at the middle of the river, where he squatted on a submerged flat rock in water up to his nipples and let the Delaware press at his back and slide along his legs and flanks, soothing the most desperate part of his weariness away.

The river by moonlight was as beautiful and mysterious as the earthly Delaware River running out beneath the full moon of Earth, and George had been evolved to appreciate what he was looking at. His brain had gone blissfully blank from the instant he entered the water. He let the blankness draw itself out, and, as he soaked at the center of the scene, even allowed a familiar blossom of joy to open cautiously in his chest, the joy of a person who—whatever his difficulties and self-doubts—has a deep conviction that he is where he belongs, doing what he ought to be doing. In the feeling was a rightness and fitness that blanked out the painful contradictions of the past hours, weeks, months. The same feeling had often come to immerse him at the village of Lake-Between-Falls, with KliUrrh and his family; and when the strong thought *KliUrrh* entered the blank field of his mind, George experienced the sudden certainty that at that moment he himself existed as a thought in the mind of KliUrrh. With this conviction, pure happiness, balm to his distress, spread down his arms and flowed into his vitals—into his penis also, which stirred where it floated like a fish in the cold water.

My whole life led to this, he thought again. His mind felt clear as the air, clear as the river. *I don't believe even Susan could have kept me from KliUrrh. He's no substitute for Susan, though, that was a false idea. If the hrossa are deceivers, then I'm unfit to judge between the truth and falseness of anything; if they're dangerous to us, somebody else will have to find out. Even all my years among Friends seem like preparation for them, for him...it can't be because they don't want us to that we don't understand them yet—I* know *that, or I don't know anything.*

But how are we to make the Sixers know it?

A truly religious person, in trouble, in a place of so much natural beauty, must feel the moment as an invitation to prayer; but George was not a praying Quaker and had not believed since adolescence in a personal God. Meeting was all he knew about prayer—something that was like prayer—and meeting required people. Still, the force of the moment was such that, all but unconsciously, he relaxed the barriers and dropped into the receptive listening attitude appropriate to meeting for worship. The thought in his mind was a simple one: *I'll need help; it's too much for me.*

What happened then was strange. He seemed to become aware of the river as a shallow denseness spread out about him, before

and behind as well, one surface passing over rocks and fallen
tendrils, the other mixing with air and briefly catching the
moonlight, edges brushing the sandy banks and native "willows" trailing their living tendrils in the water. More life than
George could have believed seemed to move all about him, at or
between the two gliding surfaces: shapes like fish and insects of
every size, darting or gliding or hovering things, all alive. Even,
he sensed where several sheep crowded to drink on the far bank
a way downstream. Beyond anything in his experience, it thrilled
him to perceive this infinite complexity of sensuous life—terri-
fied him also, for the moment threatened to dissolve his own individual consciousness like a lump of sugar where he crouched
in the water.

Terror bred vertigo, snapped the link. The river returned to
itself—a coldness through which George found himself kicking
with a certain franticness to shore. He hauled his body up the
ladder and stood on the bank, panting, heart thumping,
streaming water.

The Delaware slid along unchanging in the unchanged moonlight, pocked with upthrust stones, making little sound. In a
moment, chagrined at his panic, George caught up his field tunic
and rubbed himself down harshly. He walked along the bank to
a drier spot, folded the damp garment into a situpon, and hunkered down. He stilled the thudding of his heart.

Deliberately he set himself to relive the moments of expanded
awareness. What exactly had he felt?

The river's life, its aliveness.

Native plant and animal life had not disappeared utterly from
the settlement—otherwise the corn wouldn't have wanted weeding—but most species (if that was the word) had been sharply
discouraged by the presence of the humans and their structures,
crops, and livestock, all of which had changed the soil and the
feel of things, especially in the central area, and which were all
entirely inedible—scarcely anything bigger than a bacterium,
from microfaunum to "Mastodon," could scrounge a square
meal in the middle of Swarthmore. George had simply had no
idea there could still be this rich a population of native life in the
river.

Mentally he reimmersed himself and called back his awareness of the abundance of native life at the doorstep of his community...but the liveness he remembered had not been divisible,
fixed separately to the lives of fish and plants. The water itself

had seemed to quicken; even the rocks; even the sand and sediments.

He remembered something else. When the sheep had stood jostling in the hock-deep shallows to drink, the sense of *them* had had a difference, sharp as a scent, from the sense of the river's own life and that of the life form within.

The sheep and he were *related*, that was it. He was not related to the willows, nor to the aquatic animals. Something he had accepted as a biological fact—two wholly discrete evolutionary events—he now believed intuitively to be true.

Yet the two "scents"—or categories of scents, for the rich native life divided plentifully among itself—were less different after all than he might have supposed.

Whew! *Better go to bed,* thought George. *The library's got material on mystical experiences; I'll look into it tomorrow. Or soon,* he amended, thinking of the Sixers and the looming harvest. *And I'll tell KliUrrh about it, his people probably know a lot more about this kind of thing than we do.*

Later, as he was dropping off to sleep in Danny's bunk, his last coherent thought—a thought ripe with comfort—was that if he and KliUrrh had indeed been present to one another just before the slip of consciousness had occurred, KliUrrh might not have to be told about it. He might already know.

3   Maggie

"—I'm afraid you'll have to take our word for it, for the time being, until you get to know the hrossa. I realize it's a lot to swallow. But I doubt that any of you, any more than we, would prefer sharing that distress to putting up with the difficulties, even if you were able to justify—"

"Pause," said Jerry McWhirter crossly, and the player suspended itself obediently. "Do we need to hear the whole thing over?"

In the bare bright common room half a dozen strained faces turned toward him. The Sixer section chiefs had made their own tape and were holding their own postmortem; most were as yet too adrenalized to sleep, though all were exhausted. To be off the ship at all, to walk over real dirt, breathe fresh, unrecycled air full of natural smells, see faces not those of other Sixers, all in addition to coping with the emergency, had left the first eleven of them to land glassy-eyed at the end of their long day. Yet only Reclamation, Food Processing, Livestock, and Engineering had gone to bed.

The common room of the domicile assigned to them, an enclosed space fitted out with padded metal chairs taken off the *Woolman* as well as with large pillows in primary colors, was a relief to the overwrought nerves of the rest, and all sat by preference in the ship's chairs, in their uniform jackets and trousers of the bright color still known as Cambridge blue.

"Do we need to hear the whole thing over?" McWhirter inquired of the group. "Rather than be up all night, suppose we move on to some discussion while our impressions are still fresh. Anybody mind?"

"Why discuss anything now?" complained a black woman with a smooth hairless head, the Chief of Agronomy, Annie Sextus, cranky with fatigue. "We're too wiped out to think straight, even you. I don't *trust* my impressions. I think we ought to leave it till we've had some sleep and got a little more used to being back on the ground."

Before McWhirter could express his opinion of this he was backed up by the first officer. "No, Jerry's right," said Maria Esposito. "The captain wants a report first thing tomorrow. Decisions will have to be made almost at once, especially about whether to meet with the aboriginals, and we haven't much besides impressions to go on. And he wants to start rotating people down as soon as possible, *and* he's got to work out what to say to the UN about it all—though that's less urgent, naturally."

None of them thought this funny. The first radio report of the *Down Plus Six* from Pennterra would not reach Earth for twenty years; it was not urgent, only crucial.

"But why *not* meet with the hrossa?" Sextus said in surprise. "Taking proper precautions, of course. I mean they're all over the continent, aren't they? Whether we set up housekeeping here or someplace else we'll have to have dealings with them. Shouldn't we start off on the right foot?"

"What kind of dealings, though, that's the question. It all depends. I think," said Commander Esposito, "that the captain would be very interested in our impressions of George

Quinlan and his friends, small *f*. I know everybody's dismayed by what they've been saying, but how did they strike you tonight as people? Setting aside for the present how they've performed here and what they're advising us to do."

"I don't see why all that should be set aside, even if it could be," Frank Birtwistle, the Chief of Building and Design, put in. He leaned forward to shift his large hams in his chair. "Religious nuts don't have to be under anybody's *control* to do what these people did—remember Billy Purvis's little history lecture this evening? Hey, fanatics don't operate like other people! I mean look at the record—one time they take over politically and impose the Peace, which nobody else on Earth could ever do; another time they leave trillions of dollars' worth of irreplaceable machinery out to rust in the rain, which nobody in their right mind *would* do. Just two sides of the same coin if you ask me. Sometimes the rest of us benefit, sometimes not. But there's no reason I can see to think these abos are dangerous to *us*, based on what the Quakers say or do—they're susceptible, we aren't." He threw his weight back and folded his arms, pleased with himself for summing up the situation so neatly.

"You could be right," said McWhirter, who plainly did not believe this, "but I feel in my bones that there's a lot more behind the Quakers'—well, you'd have to call it dereliction of duty, wouldn't you?—than they've told us yet. These aliens have some hold over them, some—power, control, what have you. I'd bet my bottom dollar on that. I don't know what, maybe a kind of hypnosis, maybe not—but whatever it is, I think it's perfectly real and that it's essential for the *Skeezix* not to be contaminated by it." *Skeezix* was a corruption of *D-Six*, the ship's earlier nickname.

"I certainly agree that proper precautions are called for and should be recommended," said the first officer. She glanced at her watch; Annie Sextus stifled a yawn. "What about Quinlan himself—how plausible is he? Say you're a jury evaluating a witness's credibility." Her glance flicked around the room. "Annie, what did you think of him, hmm?"

Sextus's eyes snapped open; she pushed herself up straight in her chair. "Sorry, Maria. God I'm tired."

"Quinlan," Esposito repeated, relentless.

"Quinlan." She thought a moment. "Actually, you know, I liked him a lot, I thought he seemed very appealing. But like the baby aardvark at the zoo, that I saw once when I was little—interesting, cute, nice to be around, but on a wavelength so totally different from yours that it wouldn't even occur to you to start a conversation."

This was received with smiles. Roland O'Riley from Geology said, still grinning, "*I* thought he seemed perfectly honest but kind of goofy. I know what you mean, Annie, it's like what he wants out of life, what he's interested in—termites, whatever—is so different from what you want that you realize it's no good trying to communicate with him. You'll always be talking about different things."

Esposito raked her fingers absently through her thick dark hair. "What's disturbing to me is that everyone chosen for the mission—I mean *everyone*, aboard both ships—began by wanting exactly the same things and thinking about them in the same ways. I'm dead sure of it. Since we picked up the first transmissions from Swarthmore I've been studying the records on the *Woolman*'s personnel. Something very important has happened to these people here. And I don't entirely agree that Quinlan was being frank with us tonight," she said. "He wanted us to think he was explaining why his people *couldn't* carry out the mission, but I got the definite impression that he personally just doesn't much care about the mission anymore."

"I did too," said Maggie Smithson abruptly. "I think that's very, very shrewd, Maria. I knew George Quinlan pretty well, oh, fifteen years ago or so, subjective. He was in conflict about—something else—during the time I knew him best, and he used to talk exactly the same way *then*, trying really conscientiously to see a certain situation straight and speak truthfully about it, but always ending up speaking—even though he was telling the factual truth—in a way that was, emotionally, less than honest. He'd catch himself at it and be angry with himself, but he couldn't resolve the conflict and couldn't construct a version of 'the truth' that wasn't self-serving, which made him *feel* dishonest. It was all a bit complicated," she said hurriedly, "but the point is, I *was* struck by *déjà vu* this evening while I was listening to his discourse on the um, h'rossa. I think George was very uncomfortable then. I think he sees the situation exactly as we do, that the Quakers have abandoned the mission and that he used to mind terribly and doesn't anymore. And that part of him at least still thinks he ought to mind." Maggie had kept her eyes down through much of this long speech, only occasionally glancing at Esposito; now she looked up to find the entire group regarding her with alert interest. Frank Birtwistle was grinning like a crocodile.

"*I* thought he seemed sincere enough, just simplistic and maybe not too bright," put in tactful Nathan Levy, sitting in for his chief of psychiatry. "Sincere, I mean, in representing his community's position and beyond that presumably sincere in his religious beliefs. But I agree that compared with Purvis, who seems a much more straightforward case, Quinlan gave the impression of being uncomfortable—quite possibly conflicted in the way Maria and Maggie were saying. That's just speculation, mind, but nothing we've seen so far would rule it out."

"I think you're all being too blame nice to the guy," said Birtwistle through a yawn. "For the record, Quinlan struck me as a wimp and a phony, and I don't give two fucks what happened to him out here because I still don't see any reason to think the same thing's likely to happen to us—but I guess I'm in the minority there." He rubbed his eyes with the heels of his thick hands. "What time is it anyway, Maria? I move we adjourn to bed. We've got the whole damn job to do over from scratch here."

"No, wait a minute," said Nathan Levy. "Can anybody tell me why the Quakers are trying to impose their restrictions on us? I thought they were supposed to be so tolerant of religious differences and all."

"If the objections were purely religious I don't suppose there'd be any trouble," said Maria, "but it seems these are ethical objections. Quakers have always been great ones for minding other people's moral business." She hesitated. "I suppose I may take it that none of you accepts their position?"

There was some shuffling and shifting. Roland O'Riley spoke what most of them felt: "Well, obviously, we didn't look for this, and I don't like it one bit, but if the question is whether the natives' rights should weigh as much with us as our own right to save the race if we can, then the answer's 'no contest.'"

"That's about it," Annie Sextus said. "It's too late, we've come too far to stop now."

Levy added, "Quinlan said we wouldn't want to experience the aliens' unhappiness in order to have bigger farms and easier lives. Maybe not, but I think I might put up with it in order to make a place we could bring more people to. Though I wish it didn't have to be like that, that the hrossa didn't have to be displaced."

McWhirter, who had contributed little to the discussion he had urged upon them, now suddenly stood up. "Do we all agree with Nathan?" His eyes moved back and forth, taking in the room.

The first officer shot him a look but held her peace. "Everyone? Any reservations?"

Maggie Smithson said with some energy, "Oh, sit down, Jerry, don't *push* so! I agree in principle, but I think—I believe we need much more definite information about the natives before we proceed, enough so we can make our own evaluations and draw our own conclusions without either following the Quakers' lead *or* ignoring what they say. That was the reason the ships were sent in one-two sequence, after all!"

"I go along with that," Levy chimed in. "The Quakers couldn't tell us what the natives'll do to us when we violate their taboos. Or wouldn't," he added, with a glance at McWhirter, "but either way we know precisely nothing about the sort of empathy they're said to possess. At the moment I can't imagine any information that would weaken my resolve, but I can easily imagine some that might help me defend it more effectively. And since I don't think we can infiltrate them"—several people smiled; they had all been shown holos of the hrossa—"that seems to suggest open meetings, with our side represented by a few, ah . . . , suitably skeptical volunteers."

"Mm. It's a quandary," admitted Esposito, for the first time sounding worn out herself. "We daren't risk being taken in, yet we can't afford not to find out if we *can* be taken in. The captain will decide . . . but Nathan's probably right, a few volunteers may have to be sent on a fact-finding mission. I don't mind saying I wish it weren't necessary."

"There's another way," said McWhirter. He somehow gave the impression of standing up again without actually doing so. "Much better and surer. We avoid all contact with the aliens—they can't contaminate what they can't get at. We go right around to the far side of the continent and found our own settlement. We warn the aliens to keep out of sending range of us. Any that ignore the warnings we burn, the instant they cross a clear boundary. Also, we avoid all further contact with Swarthmore, at least till we've got our own town established. We do all that and we're bound to succeed. This place was *made* for terrestrial life!"

He stopped and glanced around at his colleagues. Birtwistle wore a considering expression; O'Riley and Levy were frowning; the others' faces were blank or averted. "All right!" he burst out. "Look, I don't *enjoy* coming on all bloodthirsty and paranoid, whatever you bozos may think!" His voice was actually shaking. "As a matter of fact, in the Quakers' place—in point position—I'd probably have tried to be conciliatory too. But I think I'd have hoped, if the abos were able to persuade me to abort my mission, that the reserve team would take a good clear look at what happened and be just as ruthless as they had to be in order to ensure that humanity secures a base here. In fact, I'd be willing to bet that in their heart of hearts a fair number of *them* are hoping we'll get clean away from here and do what we came for. Maybe you're even wrong about Quinlan, you two—maybe *that's* his guilty secret, did either of you think of that?"

Jerry McWhirter had never spoken on any topic, to any member of his present audience, with a fraction of his present emotion. The room had become charged with embarrassment, yet the speech had made an impression.

Esposito's sharp movement and question broke the silence: "Nathan, you reminded us that Quinlan claims not to know what the natives might do to us." Her eyes swept the circle. "Did any of you feel that Quinlan or the others were lying outright this evening?"

McWhirter looked up. "Were they acting as enemy agents, you mean? No," he said in calmer tones. "Not even I thought that. They're dupes, not liars—they believed what they were saying."

THE HARD RATTLE of rain on the domicile roof, an exotic and voluptuous noisiness, fetched Maggie up out of a dead sleep the next morning. She knew instantly where she was; but, after rolling out to grope beneath the bunk for the jordan (a plastic pail with a lid and handle) and use it, she bundled herself back into bed. After yesterday, after the numbing spate of contradictory impressions and sensations that made judgment so difficult, she meant to begin this day deliberately. She meant to *take in* the actuality of Pennterra, of being on Pennterra, and of the situation her people had found here. The fatigue and mental muddle of yesterday would not do. Last night, because of it, she had mixed essential with inessential information and given herself away; she wanted no more incidents like that.

I have actually arrived, she told herself, *at the planet we call Epsilon Eridani II, which the Quakers named Pennterra for reasons of their own. My job here is to help make a home for Earth's displaced people, who by now have all but certainly guaranteed their extinction on their own world. Granted that we were sent because Earth needed a symbol of hope for the future, that not one person in a million believed we'd actually get here. We did get here! Pennterra's a place,* this *place, where you are, my dear Margaret, at this moment.*

Granted that not one in a million believed we could survive the journey. We did. *Nobody thought we could live here, even if we did survive,* but we can.

Pennterra's a place to live, *dummy.* You *are going to live here now. Really and truly, you are.*

Drawing and releasing slow shallow breaths, Maggie informed herself over and over of these facts and did her best to concentrate on what they meant. Beneath the rain's racket the building around and below her was silent. Fifty-odd Quakers had moved out to give eleven Sixers their collective privacy and to provide each of them with quarters of their own, a sensitive courtesy on the part of people who had not forgotten how luxurious both privacy and elbow room would feel after the years of shipboard crowding.

After a long time Maggie opened her eyes again. She'd gone to bed by light from the open door to the corridor, too exhausted to make sense of a note explaining how to kindle the lamps in her quarters. By watery daylight she now thoroughly surveyed the room she'd barely glanced around the day before.

Her bunk, like the chairs in the common room, was off the *Woolman* and more or less identical to her own bunk aboard ship; she had slept well in its familiar narrowness and its reality was easy to accept. The exposed uprights of the room were metallic, the floor, roof, and walls, including the one exterior wall, of opaque composition sheeting. Double unframed windows of the same stuff minus the opaquer had been hung like a pair of shutters in the outer wall. The *Down Plus Six* carried its own supply of these materials, light but strong, from which shelters could be rigged until the construction people had organized a local supply of something else. Frank Birtwistle's crew knew how to build a sturdy house of anything that occurred naturally on Earth, stone or wood—or sod, or mud, or dung, or bundles of reeds—as well as brick or concrete or wattle-and-daub, substances that had to be manufactured before anything could be constructed of them. Building and Design were fully prepared to adapt whatever they found here to the same purpose; Frank's whole crew tested off the charts in ingenuity and problem-solving.

Contemplating the pale Fiberplaast walls of her quarters, Maggie frowned; her brain had begun to turn over. The Quakers had their own Building and Design people, all able to bake a brick in an earthen oven or sun-dry one if need be. Why, then, had they spent six winters in the flimsy prefab domiciles, which must have been thrown up the first frantic weeks after landing? Both stones and clay were plentiful hereabouts; she had seen the geological reports and soil analyses. Might it be that the idea of building more solidly offended the hrossa? Whether or no, the Quakers would have to take steps before long. Iron in the alloy would be rusting badly in all this humidity; the stuff had never been meant for use in permanent structures.

Besides, the domiciles were *hideous*—though whoever's room this was had made an effort, scattered sheepskins about the floor and hung a sort of rough abstract tapestry made of the pelts of a small black-and-white furry animal against the exterior wall, whether as decoration or as insulation Maggie couldn't guess. Perhaps, like medieval tapestries, it was meant to serve both purposes at once.

Apart from a few big pillows, a small metal mirror, a couple of blue plastic packing cases that had once held ship's stores, and what appeared to be a clothes tree made by twisting strips of light wood together—the only artifact Maggie could see evidently wrought out of native material—the room was unfurnished. Some shelves, now empty—probably cleared for the use of the guest—had been mounted between wall studs. Of the usual tenant's personality very little could be inferred.

Even so Maggie had lost the need by this time to impress upon herself the actuality of this room and its contents. Wide awake now, she got out of bed again, padded to the window, and with some difficulty unlatched the right-hand panel, standing well back out of view of any Quakerly voyeur who hadn't had sense enough to stay indoors this sodden morning. She shoved; the window stuck, then swung wide open, and the sudden leaping odors of wet earth and rain, the flow of the damp fresh air over her bare skin, abruptly swamped her senses.

For the space of several gasped breaths her body responded with such shocking intensity to the morning's realness that her eyes and sinuses actually burned, her heart pounded painfully, and a pulse in her clitoris twanged like an itch, causing Maggie to grip herself there. She laughed in confusion and pleasure. The sensation, comical but unnerving, was as if her sensuous self were rearing, pawing the air, breaking traces and fences and lunging forth to assert its long-denied animal rights at this first irresistible whiff of the new world *A place to live!* The world and

her senses rushed together like long-parted lovers, dragging her
disconcerted mind along with them.

A light tap at the door made her jump guiltily. She hopped
across the floor on the stepping-stone sheepskins, grabbing her
uniform coat from the clothes tree in passing. In the time it took
her to stick arms into sleeves and unpuzzle the door latch, Maria Esposito had retreated a few paces along the corridor, but the
sound of futile clicking brought her back, and at the sight of her,
"Good God, Maria, look at you, you've gone native!" Maggie
cried in delight. The first officer had donned one of the Quakers' light pullover garments and was carrying a jordan by its
handle in one hand and a mound of what appeared to be folded
linens over the other arm. Her feet were bare. She looked like a
laundress, a thin, stern one.

"Fetching, aren't I?" said Maria drily. She nudged something toward Maggie with her toe. "That's breakfast. When you
hadn't come out and found it I thought you must still be asleep."

"No, dangling out the window." She swooped down on the
basket and started to undo the napkin folded around its contents. "As weather this may not be perfect, but that there should
be weather at all—"

Absorbed in the bundle, Maggie missed Maria's look of curiosity. "You won't mind braving the elements, then. I came to tell
you the Quakers have turned their bathhouse over to us for the
rest of the morning. Nice of them, they know we're under orders not to fraternize. The men will go along later. Interested?"

"Oh, *Lord*, yes. Gosh, *look* at all this stuff!" Nestling in the
napkin were two yeasty-smelling brown rolls, still faintly warm,
butter and jam in little baked-clay crocks, a hard-boiled egg and
paper twist of salt, and a stoppered jug. "What's in this—not
coffee!" She wiggled the fat cork out and sniffed.

"No, not coffee. Milk. I gather the coffee gave out three or
four years ago, and they haven't been synthesizing. What *is*
there's as good as it looks, though. They also brought over a
bunch of these gunnysack things I'm modeling, to wear over to
the bathhouse, and some towels. We take along uniforms to put
on after, and we wrap up in these." Maria had set down her pail
and was peeling off two doubled-over squares of fabric and a
folded-up piece of plastic from the bundle on her arm. She
handed them to Maggie.

"Uh, thanks." Maggie stuffed these offerings under one
armpit.

"By the way, chamber pots are emptied downstairs at the end of the corridor next to the WCs. The biggest door is a closet with a composting arrangement, and soap and water to swab out the pails with. Try not to splash. Ordinarily they only use these things for peeing in and visit the WCs personally for everything else, but it all goes into the same pit, so follow your own inclinations—just don't throw anything else down there. The only other instruction is: close all the lids tight when you leave. It's an anaerobic system."

Sniffing at her ravishing breakfast, Maggie nodded. "I copy."

"Annie's coming; I'm on my way to tell Joss and Two Clouds. Come down to the common room when you're ready and we'll all go over together—say in half an hour? There's some bath-house instructions too."

"OK." Maggie backed into her room clutching the various Pennterran gifts to the bosom of her uniform coat. "How'd you come by all this info anyhow—did a Quaker delegation call on you this morning, or what?"

"Something like that. Hurry up, I'll fill you in later."

NOBODY WAS ABOUT as the five Sixer women, shapeless in plastic ponchos, crossed the creek by a footbridge of planks and winced in their thin ship's slippers along a gravel path that ran beside it. Near the creek's mouth a small pond had been created by a low dam of rocks and earth; next to this stood the large prefab building easily identifiable as the settlement's back-to-back bathhouse and kitchen. Pipes emerging from the dam's narrow spillway led into a shedlike structure that straddled the creek below the dam. "That'll be our hot water," observed Joclyn Justice, the Chief of Mechanical Engineering, "and look—electric lights!"

They pushed through a set of swinging double doors and entered a big warm room. "Shoes here, clothes on pegs," said Maria, "and then we get a choice. This door's the sauna; this is the shower room. You can just have a shower, or you can make a ritual of it and do the sauna first, then soap and rinse in the shower, then rush out and plunge into the pool outside. Now, since we have things to discuss, I suggest that this time we all try the sauna, with or without the plunge to follow."

"Is it *very* hot in there?" Elizabeth Two Clouds wondered doubtfully. "I get dizzy in these things."

Annie pushed the door open. "It's pretty hot. It doesn't *smell* right, Maria."

"They used native willow, there's so little real wood. Shall we try it? If Two Clouds has to leave, we'll finish up later on, but this shouldn't take long and it really can't wait."

They undressed: bony brown Maria; pale Maggie and paler Joclyn; coppery lissome Two Clouds, the Chief of Food Processing; Anne, the color of unsweetened chocolate, buxom, plump, and bald. As a group they looked like a demonstration of the Sisterhood of Woman, though this thought occurred to none of them, accustomed as they were to one another.

Maggie was first through the sauna door, but stuck her head back out almost at once to say, "Bring towels to sit on, everybody, the seats of these benches are *woven!*"

The lilt in her voice made Two Clouds turn to look at her. "Are you as happy as you sound, Mags? Tune me in if you are, I could use a little of that myself."

"One will get you ten its the long-lost boyfriend," said Joclyn wickedly. "He sounds like a perfect paragon from what I've gathered. Frank can talk of nothing else."

"It's the long-lost mud, if anything," said Maggie. "Listen, Joss—and the rest of you too—I'm serving notice here and now that I'm not going to take kindly to being teased about George Quinlan. If you have to talk about it, talk where I can't hear you." She paused to let that sink in, then shut the door smartly.

The younger woman opened it again right away and came and sat by Maggie on the towel-padded, wickery bench. "Sorry," she said ruefully. "I guess it's just so thrilling to find out that any of us has any secrets left, I couldn't resist."

Maggie smiled at her. "I know. I'm not mad, I only want it understood that this is a case where care should be exercised."

Two Clouds said, "We may all have one or two very closely guarded secrets left—what we haven't got left is any manners. We've lost the habit." She spread her towel down and sat on it, gingerly, wrinkling her nose at the heat and smell.

"True." Joclyn made a face. "But all the same, Maggie, *if* you don't mind my asking, what was that about the long-lost mud— or weren't you being serious?"

Maggie looked surprised. "Oh, I don't know. Doesn't it make you feel cheerful just to *be* someplace—back in a world, with fresh air and a sky to look at, in spite of all the problems?"

They peered at her, birds perched on a wire. "It might, if the problems were less distracting," said Maria briefly from her place at the end of the row.

"I don't mean cheerful's *all* I feel—part of my mind is still thunderstruck at being here at all, and part's worrying right now about working things out with the Quakers and the natives some way we can all live with afterwards. But there's another part that's just tickled to death about being off the ship and having real rain to walk in again, and real creek sounds to listen to. A creek that isn't a sewer!" Her voice rose irrepressibly.

"Lucky you," said Two Clouds, not snidely. "I'm real happy for you if you feel like that, but to me mud's mud. I didn't go in for it that much at home either." Two Clouds, poised gracefully on the bench in her beautiful skin, was a full-blooded Sioux who they all knew to have lived in urban complexes her entire life prior to the three years of mission training. If anything, she was more at home in artificial environments than most Sixers, and in the days before constant companionship had worn away their ability to surprise one another had rather enjoyed confounding expectations to the contrary. Certainly, every animal and plant to enter her lab kitchens had been turned into raw materials beforehand: skinned, sectioned, cleansed of mud and blood.

"I can't say I'm feeling really happy to be here—yet—either," Annie admitted, "which is odd, because I expected to be just thrilled. Smell of mud, rain on the roof, you name it." (Looking at her sidelong, Maggie suddenly smiled at Annie's resemblance to a primitive Venus made of clay—a slightly underweight one, all belly, hips and breasts.) "But as a matter of fact, when we first came out of the lander—I don't really know *what* I expected, it was so exciting yet things were such a mess too—but still, I surely did assume it would be just wonderful to stand on solid ground again. My heart was going like a jungle drum. But when the moment came, and I climbed down and looked around, it was all too sort of overwhelming to be wonderful—all that, you know, open space, all that *sky*!"

Joclyn picked it up: "All that unpredictableness! All those odd types milling around in sacks and loincloths! I *still* feel weird as hell, even though the first shock's worn off some. In fact, now I think about it, I'm sure I was ribbing Maggie just to make things seem more normal. Keep it in the family." Joclyn, at thirty-three subjective years old, was younger than most of the other chiefs by close to a decade; she had barely finished graduate school before commencing her training for the mission. Her intuitive grasp of mechanics was brilliant, but for better and worse she knew less of life on Earth, and what "normal" might be there, than any of them did.

Maggie smiled upon Joclyn with sympathy, feeling pleased with herself for getting attuned to Pennterra so much more quickly than the others but surprised that so little effort had made such a difference. Right now, for instance, her skin was beginning to flush in the dry intense heat; her heart had speeded up; soon her nipples would be burning uncomfortably. Each of these sensations delighted and energized her, yet through them she could sense Maria's tension and the uneasiness of the rest. The question of why some of them adjusted more readily than others would intrigue the psychologists, and she made a mental note to remember to record the suggestions she'd given herself that morning.

Meanwhile, best not to emphasize the contrast. To distract attention from herself she said, "Maria, should the meeting come to order? I for one would like to know what's up."

The first officer leaned her gaunt frame with its small breasts forward to make eye contact all along the row of women. "It's soon told. Catherine Kendry and a man called Bell paid me a visit this morning. Bell was at the session last night, but he didn't have anything to say—a very good-looking fellow, mid-thirtyish? curly blond hair?"

"I know who you mean," said Annie, "the chap sitting right opposite me." The others murmured or nodded; they remembered too.

"He's a chemist, if that means anything in the here-and-now. Anyway. Along with information, laundry, breakfast, and a guided tour of the facilities, he and Kendry delivered a message. The elders—that's what they called 'em—from the nearest village of hrossa, someplace upriver from here, have agreed to meet with two Quakers and two of us tomorrow. They'll fly us up in a whirligig. Their rule is that only one gig ever lifts at any one time, and these little ones only carry four passengers, so that settles the size of the delegation. I called the captain back as soon as they left." She paused, and the others watched her now with all their attention.

"He says we go ahead. Like me, he thinks it essential for us to develop our own sources of information, and like me he sees no way to avoid risking somebody reliable." She leaned again to crane along the bench, tendons standing out in her forearms, and shook her head slightly. "Maggie, I'm sorry. Quinlan's asked for you especially. The captain says OK, but this is a volunteer job, so the decision's absolutely up to you. If you don't want to do it, for any reason at all, then don't. Dick thinks Ben could take over the administrative side of Medicine if it came to it, but he says if you have any misgivings on that score either, better say no."

Maggie sat very still, her gaze locked in Maria's. Sweat slipped down her ribs. Her thighs were blotchy, the backs of her hands completely wet: time to get out anyway. The others stared from a sudden distance created by the news, half startled, half fascinated. "How fast does Dick need an answer?"

"By dinnertime tonight. He's going to find a likely person with less responsibility for the second slot and send down him or her— probably him—before supper, so you've got till then to decide. If it's no, the captain will recruit somebody from among the chiefs already down here and thinking about whether in that case we'd want to volunteer. Jerry's briefing the men."

Maggie stood up. "Back in a minute." She walked stiffly toward the door.

"There's no special pressure on you, understand that," said Maria quickly. "It's even possible that your prior connection with Quinlan makes you the *worst* possible choice for the job, but you're the one to judge that—Dick can't and neither can I."

"I understand." Maggie pulled the door to carefully behind her and—ignoring the relative chill of air that had seemed warm twenty minutes before—marched through the foyer and the shower room, slid open a small clear door leading to the pond, and stepped outside.

The rain had settled down into a steady, drenching drizzle, so cold on Maggie's superheated shoulders that she gritted her teeth. Without stopping to consider, she took three long strides and dived into the pond. Unspeakable cold received her; her right knee scraped the bottom and she kicked furiously up to gasp at the surface; but by the time she had churned across the pond and back again its waters had become refreshing and benign, much warmer than the air or the needle-shower rain. Somewhat settled down herself, Maggie sloshed up the steps and made for the door, then—momentarily turning around—started violently at the sight of a smallish poncho-hung shape watching her from the high ground on the other side of the pond.

When the shape knew itself observed it waved and called "Hello!" in what sounded to Maggie like a boy's preadolescent alto, not that she was an expert on boys. "Hello!" she called back, straining to see through the veil of rain. The boy, if it was a boy, now made a megaphone of his hands and shouted something she didn't catch. "What?" she called—realizing in the same instant that besides being stark naked (and who could tell what the Quaker views on that might be) she was violating the order against any unofficial communication with the settlement people (if yelling at each other thus could be called communicating).

Either the boy was disobeying orders too, or else he hadn't been given any. "You're—not—supposed—to—dive—in," he was shouting, and then something that sounded like "It silts up."

A needle-filled gust reminded Maggie that she was bare and freezing. Sending him one last wave, she ducked back inside and hurried—carefully, because of the slickness of the floor—back toward the sauna's heat, wondering whether the others had heard the exchange above the hum of the generator. If not, she would keep it to herself. What had been natural in fact might sound more awkward in the telling, and the question that had to be settled called for all her attention just now.

And just now she didn't mind withholding this one tidbit from Maria, either.

At any rate the swim, with its odd coda, had gotten her past the first jolt of resentment at having her choices put to her in front of Joss, Annie and Two Clouds, and at the preposterous and insulting idea of making Ben's fictional incompetence an excuse for turning the job down. Maria, who did everything she did for a reason, had done these things for a reason too. Maggie had wanted to dissociate herself from George, she had said as much to Joss, but the Sixers could not afford to indulge her; the "prior connection" might need to be turned to account, and personal considerations could not be allowed to interfere unless they might actually damage the mission's chances for success. And that was what she needed to assess now.

Her hand on the sauna door, Maggie grinned in sudden amazement and shook her head. Despite being safe on Pennterra at last after years of uncertainty, here they all were wrangling and manipulating—right back to business as usual. What a safety valve human nature had developed for itself, that yesterday's staggering marvel or shattering catastrophe should so promptly be accepted as the new day's fact of life.

4 George

The spot they had chosen for the picnic lay somewhat outside the main flow of settlement activity, a grassy area between the meeting house and the Delaware River where a young grove of walnut trees threw some patchy shade. The special delegation to the hrossa from Swarthmore Settlement stood in its coolness now with their two backs to the river, double-checking the preparations for the preexpedition lunch and briefing. Both were fresh from the bathhouse, damp of hair and clean of fingernail. In honor of the visitors, both wore rawhide sandals and brand-new belted tunics cut from bolts of cotton brought from Earth—the Quakers having found their "plain" uniforms, put on for the first formal meeting, inappropriate for continued use.

"The damn things make us look like a bunch of Yanks and Rebs at a powwow," Billy Purvis had complained; and besides, Quakers were anti-uniform by tradition.

The day was dazzling, blue and sharp as a noontime in October after yesterday's long rain and perfect for a picnic. "Everything looks just beautiful," said Katy Kendry. The kitchen squad had carried benches and a trestle table across the creek and set them up under the trees; they had then cast aside all restraint and set out the stacks of bowls and plates, and the four mugs, on a freshly laundered and ironed white linen tablecloth dug up from somewhere. On the table several round rye loaves and a cream-colored cheese had been set out on cutting boards, and there was a vast green salad in a wooden bowl. In the middle of all this a tall vase of asters and geraniums blushed and glowed.

"It really does. Just beautiful," George repeated gratefully to Ned Pedersen and Norah Bell, who had just climbed the slope bearing last-minute items: soup in a terra-cotta tureen (hot) and a large plastic pitcher of cider (chilled). "Please thank everybody for us, will you? This was a lot of extra work."

Norah put the pitcher down at one end of the table. "It does look nice, doesn't it? Do you know, I really enjoyed trying to make a table look attractive for a change. I wonder if we shouldn't try to live a little more graciously ourselves. We're all turning into pigs—shovel it down and back to the fields."

"I draw the line at ironing any more tablecloths, though, for people to spill soup on." Ned set his burden down safely at the table's other end with a grunt and stepped back to admire the effect. "Hmm, not bad. Hope it helps the cause, you two."

"It sure can't hurt," said Katy warmly.

"Whoops, here they come! Good luck!" Norah darted away down the path. Ned hung back long enough to sling an arm each around George and Katy and say firmly, "Hey, everybody knows you'll do your damnedest for us, don't worry!" and squeeze before dashing after Norah. At the bridge both turned to wave. They had not quite reached the kitchen door when the Sixer delegation arrived at the table in the shade, and Maggie Smithson had begun thanking George, a bit drily, for his special invitation.

"Thank *you*, for accepting. I so much hoped you would." George clasped her hand, then impulsively held on to it, searching her face—looking her over altogether, in fact, more thoroughly than he had looked at anybody for years and years. Maggie in her blue uniform was as trim as ever, but the fine straight brown hair he remembered was threaded now with coarser gray, and the tan had faded to shipboard pallor. Yet he felt much more pleasure than he had been prepared to feel at the sight of her, of a face known yet altered by time, not strange, yet not familiar as the three-hundred-odd faces of Swarthmore were familiar to him. He found that he loved looking at her, and not until Maggie tugged back her hand and showed signs of discomfiture did George wake up to the fact that he was being rude.

Hastily then he introduced the two women to each other and turned to greet a tall blocky young man of whom he had observed (with much relief) only that this was *not* Gerald McWhirter. Maggie introduced him now as "Byron Powell, George, from Engineering. A first-rate swimmer, presently a little out of practice apart from a quick turn or two around the bathhouse pool."

Disappointment must have shown too plainly in George's hopelessly transparent face, since Powell saluted and shook hands, then immediately said a shade defensively, "The captain tried his best to find you a farmer, sir, but all our farmers say they can't swim for shucks, so I'm afraid you're stuck with me. You did say the swimming part was more important than the farming part, if push came to shove."

Aware that he had now managed to make both his guests uncomfortable, George turned to Katy in dismay; Katy caught the look and burst out laughing as she shook Powell's hand. "You mustn't mind George, please. He's a very steady fellow and the best possible person to take you up to meet the hrossa, but it's just as well he wasn't interested in a political career. His face is a viewscreen: instant display."

Everyone smiled and relaxed, even George, who managed to look both embarrassed and rueful at once. "It's indecent to be so tactless, I'm sorry, Byron—and please don't call me 'sir.' We *were* hoping for a farmer, but we're delighted to have you all the same, and I hope you can find it in your heart to overlook my appalling manners."

Byron shifted his thick shoulders and murmured something agreeable. "Please sit down, everybody," said Katy now, adroitly playing hostess. "On that side, you guests, so you'll have the view of the river. George, you're right here." She handed him the cheese knife, briskly lifted the lid off the tureen with a pot holder, and began to ladle up the steaming soup.

"What in the world went into this soup? It's so good I can't believe it," Maggie asked a minute later.

"It's vegetable, ah, rabbit I think," said George. He stopped slicing cheese to poke around with a spoon in his own bowl. "Everything from the kitchen garden that's ready to pull, dig, or pick. Let's see. Tomatoes, sweet corn, pole beans, leeks, chopped greens of some sort—chard, Katy? or beet tops?—chard. And carrots, some potatoes, a little of the new summer broccoli cultivar—not too good, *I* don't think—and some herbs, and that's everything. The stock's probably rabbit, and the meat certainly is, because we had stewed rabbit for dinner last night. Glad you like it." He poured out mugs of foamy cider and handed them round, then picked up his spoon again.

"Do you mind my asking why you wanted a farmer especially?" Byron asked, looking from under his eyebrows at George. He had not, obviously, put the matter out of mind.

"Of course not," George laid his spoon back down, happy to be asked. "You've been briefed about our bargain with the hrossa, the restrictions we've agreed to abide by?" Byron nodded. "Well, you know, we were mostly scientists and scientific technicians on the *Woolman*. We had an agronomist or so aboard, and a good supply of seed, and viable embryos of various food and farm animals, though nothing like as broad a selection as I imagine yours is—just sheep, goats, rabbits, chickens, several species of fish, earthworms, and some swarms of bees—but we'd meant to feed ourselves, for a while at least, mainly by processing any local stuff we couldn't eat, plants, animals, carbonaceous rock, whatever, while we decided on a permanent lo-

cation and got on with building a real town, as well as collecting
all the data we could about the planet. Then later we were going
to bring some meat animals to term as we got around to developing an agricultural base for the town. That was the plan.''

Maggie had been eating steadily, her eyes on George. "But the
ban on the use of machinery put paid to all that."

"Yes, totally." George shifted his position to face her. "And
of course nearly all the real farmers were coming on the second
ship, with you. None of *us* had the faintest notion of how to set
about raising crops without tractors or cultivators or even so
much as a pair of oxen to pull the plow—the *Down Plus Six* was
bringing horse and cattle embryos; we didn't have any. So," he
ducked his head, put the spoon back in the cooling soup and
moved it around, "we wanted an expert to see what we've been
able to do here without them, just by using the computer library
backed up by trial and error."

Maggie grinned shrewdly. "The point being that if you did all
this without draft animals or agricultural expertise, we could do
at least as well and probably much better making full use of
both."

"And with trees for fences, and us to help you—precisely.
Also," said Katy, "we were quite looking forward to knocking
you flat with astonishment and admiration. We're awfully proud
of what we've accomplished here. *Eat,* George." She pushed
away her empty bowl and leaned her forearms on the white cloth.
"The first couple of years we had a truly miserable time. It
turned out we couldn't digest *anything*, animal or vegetable, that
grows naturally on Pennterra. The stuff didn't poison us, didn't
even make us queasy, but it passed straight through us like wood
pulp. And the hrossa had no help to offer but sympathy. They
couldn't lift the ban, even temporarily, even if we all died. Nobody did, but let me tell you, that first one was a hungry old
winter—we arrived too late in the year to put in a crop, so after
the supplies started to run low we lived for months on foddercake, if you can imagine that."

The guests looked horrified. Foddercake was made of algae,
a greenish-gray crumbly substance meant strictly for emergency
use. The ship's tanks could supply it endlessly, but it was no fun
at all to eat, even once. But very nourishing, and produced with
a tiny fraction of the energy that processing raw local stuff would
have consumed; and there were plenty of people on Earth who
would have been tickled to death to have it.

"The landers used to go up and bring back load after load of the stuff," said George dreamily. He sighed, shook his head, smiled. "Never mind: that was a long time ago." As he spoke he stacked the soup bowls and passed plates and small knives round the table. "We wasted no time that winter, though; we went to school to the computer every day, learning how people used to grow crops and manufacture necessities long before the industrial revolution. And we analyzed the soil so we'd know exactly how to treat it come spring and laid out the fields and pastures. And we started composting the native vegetation."

Maggie broke off a hunk of bread from a loaf, saying cheerily, "Our agronomy people should be fascinated with your setup here. It's really a living museum of antiquarian agriculture, isn't it?"

"Not exactly." George looked smug. "Our methods of working the soil are antiquated, but our seed and stock would make a neolithic farmer weep. We've got perennial corn, soybeans, and cereals, and the lab's working on a strain of perennial wheatgrass that should outproduce anything you ever heard of. Our corn produces an ear at every node, sweet corn and field corn both. And a couple of our dairy goats give almost as much milk as a Jersey cow—this is some of it, by the way; the cheese and butter are courtesy of Amathea and her many descendants. You can probably see some of them from here." He twisted round on the bench and sighted across the river. "Yes, there's a bunch of 'em, see? Straight across the Delaware, by the back fence. I imagine your livestock people will be *very* interested in Amathea. She broke records when she was younger, and now her daughters and granddaughters are breaking the ones *she* set."

Byron, polite guest, asked between bites of bread and cheese: "Can't the goats eat the native vegetation? Seems like if you can digest a tin can you ought to be able to digest an alien plant."

"That about tin cans is a myth, you know," said George a bit severely. "The goats can't make anything of the native browse either, none of the terrestrial life-forms can. No, we feed them alfalfa hay and garden wastes, and this and that. Field corn. Oats. Molasses, the years we grow cane. The sheep do well enough on pasture when they're not lactating, but goats aren't grazers by nature; they want twig ends and blackberry canes and a lot of other things we can't let them have. They got into the orchard last spring just as the pears were blooming, so this fall we have no pears and rationed apples—and no cider at all, I fear, next winter. This we're drinking will be the last of the lot. I wish, for their sake and ours, we'd brought many more apparently *non*useful plants along—for instance, we badly need a stickery shrub like hawthorn to train for hedgerows, but nobody dreamed there'd be any point in bringing hawthorn or the like—"

Maggie crunched her lettuce and cucumbers with evident relish while listening to this, glanced with heightened respect at her mug of cider, but interrupted here to herd George back to the main topic. "Can the native species utilize the settlement's crops, though?"

George didn't mind what topic he was handed, so long as it bore upon the situation. "No, and our stuff must all be just as unpalatable to them as theirs is to us, because, well, you can't tell from the soup or salad, but produce from the kitchen garden is perfectly blemish-free, always. And that's another immense advantage we have over the neolithic farmer: no stored grain losses from rodents, no losses in the field from woodchucks or deer, no corn borers, slugs, tomato hornworms, Japanese beetles, no blights or wilts, no viruses—no pest or disease damage at all! We have to work constantly at building up soil structure and fertility—it's sandy here and deficient in micronutrients like chromium and selenium—and we're at the mercy of the weather like every farming community that ever was. But nothing *else* reduces our harvest except when our own stock gets loose. Well, it's not pure loss at that, goats can make milk and hides out of pear twigs as well as clover hay. But still."

"Maggie, what's so funny?" Katy asked suddenly.

Maggie's eyes had been sparkling, and crinkling at the corners, and her mouth twitching; now she laughed openly. "George is! Oh, I don't mean *funny* really, not in the circumstances—but it is hilarious to *me*, George, to hear you sounding so wise and involved about agricultural things, when I can remember so well how my little allotment in New Haven used to bore you practically to stupefaction! You'd go on about rocks in that totally absorbed way, but in those days you thought plants were too ephemeral to bother about . . . oh dear!" She made an effort to smother her mirth. "Sorry. It did strike me funny—just a bit of welcome comic relief, no doubt." But her color had heightened and her eyes still shone.

George was taken aback—his attention had been altogether elsewhere—but after a moment he discovered himself to be rather gratified than otherwise. Nobody in Swarthmore, except Billy, had known him long enough to make such an observation. It was nice for a change to have the present connected up, through

Maggie, with the past, the personal past; most of the time it seemed to him that his present life had made a clean break with his life before the *Woolman*, a break even more absolute than a switch from minerals to vegetables, or even from Earth to Pennterra, would imply. The period to which Maggie had alluded was in fact not flattering to George—in his own view he had behaved rather badly then—but he felt a certain nostalgia even for the years at Yale, if only because they were so entirely behind him now.

Katy was regarding Maggie with a keener, friendlier interest. "You knew George a long time ago, didn't you? Tell me, was he always so sort of serious and sweet, and such a *talker*?"

"Very serious, and *very* verbal, yes indeed. Completely unable to hide his feelings, what you called instant display, always. He does seem to have mellowed quite a bit," she added, smiling broadly at the subject of these remarks.

The thought flashed through George's head that Maggie had turned the tables on him. "Let's get back on track, ladies, if you don't mind," he said, revealing most of the traits she had mentioned in his voice and/or complexion—revealing also, by the use of a gender term, that he was flustered, a fact not lost upon his fellow delegate. "We were discussing, ah—"

"The absence of pests on Pennterra," said Katy soothingly, "apart from the human sort. Do you notice, Maggie and Byron, that we're having a pest-free picnic? No ants, no flies, no mosquitoes, and you wouldn't dare leave this on the ground at home, would you?" She leaned sideways to reach under the table and draw forth a basketwork tray containing four blueberry-studded baked custards and a jug of cream.

George drew five deep breaths while his guests passed and poured busily. When they had begun to dip their spoons into the rich confection he forged ahead. "Not only no ants—no *native* creepy-crawlies either. There aren't any left in the settlement now, they can't share living space with us. Somehow the hrossa knew it would be like that. In six years the native plants have been all but exterminated in this part of the valley, except for the river willows and some amazingly tough weed-type species able to grow despite the changes in soil chemistry and the absence of other native flora and fauna. But in general they don't even put up a good fight—and that, of course, is why we've had to be quarantined. Wherever we go, even without the mass destruction we'd make with machines, we'll terraform the planet willy-nilly, just as we're terraforming the valley."

Having gathered that much steam, he eyed the engineer squarely. "As a matter of fact, Byron, *you* might give some thought in your spare time to designing us a filter system that would keep the upper valley of the Delaware from contaminating the lower valley and the estuary. Runoff from our fields and pastures is eventually going to pollute the river to the point where all the native aquatic life will die or leave. It hasn't happened yet—" his eyes unfocused as a memory of transcendent immersion flashed behind them "—but in my opinion it's bound to eventually. It would have been wonderful if we'd been able to establish a terrestrial freshwater ecosystem here, but that hardly seems possible now. I dream sometimes of taking my son fishing... which is in a class with my dream about going out to the goat pasture some morning and finding half a dozen Belgian draft horses looking over the fence at me! Eventually we might dig ourselves a pond, I suppose...but anyway, before too much longer I'd like to start experimenting with ways of purifying our alien effluents out of the lower river."

"A passive system?" Though Byron didn't sound very interested, he was attentive and spoke pleasantly.

"I'm afraid so."

"But you're raising fish for food now, aren't you?"

"In the greenhouse tanks, yes. It's not the same, believe me. The ones we put in the creek and the Delaware in cages all died."

"You keep calling it the Delaware," Maggie remarked. She had finished eating and wore a sated, slightly glazed expression. Her high spirits, now firmly in check, still seemed to leak a little brightness at the edges; but the implicit question signaled a turn toward the business before them, and the Quakers, recognizing this, squeezed hands beneath the table. From now on it would no longer be possible for George to fight off self-consciousness by rattling on about whatever came, or was put, into his head.

Luckily the long speech about water pollution had restored his balance. He nodded. "We named it the day after we landed, a sentimental gesture to our own history, like calling the settlement Swarthmore and the planet Pennterra. Hross name-words are all more or less unpronounceable—by me, and probably by the human vocal apparatus generally, though my boy may prove me wrong. He usually comes up to the village with me. He was six when we landed."

"They speak with their spiracles, like dolphins," Katy put in. "Their vocal plates and valves are associated with the respiratory system; the organs for ingestion and mastication belong to another system altogether.''

Again Maggie passed smoothly over these elaborations and hewed to George's principle: "Is h'rossa? hurrossa? is that their name for themselves, or an anglicized version of it?''

George eagerly started to reply, but Katy interrupted: "Let me talk now, so we can get going; you eat your custard. Time's getting on.'' He glanced with surprise at their empty dishes and his own untouched one, then made a wry face and dug in.

"No. We can't pronounce that either, can't even come close— well, Danny can, but he may be a special case; he's a natural mimic. In English they call themselves the People, just like terrestrial primitives used to. No, *hrossa* comes from a book by an early-twentieth-century Christian writer named C. S. Lewis, an Oxford pal of Tolkien's.'' The listeners nodded; they knew Tolkien's work, though neither had heard of Lewis. "He wrote a novel about an Englishman who gets hijacked to Mars, which he finds populated by friendly Martians that call themselves hrossa—that's the plural proper noun; it's *hross* for singular and modifier. These Martians look like seven-foot stoats with black fur—a stoat was a kind of skinny predator like a weasel, not like *our* hrossa at all—but they *were* amphibious, intelligent creatures with a Stone Age technology, and, I don't know, the name sort of stuck. *They* quite like it; they love parables and religious myths even when they find them baffling, and Lewis's novel is allegorical apparently. They love to hear episodes from Quaker history, too, though they have a hard time grasping the idea of religious persecution.''

"So do I,'' said Maggie. "And what do they call the planet? The world, I should say; I don't suppose they realized it was a planet until you told them.''

"Oddly enough,'' said Katy, "they did. I don't think they had any notion of its true size, but they knew it rotated and orbited the sun instead of vice versa. Their name for the planet sounded to one Friend, who's an amateur anthropologist and up on Amerindians, like the Sioux Indian name for the Great Spirit: Tanka Wakan. They liked that when he explained it, so now that's what we and they both call the planet when we talk about it together. It's quite a good term, in fact—sometimes when they say 'Tanka Wakan' they seem to *mean* what we might mean by God, which isn't unrelated to the Sioux meaning either, I gather.'' She suddenly looked rather sad. "We ought to stop saying Pennterra altogether, I guess, but somehow we never do.''

It occurred to George that Katy, fond as she was of the hrossa, remained clear in the pattern of her allegiances. *Not like me,* he thought, then pushed the thought away.

"Our Chief of Food Processing is a full-blooded Sioux," said Maggie, "but I doubt she could shed any light on the question."

George cleared his throat. "The hrossa will probably look pretty odd to you two at first. You saw the same pictures everybody saw, day before yesterday—did you see them, Byron?—but we figured these might give you a better idea of what to expect."

From beneath the table he brought out a loaded holo viewer and passed it over to Maggie. The Sixers bent their heads together above the screen. George and Katy watched and supplied commentary as images flicked by. There were hrossa collecting vegetable food in baskets, small hrossa swimming in the charge of a big one, a group of hrossa occupied in a small field cluttered with plants. In one holo half a dozen adults were bearing along the corpse of a huge swamp turkey hung from a pole: four stumpy trailing legs, two tiny vestigial arms, a pair of narrow blue leathern "wings" far too small to carry such a massive creature aloft, and enough meat on its thorax to feed an entire village.

In another holo two hrossa were pushing front to front, heads back, bulging eyes rotating upward, spiracles dilated. Byron said, "Is this what I think it is?"

"Copulation," George confirmed, "for lack of a better word anyway. You have a fair chance of seeing this whenever you visit a village—the hrossa are uninhibited about sex."

"Which is which?" Byron wanted to know, and at the same instant Maggie asked, "Do they come in males and females?"

"They're hermaphroditic," Katy volunteered, "and ovoviviparous, like some of our reptiles and fishes. We think *all* the higher forms of animal life on Pennterra are made like that, each individual with a complete set of everything, though we're not too clear about how that works in practice."

"The fact is," said George, "there's a hell of a lot we're not too clear about. As you're going to learn, in a frontier community nobody has much energy left over from the sheer effort of struggling to survive. There are a thousand things every one of us is dying to know about this world as it relates to his or her own field, but we're farmers and goatherds here for a good while to come. And, of course, we've been *in quarantine,* with no chance, even if there were time, to observe the ecology outside the valley—and we change it too fast where we are to observe it. But we do have these.''

He held the button down and watched the counter, then gave the viewer back. The Sixers looked at that display in silence, then the next, then the next.

"How," said Byron in an odd voice, "did you get hold of a specimen for dissection?"

"From the Lake-Between-Falls village, where we're going today," Katy replied. "One afternoon during the second winter a couple of us flew up for a language lesson. When the lesson was over, KliUrrh—you'll meet him today, he's an important elder, a kind of priest—KliUrrh said, 'We have a gift for you,' and led us down to the beach. Several hrossa were just putting this body into the lake to swim it over so we could bring it home in the whirligig. KliUrrh explained that, some time before, they'd picked up from one of us—actually from one of our medical people, Larry Shea—an intense wish to learn how the People are put together internally. Well, the villagers had discussed this and agreed among themselves that the body of the next one of them who died should be loaned to us for exploration and discovery. They stipulated only that all the bodily parts and substances should be returned to them, and that no preservatives or fixatives or stains should be used on them, so their friend could be given back to Tanka Wakan in his completely natural state."

George leaned across the table. "Four of us worked outside in the snow for a week last winter on this old fellow. These are his sexual organs, here—pouch, penises, vaginal passages, and that's the uterus, or egg chamber, where the baby develops *in ovo*—all atrophied, so as I said there's still a lot we don't know about hross reproduction. But most of what we do know we learned that week."

Maggie and Byron peered at the plate labeled *Reproductive System*. George added, "Larry asked KliUrrh whether the letter of the 'preserved' taboo would be violated if we took pictures. He was taken aback. He said he'd been speaking literally, that we were as welcome to make records of that kind—he'd seen holos before, obviously—as we were to make memories."

"And you gave the bits and pieces back when the week was up?"

"Every smidgen. Even some sponges saturated with fluids."

Maggie looked up. "You said the hrossa 'picked up' the desire for a specimen—'picked up' how?"

George and Katy exchanged glances. "Empathically," said
George. "You must have been wondering about that." He
switched off the viewer and pushed back the bench. "Time we
were off, I think. Ready, Maggie? Byron? Throw some towels in
the gig, Katy, will you? That breeze will be brisk by the time
we're done. I'll sign out the key and meet you at the pad in five
minutes."

Not more than ten minutes later they had lifted, and Katy was
piloting the whirligig, electric motor buzzing quietly, northeast-
ward toward the mountains, following the glinting curves of the
river. Below them, cultivated fields—greens of corn, soybeans,
and potatoes, the several greeny-golds of hay, barley, rye, and
oats, and the pure blond of wheat—spread out and back in a tidy
patchwork from both banks of the blue Delaware for a mile or
so upstream and down of the settlement, alien corn photosyn-
thesizing and ripening rapidly beneath the wrong sun's vigorous
blessing. Sheep dotted the newly mown half of their pasture,
white against grass-green and hay-yellow beside the blue border
of the river.

Visibility was superb, colors bright, outlines crisp. The visitors gazed and were silent. This pleasant sight, a modestly pros-
pering farmscape of small enclosures oddly bare of hedges and
thickets, had not been seen on Earth for decades, anywhere; to
their eyes it was a storybook illustration come to life. George
could guess their feelings. Accustomed to this view as he was, it
rarely failed to reconfirm a conviction that his people were
meant, perhaps deserved, to live in such a landscape, and with
active regret (grown more mechanical of late) that human stew-
ardship of the Earth had been so bungled. He knew the Sixers
must be thinking, as all the Quakers had thought in those early
months and as some did still: *People could do anything with this
world, if it weren't for the fucking hrossa.*

From up here the Quakers' immense investment of brow-
sweat was invisible; if you didn't know better, you might easily
assume this farmscape had been created by tractor power. One
much like it could be, though there would be some differences of
shape and especially of scale.

The whirligig hummed on, its beeline shadow skimming the
lower foothills. As the land rose, the signs of alien impact
dropped behind them. The river sank between the sides of a
deeper valley, almost a canyon, cutting a steep irregular course
through a low forest of fibrous blue-green treelike vegetation.
Many ponds and lakes filled the hollows in the topography be-

low; hundreds of grooves in the foliage showed where streams and rivulets squirmed to join the narrowing river; range upon range of rounded old-looking mountains came into far view, purple and mauve with distance.

Occupied with their own thoughts, the two Sixers, rapt and wordless, continued to stare down upon the passing scene, and George settled against the backrest of his saddle. All day, making virtue of necessity, he had used talk to concentrate his mind and prevent his fluttery feelings from intruding (much) upon his business with Maggie and Byron. But he needed now to let the feelings surface and be exorcised. He had learned early on that to come into KliUrrh's presence carrying concealed emotional fright invariably resulted in some sort of outburst or loss of control—a giggling fit, an orgasm, an attack of rage or tears. This was always inconvenient and usually embarrassing. He particularly dreaded a recurrence of the gentle, perplexed disappointment KliUrrh had made him aware of during the several meetings marred by explosions of his wrath. George's face was not quite the open book Maggie and Katy believed, but the effect of hross empathy upon him was such that he was simply unable to be with KliUrrh and keep emotional secrets to, or from, himself.

Not today, O Lord, O not today, he pleaded now, quoting Henry V according to Shakespeare; *everything depends on today. Let me not mess this up.* He had not even tried to avoid taking the newcomers up to meet the elders; Billy Purvis might substitute for him in the formal sessions, but no one else was nearly so close to any of the hrossa. He was the one for the job. And in fact he remained clear about what he hoped to accomplish, of one mind with his community in this. Yet whenever the flow of discussion ceased, as now, self-doubt assailed his centeredness. He would have to confront it now.

Neither of the Sixer delegates had challenged him or accused him, or the Quakers through him, of anything. Their captain, evidently wishing the picnic itself to go smoothly, must have instructed Byron and Maggie to stick to the gathering of straight information. Well and good; but in his own mind George now accused himself plainly of being more devoted to KliUrrh, for no reason he could name, than to any human or group of humans or to humanity as a whole. Gazing down into the algae-colored jungle he squarely faced up to the fact that he was guilty beyond any doubt of this crime—for he did consider it a kind of involuntary crime. But the night in the moonlit river had settled some question for him. He had gone AWOL from his mission, permanently, and very soon he would have to confess this before the meeting.

The river had also made George strangely shy of seeing Kli-Urrh. He wished hotly that they could have met for the first time after that experience on some occasion other than this one. All right: *Why am I shy of him? Why do I feel so much like a lover uncertain of his welcome?*

The answer was not far to seek: *Because in effect that's what I am. I am. I need him to love me. I do seem to need that,* and embarrassment made his ears get warm. George Quinlan had a modest, simple heart. It was relatively easy for him to acknowledge that a higher allegiance had replaced those he had once held to his own people, his late wife, or his solemnly undertaken mission; admitting to himself that he yearned for KliUrrh to love him back was another matter entirely.

More than Danny? he made himself ask, and felt with a rush of relief that at least he could answer no to that question. Score one for normality.

So. I'm involved to the point of obsession with KliUrrh, but Danny's more important. Put like that it doesn't sound so dire. But I think it probably is fairly dire, all the same. As for his reciprocating, that's pure anthropomorphism; I doubt he can.

Now about Maggie.

He pondered this. He had wanted her in the delegation because he knew and trusted her. Her coming would assure the presence of at least one fair-minded Sixer at Lake-Between-Falls. He had been almost shocked by his pleasure in seeing her and glad she should still be fond of him—grateful, too, for the contact with a person able to connect him with himself-when-young.

But none of these were deep responses. They had flared and faded, and just at that moment he felt nothing much about Maggie. All feelings of that sort had been eclipsed by the knowledge that in less than an hour he would be in the presence of KliUrrh, and by nervousness on several counts about the outcome of that meeting.

At this point there formed in George's mind a thought, complex and precise, detailing how with Maggie's help the Sixers might be persuaded to accept the hross restrictions. This was rapidly succeeded by a counterthought conveying with terrible clarity how insane it had been ever to believe the Sixers could be brought round to this, and his heart sank.

No time remained for further preparation. The whirligig had mounted above a last ridge, they had all caught sight of the circular lake that brimmed brilliantly in its basin before spilling over, giving perpetual birth to the infant Delaware, and Katy had begun her descent.

5   *Maggie and Byron*

Maggie watched the ground rise up to catch at the whirligig and for a moment felt unable to move. During the quiet flight her adrenaline had ceased to flow, and she had begun to appreciate the costliness of her situation. Her sense of extraordinary physical well-being, present from the first morning after landfall, had not much reduced either her apprehension about the coming encounter or the quandary of George; even aboard the whirligig these forces had held Maggie at the center of a three-way tension: aloft in the dazzling Pennterran day with that lovely lunch inside her, George in the saddle behind, speeding toward the mountains and the hrossa.

They were down. Katy killed the engine and unclipped herself from her harness. "We don't land near the village—no machines allowed. You can just about see it from here."

She pointed. Byron leaned forward to look and said in amazement, "You people swim all that way, twice, every time you come up here? It must be, what, nearly two klicks from here to the other side?"

"About that," said Katy, "but there's no way to walk around, and the hrossa like us to swim. That little island is our goal today, though, not far, and the water's warm."

"You'd have to use boats in winter, wouldn't you?"

"Oh sure. We don't come up that much in winter though." She opened her door and swung down onto a carpetlike growth of tiny, densely crowded plants, rather like dry moss or nappy lichen.

Maria Esposito had briefed the two Sixers. They knew: that the meeting would take place on a small island some four hundred meters out from the beach where the gig would land;

that no boat would be provided, the party being expected to strip and swim naked to the meeting place; and that only volunteers who were up to it all that need apply. At the time Maggie had felt up to it entirely, once she had seen her way clear to accepting George's special invitation. He'd obviously remembered her as a strong swimmer (or he wouldn't have asked), and this had pleased her. Now, pushing her own door open and climbing down, she wondered how she would manage even to reach the island.

"Tired, Maggie?" Katy, ever vigilant, had observed her effortful descent and came round to Maggie's side of the gig. "You must both be exhausted, all this strangeness and then the flight up here—it's fatal to lose your momentum, isn't it? Especially after a solid meal."

George and Byron had dismounted and climbed down, meanwhile, from the aft saddles. George walked down to the water straightaway and sighted toward the island, then toward the village, shading his eyes with his hand. (Through her fatigue Maggie was struck suddenly with his likeness to the figures on the cover of her college copy of *The Iliad*, which showed a frieze of Greek charioteers. In his belted tunic and sandals, all George lacked was the hero's wreath of laurel.) "Phew, what a glare! We haven't had a day this bright in weeks." He scanned the ruffled blue water, hard, then turned and walked back toward the others, untying his cord belt as he came.

"It's too soon after lunch," said Katy firmly. "We had a tail wind; we're way early. I think we should wait another half hour or so."

George was headed straight their way and they all saw his "instant display" of annoyed resistance. Maggie said quickly, "Katy's sparing our pride, but frankly we could do with some rest before the swim. I'm feeling a mite middle-aged if you want to know the truth."

Byron said just as quickly, "Hey, speak for yourself, Commander; *I'm* not tired—I'm ready to start whenever you say."

Maggie's eyebrows went up (as did George's). "Are you? Well then, it's only me. I'd been thinking I'd just tough it out, but Katy's right—things are exciting enough already, we don't need a dramatic rescue to liven them up any more."

The thought of what the accidental drowning of a Sixer section chief would mean to relations between the newcomers and the Quakers seemed to strike them all at the same instant. George slapped his brow. "Maggie, forgive me! I'm overexcited and nervous, and it's making me inconsiderate as well as even more stupid than usual. Of course we can wait awhile. The hrossa don't run on clock time, it won't matter a bit to them. I was only thinking of myself.''

Byron looked askance at George, as if he thought this was carrying openness and modesty too far. Already sweat had begun to soak the collar of his shirt beneath the blue jacket, and Katy said, frowning, ''We may as well undress at least—Byron, you and Maggie stay in the whirligig's shadow; I never till this minute thought of sun block. There's no shade on the island, you'll probably burn some anyway, but it'll be a lot worse if you get a head start now. I'm sorry, it was really dumb not to think of it, we none of us did.'' While she was speaking, Katy had loosened the belt over her own tunic and with total un-self-consciousness now pulled it over her head and kicked off her sandals. George shucked his as well and dropped it in the sand. Neither of them was wearing anything underneath.

Recalling her trepidations about the Quaker views on nakedness, Maggie smiled ironically to herself. They might be fanatics, but prudes they were not; nor was it possible for her and Byron to go through the laborious process of removing their own eight or nine garments each with a fraction of their grace and ease. The fact was that Maggie felt inhibited not by modesty but by vanity. The last time George Quinlan had viewed her naked body it had been rather better able to stand exposure to daylight—better than Katy's, actually, at Katy's age. Or fundamentally better formed; but never in all her life had Maggie been as splendidly lean and muscular and deeply tanned as Katy was now, and George himself actually looked *better* than he had at twenty-five—it was unfair, almost indecent; it and her weariness together put her at a hopeless disadvantage.

Like everyone else aboard the *Down Plus Six*, she and Byron had clocked the regulation number of hours per week in the gym, but neither had been among those who made a fetish of working out, and years of confinement had inflicted more than pallor on them both. Maggie, once a great walker, had been smitten hip and thigh by flab; Byron's large muscles were overlaid with a layer of fat. To Maggie it seemed that at the moment the two of them made a poor demonstration for the hrossa of why they should be prepared to give up a sizable part of their world to human use.

George had thrown himself down and lay now on his back in the sand, his rolled-up tunic wedged under his head, knees bent and apart, feet flat. Maggie folded her clothes as she removed them and finally sat cross-legged beside the blue pile on the yellow carpet of plants, sensing George's perfect indifference to her, grimacing in disapproval of her own acute awareness of him. Katy went into the water. Byron brought his own clothes and sat somewhat diffidently beside Maggie in the shadow of the whirligig.

The two Sixers were not well acquainted. Byron was junior to Maggie in age and rank and in Joclyn Justice's section, which interacted very little with her own. But ranks were taken none too seriously among people commissioned almost as an afterthought, and an experience of this sort was a great leveler. She gave him an encouraging smile.

"Sorry if I was touchy before," he said. "Actually, I probably *could* do with a little rest myself—I really don't feel that tired, but like the lady said, so many new inputs all at once, its *mentally* exhausting. Plus trying to be on the lookout for any funny business all the time is a strain. My head's starting to feel like a blimp."

"I know what you mean. All the same, you're a lot younger than I am. I had no business assuming you were wiped out just because I was." She leaned back on her elbows and stretched out her white, puffy legs. "What about it, anything suspicious so far?"

"No, that's why it's so hard not to let the guard drop. They both just seem like really nice, ordinary people. Well, Quinlan kind of goes on too much, but he admitted he's all keyed up, and anyway the stuff he's talking about is mostly stuff we need to know. I did think for a while he was doing a sweet innocent number on us, but now I'm beginning to think he might be for real."

"Oh, that part's for real, all right. He used to be much less quick to admit his faults, and lots of things made him angry—but of course I knew him when he was about your age, before he joined the Quakers. That was a long time ago."

"God," said large, white, podgy, hairy Byron, "don't they look fantastic? It's goddamn embarrassing." Katy had come out of the lake and stood frowning and squinting at the sun. She said something to George, who held up his arm to look at his wrist, then let the arm fall back to the sand as he replied. Both were spangled all over with bright droplets of sweat or water. They looked like what they were: people who carried out some of their ordinary activities dressed only in a tanned skin. They looked connected to their world, and at ease there.

"A year from now we'll give 'em a run for their money," said Maggie kindly, perfectly aware that Byron's imagination could not possibly project a fit and desirable image of elderly Commander Smithson to set alongside those of himself and Katy, and even of George.

"I know. It just makes me want to get going that much more."

Maggie folded her trousers over, stuck them behind her head, and lay down flat. She closed her eyes. The dry little plants were pleasant to lie upon; she stroked the ground with slight movements, feeling their aliveness. "This whole world is fantastic," she said, eyes still shut, "just to state the obvious. I'm getting *my* first good look today too, there was too much rain yesterday to see anything, and so far everything here, absolutely everything, looks beautiful to me—the farm, the trip up here . . . this mountain lake scenery is so spectacular I can't believe it's real. It's like travel posters from the old time. I'm filled with greed and possessiveness, I don't want to quarrel with the Quakers or upset the natives either, but by God—by God I intend for us to live here! It feels right to me already to be in this world, it just feels right."

"Yeah? Hunh. I think I'll be able to say that once we start building the town, but—I mean, it's pretty up here all right, I like looking at it too, but I still kind of feel like home's the good old *Skeezix*. I want our own place, a real town with real houses— Jesus, why do you think *they're* still living in those prefabs with leaky solar panels, after all this time?"

"I wondered about that. I think they've probably just literally not had time to replace them and won't even try till they're forced, when the framework starts to go—which won't be long by the look of No.6. Lieutenant, I'm going to have a little snooze. Wake me in ten minutes, will you?"

She heard an indecisive pause followed by "Right, OK," and the scuffling as Byron got up and moved away. Maggie smiled to herself: There. If the Quakers had bugged the struts of the whirligig after "forgetting" to provide sun block for herself and Byron, they wouldn't have heard anything useful. She was instantly asleep.

Not long thereafter the four humans regrouped on the little beach and waded together into the water. Waist deep, George plunged forward and began to swim with a smooth overarm stroke toward the largest of several bare lumpy islands. The others followed, Maggie using sidestroke so as to keep her eyes and one ear out of water; she wanted to see (and hear) where she was going. Her nap had done her good. A brief cheerful dream full of flowers lingered with her, and the glancing water had a benign feel to it. Every little while she changed sides. The others gradually drew ahead and were standing on the rocky ground in a line by the time she felt grit sloping under the fingers of her down-sweeping arm, groped for the bottom, and stood to flounder painfully up onto the bulge of land strewn with more of the now-familiar friendly yellow ground cover.

The island looked to be nearly round, perhaps forty-five meters across, and featureless apart from the stones scattered about the ground. George led the tenderfooted ones to a level area above the place where they had landed and told them to find tolerably comfortable seats. He shook the water from his thick gray hair, then set about stacking up a stone stool for himself, explaining that his back made it hard for him to sit on the flat ground.

"Caught between a rock and a hard place again, eh?" Katy cracked, and George grinned and replied that this time he believed he would opt for the rock. His mood had changed; Maggie could see at once that he seemed happier and more confident.

To Byron George appeared to have taken on weight and authority. The younger man approved, both of this and of the idea—wonderful to him—of swimming as a practical mode of transportation, of getting someplace you needed to go. He swept a patch of ground clear of pebbles with his hand and planted himself tailor-fashion there. He watched George clap a smooth flat stone on top of his cairn, hunker down to test its stability, seem satisfied; finally he could not help asking, "Now what? What happens now?"

George heard the eagerness in Byron's voice and looked pleased. "Well, now we wait. They'll turn up when the moment's ripe, what we've got to do is help create a ripe moment. The best way *we've* found of doing that is by getting centered together, but the goal is—well, call it a state of spiritual ease. You can approach that state by whatever route ordinarily works best for you, any simple exercise that'll clear out the static. You two know self-hypnosis, don't you? Try that. Or join us if you like."

Being told he was supposed to achieve a state of spiritual ease instantly made Byron feel tense and resentful; his eager look vanished and his voice got shriller. "No thanks. How long do we do this? What if it doesn't work?"

"Oh, it'll work. We take as long as it takes—not very long, usually. They're empaths; if we're too hyped up it'll make them uncomfortable, you see. It's OK to be a bit adrenalized, that won't put them off, but they like an uncluttered ambiance."

"But what if—"

"Byron, the way you looked just now when you came ashore here was exactly the right look. Just put yourself under a little way and think about whatever it was that gave you that look—while you were still in the water," said George, and his reassuring smile was full of private joy.

Byron shut up. George glanced round at each of the others—"All right, everybody? Maggie? Here we go then"—and reached for Katy's hand.

Except for the bump of small waves on the strand below, the island became still. Where quacking or the cries of gulls would have sounded on Earth, here there was silence.

Byron, his hand upheld, eased his bare buttocks on the stony ground and began to count slowly backwards from fifty to relax his voluntary muscles group by group. He was well practiced in these techniques, which were in general use as an antidote to stress-induced insomnia. And he tried, *faute de mieux*, to do as George suggested.

Byron had grown up in St. Louis, by a Mississippi River too befouled for anything but snapping turtles to enter with impunity, let alone pleasure, but as a boy he had passionately loved the book *Tom Sawyer*. His father had taught him to swim at the Y, in an indoor pool whose chlorine burned his eyes and nose disagreeably. Never in his life had he seen an inland body of water without roads, traffic, piers, hotels, boats, concessions, and crowds. The pastures and fields he had been shown at Swarthmore were too far removed from his experience, too *quaint*, to seem covetable or even real. But it had never been his childhood fantasy to live on an Amish farm, whereas for several preadolescent years he had hankered almost obsessively after Tom's and Huck's casual involvement with *their* Mississippi River.

The muddy stream made hazardous by currents, through which Tom Sawyer swam out to his tree-shaggy island, was perhaps not much like the clear, open reaches of this lake. Still less was Jackson's Island of the novel like this bald hump of rock with its tattered yellow skullcap of "moss," and anyway Byron hadn't thought about *Tom Sawyer* for years and years. Yet within seconds of entering the water he had recognized the source of his powerful feelings of excitement and freedom, and that a fervent childhood desire was finally, in the strangest of circumstances, being gratified.

How extraordinary to find that one could still care so passionately for what had been so entirely forgotten! Epsilon Eridani II's afternoon rays fell upon his white shoulders, drying and warming him. He sat on his patch of ground and first compelled, then allowed, his mind to be possessed by images of that old obsession; and so, sitting thus, became aware of a shift at the center of his consciousness, unmistakable as a whiff of honeysuckle on a June evening.

Byron opened his eyes. The surface of the water swirled smoothly near the island, and a shape broke clear, spouting twin jets of vapor from blowholes in its brow region. Then another surfaced, and a third. Three heads like nothing in all his experience looked up at him, at all of them, out of bulging eyes set high and just forward of the blowholes. They swam nearer and began to splash up out of the water, walking on four legs like dogs, like elephants. Byron watched the fantastic bodies emerge, two pairs of arms below the neckless head, the shorter pair held close to the body and set lower and forward of the longer, looser pair, attached as awkwardly—to his eyes—as the arms of a kangaroo or a tyrannosaurus. He saw a smooth, mottled tegument, a bulge where the lower chest of a horse would be, or the groin of a man, between widely set sturdy forelegs articulated like a man's, with forward-bending knees. The back was short and sloping as a hyena's and the relatively short, slender hind legs folded like a dog's, though set higher on either side, crocodile-fashion. The broad feet were furnished with some sort of webbing whose structure Byron strained but failed to see. He wished for a slow-motion camera as the three hrossa ascended the slope from the beach, and yearned to study the engineering of the creatures' skeletons, build a scale model showing the articulation of those extraordinary limbs.

He felt no fear at all. In a day of novelties in numbing abundance, the hrossa were by a long way the most diverting and novel of all.

One of them blew its spiracles clear with a rude noise and said, huskily but plainly: "Friend George."

"KliUrrh," said George, and his face broke into a beaming grin.

The hross climbed nearer and settled beside George, kneeling on its front legs and tucking the back ones up at the sides of its tapered torso, a process Byron observed with rapt fascination. It exchanged a brief greeting with Katy. "[WikhKiah] and [HaahKoob] are here, as you can see," it said. "We were to be four, like you, but [PaahOokh] could not come; the trance tired him very much." To Byron the hross names were double bursts of noise, barely distinguishable from one another, but George looked at each of the other hrossa in turn and said gravely, "WikhKiah. HaahKoob."

He then laid his hand flat on KliUrrh's flank. "These two are Margaret Smithson and Byron Powell, from the Earth ship *Down Plus Six*."

The hross turned its bulging eyes upon them and after a moment said, "[KliUrrh]," which Byron recognized, barely, as the name by which Katy and George had referred to it, a click and little squeal followed by a gargling purr. "MaahrrGett," it said experimentally. "MahrrGahrrrt. ByRoonh." The great eyes in their circular "lids" rolled back toward George. "The man ByRoonh is young."

"Yes. But he speaks for his elders faithfully."

The hross looked Byron over, then let the issue drop. It shifted sideways, snuggling up to George, who slid his warm arm around KliUrrh's cool wet withers; discounting KliUrrh's own arms the picture they made together resembled that of a primitive child and his very large, very peculiar-looking dog, or a naked virgin with a unicorn. The two hrossa that had been standing slightly apart now came up and settled themselves on the ground nearby. One of them stroked Katy's shoulder with an upper hand in passing and Katy put out her own hand so the hross's flank could rub against it.

When all were settled a decorous silence fell.

Maggie used this silence to try to get her shattered balance back. The visible togetherness of human and hross disturbed her, profoundly and fundamentally. She understood at once the erection she could see on George, for the arrival of the three hrossa had affected her own nervous system like the sun's heat after half an hour in the lake, deliciously. Yet even now, bathed in the sensuous pleasure of their presence, she found the hrossa's ugliness desperately disconcerting. Unprepared for her reaction—she had, after all, seen the holos—Maggie fought silently with herself, not able to tell whether it was George or KliUrrh she envied, unsure if it was envy she felt or revulsion.

KliUrrh said to George: "Will you speak for the new ones, or will they speak for themselves?" The words were perfectly clear; the unpracticed way he had pronounced their two names must have been due to the fact that these words, like their owners, were "new ones."

George turned to Maggie, looking his question. "For ourselves, certainly," she told him, as stoutly as she could.

"Very well." KliUrrh fixed his goggle eyes on Maggie. "We say to you what we said to the first of your kind when they came here. You must live in the valley Delaware, there must be no more of you, there must be no machines. This is all the law. Do you understand it? Will you obey it?"

"We can't obey it. I'm sorry. We must obey our own laws, which order us to build a town here, establish farms, build up our population and if possible bring more people here from Earth. We'll put the town wherever you like, but we have to build it, and the valley isn't big enough—we'd soon outgrow it if we tried to settle there. You must tell us where else you prefer us to put the town."

KliUrrh waited, seemed to sample the silence. Then: "This is a mistake. You are not in your own place, your laws do not work here."

"They work for us," said Maggie firmly.

"They will destroy you, you do not understand where you are." KliUrrh startled Maggie by swinging his grotesque head and "shoulders" in apparent distress, an impression confirmed by the downward shift, a darkening of emotional color, felt by each person present.

One of the other hrossa spoke now. "The new ones are not KwaaKurrhs? They do not center down? We here would save much trouble and...wrongness if we could unite together as for worship now; the man MaahGrett is not peaceful, and both are stiff that they should not be changed." His accent was not as good as KliUrrh's and his English was less idiomatic.

George said, "It'll have to be words, I'm afraid."

"I will use them, but they are faint. Listen, ByRoonh and MarrGarr," said KliUrrh's breathy voice through the writhing holes behind his eyes. "Open yourselves now, I will speak as clearly as I can:

"This world Tanka Wakan is everything, and everything is Tanka Wakan. Understand this. Long ago he made himself into living things, past counting, before he made himself into the People. Friend George, you have said that because of the hrossa the Quakers knew they must tell other humans not to follow them here. Ahhhh. True that we are more wise than the rest. But still Tanka Wakan used only a very little part of himself to make us. If you had come and found that he had never made us at all, you would have called the other humans from Earth with a peaceful heart. Yet the [*********] would have been here, and the flying [*******], and more, and I tell you that you would have done as great a wrong as the wrong that for love of us you are trying to stop. For even these rocks and this water are alive, for even they are made of Tanka Wakan.

"You have said that your world is nearly dead, your people are dis-pair-ing. To us it is astonishment. The humans are truly very strong; it may well be that they are strong enough to kill a world, but how did it come about that they could wish to? And why did Earth not protect himself and his other children from you? Among ourselves we have said: maybe, when you turned against him, his heart was broken and he had no feeling to live longer. But Tanka Wakan is strong," the recumbent hross sighed slowly, "and you cannot break his heart, for you are not his children.

"You new ones must tell your elders: stay in the valley, he will endure you there. Tend your crops and your animals. But do not tear his flesh with machines, as the Quakers did in the beginning, and make only as many children as the valley can keep. And tell the ships of many humans not to come here, for if they come these humans will die, and you will die with them before your time, that is what will happen, they will come so far and die! It will be terrible for us and terrible for them, and in the end all of you will certainly be dead."

He stopped, rasping. Even George and Katy looked shocked. Maggie blurted, "Will the hrossa *kill* our people if we refuse?" The idea seemed preposterous, the old hross, repulsive as he was, looked like an illustration from a child's bestiary. Yet the force of his feeling was terrific, like being hit broadside by a wave.

"We? No. Tanka Wakan will kill you himself. Many of us may die as well beforetime, and many plants and small things, insects and water things, before their time of rep-li-ca-tion. Quakers may die, I do not know."

"*How* will he do it? How will he kill us?"

"I cannot tell you that. Does it matter? You will still be dead."

Maggie leaned urgently toward him. "Of course it matters! How can we simply take your word about a threat like that? If you'd explain why you think Tanka Wakan's going to kill us, and how, we could consider this and come to some conclusions about it; as it is we can't see any reason to believe you, you've given us no evidence at all."

The emotional atmosphere fluctuated, grew heavier. "I said that words are faint. I do not know ev-i-dence, MarrGarr."

George broke in: "Maggie, the elders don't argue that way. Won't you consider an empathic link? Under the circumstances? This is news to us too, we all need to find out what it means."

Maggie glanced at Byron, who shook his head. "We're under explicit orders to resist anything of the kind," she said, "and quite frankly, even if we weren't I wouldn't feel easy in my mind about it."

"Well, at this range the rest of us can't form a link without including you." He made no further attempt to persuade her. KliUrrh sighed and shifted within George's embrace. "Can you tell me why nothing of this was ever mentioned before today?" the man asked him, and again the hross swung his head in agitation.

"Ahhhhhhhhhh we did not know it! If the Quakers had been a danger to the world, I would have known," said KliUrrh, "but they were not. They were not. Until you told us the second ship was coming, I grieved for your people and your world but I felt no trouble about mine. But your own worry told me what could be coming here. And so I united with these elders and [Paa-Ookh], and with others from our village, and villages beyond the ridge. We knew it only then, what must happen if this law we learned for you is broken." He lurched onto his four legs, and George's arm slipped off his back. "It must be as we have said. One valley. Few humans. No machines with engines, except only the whirligigs." He rubbed his head on George's shoulder, a weirdly doglike gesture. "Forgive me, George, Katy, we must go. The trance tired us all, we cannot keep you out." The two silent hrossa had risen also, and now all three descended the short slope and began to walk into the lake.

"We'll call a meeting tonight," Katy called after them, "won't we, George? Will your people unite with us then, KliUrrh? If we can understand the danger we can try to explain it to the captain of the new ship. Forgive me for speaking in a council of elders," she added.

KliUrrh's forequarters had thrashed the shallow water as his ugly froglike head swung back to look at Katy and George. As he paused there, half-submerged, a breezelike breath of sorrowful well-intendedness came and brushed against them; even the two skeptics, catching the fringes of it, understood why tears spilled instantly from the eyes of the Quakers. "Yes," he said finally. "You are right. The meeting should understand this now. But these new others who do not center down, it may be—it may be, Friend Katy, that there is no other way for them to see. But we will unite with you, and you will try." He turned again; the three swam out a little way, dived smoothly as three walruses, and disappeared.

Maggie forcefully exhaled the breath she had been holding. "God Almighty, George! Don't tell me you really knew nothing about an extermination threat before today!"

"Maggie, as God is my witness," said George. He wiped his eyes, looking stunned.

"I wonder if they could injure us by some sort of mental projection," Byron wondered. "They sure can stimulate the pleasure center like nobody's business—easy to see why anybody'd want to stay on their good side."

"Meaning us?" Katy scrambled up, glaring with un-Quakerly hostility. She brushed angrily at her wet cheeks. "That's really a cheap shot, you've no right to say that! Weren't you listening? He said Tanka Wakan will kill the humans himself—the hrossa won't have anything to do with it! I don't know what he meant either but I do know there isn't going to be any hross uprising."

Startled, Byron shot back defensively, "Oh sure, because he said so."

"Yes because he said so! We have to find out what he *meant*! We'd know *now* if you two hadn't been so scared you'd get brainwashed or something."

"Well goddamn it, it's *time* somebody got scared!" Byron shouted. He got up hastily, scattering pebbles. "There has to be *some* reason why you people take all this 'the Great Spirit is angry' garbage seriously—you're trained scientists, for God's sake! Even if you do believe in God."

"Stop it, both of you," said George. "Name-calling isn't going to get us anyplace but divided."

"I'm trying to think up a way of finding out whether the hrossa are controlling you more than you think they are," said Maggie in a strained voice. "It does seem that they could if they chose to, though it doesn't follow that, because they could, they do—or ever would. The question is, how can we know for certain? It makes all the difference."

"Why?" Byron's face was flushed. "Either way they mean to hold us in the one valley and close the ports. No more people, under any conditions, and no machines. Serf labor in a concentration camp, for a subsistence living, and the rest of humanity gets flushed out the vents. I think that about settles it, don't you?"

"Lieutenant, that's enough. Get hold of yourself," Maggie snapped, and Byron turned from red to white at this second reprimand.

George shook his head. "You're missing the main point, both of you. I'm telling you, if KliUrrh says Tanka Wakan can kill us all, there's something to it and we'd better find out what. Our being or not being controlled by the hrossa is a red herring, it's a side issue."

"But it's not," Maggie insisted. "George, we don't know whether we could trust *any* finding of yours, don't you see? To me, the most striking thing about that little scene we just played through is that in spite of the surprise they sprang on you, your faith in the hrossa seems completely unshaken."

Katy broke the snapping silence. "Anyone's welcome at meeting," she pleaded, "anyone from the ship, anyone at all! It'll be easy to hear tonight with all of us receiving. Can't some of you attend?"

"I don't see how that would settle the question either way," Maggie replied, and now she too stood up. "It's not your sincerity that's in doubt, it's your credibility. Our people are all concerned about being influenced by the hrossa if we let ourselves be exposed to them—we're still committed to resettling humans on Pennterra if we possibly can; you're not, and we're dead determined not to let ourselves become like you. We were hoping to work out a compromise. Since that's clearly out, what we have to do now is somehow assess the hazards of proceeding according to plan. Hazards to you as much as to us, maybe." She rubbed her face with both hands, a pale tired woman with sagging breasts and shapeless thighs, inadequate to this situation. "I don't know how we're going to do that. But not by going to meeting."

There seemed no point in prolonging a debate that entangled them in complications at every turn, and the sun was getting lower. The swim back seemed endless. All were chilled and tired when they straggled up the beach toward the towels and clothing, and Maggie again felt exhausted. She glanced at George dispiritedly rubbing down, at his shriveled penis and anxious, pensive face, and realized she had absolutely no idea whether his obvious feelings were self-generated or infused into him by the perplexing water beasties she had seen at the island. She was sure only of her determination not to share them. "You like the hrossa better than you like us," she said impulsively.

The look George turned upon her was so filled with guilt and pain that Maggie took an involuntary step backward; but Katy, squirming on her bare left foot to tie her right sandal on, failed to see it. "I do too," she said. "Though I never think of it like that. To an extent it's a case of apples and oranges. They completely lack some of the most attractive human qualities—they aren't curious or witty-clever, and they aren't charming. And I don't think they'll ever achieve anything *we'd* call civilization or science or even much of a material culture, let alone high technology—I just can't imagine they *ever* will, though at the same time they're very wise in ways we're not." She stood, half shod, and gazed thoughtfully across the lake toward the village. "I think I like them—love them, really—because they're *nicer* than we are. Maybe if you feel each other's feelings you can't help being gentler, more sympathetic, less competitive...I don't know."

She sat down and tied her other sandal, then hugged her knees and looked up at the others. "I'm positive of one thing anyway. They couldn't force me to like them any more than you could force me to like you." She glanced at Byron, who looked down. "All they can *make* me do is know what they're really like— know directly, like knowing a flavor or a smell. If I didn't respond to that, or responded with disgust or whatever, they couldn't do a thing about it. They show you exactly what's there; they don't deceive you. I'm sure they couldn't, aren't you, George? We feel just what they feel, no more and no less."

"And vice versa, only more so," said Maggie.

"Yes." Katy crossed her legs and stood. "Please come to meeting, Maggie. Somebody your people trust has got to experience the union and report back. They'll never believe what *we* say."

"It wouldn't prove a thing," Maggie insisted again, but she had understood by now that the idea of "uniting" with these bestiary creatures, of an emotional intimacy like the intense physical intimacy she had recognized between George and KliUrrh, threatened her profoundly—as if her self-control would be snatched away by a contact so strange and invasive, whether or not the hrossa actually meant to take it away. "Katy, even if they converted me, Jerry McWhirter—and he wouldn't be the only one—would just view me as a casualty lost to thought control, and I wouldn't really blame him."

The excuse had the virtue of being true. Katy turned away, disappointed. George, who had been watching them, wearily caught up his damp towel from the ground and moved toward the whirligig.

But when they had landed back at the settlement, and climbed down, and were walking single file along the footpath toward the guest domicile, Byron suddenly blurted, "I'll come. To meeting. If the captain gives me permission."

6 Katy, Byron, George

Katy stood with Byron outside the meeting house to brief him before taking him in. "What made you decide to risk getting brainwashed after all?" She drawled the offending word to make it sound ironical.

Byron's hands were pushed deep into his pockets, in one of which nestled a recorder. He shrugged. "The ship needs a guinea pig, I'm expendable. We'll have a better idea what we're up against, no matter what happens to me."

Katy looked unconvinced; in her professional judgment Byron was not the kamikaze type. "Do George and I act brainwashed?"

"Well, not *act*. But you're siding with the natives against your own people, that you came all this way to save. Nobody on the *Skeezix* can understand that, except in terms of thought control."

"So how do you expect to know if *your* thoughts are being controlled—by whether what happens in there changes your mind?"

He fended off Katy's hostility with vagueness. "I'll wait and see. Shouldn't you be telling me what's going to happen? We haven't got all that much time."

Quakers were beginning to come along the gravel paths, by ones and twos from the domiciles, in small groups from the dining hall. A larger group of ten or twelve, carrying covered pails on yokes across their shoulders, trooped over the bridge from the goat barn and went into the kitchen; they came out without yokes or pails and turned into the path to the meeting house, rolling down their sleeves and glancing at the sky, where purple thunderheads were beginning to pile up over the mountains.

Byron kept his eyes on the goat squad, not on Katy, while she started to describe the silent meeting. "It'll be like what you saw us do on the island, only on a grander scale. We go in and sit down. Nobody talks. Sometimes people hold hands, or close their eyes, or bow their heads—however they're comfortable is OK, whatever helps them center down. 'Centering down'—that's the term we use, it goes way back—physically it works like a lot of other forms of meditation that produce alpha waves and slow down the rates of pulse and breathing. OK so far?"

"Sure."

"We're all used to doing it, of course—individually we move pretty smoothly through the stages of getting centered by our different methods, I won't go into those now. But when a lot of us have achieved that sort of relaxed-but-alert condition *as* individuals, something else happens: the separate people merge—or unite, that's the jargon word—into a whole, and then we say the meeting is 'gathered.'"

She paused doubtfully. Having lived in an isolated community of Friends for so long, it wasn't obvious to Katy what an outsider would find strange. The Quakers themselves were familiar with the experience of the gathered meeting, knew certainly when the quality of the silence changed, knew the change—wrought in, and also by, each person present—to be of a corporate power greater than the sum of its personal parts. But how account for all this to someone who had never been to meeting before? Katy had never tried. It was easier to describe it without explaining.

"Question," said Byron. "Is every meeting 'gathered'?"

"On Earth, no, not always. Here—it's different here. We need each other so much, we've had to work so hard . . . I can't remember offhand the last time we didn't have a gathered meeting. I guess we sort of take it for granted now. It's like good cooking or good sex, if you get it all the time you forget there's any other kind."

Byron ducked his head, grinning tensely, and Katy was suddenly, sharply aware of how afraid he was. Her conscience pricked her. Could she be wrong about Byron? Without being able to like him better, or think him much less cloddish, respect for his courage now stirred her for the first time to something like sympathy. "So everybody just sits there for an hour or so?" he was asking, and she tried to put some kindliness into her reply; being a sincere Quaker, she also honestly tried to feel more warmly toward Byron.

"Oh no, if somebody feels an impulse to speak, they do! Speaking in meeting is *supposed* to be strictly spontaneous, and usually it is, here in Swarthmore anyway." She gave him the friendliest smile she could manage and got a weak one in return. "The early Friends six hundred years ago, who had grown up imbued with Christian tradition, used to say they were guided or led of the Lord to speak, or pray aloud or whatever—sing, sometimes!—and *they* knew what they meant! Nowadays you couldn't get most of *us* to say what 'the Lord' is, though everybody's familiar with the history of the Society's thoughts on the subject. But come to think of it, nobody'll speak tonight anyway because the hrossa will be uniting with us and we hear much better in the silence. So you can forget all that part."

"Don't Quakers believe in God? I thought they did."

"Oh sure. But at various times we've defined God as love, the source of everything that is, the ground of being, the first mover, the life principle, humanity's best nature, entropy's creative antithesis, and on and on. You don't have to 'believe in God' in any traditional sense to be a good Quaker; we're very tolerant about stuff like that, doctrinaire stuff. What's important to us here is the reality of what happens in meeting. Something does really happen, not just between each of us and God, whatever God is, but between all of us *together* and God. There've been theories that it's to do with telepathy, or the collective unconscious or group dynamics, but really we don't any of us know how it works or what it means, just that it keeps us going and we'd be sunk without it."

"Could whatever it is be happening just among all of you, leaving God out of it?"

"George Fox, the founder of the Society of Friends, used to say there was 'that of God' in everyone. If you look at it that way, God can't *be* left out."

People were glancing at Byron curiously as they went by. Though there was sometimes sympathy and never antagonism in the looks, he felt conspicuous, and hunched his bulky sun-burned shoulders. The meeting was filling up; they would have to go in, but he had one important question left. "What *about* this 'uniting with the hrossa' that's supposed to happen?"

"It'll be a lot easier to experience than explain, but—well, briefly, we found out early on that when we were united in meeting for worship, and the meeting was gathered, was when the hrossa were most audible to us and we were most receptive to them. The *human* capacity for empathy, such as it is, seems to be greatest in that centered, corporate state. Anyway, KliUrrh will have been in contact with several villages, and they can reach us collectively even at this distance when the whole settlement's meeting to receive collectively.''

Again Byron smiled weakly, remembering the island and a sensation like a whiff of honeysuckle.

"We don't do it much, it's hard on the hrossa." Katy looked around, then nudged his arm: "OK, better go in now."

The meeting house, a large, hexagonal, one-room building, had been the first permanent structure built in the brand-new settlement. The Sixers had been told already how its steel frame had been raised and its concrete floor poured before the hrossa came, and how afterward the wall panels had been bolted to the frame by hand. Inside were curving benches set concentrically on shallow tiers around the whole circumference of the room. The central space, the bull's-eye, was empty.

Here Byron felt even more conspicuous. Every person seated anywhere in the room could see everyone else; everyone could see *him*. But hardly any heads turned as he and Katy took their places, and after a moment he relaxed slightly. To his surprise, and sharp gratitude, Katy tucked her hand into his—checking his face as she did so in case he objected—before closing her eyes and settling into the stillness that characterized each person in the whole roomful of people except for Byron himself.

He looked warily around, his cold hand linked with Katy's warm one, aware of her, and of the silence, but chiefly of his own apartness from the several hundred Quakers seated around him, whose unity and common purpose even he could sense dimly. He was impressed; at the same time he felt lonely and young, and steadily more nervous about what might be going to happen. In a couple of minutes he had to make himself relax his grip on Katy's hand.

Too late to back out now. Well, he had gone into this of his own free will, or at least his own free impulse. Now he had a job to do, which could not be done effectively in his present state.

Byron took a grip on himself. He got as comfortable as he could on the padded bench and then initiated the self-hypnosis exercises. At first his concentration was poor, but after a while the familiar discipline began to have its familiar effect, and he arrived in time at a plane of calmness where he switched to a mantra, coordinating it with the slow rhythm of his breath.

And then at a certain moment he distinctly felt the character of the silence change, become at once deeper and more vital. He sensed the people all about him collected into one thing, an entity, a felt union that neither included nor excluded him. And as the deepened silence rang in his ears, and rain began to clatter on the metal roof, for the second time that day he experienced a shock of recognition.

The summer he was twelve, Byron had spent two weeks at a Boy Scout camp squeezed into a bend of the Mississippi bluff behind a fifty-mile belt of enormous cornfields. By day the Scouts hiked along the muddy riverbank or the country roads, or rowed the camp's several battered rowboats where the river's currents were not too dangerous; by night they often clustered at the fire circles to roast marshmallows and sing the sentimental folk songs traditional at that camp. Sometimes a counselor or a visiting professional Scout would speak to them: the world was in deep trouble, they must try to help—do what they could now and more when they grew up. All the firelit faces would be turned toward the speaker; all the boys, kneaded to responsiveness by song and romance, would feel his idealism stir to life in them.

This was amazingly like that. But this time he was not part of it; there was no campfire, no wise leader, not even words. He couldn't tell where to focus what he felt or how to be part of the emotional collective, though desire to submerge himself in it swept through him now.

Gripped thus by childish longing, Byron's isolation was breached by a swelling sense of what he recognized at once as hrossness when it filled the room, filled the gathered Quakers, filled his own hypersensitive self with presence and authority, authentic beyond question.

The hrossa were afraid. They were distressed for their own people, and for the newly arrived humans and those who threatened to come after they were full of cold fear. That all these humans would perish was a fact, a certainty colored all the stronger by their own impotence. The hrossa could not protect them, Quakers too might die, turmoil and grief would follow—there came a sense of chaos, of disruption, of overwhelming power like that of a natural disaster, a volcanic eruption or a tidal wave.

Byron had no resistance to this sending. As the shattering impact slackened, he struggled furiously to get himself in hand. The

Quakers, nearly as shaken as he, sat looking at one another—still speechless—until two women across the room from Byron hastily shook hands, upon which a stir and murmur moved through the room. When George Quinlan stood up they all fell silent again. "What in God's name was *that* about, George?" asked a voice, and George shook his head.

"I'm blessed if I know. That sense of immense power outside the control of the hrossa, almost outside their grasp, is a new one on me. Anybody else have ideas or suggestions? Katy?" Next to Byron Katy wordlessly signaled *No*. "Bob? Tony?" He cast about the round room. "Who else has spent time at Lake-Between-Falls?"

A boy sitting by himself on a middle tier on the other side of the room from Byron and Katy said, "Dad?"

"Danny? What is it, have you got something to say?"

The boy stood up, looking scared in the way the adults did. "I think they mean [TuwakhKawan]—you know, Tanka Wakan." His mouth and breath moved strangely, forming the hross word. "This planet. This whole world, Pennterra. I think what they mean is, somehow or other [TuwakhKawan] will kill all the Sixers if they try to live outside the valley here, or if they live in the valley and use machines, or have too many kids." His father looked at him blankly without responding; Danny's voice got higher and more plaintive. "Well, you said that's what [KliUrrh] *said*. You all think that was just a way of talking, but I think *they* think it'll really happen—the *planet's* going to kill the people that don't act right."

The boy sat down. Nobody said a word.

George roused himself, finally. "He might be onto something at that. Say for the sake of argument that the hrossa believe the Sixers . . . will be destroyed by some natural calamity, as punishment for breaking the law."

"Pennterra's answer to Sodom and Gomorrah, right?" someone cracked, and there were nervous titters. "Locusts? Frogs? Boils?" improvised someone else.

"More like an organism fighting off a disease," said George, frowning slightly at these witticisms, which he clearly considered inappropriate to the occasion. "The hrossa always speak as if the planet were a living being. KliUrrh said today that even the rocks and water are alive because they're part of Tanka Wakan."

"Should we discuss the possibility that KliUrrh might be right?" a woman in front of Byron wondered, "or is that too absurd? I mean: is there any sense at all in which an entire planet might be said to be alive, literally?"

"What do the biologists say about that?" George looked about the room to spots where, presumably, biologists were seated.

None of these was quick to speak. At length one said slowly, "Pennterra's got an ecosystem—or is an ecosystem—which makes it alive in a sense. But I don't think that can be what the hrossa meant, do you? I don't know of any way an ecosystem could take purposive action."

"Maybe the law was laid down to protect *us*, not Pennterra—maybe conditions aren't safe for humans outside the valley," a second biologist suggested in response to George's prodding.

"What kind of sense does *that* make?" a third objected. "We've scanned the planet thoroughly, there's nothing that special about this valley. We chose it pretty much at random if you remember, just as a temporary base."

The discussion now became general. "Could there be viruses lethal to humans outside the valley?" The biologists all said no, no, looking exasperated: none of the native life forms can interact biologically with ours in any way, or at least we have no reason whatever to think they can.

"Well, if not purposive action, what about automatic action—what George said, an organism's immune system fighting off a disease brought here by us? Like, uh, an automatic reaction of the soil to being worked with metal equipment, or to the vibrations of the heavy machinery?" This was the cue for other experts to look disgusted and say no, no!

This speaker persisted: "No, hang on a minute! On Earth, when somebody hikes way up in the mountains without packing stuff like extra clothing, a poncho, water and food, and a first-aid kit with stuff to start a fire, he's breaking the laws of mountain hiking so to speak, right? Then if there's a sudden change in the weather or the guy sprains an ankle, you could say the mountain imposes an automatic penalty, like hypothermia." A few people were interested in this, if doubtful, since no one could see normal bulldozer activity as analogous to that of an improvident hiker or—say—of those who build cities on a geological fault line. Where, in the former case, was the risk? "That's for us to find out," said the speaker, an earnest young woman, and several others felt that there might be something to her idea; but others—chiefly experts—flatly disagreed.

Byron abruptly let go of Katy's hand, which he had forgotten he was holding. The discussion circled on about him. The recorder was getting it all down, but his own on-site observations would be crucial when the captain came to interpret what had been recorded, and he concentrated all his attention now in an effort to detect signs of duplicity mounted for his benefit in the ongoing debate.

He could find none at all, and after his partial linkage with the gathered meeting was far less inclined to think the Quakers would, or could, deliberately deceive him. But the degree of trust they seemed to put in the hrossa was astounding. The questions ran consistently: What is it they know? In what sense could it be true? Never any hint of: What are they trying to pull? At that very moment someone was saying yet again, "Well, dammit, the hrossa obviously know something, the question is *what*."

"The other question is *how*," said a woman who had not spoken before, "if they do mean something literal, which I too find absurd on the face of it."

"How do the hrossa know anything?" Billy Purvis asked rhetorically.

"How do they get the swillets to volunteer to be a casserole?" said the young man George had addressed earlier as Tony. "I've gone down in diving gear and watched them collect swillets, several different times. They don't *order* 'em to pop into the baskets! Also, I've never actually gone on one, but something very weird seems to happen on some of the hunts . . . Pennterra just doesn't *work* like Earth, the same rules don't apply, I've felt it all along."

"The laws of nature are universal," an older man objected.

"The laws of *physical* nature, yeah, but how can we be sure the laws of biology are, when all the life-forms we really know anything about evolved on Earth?" Tony began to sound excited. "We know our biochemistry and Pennterra's are similar, OK, but we don't *really* know *anything* else about the native life on this planet—not one damn thing!"

"It's perfectly true, we don't," said another man. "Could be it's about time we found some things out. Would you talk to KliUrrh about it, George? It seems we've reached a point here where we've got to know more than we know."

"I will, if that's the sense of the meeting." He waited; no one demurred, and a number of heads nodded agreement. "All right. I have an idea he may go for it, actually. We might have tried it even sooner, only it never seemed like we could spare people for a field trip; but I guess our priorities have shifted around some now."

Billy Purvis said, "About the Sixers, is there anything in this sending that's going to persuade them to scrap their own plans and come in with us?" The meeting fielded this question briefly but discussion was dispirited; it was as obvious to the Quakers as it was to Byron that nothing had been gained to that end, nothing in the way of evidence. Rationally, they were far from convinced of the danger themselves. They knew what the Sixers were bound to make of the warning.

George spoke directly across the room to Byron at last. "I guess the ball's in your court now. There isn't anything we can do fast enough to build a case. You heard the sending?"

"Yes."

"And you'll tell Captain Harrison?"

"I'll tell him."

"—SO WE CAN RULE OUT thought control as such, in my opinion," Byron reported to the section chiefs and ship's officers, back aboard the *Down Plus Six* the next morning, "but feeling somebody else's strong feelings is just incredibly persuasive. The Quakers have had six years of rapport with the hrossa. After all that time I can see very well why they keep on trying to make sense out of this idea of the planet being alive, instead of just taking it as superstitious claptrap."

Justice leaned forward tensely. "But you can't see any sense to it."

"They didn't get to me, boss, of course I don't. But I *am* convinced that the hrossa do actually believe the planet can punish us."

"And the Quakers are trying to decide whether or not there's any truth to that? Christ Almighty!"

"Well, you heard the disc. They're dead sure the hrossa wouldn't be that upset unless there was *something* to it. See, they're in a bind. They have a big, big investment in the hrossa and they have to protect that, but at the same time they don't see any more than we do how the planet can be literally alive, or conscious, or able to do anything to us on purpose—they're not that crazy. And they haven't had time to find out what other kind of truth there might be to it. Like I said, I don't go along with that, but you have to understand: after six years I know my resistance would be a lot weaker. Anybody's would."

"He's right," Maggie remarked morosely from her place. "I see some of you looking skeptical and superior, but I can assure you that he's perfectly correct."

Nobody bothered to contradict this. "I learned something yesterday," said Byron in a moment, rather bleakly. "I always kind of liked the idea of esping, I figured it would make the truth easier to get to. But all it really tells you, or all this hross-type empathy tells you, is how somebody *feels* about something—doesn't matter if they're prejudiced or misinformed, to the extent that they're sincere they're still going to be very, very persuasive." Uncomfortably he hitched himself around in his chair. "It's better to keep out of people's minds."

"Very much better to keep these hrossa the hell out of ours," Captain Harrison said grimly. "Do they only feel feelings, Lieutenant, or can they read thoughts as well?"

"George Quinlan says they pick up images and single words sometimes—in the first couple of months one of them embarrassed Katy Kendry by suddenly asking her what a frog was and whether it was dangerous." Several people smirked at this, thinking of the goggle-eyed creatures in the holos they had been shown. "Complex ideas and technical stuff doesn't transfer in either direction, though, according to him. The hrossa were nearly as blank about the nature of, say, computers or nuclear fusion after one of those 'uniting' sessions with human experts as before, he says."

The captain had started and flushed angrily. "*Nuclear fusion?* What the flaming hell were they thinking of, to take a security risk like that? It may be a neolithic culture down there as far as we can tell, but there's too goddamn much mystery about these goddamn hrossa. That just plain wasn't sensible, it was—indiscreet!"

"It was," Frank Birtwistle agreed. "Tell you the honest truth, I'm not sure it wasn't downright treasonous." He thumped his fist on the arm of his chair a couple of times, saying, "If we'd had the tiniest suspicion there might be sentients out here I'd have raised hell about sending Quakers in the first ship, but that's water over the dam now, worse luck." There was general approval of these sentiments; the Sixers were already forgetting the long suspenseful voyage during which they had not even known if the world out there was habitable, let alone who else might already be living on it. Maggie, slumped in her corner, folded her arms and looked down.

Seeing her, aware of her unhappiness, Byron found he had nothing more to say and that he badly wanted to get off by himself, away from all these officers who were plainly quite prepared to confer for hours before coming to the only possible conclusion. Despite his exhausting day he had not slept very well; he'd been too charged up, and his sunburn hurt. And he felt agitated clear through: about the hrossa who had twice breached his defenses, about Katy in proportion to the strength of his attraction to her, and about his own display of weakness in meeting. He winced and swore inwardly to think how he had clutched at Katy's hand and shed tears of his vanished childhood.

Almost the worst thing was how much he had liked them all—Katy, George, the other Quakers, even preposterous KliUrrh. It struck him that the hrossa and the Quakers made a weird kind of sense together, they *fit*. The Sixers didn't fit, and that included Byron Powell.

It included Maggie also. She sat in a fog of misery and watched Byron, wondering how the others could bear to go on grilling him like that. They had been mercifully brief with her, but Byron was the hero of the hour. They made him go back over and over the details of the meeting, playing back bits of the recording, asking him to comment and elaborate, while beneath his false face of pink, and superficial pluck, he grew steadily more drawn.

By contrast with her own high animal spirits of the days before, Maggie herself was in much worse shape than he. She had discovered more about herself in the intervening hours than she'd learned in the previous decade, and all the news was bad. One: she had proved to be exceedingly susceptible still to a man with whom she had had an intense, painful love affair when he had been newly married to somebody else, who had chosen against Maggie when push came to shove, and who apparently had no more space in his life for her now than before; the vacancy left by Susan's death was tenanted. Two: she had proven to be both xenophobic and a coward. She ought to have agreed to attend the meeting when Katy begged her to. Byron had volunteered despite his fear; Maggie had ducked and made excuses.

She didn't trouble to reassure herself that no volunteer for the *Down Plus Six* could in strict justice be called a coward. Up to a couple of days before she would have hotly denied possessing the weaknesses that George and xenophobic aversion between them had exposed, that was the truth of it. She felt awful.

"Oh, let the poor boy go," Maggie snapped suddenly. "He's told you what happened twenty times over. Stop squeezing to see if there's another drop left in the flask!"

GEORGE LIFTED THE WHIRLIGIG toward the mountains, his brain dull. He too had been sleeping poorly. Beneath his craft the rye harvest was in progress, a charming biblical scene, laborers with sickles cutting, binding the shocks, stooking them in the fields. The straw, left fairly long, would be scythed later and stacked: B-grade winter fodder for the animals if needed, bedding if not. In years to come, rye straw would be turned to other purposes: thatching perhaps, straw rope certainly, baskets, hampers, tubs, mats, beehives...when they learned how, when they were forced to learn.

Every hand was needed now, and George's heart was not in his role of political negotiator at all. The theoretically leaderless Quaker community, which derived its strength from a corporate love and trust reconfirmed at every meeting, in fact looked chiefly to him to steer it safely through the present mess. Supported by the love, filled with the life of the meeting as he regularly was, in the present circumstances of inward and outward conflict George felt their trust as a too-burdensome thing; he was tired. They were bone-tired, all of them. Harvest time was no time for any crisis, let alone one of this magnitude.

"How much do you remember about William Penn?" he asked his passenger.

"He founded Pennsylvania," said Danny. "Why?"

"How did it all turn out?"

"How did all what turn out?"

"Pennsylvania. All that."

"What do you mean? It's still there, isn't it? Oh, you mean the *Quakers* in Pennsylvania." George smiled without taking his eyes from the passing terrain. "Um, I don't remember that much about it—something about William Penn's sons cheating the Indians and the Quakers having to get out of the government, but I forget why. Pennsylvania," he said a bit plaintively. "Seems like it's a long way from here."

"Penn bought land from the Delawares even though he had a charter from the king of England; he recognized the Indians' land claims as legitimate. Friends ran the legislature for years on a principle of equality and nonviolence and kept everybody happy. But as time went by, more and more non-Quakers kept pushing across the mountains and homesteading the western part of the territory. They'd just squat there—put up cabins and clear a parcel of land, and when the Indians objected they'd howl to the colonial government for protection.''

"I'd say it was the Indians that needed protecting."

"Um-hm. By that time, though, Quakers were a minority in the legislature and the colony, and there were other pressures on them too. To make a long story short, Friends still in office were crunched between the peace testimony and the obligation of any government to protect its citizens from being massacred. They couldn't resolve the contradictions. In 1756 they gave up their authority and stepped down. Quakers have never been much good at politics, politics and pacifism mix like oil and water," said George, his voice hollow with gloom.

"What about the Peace?" Danny objected.

"Touché," said George, and this time smiled directly at his bright child. "But the circumstances were unique. For once people really wanted to be kept from fighting; *nobody* stood to gain more than they would lose from *that* war. But no country kept Friends in the highest offices for long, even so."

After a while Danny said, "Did William Penn know the Indians were there when he went to Pennsylvania?"

"Sure. Is your history that bad? Columbus was 1492, Penn's charter was 1665."

"Well—what did he think would happen? After he was dead, I mean—say in a hundred years or so?"

"He didn't think," said George. "Nobody ever seems to look that far ahead. He started something he couldn't see to the end of. Oh, his conscience was clear enough; the Delawares thought very well of him—of Quakers generally, matter of fact. But," he said, "it didn't occur to Penn that where Friends had led, others were bound to follow. And get out of hand. It probably didn't even occur to many Indians, at least for a while."

"Are you thinking he compromised the peace testimony by coming to America at all? William Penn?"

George glanced quickly at the boy's entirely comprehending face, then took one hand off the controls to squeeze and rub gently the back of Danny's thin neck. "Nothing's ever that simple," he said. "The English would certainly have come to Pennsylvania around the time Penn did. Charles would have just given that little piece of his empire to somebody else to play with. Want to sail over today? I don't think I'm up to a four-klick swim on four hours of sleep."

Danny reckoned he would swim while the warm weather held, and after they were down he splashed off cheerfully enough while George uncovered and rigged the little cat-boat stored for the season in the shed at the landing's edge. The hull was fiber-reinforced plastic, lightweight and tough and irreplaceable; it slid easily down the slope and sandy beach into the water. George tossed his clothes on the sand beside Danny's, stowed the oars and the packet of sandwiches, and launched the little craft with a sudden, unlooked-for (and irrelevant) lift of pleasure; he hadn't sailed the lake in summer for years and years. He lowered the rudder and leaned back, tiller tucked beneath his armpit, back strain adjusted for, while a light breeze rounded out the single sail. The sun-bright water, the childish, exhilarating, skimming flight toward the village—these sensations soothed and consoled him, and he felt absurdly grateful. For the first time in more than a fortnight he felt as though he were living his own life again, instead of scrutinizing or defending it. He tacked to intercept Danny's course and cheer him on, then set off directly across the diameter of the lake before the still-favorable breeze.

As he neared the village, and as his spirits had just begun to flag again in anticipation of the meeting there, a head broke the surface and KliUrrh's offspring SwikhKarrh (whose name, with its kissing smack in the middle, none of them but Danny could begin to say correctly) stared up at him. "Hi, George," he gargled and blew his spiracles clear: "Phew! Sorry. I saw the boat from below and recognized you. It's bad news, isn't it? Can I help at all?" He matched the sailboat's speed easily, legs churning the water.

"Hi yourself. I didn't feel you coming, I was preoccupied. Yes, the news is bad. If you really want to do something, you might just go check on Danny. He's swimming, and the breeze seems to be freshening a bit."

"OK." Pleasure broke upon George like a small wave, for SwikhKarrh and Danny were very good friends. "Could you take these back to the house for me?" He held a nearly spherical lidded basket up out of the water.

"Been on a swillet run?" With some difficulty George took the heavy sphere from the hross and wedged it upright under a thwart.

"On my way back from a sex run," said SwikhKarrh, and his Danny-pleasure was overwashed by pleasure of a livelier sort that crowded into George's senses. "To [******] village, you've been there a couple of times I think. I may be fertile this season, you know—time I was looking around."

Had George been less distracted and anxious he would have responded physically to the young hross's vivid memory. But he felt nothing now. He thanked SwikhKarrh, furled his sail, set in the oars, raised the rudder, and doggedly rowed between the rocks until his prow grounded on sand.

KliUrrh had seen the boat before sensing its approach and had come down to greet him. George stepped out and pulled it up on the beach. Then he turned without preamble to his friend and said, "You know already what I've come to say. I apologize for not swimming, I'm very tired."

"Let's go to the house," said KliUrrh, "and shall we bring the [swillets]?" George had forgotten them. He pried the basket loose, picked up his own lunch in his other hand, and followed KliUrrh up the short sandy path, past other lodges and other hrossa, to the familiar dooryard. Both lay down there at once—no need to watch each other's faces—and George opened himself easily, so that the hross's kindly sympathy flowed unimpeded through him. Impersonal kindliness, and something more. All George's maidenly quiverings of two weeks before had been quenched that same day in the living waters of the lake; there was no awkwardness in his manner toward KliUrrh, only the heaviness of his message.

"I wonder now why I ever thought we might convince them," he said and sighed. "The Sixers aren't evil, they aren't bad people. Even the ones I don't much like" —a picture of McWhirter formed in his mind, and KliUrrh made a sympathetic razzberry noise—"all freely risked their own lives to come here, and if humans and hrossa could coexist they'd rather have it that way. But they mean to do whatever's necessary to carry out the mission. They *might* have given up the machinery, if that were all, but they won't give up the future for humanity, and they say the hrossa will have to get out of the way if they don't like it."

Because of the swelling regret emanating from KliUrrh, for a moment George was unable to speak past the ache in his throat. He swallowed hard and drew a deep breath. "They're going to leave Swarthmore and start fresh. They've picked a site on the coast, way to the east of us. Construction gets going right away. A lot of them will winter over in the ship, then come down and plant in the spring, when the houses are finished. They'll certainly radio Earth to start readying the emigrant ships—though we'll go on insisting they mustn't in our own transmissions, of course. Also," said George, "they've offered to help us refit and supply the *Woolman* in a year or two, and to make us some fuel. We'll be able to go home if we like. But going back wouldn't stop ships from launching long before we could get there, and I don't know which of us will go, now that that way has opened after all."

KliUrrh's response moved painfully in George, supine beside his friend. "These humans are too strong to be stopped," said the old hross slowly, "but Tanka Wakan is stronger than they are. I tell you again, Friend George, he will not permit it. I am glad these others have decided to leave the valley, for if they had not you might all have been destroyed together. But more than Sixers will die over there." The emotional undercurrent of his statement said: *It would have been better for this world if humans had never come here.* Yet it also said: *But then I would not have known you.*

"KliUrrh," said George, "you've told us again and again that Tanka Wakan is a living being, able to kill lawbreakers. You know that this is as hard for us to understand as it is for the Sixers. Neither we nor they can see how a whole world can be alive. This world is like ours in so many other ways, and ours was never alive."

KliUrrh rolled over to look at George with his eyes, and his feelings surged perplexingly. "You are sure of that? You would certainly know? Yet to us it is impossible that Earth never lived—the People know that Tanka Wakan who made us is alive. Who then made you? We have wondered very much at this, George. Your people were stronger than your world, that much is clear. Your demands were too great. You finally grew to care nothing for Earth, so he could not care for you any longer. You forgot you were his children. But how did it begin? We cannot understand how such a terrible thing could happen, that Earth and his children—his wisest children, just as we are Tanka Wakan's—became so far apart in spirit that the children forgot who their parent was, and turned from him, and finally killed him." And now through the kindness and sorrow George detected a strange emotion in KliUrrh: anxiety.

"We have said to each other that Tanka Wakan may be wiser or stronger than Earth, and therefore a wiser parent, or more lucky in his own nature, or happier in the lessons of his first experience. But still, we wonder very much. It is said," KliUrrh breathed harshly, "that Tanka Wakan has also made certain People in his time who were at odds with him, as the humans are

at odds with Earth. I thought I understood this and believed it.
Now I see that until the Quakers came I took it for a story. I
never imagined a thing so terrible could happen in truth."

At this point, beneath the combined stresses of KliUrrh's
unease, grief, and sympathy, and his own exhaustion, George's
self-control broke down. When Danny rode up out of the water
on SwikhKarrh's back, he found his father still lying on his back
beside KliUrrh, chest rising and falling, tears slipping steadily
from the corners of his eyes. He slid off and ran toward George,
crying, "What's the matter? What's wrong, Dad?"

George sat up and hugged him. "Just something sad about
parents and children," he said, and KliUrrh heaved upright and
shoved himself front to front against his own child.

Danny rode back later in the sailboat with his father, squinting against the setting sun and its dazzling reflection on the lake.
He didn't chatter and seemed thoughtful. After a while he asked
what was going to happen to the Sixers now.

"KliUrrh doesn't know, but he still swears something will."

"Do you think it's true?"

George groaned. "Oh, God, I wish I knew what to think! I'm
stuck between my scientific training and faith in KliUrrh and the
elders, and can't discredit either side, can you? We've got to have
more information, a lot more. We've got to figure out how the
two things connect to each other."

"And get some answers." Danny nodded. "Can I sail the boat
now?"

They switched places carefully, and George sat in the bottom
under the boom, bracing his back as best he could. "The Sixers
are going ahead now in any case," he said presently. "They've
made their minds up. We'll offer to keep anybody who wants to
stay with us, and then I guess we'll just go on with our own lives,
and wait and see. Did you know they're leaving us some horse
and cow embryos, and sheepdogs, and a big stock of shrub cut-
tings and hardwood trees? Next spring should be the last one any
of us spends harnessed to a plow, thank God, and the fencing
problem's as good as solved."

"Thank God," said Danny.

"Thank God," said George. "But once the harvest is in we'll
have to try and find out what it's all about."

"How're we gonna do that?"

"It'll have to be worked out with Lake-Between-Falls, but
KliUrrh agrees in principle and thinks the other elders will go

along, and if they do, maybe a few of us will come and live up here for a while this fall."

Danny's whole body stiffened with incredible possibilities. "Are you coming? Can I come too?"

"Probably, but don't bug me about it yet, OK?"

Utter delight suffused Danny's face, but he obediently did not exult or pester for details and assurances. In a few minutes he said, "Do you think any of the Sixers *will* want to stay with us?"

"Who knows?" George sighed and shifted his position. "They've got that quasi-military setup on the *Down Plus Six*. Even if anybody wanted off, I doubt they'd be allowed. We'll offer, though."

For a peaceful time they sailed on into the sun without talking. Gradually, without realizing it, George began to feel as if the immediate crisis were over. Water lapped placidly against the hull, the sun shone, the breezes blew. Danny brought the little boat about again and again, tacking toward the far shore. He worked competently and seriously, now frowning, now illuminated from within by secret hopes, and George grew happy watching him. After a while the boy said, "Are they going to leave us alone, Dad? After they get their own town built, if [TuwukhKawan] doesn't zap 'em first, do you think there's any chance they might . . . well, bomb Swarthmore or something?"

"We've discussed the possibility," George replied reluctantly, "but everybody seems to doubt they'll see enough of a threat to their own operations in us. We think they'll probably just carry on as if we weren't even here. Oh, I expect they'll try to jam our radio transmission to Earth, that's the biggest mischief we're capable of from their point of view—trying to nix the sending of more ships."

Danny's intelligent eyes rested upon him with terrible clarity. "Even if you keep trying to stop them, do you sometimes catch yourself hoping they get away with it, Dad?"

George's heart lurched, and for the second time that day he felt his self-control about to fail him. He squinted into the sun and in a moment was able to say steadily, "If they succeed it'll be in spite of everything I can think of doing to stop them," but he could not meet those knowing eyes. After a bit Danny looked away, out over the water; but when they had landed, and dismasted the boat and stowed it away, he butted his hard head against George and put his arms around him.

"I don't expect you to understand," said George painfully, holding his naked son against his naked self.

PART TWO Lake-Between-Falls: Field Study

Field Notes: Firstday, 25 October 2233 Absolute (George). These pages are to constitute the official report of our field expedition to the hross village Lake-Between-Falls. We have taken Kli-Urrh's suggestion to keep all our records in written form, both to obviate the need for recharging our DisCorders up here and for privacy's sake—he thinks we may soon be bothered by lack of privacy, and we are inclined to trust his judgment, at least initially. All these notes and reports will eventually be fed into the settlement computer. The plan is for each member of the team to take roughly in turn the chore of writing the public record. Also, the two of us—Katy Kendry and myself—who have the habit of keeping a journal will make private records as well, in the expectation that these may supplement the Field Notes at some future date, in ways and for reasons that we can't now foresee.

Swarthmore Settlement has been plentifully supplied from the start, alas, with experts whose expertise was of no use to the task in hand. We, and our task here, are no exception. None of us sent to live among the hrossa has had formal training in anthropology or ethnology. In the past weeks we've all put in as much time as possible at the library, but none of us really know how to go about describing a culture scientifically. First frost was only two weeks ago, and the Sixer fracas set us back. Still, band of rank amateurs that we are, we have these advantages: that our subjects understand *us* disconcertingly well, and that they are eager to amplify our inadequate understanding of them and of their world.

Since the team had to be kept small enough to be housed together in a single hross lodge, we are only five. We'll be here till Christmastime, with a break at Thanksgiving for R&R, replacing our store of supplies, and delivering an interim report back to Swarthmore.

Members of the team:

Katy Kendry (age 34). Her training in psychology exposed her to all the social sciences along the way; also, she has logged a lot of time at this village already and is on excellent terms with a number of hrossa who live here.

Bob Wellwood (32). Chosen for his considerable knowledge of various Amerindian cultures, acquired and deepened steadily from early adolescence clear up to the time of his preflight training. The nearest thing we have to a "real," if amateur, anthropologist, and equipped—as a builder—to make sense of hross dwellings and artifacts, or better sense than any of the rest of us.

Alice Flower (47). Exobiologist. The one of us most able to pursue rigorously, as opposed to impressionistically, Tony Comfort's hypothesis that here on Pennterra the laws of biology are different from Earth's biological laws. Last winter she assisted at the dissection and analysis of the old hross from this village.

Myself, George Quinlan (44). Hrossophile.

My son Danny (12 ¾). Interpreter and general handyboy.

The five of us and our supplies made three full loads for the whirligigs that ferried us in shifts up to the lake this morning. We spent a couple more hours sailing back and forth from the gig landing to the village, transporting our food, extra clothing, soap, toilet paper, stove, lamps, bedding, my chair, etc., etc., etc., and stowing it all in the lodge built for us a little way along the lakeshore from the cluster of hross lodges. (KliUrrh thought both groups would be more comfortable, clearer of each other's emotional static.) Bob and Katy dug us a latrine and collected deadfall wood for the stove, after getting permission to do both; Alice and I took charge of the housekeeping arrangements, which she's still seeing to as I write this.

We are all in excellent spirits despite the urgency of the crisis that pushed us into mounting this expedition. I feel myself as if I've come on holiday: free, relaxed, exhilarated, relieved of responsibility, only too happy to put up with the rough conditions—and they *are* rough; our lodge will keep the rain off but as yet it doesn't even have a door. A lot of our gear can't be hung up on hooks, and the hrossa don't go in for shelves or cupboards ... we should learn quite a lot about the way they think even while adapting their basic house design to one more suitable to our own needs.

I'm not being very systematic here. Perhaps I'll get the knack of this better as I warm to the work.

We expect to evolve discrete individual areas of investigation, as we become more familiar with village life and less ignorant about what it is we need to know. But starting tomorrow morning Alice will be taking little nature-oriented field trips with any hross/a who feel/s like helping her, Bob will be surveying the material-culture (houses, tools, implements) aspects of village life, Katy is to focus on food, and I'll try to clarify our still quite muddled picture of hross reproduction and the life cycle. Danny is the expedition's cabin boy; he'll help wherever his knowledge of the language is needed and do any odd jobs he can handle as they arise.

Our work here is both simplified and made harder by the season: simplified because the variety of activities is so much reduced as compared with summer, made harder because the picture we assemble will be so partial a picture. The hrossa are neolithic-type hunter-gatherers with a bit of agriculture thrown in, but there's precious little to gather just now and their gardens, like ours, are effectively finished for the year. On the other hand the cold doesn't trouble them—they lay on heavy subcutaneous insulation in winter, I put my arm around KliUrrh this afternoon and could barely reach across his back—or slow them down. There's a tremendous amount of sexual energy in the air; we wonder for the first time whether the hrossa are primarily seasonal breeders. If they are, we should finally be able to get answers to some of our questions.

In fact, it's by answering such questions as we know enough to ask—What do the hrossa eat? What accounts for the design of their lodges? What about family life?—that we hope to blunder/intuit our ways eventually to the questions we *don't* yet know how to ask. It's to identify, so as to ask and get answers to, these questions that we were sent up here, even if it feels like a camping trip.

Which it does. All at once the work we've longed to do since we landed, and had no time or strength to spare for and/or opportunity to undertake in quarantine, has become the work we *must* do if we're to ensure our survival here or discover whether any real danger threatens the Sixers. I expect that accounts for the exhilaration we all feel: despite the desperateness of our case, our self-denial has been reversed at a stroke. We're actually *commanded* to our hearts' desire.

Personal Journal: Firstday, 25 October 2233 (George). I wanted to come so badly that I still can't believe I'm right to be here. Nothing but a clear breakthrough will relieve my doubts on that score. I'm quietly frantic to prove to myself that my allegiance to the hrossa can be of service to Friends, that my shift of primary loyalty works in the long run to Swarthmore's advantage, even to humanity's. Then everything would be lined up in the same plane, and I could have some peace. I said in the Field Notes that we are commanded to our hearts' desire (bit high-flown, that! yet it's what I feel); I see that what I want for myself, above this, is the assurance of being commanded to love the hrossa more than I love humankind, *in the service* of humankind.

"Commanded" by whom, indeed? It's all the sheerest foolishness. I know, I've known unalterably since that blissful baptismal swim over to the island with Katy and the two Sixers, that this role is what I'm *for*—I can put it no better. Yet the other reality of guilt and doubt continues to superimpose itself on the reality of what I know, or know while immersed in Pennterra's life-filled, life-enchancing waters.

I go on and on longing for these contradictions to resolve themselves into one focused and proportionate picture. An entirely self-serving wish: it's important to me to feel virtuous in *all* the worlds I have to live in, and even in the world of Swarthmore I feel guilty, let alone that older, farther one in which I vowed to carry out a certain mission. The picture at present is layered, without the depth of focus I require, and I can only make sense of it one layer at a time. It's not enough for peace.

Danny has looked simply *vivid* with joy all day, even while staggering up from the beach with loads far too big for him, determined to prove his right to be here. I'm not sure Alice is altogether pleased that I brought him along, but Katy and Bob seem to be, probably because they can see more readily how he'll make himself useful to them. And in fact we do need him, as much as he needs to be here.

All through the harvest I spared no thought for the Sixers once they were gone. Nothing like a piece of work that straightforwardly basic—safeguard the crops, survive the winter—to simplify life: you just pile pumpkins in straw all day till you can't see straight, and then you fall into bed. Yet now, up here, there's room in my head again to wonder about Maggie and Byron—with detachment, I'm afraid—and how they're getting on. I do think we did all we could, and were in error only in failing to see how pointless it was to expect to persuade them, and through them everyone else aboard the *Down Plus Six*, a thousand strong! to do as the planet's rightful owners had enjoined. There was *never* a chance that they would.

Yet even that failure to see the hopelessness of trying meant we tried all the more sincerely and so kept our honor bright, for what that's worth *sub specie aeternitatis*. (Worth something, obviously, to me.)

To complete this list of guilts and self-contradictions I'll just add that my honest effort of persuasion comforts me now for what I've since recognized—as has Danny, I'm sorry to say—as a small, sneaking, intermittent wish that the Sixers *may* succeed without us.

—This despite the fact that although we are at Lake-Between-Falls chiefly in order to learn why the hrossa believe the Sixers cannot succeed, under no circumstances will anyone at Swarthmore lift a finger to help them succeed.

Field Notes: Sixday, 30 October 2233 (Bob). A hross lodge is a sort of large, straight-sided, inverted, openwork basket woven of willow poles. (Query: same species as our Swarthmore willow?) It is between three and four meters in circumference and is anchored in place by being guyed to shallow tree roots with hide ropes. The bottom poles aren't pushed into the ground because right here the soil cover over the rock isn't deep enough to hold them securely. Instead they finish the lodge off with a rim, tie it down, then pile loose stones around the base. The whole thing is covered with skins sewn together. It's all beautifully done, both the weaving and the stitching, but you still get a feeling of primitiveness because the interiors are so bare. There's no smoke hole—the hrossa don't use fire at all. (Did we know this before?) There's no furniture either except for the low sleeping platforms and racks of pegs that implements are hung from. The dirt on the floor is so thin it wears loose before a house has been in use very long and is soon swept out, leaving smooth bare rock behind.

Because the material culture is rudimentary you somehow expect it to be slipshod, but the opposite is the case. Everything I've looked at and handled—tools, baskets, nets, stone knives, bone needles, everything—is beautifully crafted, but nothing's decorated. Invariably they're surprised when I admire the elegance of these articles, as if they didn't know and couldn't conceive of any way to make anything *other than* excellently.

It's possible that the hrossa see excellence of form—integral adornment, so to say—as enough. The idea is attractive to me personally and has characterized some human cultures (Japan and Sweden come to mind) but no primitive societies that I know of. Among us, it's an attitude that only appears to develop at a high level of civilization. There's a seeming paradox here, or maybe several paradoxes.

The fact is, they live a lot like *animals*. It's not insulting them to say this; I just mean that they *could* do without any agriculture or material culture at all if necessary. For starters, they're free of the need for clothing and fire in temperate/montane climatic conditions, and they know how to live off the land.

Or am I right about that last part? They're hunters besides being gatherers, and I know Tony Comfort was up here during some hunts and got holos of a group of hrossa coming back from one, but I haven't seen any bows or arrows or lances, so what do they use to capture the game? Snares, deadfalls, bare hands (all four of them)?

I have to try to get invited out with a hunting party.

Field Notes: Sixday, 30 October 2233 (Alice). Already obvious no use my trying to investigate flora in field (all dormant)—hrossa refuse to permit specimen collecting of flora *or* fauna—I'm shifting my attention to food items; at least they'll let me cut up a dead swillet before it gets eaten.

Field Notes: Sevenday, 31 October 2233 (Katy). Less than a week into the project we've reoriented ourselves so that all of us but George are focusing upon food: what it consists of and how it's acquired, stored, and prepared.

Lake-Between-Falls village has 31 full-time inhabitants: children under ± 10 (?), breeders, adults, and elders. That's a lot of mouths to feed. The hrossa are omnivores and get their food by three means: collecting, cultivating, and hunting.

WikhKiah showed me several "root cellar" caves in which garden produce is stored. He says there are three major crops: (1) a big yellow tuberlike item, hard like a sweet potato but much bigger and hairier, (2) a hard, husked fruit like a very thin-shelled coconut, soft inside, and (3) an apple-sized fruit, also very hard, bright blue in color.

I've been in the gardens at various times over the years but can't now connect these three foods with the three types of plants I must have seen being cultivated there. Not only do I have no clear memory of what they looked like; I can't recall seeing either of the fruits on any of the plants! Excuse/hypothesis: each year since we landed, we've been far too busy with our own harvest to visit the village at the time these crops were maturing. Understandable, but frustrating. Every answer raises a dozen new questions. All I do remember is that the three plants grow all intermingled, like the "three sisters" (corn, beans, squash) of the Amerindian agriculturalists, and so are presumably equally complementary in their use of soil nutrients and available sunlight.

Hross "dentition" is internal, in the first compartment of the alimentary canal. The elder we dissected had a gizzard like a bird's, full of grinding edges and grit. His "mouth" was lined with bony ridges theoretically capable of crushing/shredding both apples and sweet potatoes (the coconut splits easily by hand pressure so the insides can be scooped out). But the village hrossa chop things up before ingesting them. And that's the only processing the garden produce gets, as far as I know. Like all hross foods these things are eaten raw.

Apples, sweet potatoes, and coconuts between them probably couldn't carry the whole village through the winter, but they don't have to; hrossa eat a fair amount of animal foods and some wild vegetable ones too. In late summer, for instance, they gather hiding nuts and "berries" (things that look like dark red raisins when sun-dried): big squirrel-hoards of both. Nuts go into baskets stored in the caves, berries into hanging lidded baskets in WikhKiah's house and, he says, in everybody else's. They also gather several kinds of foliage in late spring after the new growth comes in, and lots of wild fruits all summer long. I don't know if they dig for roots, or what else they may pick up. Hearing about it is no substitute anyway for coming along on a foraging expedition. We should make a point of that if we can get up here for a day or two in the spring.

Animal foods haven't been much in evidence this week, apart from the ubiquitous swillets upon which the hrossa practice a kind of husbandry. (Swillet is just about the only hross word I know that sounds in English pretty close to how it sounds in Hross.) They routinely keep large schools (?) of swillets in underwater holding pens in the lake, where they reproduce naturally and, one gathers, perpetually. Collecting swillets from the pens is one of the regular chores. Rights to collect them rotate among the twelve households. I've never yet seen whether the hrossa kill them or simply let them die out of water before cleaning and cutting them up (into rounds, like small eels) with stone knives. They then put the pieces into stone bowls and combine them with hiding-nut flour and/or chopped vegetables into a sort of cold raw stew—the very idea makes me shudder, hard though I hold to the thought of pickled herring. Luckily this squeamishness has not offended WikhKiah; he can understand it in the light of his own unhappy reaction to the idea of cooking fish—or vegetables, or meat, or anything.

It's no use yearning for a biochemical analysis of these food items—some year we may get to that point, but it's hardly within the scope of the present project. The impulse to overdo is almost irresistible, though; after all this wanting and waiting we're all guilty of intellectual greed.

Personal Journal: Sevenday, 31 October 2233 (Katy). The tremendous sexual ferment in the air has begun to bother me considerably, if *bother* is the word I want. Nobody's spoken of it yet—it could be that Danny's presence makes us reticent—but I'm pretty sure some or even all the others are as distracted as I am by being empathically kept in a constant, undirected state of semiarousal. The reason I think this may be so is that for the first few days we met together for worship every morning and evening, and yesterday by unspoken agreement we skipped over the evening meeting. It's just too hard to sleep, after opening ourselves up to the full force of the breeders' feelings at such close range, while on terms of such intimacy with one another. We're overstimulated enough by our new license to pursue intellectual interests, even though clumsily and in areas outside our fields of expertise, without adding sexual stimulation to the total charge.

I wonder if KliUrrh had this in mind when he said we'd feel our privacy invaded before long. The distance doesn't help that much really. One of us will have to speak up about this soon, I'm sure, and it may well be me if things go on this way—that is, if I don't get acclimated to it first. Just as well it's winter and we're always either bundled up, getting dressed to rush out for morning chores, or getting undressed in the semidark to rush into bed. In the circumstances the lack of personal privacy is especially trying. Twice now I've had erotic dreams with spontaneous orgasms that woke me. It's a problem that'll need to be dealt with before it starts interfering with the work, but I'm not even sure how I'd *prefer* to deal with it. Sleep with George, probably—but when? where?? how??? (even) how often???? Judging by the way I feel this evening, twice or three times a day would be just barely often enough.

Horniness aside, I have to say I absolutely *love* being up here. I feel the way Danny always looks: intensely delighted, energized, in wonderful spirits. Things like my petty revulsion at raw swillet stew, or at watching the hrossa ladle the stuff into mouths that open so disquietingly along a *vertical* line, while they go on peaceably chatting (no such social error here as talking with your mouth full!), don't even touch, let alone damage, the fundamental joy. Lack of properly heated living space, of hot showers, of laundry or kitchen squads—none of *that* reduces the intensity of the pleasure of being here one bit. Sexual arousal may even *enhance* this for all I know. (Up to a point.) I feel I'm right where I ought to be, doing exactly what I ought to be doing: probably a basic formula for the sort of intense well-being I've experienced since the day we got here.

What if the meeting hadn't seen fit to send me? What if I'd missed out on all this? I can hardly bear the thought.

Of us all, I think only Alice fails to share in the general glee. She's the only non-amateur aboard, the only one who knows exactly how she wants to proceed and the one who keeps running up against major obstacles and impediments: the plants have gone completely dormant, they can't be collected for study, neither can the animals unless destined to be dinner, she has no lab equipment here, let alone a lab. She's been dissecting and photographing swillets and whichever vegetable items are on the menu each day, but it's madly frustrating for her. If she had a tankful of swillets in a lab, or even a glass-bottomed boat! and could observe them carrying on their daily business—but she hasn't and can't. This is just the wrong season for the sort of field work she wants to do, and even the sort of lab work that would be permitted isn't possible to do up here. I hope she gets a break soon. The rest of us are happy in our ignorance; Alice is neither ignorant nor happy. (Bob said today that he's going to try to *weave* her a lab, if he can get somebody to teach him the technique.)

G. is doing his back exercises, his last activity before bedtime. Better leave this for now, though I seem to have lots to say.

Personal Journal: Eightday, 32 october 2233 (George). Danny and I were kitchen squad this morning. The others went out one by one before we'd finished, and when we were alone in the lodge Danny—who'd been very quiet at breakfast—said: "Listen, Dad, I have to talk to you about something." From the embarrassed way he ventured this I was pretty sure of what was coming and braced myself. He said, "My penis has been driving me *crazy*. It's hard *all the time*, and *stuff* keeps coming out of it. My bedroll's a mess, and all my underwear's a mess, and the worst is when I'm out helping Katy. Every time she touches my knee or puts her arm around me or something, bang—off I go." He was half sheepish about it but the other half was pretty upset. Whatever sexual feelings he's felt before must seem like a gentle breeze by contrast with such a storm.

Oh me. Danny knows everything there is to know about the sex lives of livestock, and he's known for years that when he reached puberty he would undergo various physiological changes, but it would have to happen up here. I told him it was just bad luck for him that this milestone in his career should be passed at Lake-Between-Falls, since it would be hard enough to endure even without being tuned in to the breeders' fever-pitch excitement. I said *my* penis has been driving *me* crazy too—God knows it has, I'm working *with* the breeders!—so I could imagine what it must be like for him, that he must hardly be able to think of anything else. He seemed relieved to hear *that*. Then I said I had half a mind to send him home; but at the very idea such a howling and wailing arose that I withdrew the suggestion at once.

Still, we shall obviously have to take steps.

It occurs to me to wonder whether the timing of this onset *is* just Danny's bad luck, or if being exposed all day every day to so much sexual static has somehow evoked it, brought it upon him a little before its time. Certainly he's grown since the summer and his voice may be huskier, but I'd have thought he had half a year to go at least.

This development forces me to think, again, about Danny's social situation in the settlement. He has virtually no peers or older boys to hang out with and learn the ropes from—nobody else brought an infant aboard the *Woolman*. Jack Wister's what, sixteen? but he and Danny have never seemed to hit it off. The Shippen twins can't be more than ten, and Rachel Heineman was nine in September. And all the other kids were born on Pennterra.

Well, Jack Wister got this far through it on his own, so presumably Danny can too. But I wish he weren't up here, vulnerable to such a saturation bombardment of *external* lust. Overloading those circuits can't be the best thing for him. He's too new at the game to be pushed into playing so hard.

Why can I never seem to *anticipate* (and so prevent) a problem anymore?

LATER. SOMETHING'S HAPPENED to put the fat even further into the fire. I was walking along the trail above the falls and the root-cellar caves, "lost in thought," when I rounded a curve in the path and there stood Alice. She was leaning with her back against a tree. Her face was flushed. There was no doubt in my mind what she'd been doing when she heard me coming. It might have been one of those embarrassments that neither of you can ever really forget nor forgive the other for, but somehow it just wasn't. I went straight up to her; she put her hand on the lump in my pants as soon as she could reach it, each of us undid the other's fly, and without further ado we proceeded to fuck standing up—something I never did before in my life—till both of us came, a matter of maybe thirty seconds.

Afterwards, neither remorse nor recriminations. I felt fantastic, as if I'd finally done the right thing about The Problem after a whole week's prudish folly. Alice grinned like her tough old self for the first time in almost that long. We separated, and for about ten minutes I was perfectly sure we ought to take a leaf from the hrossa's book and adopt a program of friendly promiscuity for the duration, for a brief trial period at the very least.

When the ten minutes were up my high had subsided enough for me to realize that I don't *at all* like the idea of Danny going through this part of his life surrounded by wildly rutting adults, even though I've surrounded him myself with wildly rutting hrossa. However careful we were, he would know. I dislike the idea partly because it's unseemly and partly because it *excludes* him: the one of us with arguably the greatest need would be the only one denied relief. I can't make out what to do about this. Ultimately I guess the decision's got to be mine; but tonight after supper I'm going to ask for a meeting for concerns, and as soon as he gets back I'll take the whole thing up with KliUrrh.

Field Notes: Firstday, 1 November 2233 (Bob). I've been systematically examining tools. There's a complete set of personal-use tools hanging up in the different lodges and a collection of community tools in a small lodge that serves as a garden shed. *Everything's* hung up, either from hooks fastened to the wall or from freestanding "clothes trees." The bowls, which can't be hung up, are stacked outside (little ones are hung up in nets). The floor of a hross lodge is never littered.

Here's what seems to be the basic equipment for a household:

- 2 or 3 different-sized needles of bone or shell, for stitching and mending things like house covers and skin bags
- assorted flake knives, for skinning, dismembering, and cutting up various food articles—sometimes a stone sliver will have one end wrapped neatly in hide strips for a good grip
- a hatchet with a stone blade and willow handle
- 1 or 2 digging sticks carved or ground out of pieces of wood preserved by swamp water
- 3 or 4 ladles, the basic food-serving and eating implement, also cut from preserved swamp wood
- lengths of hide strips and sinews (?)
- several plant-fiber fishnets
- a broom of tidily bundled dried reeds, with no broomstick, for keeping the bare rock floor swept clean
- assorted willow baskets, with and without lids, some of a very tight weave and some openwork
- 2-3 hollowed-out stone bowls, quite large, and several smaller ones (none of clay or wood)

That's *all* the standard stuff. Some of the elders also use a kind of mattress made of skins stuffed with dried vegetable material to put not on but *under* the sleeping platforms at night, to create a dead air space below the open weave of the platform. They sleep warmer that way, but no softer. The mattress is stored on top of the platform during the day.

Implements owned and used collectively:

- blunt stone hoes with short handles of braided willow
- dibbles of something like horn
- long sturdy poles and padded yokes, for carrying heavy game back to the village
- large fishnets

- 3 heavy clubs covered with stitched hides, like baseballs

Hardly anything in the whole village has any straight lines or right angles to it. Just about everything's curved, rounded, or shapeless.

I looked it all over carefully and holographed everything, and then I asked PwiUpp (who's been helping me) how the hrossa kill their quarry when they go hunting—because nowhere have I seen anything like a lance or sling or harpoon, let alone a bow and arrows, and I couldn't figure it out. He said, "We strike the creature with one of these," pointing to the clubs.

So do they walk right up to some mesmerized animal and bash it over the head? Do they use pit traps and deadfalls only? Or maybe *throw* the clubs? I decided not to press PwiUpp because there's a hunt in a couple of days and I'm going along. Danny is too, to interpret. I couldn't find out which hrossa will make up the party, but I'm guessing the breeders are out of action for the time being except for breeding and the elders are too old.

I'm pretty excited. If they can catch game without weapons, couldn't they wage war without them? We may be about to learn something of crucial importance.

Personal Journal: Seconday, 2 November 2233 (Katy). Day before yesterday while I was taste-testing garden goodies (sweet potatoes = astringent, ghastly beyond belief; coconut = fibrous, rather pleasant) outside the lodge of friendly old HaahKoob, to his considerable entertainment, there came a mild commotion, and at the same instant I felt myself positively seized by lust, like an itching coal at the crotch. I almost choked on my bite of whatever-the-hell-it-was. A couple of breeders had begun to copulate just out of sight on the other side of the lodge, and we were being drenched in empathic waves of the wonderful time they were having. HaahKoob's head stretched back and his eyes disappeared, and *he* started having a wonderful time all by himself. I sort of staggered to my feet, and just then Bob emerged out of the next house, PwiUpp's, with a wild gleam in his eye. He saw me, and the next thing either of us knew he was yanking at my pants, and the *next* thing we knew we were on the ground, taking part in the wonderful time.

Whew. I have never, but never, experienced an orgasm quite like that one. In a class by itself it was. Incandescent.

When we came to ourselves, so to speak, PwiUpp and HaahKoob and the two youngsters had gathered round us, very pleased and *most* interested, and one of them said, "We made it better for each other, that time!" Cheerful feelings all round. Oddest of all, I wasn't the least little bit embarrassed and neither was Bob—not on account of the public spectacle we'd made of ourselves and not on account of having done it with each other, when we'd never even thought about each other that way before. It was both extremely friendly and extremely impersonal somehow. All I really minded was the *uncontrollableness*, the sense of being swept away without my consenting to it, and even a little bit *against* my consent. But it all seemed merely funny and cheery afterward. The past week of resistance made a much more serious and important thing of it than the brief little frenzy of giving in made it seem worth. In fact we both felt 100% *better*, and I couldn't for the life of me think why we'd been struggling so hard not to give in.

Then I saw Danny, and right away his being there skewed the whole thing into another shape. Bob said, "Oh, Jesus." Danny didn't say anything, just stood there beside SwikhKarrh, with his eyes glittering and an excrucied expression on his face. What I did then was done purely on instinct, impulsively: I went right over and put my arms around him, and he wrapped his tight around me, pushed his face into my neck and his groin up against my thigh, and I felt him jerk and that was that. When it was over he let go and said, "Oh, thanks, Katy, thanks a lot," and gave me another fast hug before taking off with his pal SwikhKarrh; but his face looked all beamish again, and I felt fine and was certain I'd done the right thing.

BUT. When we assembled for supper, before I'd had a chance to bring the subject up privately with George, he made a general announcement that he reckoned the time had come for us to discuss the effects the hross sexuality was having on us. *Everyone*, as it turned out, had reason to agree; it seems that George and Alice had had an experience similar to Bob's and mine that same afternoon. We held a meeting for concerns after supper, beginning with silence—very full of one another we were that evening too, I may say—and each of us told how we'd experienced the breeders' feelings and discussed how we should attempt to cope with our states of chronic arousal.

Right away it was obvious that we'd have had no problem at all reaching consensus except for Danny. Or rather except for George, who wasn't one bit pleased when Danny and I related what had happened between us, though both Danny and I still felt great about it. I guess George had had quite a different idea about how Danny's sexual awakening and first experiences with girls were supposed to go, and dry-humping a woman old enough to be his mother wasn't part of the program.

If I know Danny's father, right now he's busy accusing himself of not managing things well enough and trying his best not to be furious at me for taking liberties with his boy. We're all a bit out of sorts this morning. Even though it's Seconday, we're knocking off for the day and will keep a meeting for concerns going till we work out what to do. That's our most urgent business right now. Interesting that discord among ourselves turns out to be a whole order of magnitude more disruptive to our work here than being continually turned on.

It's also raining, after a week of overcast but unproductive skies. I've been writing this in my bedroll on my sleeping platform. Bob and Danny are finished washing up from breakfast and are working on a counter-cum-table for the lodge; George is sitting in his bad-back chair, writing Field Notes on the other writer; Alice is doing something to a big garden apple and frowning.

All's serene outwardly. Inwardly, each of us is uncomfortable.

Field Notes: Seconday, 2 November 2233 (George). I'll try to summarize, impressionistically, everything I've learned so far about hross reproduction. At some point Alice will have to go over what I've said here, looking for blanks and errors.

A baby hross, a perfect hermaphrodite, is born in late spring after a gestation period of (I'm guessing) some 225 days—that is, he hatches out of the ovum which has been retained in his parent's abdomen after about that long and emerges into the world. How an egg—a closed system—supplies a fetus with air and nutrients for such a long time is a mystery I haven't begun to penetrate; there may well be a supply system we don't know anything about, indeed I think there must be. The baby is carried inside of where the rib cage would be on a terrestrial quadruped, and is born through a slit in the ventral abdominal area, about where the lower ribs would be. Unlike the arrangement on Earth, fertilization is accomplished (when it is, if it is) by means of one set of orifices, and parturition through a different orifice—more like the alimentary than the reproductive solutions arrived at by Earth's animal life.

The baby completes most of his growth that first summer and achieves full physical size in only three years. But he is still considered a child for a number of years after that—I don't know how many and suspect it varies, but on the order of 8 or 10—until the adult members of the community, as well as the child himself, all recognize empathically that he is becoming a breeder. Children can't be distinguished from breeders (or, at any distance, from adults) just by looking (or listening—no vocal cords to change), as they lack discernible secondary sexual characteristics. The external sex organs themselves are structurally adult from the time the child reaches his full size and stops growing. Beginning at that time he copulates with other kids and with everybody else, young and old (except the very old, the elder elders), all the year round. When he reaches late elderhood, the reproductive organs atrophy and his sexual recreation becomes vicarious. I've *no* accurate idea of how many years he spends as breeder or adult, or indeed what the standard life expectancy might be, because *they* have none.

Like the earthworm and the tulip, each hross has a complete set of both "male" and "female" sex organs, which are carried in a pouch on the lower thorax, between the forelegs. When an individual copulates, both sets of organs are involved in the act. the pouch contains three small penes—that is to say, three erectable pronglike structures, which I've been calling *penicles* (from L. *peniculus*, little penis; the analog is testicle) and three vaginal sockets for the penicles to plug into. The plugs and sockets are arranged thusly:

X O	X O
X O X O	X O X O
hross 1	hross 2

To see how the copulating individuals fit together, fold the page along the midline.

When not erected, the penicles are tough and nipplelike in texture and appearance, and the pouch folds snugly over them. Arousal causes the entire area to engorge with blood, and as the lower penicles stiffen they push the fold of skin beneath them out of the way. I've had no opportunity to measure these structures in either state, but when erect they look to be about the circumference of an average man's forefinger and about as long.

The three vaginal openings lead to a common passage, which in turn conducts to the chamber where the egg is incubated (and produced?); cf. holos of the dissected elder. Hrossa copulate by pushing up hard, neck to neck and chest to chest—always bearing in mind that they have neither necks nor chests, properly speaking—each plugged three ways into the other. Orgasm propels genetic material from each individual into the other, so that children engendered in both partners by the same coupling would be as closely related as full human siblings, or the "cousins" born to both couples when identical twins marry identical twins.

Hross orgasm feels just like human orgasm, at least to humans. Stimulation to the point of orgasm is achieved by pressure alone rather than friction and pressure combined. The pre- and post-breeder-stage hrossa also experience orgasm, but we assume they either don't ejaculate or that the ejaculate is infertile.

The hrossa are seasonal breeders. Pregnancy lasts through the winter, and the babies are born in spring. We knew breeding activity during autumn was intense, in both senses, but were misled by the fact that we saw copulating on every trip to the village into thinking that, like us, they could conceive at any time of the year. In fact, for them—as for members of the deer family—Autumn is It.

That was one of the big surprises. The other was that according to WikhKiah the overwhelming majority of hrossa have *one* child, and only one, in all their lives. This, if true, gives rise to literally dozens of questions. What possible evolutionary purpose could so much copulating, and waste of genetic material, serve? With a birth rate that low, why aren't the hrossa extinct? What, besides old age, do they die of? What's the birth rate among other species? Which hrossa do have more than one offspring, and why? How many more? And so forth. KliUrrh will be back from White River Rock tomorrow, and I'm extremely eager to hear his views on all these matters, and others.

"The Social Implications of Sex" is a peculiar topic in a society without gender. There do not seem to be *any* sexual mores or prohibitions here, of the sort we're familiar with. Incest, infidelity, promiscuity, rape, child abuse, prostitution, exhibitionism, "lewd and immoral conduct"... none of it exists. Sex is the universal recreation; everybody enjoys it and everybody does it, except those under three—and the under-threes are casually and affectionately masturbated all the time, the way a human child would be tickled or played peekaboo with. I have to conclude that sex among *these* hrossa—and we have no reason to think they're atypical—is much more social than "sexual" in its significance, the fact of orgasm notwithstanding. Copulation functions here more like hugging and kissing among the members of a warm family group than an activity designed primarily to perpetuate the species. I should add that I am deeply suspicious of this conclusion, also that much of the foregoing is conjecture based on circumstantial evidence and very much in need of further study.

Personal Journal: Thirday, 3 November 2233 (George). Pouring cats and dogs this morning. I hope to Christ KliUrrh isn't delayed. There's a trickle of water running right down the middle of the lodge; now we know why the hrossa keep their stuff up off the floor. We wear Fat Wellies and duckboots everywhere we go, and the damp's gotten in both writers—hence this longhand script.

I guess I'm licked, and I guess I was wrong all along to be so unyielding, but damn it all anyhow. For the first time in my life I can sympathize with those hateful, heavy fathers cracking down on a son who had decided he was gay or a daughter in love with a black/Jew/Parsee/whatever. Unfortunately, being able to see the resemblance doesn't help me break free of it.

Why not? What is it that scares me so much about Danny's spending these tender years, or this little part of them, free of the sort of misery I endured? All that urgency, nothing to do about it. I don't know; but I know that at some deep atavistic level I'm truly offended and threatened.

The whole field team spent a long time yesterday in meeting, trying to get clear on this. To make a long story short, everyone agrees that (A) we'll *have* to stop swimming against the current and just screw each other whenever we feel like it if we're to get on with our business here, and (B) while the breeders are so active, Danny should either be (1) accorded full adult status in this regard or (2) sent home. Katy was all in favor of B1, and Bob was too. Either way would suit Alice. But it was unanimous that it would be impossible for any of us to work effectively without A (and silly to try to), and equally impossible to have A but not B— that is, to let Danny stay yet expect him to keep out of the sexual free-for-all.

It took a while to arrive at that formulation of the question, but once we got there I was already licked, because I could see they were right, and I simply don't have the heart to send him home.

I need to go over all this with KliUrrh.

I repeat: why the thought of a sexually promiscuous Danny, my son, not quite 13, should wrench and grind at me so I simply don't understand; but it does, by God, it really gets to me.

Then this. I lay awake for an hour or so last night, but finally dropped off. Sometime in the night Danny woke me. He was shaking. I pulled him into bed with me, all bony knees and elbows and cold feet, and amazingly *long* stretched out straight against me. He was trying hard not to cry, but having the covers tucked around him and my arm under his head made him too much the child, and he couldn't hold it back. He said, all choked up, "It just happened again, it keeps happening, every night, I don't *like* it, it's not supposed to be like that, there's supposed to be somebody else—" He had turned against me, and I could feel the warm wet spot on the front of his pajamas through my own. Then he just gave up the struggle and put his face against my chest and cried like I haven't known him to cry in years, very quietly but shuddering and gasping. I felt simply dreadful— helpless—angry—stricken—able to think of no way to fix things for him.

After a while he calmed down. I held him and stroked his head as if he were five again. He got very quiet and seemed to be drowsing off, but then he whispered, "If you made me go home, I don't think I'd ever forgive you—and if you said I could stay but not do sex with anybody I'd have been mad at you all the time, and I'd have tried to do it with people anyway. It would've been awful, Dad."

Awful is right. He's never yet disobeyed me about anything important.

"But since you gave in, well"—big breath—"if you *really* feel *terrible* about it, I promise I'll just do it by myself. I know that's the wrong way, but I'll still do it that way if you say so. I don't want to make you feel rotten."

I'm sure he meant this, and I confess I was briefly tempted. But justice and sanity returned; I thanked him, quite calmly, but said I didn't want *him* to feel rotten either, and I was pretty sure it was my attitude, not his, that needed to be worked on. (Was I going to let the kid behave more handsomely than me?)

In the midst of my parental distress I do feel considerable parental pride at the grown-up way in which he worked the moral niceties out for himself.

Even that wasn't quite all. This is hard to write. We both dozed off. Sometime before dawn a wet dream woke *me*, as one has been doing most nights nowadays. I'd been dreaming about SwikhKarrh and KliUrrh. They'd been copulating, in the middle of one of the garden plots, just as I've often watched them do. When I woke I found myself pushed up hard against Danny's warm thigh, midway through my orgasm, brim-full with sensations of utter sweetness. Danny didn't wake up.

Needless to say, the experience did *not* make my thoughts and feelings on this subject any less confused or disturbing and afterward I couldn't get back to sleep again.

Field Notes: Fourday, 4 November 2233 (Alice). Am now quite certain that the hross garden staples we've been calling apples and coconuts are not designed to contain seeds, i.e., structures by means of which a plant can propagate itself. Ditto hiding nuts. And, after a week, that's almost every blessed thing I do know. The raisins get shriveled in the drying process, and anyway they're too small to see with a hand lens. The power lens, like the writers, is kaput—damp in the cells. Conditions could not very well favor a plant study less.

Swillets are also too small to examine properly, but I do have hopes that if the hunt planned for tomorrow is productive I'll at least be allowed to look at/cut into the results of it before they go into the (metaphorical) stewpot.

I've been reluctant thus far to use native informants, preferring as always to make my own observations in the field to eliminate a certain class of error from the outset. But I'm beginning to think I'll have to risk it, or else go home nearly as ignorant about the flora as I was when I came.

When I reflect that for six + years I might have been scrutinizing the river willows through every season—that I *thought out* experiments to set up, yet never found the energy or time for the extra effort—I just grind my teeth. If I'd carried out the simplest one or two of those experiments I'd have something to go on now, instead of nothing. I'd give my eyeteeth to be going on this hunt in Bob's place but am all too clearly not in shape for an all-day mountain expedition—equally my own bloody fault; NO middleaged woman has any business allowing herself to spend week after week sitting on her arse in a laboratory.

Field Notes: Sixday, 6 November 2233 (Bob). Yesterday shortly after daybreak Danny and I left the village with five adult hrossa. We went in Indian file up the main trail onto the mountain, us at the end. We were going for big game, a large land creature I'd never seen, called a *folyokh* or something like that (this is how Danny says to spell it), whose habits are solitary. I was bursting with excitement and questions, but SpikhKai said (through Danny) that he'd be glad to talk after the hunt but not before and that because of my excitement I'd have to keep well back so as not to make things muddled. I thought at the time he meant that I'd put nervous static in the way of hunters trying to sense where the quarry was, but that turned out to be off the mark.

Until yesterday I'd given zero thought to the question of how hross empathy might be employed in the pursuit of wild food. Did they lure game to them, or track it, by empathic tricks? Both seemed possible, especially since we set out carrying two poles, two sets of yokes, several lengths of cord, and a club—nothing to kill anything with from a distance, unless they threw the club. All the hrossa also brought knives in carry-bags hung on cords around their "necks," but I didn't think they could bring down a *big* animal by throwing flake knives at it. I thought they would be for dressing the meat, and that was a right guess.

We climbed higher and higher into the trees and the trail became just a little track and then, on top of the ridge, pretty much disappeared. Wherever there was any soil cover over the rocks the ground was still sodden from the heavy rains, and in one boggy place we were shown folyokh tracks. It looked like an elephant had gone through the swamp. I asked, was it dangerous? Danny translated, but nobody wanted to get into that, and I got the impression they viewed the question as irrelevant. That was a right guess too.

We made a big party, and we might have had trouble slipping from tree to tree like Mohawks even if we'd tried, but the hrossa made absolutely no effort at concealment, in fact they acted as if they *wanted* everything within earshot to hear us coming. There was no collective sending except hunger, the idea of hunger, which sort of emanated steadily from the group but without any force behind it to speak of.

We broke for a rest around midday, next to a stream. Danny and I ate some lunch we'd brought with us. We'd seen nothing but the one set of tracks all morning, and my excitement was under much better control by this time, in fact I couldn't see the point of all this casual strolling openly about on top of the mountain. Danny hadn't overheard anything that would shed any light because they hadn't been speaking much among themselves on the climb up to the ridge. Then one of the hrossa said in English, "Friend Danny. A folyokh, there," and waved, and I saw an immense black thing the size of a rhino—the animal we call a mastodon, known to us only by a couple of sightings up to now—walk on *six* legs right around a hunk of rock and down to get a drink from the stream. It drank by scooping up handfuls of water, bending its head back, and pouring the water into the buccal slit that gaped when the head went back. I saw this from maybe 20 meters away. The hrossa made no move to kill the thing, and certainly it showed no fear of us by any of its actions. It drank for a while, looked us over good, then went away.

I couldn't figure out what was going on and asked SpikhKai point-blank why we'd hiked all morning looking for a folyokh, then let one just walk off unscathed. His reply was: "That one has not made another one inside himself yet." I thought they must be scarce if we were looking for an older folyokh, on the same principle as not shooting does. Wrong guess again.

Anyway, we did find one. Or rather one found us. We went on in single file, wandering seemingly at random, broadcasting hunger on low volume, and along about midafternoon another folyokh came toward us out of the trees, making a lot of noise—they're gigantic animals!—but not hurrying. The hrossa and the folyokh both stopped and looked at each other, and some complicated empathy took place (I'm next thing to certain that it took place between the hrossa *and the folyokh*), and then the folyokh walked right up on its six legs to the hross who was carrying the club, KwakhOomh, reared up to expose its pouch, and copulated with him. Symbolically, anyway. Their organs erected out of their pouches, and they touched genital areas, though the incompatibility of size must have made actual copulation impossible. Our eyes, mine and Danny's about bugged out of our heads when we saw what they were doing, yet it was obvious from the way the other hrossa reacted, both in behavior and in the feelings we picked up from them, that this was no more than the ordinary procedure. What they did was form pairs and copulate too, in such a stately way it seemed almost like a ritual (the

Kiss of Peace?). Danny and I entered into the spirit of the occasion, but we didn't come, so I don't think the hrossa did either; we would have if they had.

When the symbolic copulation was finished KwakhOomh swung the club with his upper pair of hands and killed the folyokh.

Right afterward the hrossa all slumped down on the ground, apparently to recover from the experience, which had been emotionally draining. I'm not clear about the oddments I picked up—I was too amazed for a while there, and my feelings were completely out of phase with theirs. Danny thinks the atmosphere was sort of like a gathered meeting but I can't confirm that.

After some minutes they got up and started to cut up the folyokh. I had never seen that much Pennterran blood and had forgotten that blood is red here too. I roused myself to ask them to bring all the internal organs back for Alice to look over. It seems to be the custom to leave the parts they don't use on the site of the kill; however, they weren't at all adamant about leaving the offal. They did carve the heaviest bones right out of the carcass and leave *them*, so that what remained—including the paunch of guts—made two burdens of a size and bulk they could manage. These were bundled up in pieces of skin, the bundles trussed to the poles, and the ends of the poles fitted into the saddle yokes, and off they went: four to carry and one to spell the bearers in rotation, like a spare tire.

We followed the hrossa down the mountainside. They were happy and fulfilled-feeling. My brain kept whirling the same questions around: *Had* they hypnotized the folyokh into committing suicide? *Could* they do the same to us or the Sixers? In that case, why had Danny and I been allowed to witness this, except as a warning? But equally in that case, what was the formal, sort of sacramental quality of the proceedings all about? As for the meaning of the symbolic sexual contact between hross and the folyokh (Hail Caesar! We who are about to die salute you!), I drew a complete blank on that. I felt like my own worst fears might have just come true only I was too dumb to know it.

Partway down the mountain the spare-tire hross relieved SpikhKai, and he dropped back to walk with us. The trail had broadened out some by this time. He talked, Danny translated. The gist of it was that he knew I'd been upset by what I saw and wondered what I'd expected to see instead.

I decided to describe a deer hunt from the Lenni Lenape point of view, how the hunters prepare themselves physically and mentally, get their weapons ready, track or stalk the deer, sneak up on it or wait in hiding for it, and kill it by shooting it full of arrows.

It seemed to me that this story made me more alien to SpikhKai than anything the humans have done yet on Pennterra. The emotion smoking off him felt as close as shock, to me, as a hross ever comes. He mastered himself and asked some questions. Was meat commonly obtained that way, by trickery? I reminded him that *our* meat animals are grown like plants or swillets, for the purpose, but explained that at one time long ago humans had all been hunters.

But had I ever personally shot a wild deer? I told him in a general way what had become of Earth's deer herds. But in the days when deer were killed for food—*which* of them were taken? Elders? Children so young they hadn't yet reproduced? I delivered a short lecture on deer, emphasizing the sexual dimorphism of earthly life forms. To tell the truth his reaction was making me jumpy, he was so obviously upset. I explained that in the wild bucks didn't normally get to breed until they were seven or so and that does often bred from their first season but were smaller and somewhat less desirable to hunters. I explained about population explosions of game animals created by a lack of natural predators.

Everything I said got me deeper into hot water, but out of it all SpikhKai cleverly plucked the essential point. "Do you mean every doe might have many duplicates, and that some of these might be killed as children?" I said yes, if the predators could catch them. "Didn't they taste bad and make the killers sick?" No. "Did they then not offer to be killed like the folyokh?" No, they tried as hard as they could to get away. "The young ones, yes, but the elders who have bred—did *they* not offer to be killed."

I said, "What do you mean when you say that the folyokh *offered* to be killed?" I thought Danny's translation must be off.

SpikhKai's feelings were a mix of astonishment and confusion. He said, "This one was ready. His child is a breeder now, it was his time," as if that explained everything.

I asked if all hross animal food behaved like this, and he said yes. "Every young animal tastes bad until he breeds. When his child is grown up, then his flesh sweetens and he offers himself when he is ready." I said, would an animal offer himself to another animal or only to the hrossa? SpikhKai said, "A hross is an animal like any other." Then he thought a bit and said, "We knew you kept animals for food, but we thought it must be with you as it is with us."

"Well," I said, "we made the same mistake. The hrossa keep swillets as we keep sheep and rabbits, but only eat the ones that offer to be eaten, is that it?"

"And the Quakers keep animals that breed repeatedly, and eat their children?"

So we got that sorted out. After some thought I said, "A folyokh has only one child?" "Yes, like us, and the swillets too." "But suppose that child dies—can it have another one?"

He emitted agitation again—"A child almost never dies!"— but then said: "If it happens, the parent may have another if he is still a breeder; it depends. And sometimes, not often nowadays, a parent has a second child, even a third, though the first one lives. No one knows why. It is not a happy thing."

Think about it: it's like applying binary fission to animal husbandry! You have two thousand quick-breeding swillets in a pen. Each makes a baby swillet. Over a period of several weeks you harvest two thousand willing adults. The babies grow up and make two thousand more babies. You harvest the adults . . .

Very rarely a baby dies; once in a while a swillet produces more than one baby. The population remains stable.

How do you enlarge the herd?

I wonder: does the one-child rule apply to all, or even most, of the animal life on Pennterra? If it does, how long since life developed here? This world is *old*.

I'll have to finish later, I can't write any more right now—fingers too cramped and mind too muddled.

AFTERTHOUGHTS:

At some point I asked what happens if an animal doesn't offer itself to be eaten. According to SpikhKai that's like saying "What happens if a child doesn't grow up?" It's in the nature of things that a Pennterran creature knows when it's time to die back into the world.

At another point I asked what the hrossa do when the time comes for them. He said: "The People feed the ground."

Field Notes: Sevenday, 7 November 2233 (Alice). I try to imagine doing natural science in the days before electronic microscopes and stained slides, to keep my courage up, but some days the frustration is nearly intolerable. At the gross level it's possible to observe only enough to madden one with curiosity.

The internal organs brought back from the hunt are fascinating. The chilly weather refrigerated them nicely, and I had all day yesterday and most of today to dissect and photograph them before KliUrrh very courteously suggested that it was time to give them back to Tanka Wakan.

The folyokh is ovoviviparous like the hross, though the use of six limbs for locomotion, plus factors of general appearance, suggest that the relationship isn't close. I'd love to have had a complete skeleton to make a scale model from, but this team isn't equipped to do anything that ambitious even if all the bones had been brought back to the village. I'd have given my right arm for permission to take samples of blood, digestive juices, organ tissue, stomach contents, etc., but *nothing at all* of that kind is acceptable to the hrossa. So I decided to examine the digestive and reproductive systems as carefully and thoroughly as possible given these limitations, and here are my findings:

Like the hross, the folyokh has a long esophagus and a stomach with two chambers: a muscular gizzard-like anterior sac lined with grinding surfaces, where food is broken down into small bits, and behind that a larger thin-walled stomach where digestion and absorption take place. Long ropes of intestines are absent; the larger stomach appears simply to retain food until all the nourishment is extracted, then to bundle the indigestible residues into a short cloaca. The dissected hross's posterior stomach was lined with tissue that presented the largest possible surface for absorption, like our intestinal epithelium; no doubt this tissue is much the same. It seems a primitive system, unsuitable for a high order of being—rather more froglike than mammalian.

The hrossa, for instance, eat once each day, in the evening. They also defecate once daily, just before dinner. It would appear that this type of digestive system is designed to cycle through completely before starting fresh. All waste goes out the same way; no sign of a urinary bladder or anything obviously analogous to kidneys.

If their cell chemistry were like ours the system would be a monument to inefficiency, so I must assume the tissues utilize their nutrients in a more sustained and gradual way than ours do; but how are we ever going to find out?

Of course, as I write this I know the answer perfectly well. We *aren't* going to. The Sixers will find out and tell us and have all the fun. It makes me want to bite somebody, birthright Friend though I am.

At all events we'll have stolen a march on them as regards reproduction. Unlike ours, that system is anterior to the digestive system, in the folyokh as in the hross. I've examined it very thoroughly and am perplexed at my conclusions, which are these:

Our dissection and lab analysis of the hross elder taught us less about reproduction than we'd hoped—he was very old and his organs had been atrophied for a long time. But we were able to identify certain structures, and we made inferences about their functions. For instance, we saw what appeared to be shriveled glands behind his penicles, which we took to be gonads analogous to testes. We couldn't stain the samples of that tissue or slice them thin enough for perfect viewing, but what we saw tended to support that hypothesis, or at least not to contradict it in any obvious way.

But this folyokh, though past the breeder stage, was (relatively) much younger at the time of death than the old hross, and its genitals and interior organs were in much better condition. It was possible to see that each of the testes was connected by a long, extremely thin, almost hairlike duct to the neighboring vaginal passage. We had not observed this when we dissected the hross; these ducts either weren't there anymore, or had never been there, or we missed them. I incline to the third explanation.

Take a pair of copulating folyokhs. When the penicles of partner #1 push into the vaginal orifices of partner #2, and vice versa, it looks to me as if the testes of #1—instead of squirting ejaculate into #2—are squeezed or otherwise encouraged by #2's penicles into squirting the stuff *backwards*, into its *own* vaginas, and thence on down into its own egg chamber (and vice versa). In other words, each folyokh when it copulates fertilizes itself.

I sliced carefully into each penicle and found that all lacked a central tube leading from the gland out to the tip, which we had stupidly assumed to be present because of the structural similarity to a penis or the nipple of a breast. Of course such a tube might exist for a time, then grow closed when no longer in service. The hand lens I'm using just isn't powerful enough to show cells.

I then approached two breeders who had just separated and politely asked to see their genital pouches. They were happy to comply. There was no evidence of any sort of ejaculate on either one. They asked, through Danny, what I was looking for. We explained (and demonstrated) how semen is produced in human copulation, and they were very entertained and interested, but claimed to know nothing about any such material among the hrossa.

This is immensely, maddeningly far from conclusive or complete. There is, after all, the matter of the physical arrangement of these structures: if tubes analogous to urethrae were present in the penicles, any secretions produced by the testes would flow readily from each partner into the vaginas of the other. In some species, or in many/all species under some circumstances, this may well happen.

Self-fertilization could be a late, or intermittent, evolutionary adaptation—indeed it's impossible to understand how speciation could occur otherwise, if Bob's and George's information about the average birth rate of one child per parent turns out to be both true and general.

The egg chamber and birth valve are in all aspects similar to those we saw in the hross elder. No sign of anything like an ovary.

I intend to enter my statistical records on the folyokh into the computer when we go back to Swarthmore for Thanksgiving; I won't copy them out here.

We have been generating quite a lot of random data. I believe we should take time to consider, before going very much further, how these disparate facts add up to a whole picture.

One pleasant addendum that the Ancients would have appreciated: in both folyokh and hross the controlling organ of the central nervous system is also the pump that circulates nutrient-rich fluids through the body and carries away metabolic wastes. In other words, in these two species the heart IS the seat of reason. Whether it's also the seat of empathy I wouldn't care to say. It is located in the peculiar thick "neckless" region of the upper torso, or shoulder, of the hross; the folyokh has a bit more of a neck, but the position is roughly the same.

The next time a specimen is brought to the village I shall concentrate on the respiratory and circulatory/nervous systems or their equivalents; I'll only mention now the interesting fact that the folyokh breathes and emits sounds through a pair of flat nostril openings on the head, which—belonging as they do to a land animal—bear little resemblance to the mobile and supple spiracles of the hrossa. It rather suggests that the hrossa's ability to form words is an accidental by-product of their having evolved as amphibious creatures.

Field Notes: Sevenday, 7 November 2233 (Katy). I've worked out the patterns of households for the village. There are 31 inhabitants, including 8 elders (early and late), 10 adults, 6 breeders (only 6! hard to believe, considering the sheer quantity of lustfulness they generate), and 7 children, distributed in 12 family lodges. Thus:

I	II
#1 early elder (KliUrrh)	#2 early elder (WikhKiah)
#9 unrelated adult (SwiAakh)	#20 breeder
#19 breeder (SwikhKarrh)	

III	IV
#3 early elder (HaahKoob)	#4 late elder (PaahOokh)
#10 adult	#11 adult (PwiUpp)
#21 breeder	#25 child

V	VI
#5 early elder	#6 late elder
#22 breeder	#12 adult (SpikhKai)
	#26 child

VII	VIII
#7 late elder	#14 adult (KwakhOomh)
#13 adult	#28 child
#23 breeder	
#27 child	

IX	X
#8 early elder (HrukhKeeb)	#16 adult
#15 adult	#24 breeder
#29 child	

XI	XII
#17 adult	#18 adult
#30 child	#31 child

Note: breeders from other villages are in and out of Lake-Between-Falls these days, and our kids are traveling and visiting other villages too. (If each individual fertilized himself, there would be no point to this immense extra expenditure of energy;

I don't see how Alice can be right.) The chart reflects the *visual* household composition.

A number of observations can be made by looking at the schematic representation above:

1. Households are ordinarily composed of two or three family members of different generations in linear descent.

2. In no household is there more than *one* member of any generation. May we conclude that parents and children never belong to the same life stage at the same time?

3. Every household includes either a breeder or a child (but in only one case both).

4. Only two households lack an adult. Note, however: KliUrrh's household includes an adult who is not related to him and SwikhKarrh. This adult, SwiAakh, lost his child and was unable to have another. When his aged parent died, he was adopted into KliUrrh's family. (KliUrrh gave me this information himself.)

5. Individuals do not (ordinarily? ever?) live alone.

COMMENTARY

As usual, everything we learn leads to a host of questions we can't get fast answers to, or any answers at all. The hrossa have eight limbs and eight fingers; they figure from base 8 to 8^2, but that's all they've ever done with numbers. They count objects, but not periods of lapsed time, at least not at Lake-Between-Falls. The difficulty this presents for us in the present context is that they don't know how old they are. Their empathic sense of an individual's situation in life is doubtless a lot more precise than a number would be, but it's frustrating to us. How long does childhood last? How many seasons does a hross spend as a breeder? Does he usually conceive right away, or does that vary a lot? After a baby's born, is it common for the parent to develop rapidly into an adult, or does he spend several more years being swept up in the (almost always *un*productive) breeding frenzy every fall?

Etc. SpikhKai told Bob that sometimes a breeder who loses a child can have another. Breeder #23 in Household VII has an undersize child, probably born last spring, and #23 is certainly participating with gusto in this season's festivities. If we keep on collecting items like these, and if we monitor the village over the next decade or two and make a new chart every year, we'll have all the answers in the end; but the thing is that we need them NOW.

I've watched SwikhKarrh change from child to breeder since we came to Pennterra, but there's no knowing how old he was in 2227. The hrossa have no calendar; they don't even keep track of the moons.

One village child was lost and not replaced—there used to be 13 lodges here and now there are only 12. No household at present has two children in it. But that could change if I read correctly between SpikhKai's lines. Even so, the population seems stable to the point of ruinous stagnation; I simply cannot fathom what keeps it viable, or what that tremendous expenditure of sexual energy can be *for*.

Personal Journal: Seconday, 10 November 2233 (Katy). I want to record that things are vastly improved among the five of us since the decision to let Pennterran nature have its way with us. The "nature" in question is *very* different from anything I'd experienced up to now, on Earth *or* in Swarthmore, so maybe it's *hross* nature I mean; but anyway, on the presumption that we're as likely to learn what we need on this topic through introspection as through observation now, I've set aside time this evening to mull over the results to date of our experiment in going native.

I've now had repeated sexual contact of some sort with every member of this team (pardon ghastly pun), which includes a middle-aged lesbian and a boy just entering puberty. Now, up to the time of this field trip I'd never experienced what might be called "casual" sex, or "deviant" sex either, with anybody—all my partners had been genuine lovers (Charlie, Andy, Kjell) or dearly valued friends (Jonas at Pendle Hill, George). Much as I dislike the expression "make love," one sort of love or another was what I was making with all those men whenever I went to bed with any of them. In my mind, or psyche, sex has *always* been connected with love. The idea of bedding men I didn't care about has never appealed to me at all. (According to Alice, this is a relatively young, relatively satisfied woman's view of the subject. She says she used to be "fairly fastidious" but later on would sometimes get so horny, at times when there were no appropriate partners available, that she could have dragged total strangers in off the street. But she's had a rougher time than I have.)

It's become my considered opinion that the empathic jolly lustfulness of the breeders is just not *about* love. It's about friendliness, pleasure, and good fun—the whole village looks forward to the rut the way we looked forward to Christmas when we were kids. Ultimately—but, as with us, a long way from consciousness—it's about babies. But for a hrossa copulation is a happy commonplace, *not* implying deep meaning, commitment, any of that heavy stuff, not at *all*! I'd say it's like animal behavior on Earth except that the hrossa are so *jolly* about it! Their sex does have all the amorality of animal sex, but it's combined with a more human sense of fun: there's nothing frantic about it, nothing of the ram or billy goat (just to name the animals whose approaches to breeding I'm most familiar with).

I'd say that for the hrossa sex is what a bear hug would be for us if a hug had more of a kick to it. As far as meaning goes, I mean. But even that may overstate the case; we're a demonstrative bunch in Swarthmore and I know that quite often, among us, a hug has much more to do with love than these Rabelaisian delights do. And it isn't that love doesn't come into our relations up here, either. I've loved both George and Danny for years and still do. But under the spell of the breeders, loving them is *apart* from having sex with them, except for that very first time with Danny. When I used to sleep with George sometimes in Swarthmore there was love in the act; up here, there isn't. It's as if that aspect of human sex is unable to be expressed up here.

I figure *that's* why the hrossa are so uninhibited about copulation. Why wouldn't they be? There's no pair-bonding for sex to threaten or enforce. The deepest relationships aren't between sexual partners but between parents and children. In themselves the sexual partnerships have no future—they hardly have a present, and they're at the opposite extreme from exclusive.

All this may be simply to state the obvious, but I wanted to spell it out.

I already said how awful resisting the breeders was, and now I'll say that giving in to them is just delightful. For the duration, we're free of all our own sociosexual baggage and junk: guilt, embarrassment, shame, jealousy, possessiveness, inhibitions and taboos. You're grabbed by a letch and you just gratify it straightaway, with whoever's similarly inclined, and somebody always is. It's equally great with everybody, so preferences don't form and rejections don't occur. Alice's hand is about as much to the purpose as anybody's cock. We hardly even break stride in the satisfaction of these abrupt arousals—we do it leaning against something, sitting, lying down, and except at night we do it fully clothed (thank God for the invention of the crotch fly!). It only takes a minute anyway.

Physically we all feel wonderful. Emotionally the only effect seems to be that we're in supremely good spirits almost all the time—even George! even Alice!!—and full of energy and getting along splendidly together. I'm quite sure none of us fancies s/he's in love with one of the others—that whole side of things is as dormant as the vegetation on the mountain.

I really doubt whether any human culture could ever have sustained precisely this attitude toward sexual congress for long. I'm aware that free-love cults have sprung up from time to time and place to place, but the *meaning* of the sex, the charge on it, must have been different. Among us there were always men and women, with all that that implies; and where the pockets of license were homosexual they were clearly separate from the mainstream. The oldest cultures we know about were horrified by incest. Competition for and possession of sexual partners went on everywhere. None of this is true of the hrossa, who have no spouses, no genders, and no possessiveness, and where sexual contact between parents and children is common but fertilization of a child by a parent impossible, assuming—as I think we safely may—that breeders alone are fertile and that no parent is still a breeder by the time his child becomes one (supposing for the moment that the hrossa do *not* commonly fertilize themselves).

We're able to enter fully into the spirit of this life and enjoy it, so long as we're under the strong influence of the breeders' feelings; but even now, basking in the sense of well-being whose source they are, I *know* this isn't a human thing, a thing *for* humans. I mean that it's not something humans can generate and sustain on their own. When we go back down to the settlement again—or even if we stay up here till after the rut has run its course—our sexual urges will alter and our behavior readjust to patterns appropriate for a people with two genders, long-term fertility, and the abundant hang-ups thereto appertaining. I don't mean we'll be exactly the same as we were before, because how could anybody go through an experience like this and not be changed by it? But we won't be all that changed. The community will reassimilate us and we'll revert to normal, whatever that is for each of us.

And I won't be sorry at all. This has been a marvelous vacation from human hang-ups; I never enjoyed myself more. But I'd

hate to trade human sex in permanently for all this yummy freedom. It's *nice* to have a physical way of loving other people. We
need one; *we* aren't empaths. It would be great to get permanently rid of jealousy and possessiveness and the like, vices, but
they come in the package deal and we're stuck with them, even
when we call in judgment to whip the bastards into line. You take
the rough with the smooth.

The hrossa don't; they don't have to. Sexual feelings don't
create social problems for them, don't goad them into behaving
badly—nor, for that matter, does anything else. They're like
unfallen creatures, wise innocents or (again) animals. What
problems *have* they got? Well, eating enough. Raising healthy
babies. Neither of those is ordinarily very much of a problem;
what else? Do they have diseases? Natural enemies? Parasites?
Nobody on Pennterra appears to have what we'd call natural
enemies if the hrossa know what they're talking about. Things
eat one another, but only by consent of the eaten.

Hmm. If nobody competes for food or sex...then what is the
evolutionary mechanism here? Because it can't be natural selection. Is it possible that these life-forms *don't* evolve—is that the
difference Tony wanted us to look for?

Field Notes: Thirday, 11 November 2233 (Bob). Last night round
the old stove Katy looked up from writing in her journal and
said, "Hey, natural selection can't be the evolutionary mechanism here." Alice sat still and blinked a couple of times, and then
she said, "Out of the mouths of babes. Maybe not. I must be
getting old."

Katy said she wondered if the life-forms here don't evolve, but
Alice and George both said that barring special creation that's
just not possible, that maybe this could be a very static period in
Pennterra's evolutionary history, but where there's life there's
change, always.

Inspired by this crystallization of what we've been groping toward ever since the hunt, and ever since Alice came up with her
self-fertilization hypothesis, I'm going to finish writing up my
report. I'd have done it sooner if the writers worked, but I've
been learning to weave and my fingers are sore.

The more we discussed Katy's idea about natural selection, the
more we realized that practically all our "information" is un-
confirmed hearsay. We don't *know* that each Pennterran animal has only one offspring. Still less do we know that it fertilizes

itself. Proper investigation is impossible when you can't collect specimens and do what you want with them. If Alice could have put one of that folyokh's penicles and testes under a powered microscope, after preparing the slides properly, she'd be able to hazard a good guess as to whether it—#1—had ejaculated into folyokh #2 at some point in its existence; if she could do vivisection on a folyokh *breeder* she'd be home free. But she can't, and in most ways I'm sure that's just as well. But the point is, we don't know anything much for certain.

Theorizing about how the planet's biology works after looking at one hross and one folyokh is like building a dinosaur model based on one toe bone. So I know this is going way out on a limb.

But say it's true that most fauna here have only one offspring, by what amounts to parthenogenesis or cloning.

Say the phenomenon Danny and I witnessed—the folyokh delivering itself up to the slaughter—is typical, as SpikhKai says, and not some weird aberration.

He also says—I asked—that the one-child rule is general, true of all the faunal life forms the hrossa know a lot about. I don't know if that includes only animals they eat. The Amerindians knew a lot about the animals they utilized and the ones they were afraid of or annoyed by, not so much about the others. But say he's right.

Say that all animals from the lowest to the highest forms are immune to being eaten until they have produced their single offspring and made it self-sustaining, but then afterward all give themselves voluntarily to whatever preys upon their species. (I guess *preys* isn't really the word.)

By Earth standards, what you'd have seems like a formula for evolutionary stultification. You wouldn't need strength to compete for a mate or allure to attract one; you wouldn't need stamina or agility or speed to run away from predators or catch prey; you wouldn't need intelligence to outsmart either. You wouldn't "need" *anything*, so none of those traits would be selected for. Species would never adapt in response to environmental pressures. Change would come about only through mutation, and every noncrippling mutation would be about equally viable.

If all *that's* true, then almost everybody survives and passes on his genes, but only once. There's no "success" in the large-scale Earth sense, no alpha male passing his genes on to every child of the next generation and cutting many other males out for keeps. That perception you get in the study of biology, of every crea-

ture madly *struggling* to survive (eat, avoid being eaten) and to
beat out the competition for breeding opportunities, would be
missing completely. Everybody survives to reproduce himself.
Everybody then generously offers himself to feed others. A slow,
coordinated dance of inter- and intra-specific cooperation.

I don't buy it. There are too many problems.

For one thing, I can't see why intelligence would ever evolve.
All this may be consistent with the feeling we've always had that
the hrossa are—by human standards—a dull, incurious people
for all their spiritual depth, but there's no question they're intelligent.

And I don't see how there would be enough food, even if they
do expend a lot less energy getting it than some (most?) terrestrial species do. It's true that the village has taken all this time to
finish off the folyokh, and I think the hross metabolic rate must
be slowish for a warm-blooded animal of that size. (A new hunt
soon.) But even so...

The main objection is that the hrossa *are* so obviously adapted
to their amphibious lifestyle. (See also Alice's note for 7 November, contrasting hross spiracles with folyokh nostrils.)

Maybe natural selection as we understand it didn't produce
that body shape and breathing system, but something did. We
have to keep plugging away at this. Just as well the emergency
(the Sixers I mean) tends to fade out of mind while we're plugging. I don't think it would help us any to *feel* the pressure of the
deadline we're working under, though Oppenheimer & Co. might
tell me different.

Query: what might the biological role of *empathy* be? We may
have seen it operating on the hunt. If the folyokhs are empathic
too, then I think the hrossa were just looking for one that was
ready and projecting hunger as they went along so *it* could find
them. There was something else after it did find them, but since
we can't "hear" the lower orders at all, it was like listening to one
side of a conversation. If the folyokh said anything I don't know
what it was.

*Personal Journal: Fourday, 12 November 2233 (George). Nine
days* since I wrote in here! It won't do; I must create opportunities even in the absence of convenience or need. I'm convinced
that these personal records Katy and I are keeping *will* supplement the public one in important ways, and it's not as if I've been
draining all my strength into the Field Notebook, either.

I've been with KliUrrh most of every day since he returned, working mostly in that way on the question of hross sexuality and the effects of its empathic aspect on us. And I've been biding my time and doing a lot of thinking; but *some* sort of progress report could and should have been put down here before now.

Most of the team's work has been done by watching and politely poking into things, not by asking questions. Mine is an exception; I've been talking (or communicating) with what a real anthropologist could only call a reliable informant, for many hours each day. I think he may finally be getting somewhere with me.

For instance. Yesterday Katy and I were the kitchen squad. A couple of breeders gamboled by outside while I was sitting in my chair scraping carrots and she was standing at the "counter" cutting up potatoes. Naturally we both sprang to attention, erotically speaking, and since her hands were cleaner than mine she fished me out of my trousers and straddled the chair facing me; I didn't even put down the carrot or the paring knife. At the same instant Danny banged in with a load of kindling. He dumped it in the basket and rushed over to us, unfastening his pants as he came, while Katy was opening both her shirt and mine. He pushed between us. Katy pulled him in with one arm around his waist and one around my shoulders, his cock squeezed between her breasts and my bare chest. In seconds he had ejaculated, and as he did I felt Katy's contractions go, which triggered my own.

We've all got used to living amid puddles of semen and in clothes that have dried crusty with the stuff, and we've gotten very adroit at scratching and then promptly forgetting these sudden sexual itches. Danny fastened up his pants again, already talking animatedly about something he'd just remembered that happened on that hunt with Bob. Katy swabbed at our two chests with a kitchen towel, buttoned up her shirt, got off me and blotted her crotch a couple of times, then pitched the towel in the hamper and sealed her fly, all the while listening attentively to Danny and asking questions; she might have been briskly cleaning off a table after a family dinner. I pulled my own clothes together with two fingers and resumed scraping the carrot as I listened too, and *even I* made nothing of any of this at the time. Yet only nine days ago I'd have been desperately upset at the prospect of any such scene as that one.

What changed me? What's been going on? That's what I finally feel ready to try to get down here now.

When he got home on the first, KliUrrh found me in a state, and he does so hate a state. I thought he should rest before we conferred, but he said, "Better to make you peaceful if it can be done; then my rest will be peaceful too." I offered to take myself out of range, but he said no. He'd just come across the lake and was wet. "Get a towel then and rub me down," he said. He wanted to hold me, and that was what I wanted too.

When he was dry we walked along the beach, away from the village. There's a fallen tree I can sit astride down there, without putting strain on my back, and that's where I've spent much of the last week, when I wasn't monitoring breeder activity and it wasn't raining.

We got there. I mounted the tree. KliUrrh hunkered down on the sand with the upright front of his body against the whole length of my left side: thigh, hip, ribs. My left arm was around him. All four of his arms went around me, at waist and chest level, and his face was against my neck.

It was absolute bliss. The agitation and misery of the past few days began to drain right out of me, as if I were a hurt infant finally nestled in my mother's lap again, where I belonged. God knows why it doesn't embarrass me to write what must strike anyone else as cloying beyond endurance, but that was truly how I felt.

For several minutes we stayed like that. I had an erection, but not the kind I wear constantly when associating with the breeders—the itching, tickling kind that insists on regular relief.

After a while KliUrrh said, "Now, tell me." When I'd finished he was quiet except for the slow flow of comfort, very loud, against my left side. Then he said: "You want Danny to learn everything that is right for him to know, and you are thinking that if he does too much as we do, it will make the lesson hard."

"Yes, exactly."

"George. I know Danny. It will hurt him too much if you make him go back. Ahhhhhh it will hurt him a little if he stays. But that hurt is only short. He belongs here even more than you, because he is young. Being with the breeders now, when he and they are so... attuned, he will learn this one thing very well and remember it very well."

He picked the word *attuned* out of my head. As clear an instance of this kind of thing as we've had—but he and I were exceptionally attuned ourselves at the time. I said, "I can see that

that might be important," and I could. Danny's more inte-
grated into the village life than any of us, and the more he understands, the truer that will be.

"SwikhKarrh loves him to be here, that I know. You already
have decided he must stay, and I think it is right. But you feel it
may not be."

I said, "KliUrrh, my problem is that I think one way and feel
another. Among my people it's a crime for fathers to have sexual contact with their children—a child could easily be harmed
for the rest of his life by such contact. I understand that what you
and SwikhKarrh do together is not in any sense a crime, that for
the hrossa the same act has a different meaning. But I *feel* that
sexual contact between Danny and me would be utterly wrong,
even if we were only 'playing hrossa,' and sexual contact will
certainly take place between us if he stays."

"Something already happened between you."

"In a way."

"You felt bad because it was pleasant? This is a human thing;
I may not be able to help with this. Did the pleasure disturb
Danny?"

"No. He was asleep."

He went quiet again, thinking it over. I didn't try to explain
further, but only basked in his embrace. I remembered how I had
once fretted myself because I thought KliUrrh wouldn't be able
to love me as I needed him to. His way of encompassing me in his
feelings may not be just what I had in mind in those days, but it's
all I need and even all I want.

After he had thought it through he leaned away from me and
drew open his pouch with one upper hand and erected his penicles by putting the fingers of the other hand into the two lower
orifices. He rotated his huge eyes around and curved his body
down to observe them; then he put one hand on my erection and
said, "Let me look at this, please, George." Wordless, I slitted
open my trousers and presented myself in the chilly daylight for
his inspection.

KliUrrh drew my left hand down, and for the first time ever I
inserted three fingers into the puckered satiny holes there, each
too small to accommodate the penis of an adult human, but just
about right for a finger. And KliUrrh made the best cylinder he
could with his hand and slid it carefully around my erection,
which had wilted somewhat under the stress but revived at this
warm handling. For a bemusing few moments nothing else occurred. KliUrrh stroked me and "listened" to my feelings and

responses; I withdrew from the vaginas and handled the triangle of tough black penicles, "listening" to his. If rutting breeders had happened by we would both certainly have responded to that, but none did. It didn't signify. Though I don't really want to repeat the experience, it was not disagreeable at all. Just odd.

When enough time had passed we put our assortment of genitals away, and KliUrrh embraced me again. "Truly we are made as different inwardly as out. But George, do you see that *this* is the first truth about you and me? The touching of *these* parts of us is not important." By "this" I knew he meant the surge of mutual feeling when he pressed up against me; physical contact always makes the empathy stronger; the larger the area of contact, the louder the music of empathy plays. "At breeding season you are all become like our breeders, here," patting my groin, "and like the breeders you give each other pleasure. But it is not *important*. It is only *pleasure*! The pleasure stops. Everything important goes on without stopping."

And then he said something I hadn't realized: "The People do not hold each other like this, you know. We do not need to." It's true; I never saw two hrossa with their four arms about each other. Genital touching is just about all the touching they do. I knew he meant that the People communicate through empathy everything he communicated to me by wrapping his body around me like a mother.

I think now of the warmth of his strange hand on my cock and it twitches at the memory. Through most of my hundreds of hours in KliUrrh's presence I've had an erection; in every way he makes me more sensuously alert to myself and everything in the world around me. All of Pennterra does that, when I'm open to it, and always did. Above all, when I'm swimming in the lake or the river. But *then* it's as if the erection were a sort of radio antenna, not a nose about to sneeze! *That* enhanced sensuousness is *important*. All *this* maniacal tingling and spurting is great fun, I've had a first-rate time whenever I've been able to stop fussing about things, but it *doesn't matter*. Not for me, and not in the long run for Danny. That was what he meant.

Yet Danny's bound to have some adjustment problems when we go back, because for him the cart of permissive release had been put before the horse of adolescent frustration. Out of range of the breeders the rest of us will subside to normal; he won't, not entirely. For him, for now, abnormal is normal, so he's going to have to learn control when we get home, poor kid. The pressure will change more in kind than in intensity. He'll need lots of tact and talk. But I think and hope and trust that it'll be OK.

(Having said all this, I confess I'm still relieved that Danny and his mother didn't have to sort this one out between them—and for my own sake, that Danny's a son and not a daughter. No leopard can change its spots that much, that fast, not even with help from KliUrrh—how on Earth could I explain Freud or Skilken to KliUrrh?)

For days I've been thinking about sexual passion, seeking back under twenty layered years of memories in an attempt to recapture the sense of how I felt about Maggie when I was 25—the one time I'm certain of when the physical love of somebody reached its highest pitch in me, the highest I was ever capable of I think. Sex with Maggie wasn't "fun," it was a kind of sacrament. We had only six months or so of furtive meetings and I'm sure it would have gotten to *be* fun (too), later on, if we'd had the time and if there hadn't been so much pain and guilt mixed up in it because of Susan. But I've been realizing that if you take away the pain, the experience could very well have been broken down into the components of breeder-assisted orgasm on the one hand and the sort of transcendental love I feel for KliUrrh on the other. And that for the hrossa these elements are naturally discrete, whereas the ability to combine them is a fundamental part of what being human is: our great refinement on animal reproductive behavior.

Only, all hrossa have extensive experience with both components, the orgasmic and the transcendental; whereas only a few lucky humans get to experience their product more than briefly—passion being a most unstable compound, as we all know. And it's my impression that neither intense love nor terrific sex is all that common on Earth. Quakers have always drawn together partly to supply a lack of the former (how well we have ever dealt with the latter need I couldn't say). Human sexuality is a seething cauldron; hross sexuality is a fine old time—but a passionless one. But who needs passion, if you're a hross and an empath?

No passions of that sort have appeared among the members of our team. We're held in corporate love, brought in large part from home and strengthened by this extraordinary shared experience, *and* we have sex together every day, all of us with any and all of the rest of us. But as KliUrrh said, we are become hrossa in this; the two things are unconnected with each other, and it's the love that *matters*. Meeting for worship is the only thing "sacramental" about our life up here.

It's a fine life, clear, lacking the messy, disturbed quality of our "real" life back in the settlement; but it's also taught us something about the human condition, and I think we'll all—as it were—re-embrace our humanity when we go back with an altered appreciation of what the price we pay in inner ugliness entitles us to.

Even I will, I think.

Still, God knows the differences between us and the hrossa are less to be wondered at than the likenesses.

I must add a final personal truth to all this high-sounding palaver: that however my vision of human nature clarifies, however I feel my engagement with the rest of humankind refreshed, still there's something beyond and behind whatever I say, surpassing everything but the bond of blood with Danny, and that's my feeling for KliUrrh, which in quality and power is perfectly unique in all my experience.

Anyway, a couple of days after the therapy session on the tree, Danny and I were talking with KliUrrh in front of his house when SwikhKarrh came bounding by, and swung out of his way to dash over and copulate with his parent. As they connected—WHUMP!—Danny whooped and threw his arms around me at the instant the letch struck both of us, and by the time I was able to think about it it was over. The kids ran off together and left me standing there flatfooted with my pants full of guck and a dopey grin on my face. And I think that a fortuitous event, since whatever occurs in KliUrrh's presence, beneath his benign attention, can only seem agreeable to me. I pulled out my handkerchief, cleaned myself up, and from that moment ceased to mull and fret.

Field Notes: Fourday, 12 November 2233 (George). This will be a summary of what I've learned about hross reproduction, both by direct observation and through discussions with KliUrrh. It supplements Bob's report of 11/6 and Alice's of 11/7, as well as my own of 11/2.

Alice tells me that in one species of hyena the genitalia of the males and females are identical in appearance—the female has a greatly enlarged clitoris that can be erected, and fleshy pads that look exactly like testes. The members of the band lick one another's erect penises as a ritual of greeting whenever they meet, but the female's "penis" is not erected when she mates. A bit suggestive, if only a bit, of what the hrossa do.

OK. I've been monitoring the activities of the seven breeders (four Lake-Between-Falls residents—#19, 20, 23 and 24—and three guests), trying to discover any evidence of ejaculated material. So far I haven't seen (or felt) any (they don't mind in the least having my fingers stuck into them). I've probed pretty far down and never felt the least trace of dampness, not even down where I'd expect to encounter some if the ejaculate was going backwards through the ducts into their own vaginas, down near the egg chamber. The vaginal passages aren't lubricated during copulation, presumably because for them stimulation is by pressure rather than friction. Incidentally, human digits and erect hross penicles are both twice as long as hross digits—I'm quite sure a hross would be unable to fertilize himself manually.

The season's well advanced by now, and so far none of the seven breeders is pregnant—I'm told that when one conceives his awareness of this is instantaneous. KliUrrh says WikhKiah's youngster is the likeliest to conceive this season, but he doesn't really expect any new babies to be born next spring. He's perfectly calm about this. To me it seems unimaginable that so much energy could be entirely unproductive. KliUrrh says that in the first place it's unproductive only of babies, and in the second there have been no deaths this past year, so he doubts that a new life will be generated.

It's a fact that sexual energy on Earth produces large, sometimes very large, numbers of young, few of which reach maturity to breed. From the individual's own point of view I suppose *that's* wasteful, if not from nature's. KliUrrh shares the shock SpikhKai expressed to Bob at the idea that young creatures on Earth are killed and eaten as a rule. He confirms that one-child-one-parent is the rule, all over Pennterra, for every creature he knows of from the least to the largest, but cautions: "This is in our time. Long ago they say it was different."

But apparently populations *do* grow a bit (and shrink a bit) from time to time, even though the ordinary thing is for a death in the community to "trigger" a replacement. Child #27 was conceived after the late elder we dissected, from Lodge XI, died; child #26 was conceived after the loss of SwiAakh's offspring. The number was 31 in 2227, and it's still 31. But six years from now it might be, say, 33 or 28. Those numbers probably define the range of fluctuation; I doubt that the village ever gets smaller or larger, though this is a conclusion based on anecdotal evidence and may be shaky.

The hrossa are at the top of the food chain, and—unlike *every* other sort of creature here, says KliUrrh—they don't normally "offer themselves" to be eaten by any other species (except microorganisms). Thus three generations may be alive at the same time or, rarely, even four (as now in Lodge VII). Generally, when the child becomes a breeder—which takes anywhere from a few days to a number of years after birth, depending on the species—that's the signal for the parent to retire. But not among the hrossa—to that extent even they have transcended the natural order.

The following questions and answers are paraphrased and summarized, except as indicated:

Q. Does a breeder invariably bear a healthy child?

A. Almost always. Infertility is as rare as a child that dies, and a tragedy for the individual.

Q. Other than old age, what are the causes of death among the hrossa?

A. Accident. Starvation. Natural catastrophe (causing injury or starvation). Very rarely a child like SwiAakh's is born, that "cannot live well in the world."

Q. Any deaths from illness or disease?

A. [Incomprehension.] Apparently there are no hross diseases—no microbes that make a living in that way.

Q. Couldn't SwiAakh have borne another child?

A. No. He hoped to, but it must have been just too late. "He is the end of himself, and that is the greatest sorrow we know but one."

Q. "And the greatest of all?"

A. "Disharmony between a parent and his child." (—which makes *our* kind of evolutionary sense. Except for the linear parent-child-grandchild relationships there *are* no relatives here, no siblings, aunts, uncles, cousins: no horizontal family. All the genetic eggs are in one basket, unless it turns out that cross-fertilization does take place after all somehow; and even if it does, there's still no bond to rival that between a parent and the single child he is ever to carry, commune with throughout the gestation period, and give birth to himself.)

Q. When are second children conceived, and by whom?

A. It happens sometimes, no one knows why. [Uneasiness.] (It appears that multiple births do not *ever* occur.)

Q. Are such children likely to have more than one child themselves when they become breeders?

A. "I never knew such a child. I heard it said once that both the children of a hross from a village to the north grew up strong and well." [Uneasiness.]

Q. Have you ever heard tell of a third child being born?

A. In old stories only. [Uneasiness.]

Q. "KliUrrh, why does this subject cause you discomfort?"

A. "I hardly know myself. The People believe that one child is best, much better than two or none."

This incident was only the second time I've known KliUrrh's serenity to be disturbed by anxiety. It must be important, but at this point I don't know what to make of it.

I wonder if the hrossa are built to bear more than one child ordinarily. Could those able to do it be throwbacks to an earlier time? It would help immeasurably to be able to look inside a breeder. But, until one of some species dies an accidental death, that won't be possible; and KliUrrh just doesn't *know* any child or breeder physiology. He knows everything there is to know about adult animal physiology at the macro-, or butcher's, level, but by adulthood the reproductive information we want is no longer obtainable.

We'll put the problem to the computer when we go back: if no species here is prolific, how does anybody get enough to eat? One probable answer: I asked KliUrrh, and he says that as far as he knows there are no strictly carnivorous species in the world. Everybody that isn't a herbivore eats everything. We can't study plant reproduction in the field till summer comes, but we now expect to find fundamental differences between what we're used to and what happens here.

We also think that the mean metabolic rate of the faunal biomass is probably going to turn out to be quite low. Outside breeding season you never see a hross hurrying to get anywhere. I have the impression—for what it's worth—that land animals are generally largish, and I know a fair proportion of them hibernate, and that many who don't are said to choose late autumn to surrender voluntarily to their... I was going to write *enemies* when what I mean is only *eaters*.

The fact is, we need a permanent station up here. We need to see nature on Pennterra operating at full tilt, not the stripped-down and partial version we see now. But I don't know if Lake-Between-Falls village would like that or permit it, and I'm not sure if the loss of several full-time farmhands would be tolerable to Swarthmore either just yet. Mustn't rush it. Our being up here *now* is justified by the Sixer crisis; but in fact—between sexual seizures and the greed for information, a sort of frustrated-scientific gold fever—I doubt if any of us has given the Sixers and their fate more than passing thought since we got properly going. I can barely tolerate the prospect of going back for Thanksgiving in nine days' time, even for a sauna and shower and my first real turkey dinner in eleven years (turkeys, of course, courtesy of the *Down Plus Six* embryo lockers. Nothing in this life is simple.)

Field Notes: Fifday, 13 November 2233 (Alice). I readily confess that *my* only thought for the Sixers had been to curse the advantage their lack of scruple gives them. *They'll* go out and collect a folyokh breeder and dissect it whenever they damn well please. But if Katy's wrong, and I *am* on the right track here, we ought to be thinking about them all the time, because if they start collecting immatures or breeders of any species indiscriminately they could have one hell of an impact on population numbers, and the ecological balance, in no time flat. Balance depends entirely on the proposition that no creature is eaten by another until it has reproduced itself. The low birth rate is only feasible given this arrangement. Up to a point the deaths might be compensated for, but not if *many* breeders and children were to be killed.

Whether to give the Sixers this information will be for Swarthmore to decide. If we don't, they could do a lot of damage without realizing it. If we do, they could accuse us, quite rightly, of jumping to a lot of conclusions on the hrossa's say-so; or they could joyously set to work and wreck the planet's ecology on purpose, using the weapon *we* had delivered unto their hand. I renew my proposal that we cease to gather new data a few days before Thanksgiving at least, so as to ponder the implications of what's been learned thus far before we go home to report to the meeting.

I spent the several days between finishing work on the folyokh, and waiting for the arrival in the village of another folyokh or some other meat animal, inquiring into the matter of *seeds*. I asked KliUrrh who the best gardener in the village was, and he said old HrukhKeeb is as good as they come. Accordingly I approached HrukhKeeb via Danny, and he willingly agreed to discuss the growing of crops with me.

I began by suggesting that the vegetable stores in the spring-house caves are not seeds. No indeed, he said, emitting amazement and amusement at the very idea. I then asked if I could *see* the seeds for next year's crops. I knew already that I wouldn't be allowed to have any to cup up; as a matter of fact I felt I knew—once I'd begun on this line of inquiry—what I was going to be told.

The seeds of the three garden plants are large, with tough rinds—golf ball size, I'd say, though egg-shaped rather than spherical. They don't look a thing like the edible fruits or tubers, but resemble one another markedly.

According to the informant, each plant produces many edible fruits or tubers but only one seed. The seed tastes terrible and is never eaten, not by pests and not by hrossa. It is always viable, or as near to always as makes no difference. It begins to form on the plant as soon as the first leaves appear in spring. These earliest leaves are also bad-tasting; in fact the plant is not bothered by pests at all until its seed has completely formed, early in the season. HrukhKeeb was unfamiliar with the concept of flowers, so "pollination" (or the equivalent) will be by wind or the problem will have developed entirely different solutions here. And guess what: very rarely, a plant will make two seeds instead of one, or even three.

After the seed is made the plant produces many more leaves, which the hrossa protect from "too much" pest damage, and fruits. Seeds are fairly safe from insects anyway in their hard husks. Insects are kept off the leaves, and larger creatures off the fruits, by hross "scarecrows"—live ones—who sit in the fields in shifts round the clock, projecting empathic discouragement!

After the fruits and tubers (which seem to be underground fruits and not tubers in our sense, despite their roothairy appearance) are gathered and the seeds secured, the plants are left to manage themselves, and anything that cares to eat them does. When the uneaten ones die (at first hard frost if not before), they "feed the ground." All three garden plants are obviously annuals. The seeds, though set in spring, are left on the plants all summer. When I asked him why, KhukhKeeb replied that both the parent plants and the seed children are happier that way.

Now, all this exemplifies why I prefer not to work with informants. Little if any of it can be taken at face value. How, pray, is the plant's self-interest served by making fruits *after* the seed has set? There's just no substitute for firsthand observation, and in this case firsthand observation is exactly what can't be made for another four to six months, if then. There's nothing TO observe in the field, except flokh trees with their limbs retracted, and nothing we're permitted to observe anyplace else. Sorry to keep obsessing about this, but it's like starving to death on a mountain of walnuts, with a hammer I'm forbidden to use clutched in my hand.

I asked whether too much pest damage ever kills a plant. The informant said, Oh no, that when the stress to the plant reaches a critical level (I'm paraphrasing freely) the leaves turn badtasting again. But the hrossa don't usually wait for this self-protective device to kick in, because the more leaves there are the more, or larger, fruits there will be; so they broadcast at insect frequency too over a wide band that also affects the Pennterran equivalents of rabbits and woodchucks.

Field Notes: Sixday, 14 November 2233 (Katy). In a burst of inspiration I decided to ask KliUrrh for a story last night. I can't imagine now why we never thought to before. We'd been invited to his lodge after supper and as ours was hung full of wet wool socks etc., and smelly-steamy, we were just as glad to get out. Danny and George and I went over, and all six of us snuggled up together on two of the sleeping platforms—it's turned very clear and frosty—and I suddenly thought: what kind of anthropologists would let so much time go by without collecting a creation myth or two at the very least? KliUrrh seemed agreeable, so I went back for the DisCorder, which we've hardly used since we got here, so it's still full of juice *and* still working (unlike the indoor-type battery-powered equipment), and he recounted the following in his own language, here transcribed by me with lots of help from Danny and stylistic assistance from George, a team effort:

How the World Got Started

In the beginning was the sky, full of dust and sand, like when you stir the shallows with a stick. No sun. No moon. The world had not been made yet either. For a long time there was nothing anywhere but the sky, with little pieces of drifting grit in it.

Then someone came and changed all that. We call this person The One That Loves Life, but he is not here anymore and no one really knows anything about him. The One That Loves Life swept up the dirt and grit, and wet it so it would stick together, and then he shaped it into mudballs. He made 48 mudballs of all different sizes. We don't know why he didn't make them all the same size. He gave them all names, but most of the names are secret.

The biggest ball he set in the center of the sky, saying, "Life needs light." And the big mudball dried out and started to burn. Then The One That Loves Life set the other balls to spinning about the burning ball, as we might spin apples on the lake, and watched to see what they would do. In a while, each ball was going around the burning one in the place it liked best/felt best in, some nearer, some farther away. But the two that found the best places, because their natures were most life-loving, they were Kreeb and Tanka Wakan. "Only two?" said The One That Loves Life. He had hoped for more; but so it was.

Now all the balls had become alive after The One That Loves Life had handled and named them, but they were entranced; only the sun had become wholly awake—that burning ball is the sun, you see. But now The One That Loves Life woke Kreeb and dealt with him. Then he woke Tanka Wakan. The One That Loves Life told him what was going to happen: that he would give Tanka Wakan power to make living things out of his flesh of living mud. He told him how to do it and how to instruct the creatures that came of him. He made him understand everything. Then he copulated with him.

That was how it all started. Tanka Wakan began to breathe. His blood began to circulate. Out of his flesh the waters were born, and from these the plants, and from these the animals. But The One That Loves Life never saw any of this; he told Tanka Wakan how to do it, and then he went away. He trusted Tanka Wakan to start things up and keep things running well. Usually they do, not always.

That was how the world got started. [End.]

As a PICTURE of the formation of this system this is astoundingly accurate, right down to the number of planets and satellites—far nearer the mark, in fact, than any creation myth we ever heard of on Earth, though virtually any of them makes a story of more intrinsic interest *as* a story, at least to humans. Indeed, as myth this is desperately dull stuff.

Now, what accounts for that?

Alice and I discussed it while baking this morning. As I understand it, in human cultures the chief purpose of myth is to explain the mysterious, provide people with some sense of con-

trol over the phenomena that make them feel anxious and fearful. Where did we come from? What happens to us when we die?
What if I sleep with my mother? and so on. Stories that don't
engage these deep universal fears, that attempt to explain lesser
mysteries (How did the leopard get his spots?), are designated
folktales and are for entertainment, not reassurance or cathar-
sis.

By that definition the story KliUrrh told is a folktale. The only
feelings I picked up throughout the telling were mild wonder
and . . . confidence, I think. Yet "Where did we come from?" is
invariably a mythic theme among human cultures. And a human psyche would surely not tolerate loose ends like "We don't
know why he didn't make all the mudballs the same size" or "No
one knows anything about The One That Loves Life." A human myth would *explain* such matters; explaining would be the
whole point!

We realized long ago that the hrossa have almost no monkey
curiosity, and in our investigations up here we run into this clash
of natures continually. But it hadn't occurred to me till today to
wonder whether they *have* any terrors, guilts, night sweats, etc.,
equivalent to those we experience. Not about where they come
from they don't, on our skimpy evidence. They die voluntarily,
hardly the practice of a people who fear what will confront them
beyond the grave. What *do* they fear, then? What *does* cause
them anxiety? Do they experience guilt? Remorse? We realized
we have no idea.

When George came in to lunch (Bob and Danny are out with
the hunting party), we put all this to him. The ensuing discussion generated a short list of common sources of troublesome
emotions among us, all of which the hrossa seem immune to:

1. Origin (of cosmos, of self)
2. Death
3. Sex
4. Sin/Wrongdoing
5. Violence
6. Anger
7. Pain (physical, emotional)
8. Humiliation
9. Bogeymen, monsters
10. Purpose of life
11. Etc.

Is it just that they lack imagination? George was the only one of us who could remember ever detecting something like anxiety in a hross—anxiety about the hross's own life, uncomplicated by us: KliUrrh, when he was answering George's questions about exceptions to the one-child rule. We all remember their collective fear when they sent to the meeting Byron came to, and George says KliUrrh was also anxious when they were discussing how we humans could have killed our own world. But those are matters introduced into hross society by the alien invaders, not native to hross psychology.

If we just asked point-blank what they fear, would they be able to say? I doubt if an untutored human could whip off our list, above, just like that. Instead, we've decided to try some of our own myths on the hrossa with the best English. We told them lots of stories early on, during the language lessons, and they loved that (and no wonder, either, if this one's a fair example of *their* efforts along those lines!), but we were much less skilled at "listening" to their responses in those days. Now it seems to offer us a way of finding out whether, or to what extent, they resonate to any of the same anxieties we do—or whether (as G. suggests) they simply climb aboard the vehicle of narration and climb off when the ride's over, indifferent to where they've been.

LATER. THIS AFTERNOON we invited a group of adults and elders (no breeders—too rambunctious and distracting) to a story hour on the beach. They were quite pleased to accept, and with all of us huddled together it was tolerably warm. (I'll just note in passing that when three humans and eleven empathic hrossa in a tightly packed group all achieve orgasm at the same instant it's a memorable experience—but also that these experiences appear to be somewhat on the wane. None yesterday, just that one today. The breeders may be winding down at last.)

George told them the story of Adam and Eve in the Garden of Eden: how all the animals ate grass and fruit and didn't have to kill anything, how Adam and Eve were naked but didn't know it, but everything was peace and natural harmony. He told them about God's one instruction and the penalty for not following it. Enter Satan; enter temptation, disobedience, shame, expulsion from the garden. Enter sex and the next generation. The animals commenced to kill one another. Adam went to work for a living.

Those were the points he emphasized. Alice and I listened as hard as we could to whatever feelings the hrossa were giving off in response.

It wasn't too productive. They did enjoy themselves, but when George got to the part about the serpent, nothing happened; they didn't appear to recognize that as the crucial turning point in the tale. From their point of view it must have seemed like an amazing lot of fuss about nothing.

George has a theory that they take their cue from us, and that we three no longer feel the force of the myth, the elements that make it work *as* myth: shame, guilt, yearning for perfect innocence. Hardly any of the details apply to hross life. The point about yielding to temptation though—wouldn't that be expected to hit home? What happens when this little community finds itself under stress—when there isn't enough food to go round, for instance?

Answer: nothing. They bear one another's burdens because they feel one another's feelings. For a minute there I was forgetting.

The point about falling out of harmony with nature also failed to get a rise. Harmony with nature must feel like the force of gravity to them—something they've never consciously noticed, let alone feared losing. We'll have to pick a likelier story and try again.

Bob asks me to add that two swamp turkeys were procured on yesterday's excursion and that in every significant way this hunt was like the first. The hrossa, followed by Bob and Danny, walked along the lakeshore, working their way through the thick stands of flokh trunks and willows at the water's edge, and after a while a gobbler approached them and communed and copulated with the leader, who then clubbed it. Ditto the second turkey. Both sets of internal organs are just inside the lodge door here, so they'll keep cold and safe from little scavengers but won't freeze before Alice has a go at them tomorrow.

Field Notes: Sevenday, 15 November 2233 (Katy). We've agreed to reserve the 18th and 19th, as Alice suggests, for a meeting for concerns. The purpose will be reflection, assessment, assimilation of, and clarification about, what we've learned here. We leave for the planned four-day Thanksgiving break, in two shifts, on the morning of Fifday the 21st. None of us really wants to go, but our stores are almost exhausted and besides that everyone in the settlement will be dying to hear what we've found out.

If we save the 20th for winding things up here, that gives us two more full working days after today.

This morning Alice went off with her bundle of swamp turkey innards, accompanied by Danny with two lanterns and a tool kit, to the new lab Bob finished weaving for her a couple of days ago. The rest of us sat around trying to draw up a list of classical tales that still have power to move us and at the same time seem likely to have some relevance for the hrossa. We thought of Old Testament stories, Greek plays, Shakespeare's tragedies, fairy tales, legends of monsters (Grendel, Dracula)...too bad Friends have always been so overwhelmingly Anglo-Saxon, apart from our smattering of Jewish converts.

It still makes a largish pool to fish in. We realized quickly enough that a huge number of these narratives attempt to cope with tensions of all sorts between parents and children, often with tension between siblings thrown in for good measure. Plenty of wicked stepmothers (plus stepsisters, plus Hamlet's uncle) for purposes of displacement. Another set of tales defends against the Terrifying Unknown. Another deals with crimes and punishments or sin and retribution. We're blank about what the hross concept of sin might be, if they have one, and yesterday's session of Adam and Eve didn't enlighten us. Siblings they *don't* have—what murderous fury in some of *those* tales (Cain/Abel, Esau/Jacob, Joseph/brothers)! But they do have offspring, and KliUrrh told George that disharmony between parents and children is a deep sorrow to the hrossa just as it is to us.

So here's the preliminary list we drew up, of stories whose theme is parent-child discord/grief/injury:

1. Oedipus the King
2. Abraham and Isaac (God and Jesus)
3. Noah and His Sons
4. David and Absalom
5. The Prodigal Son
6. King Lear
7. Hansel and Gretel
8. William Penn and His Father

Judged as narratives, with a beginning, middle, and end, 3 and 4 don't work too well. *Oedipus* is about parricide and incest, both irrelevant here. All in all, we think 2,5,6, and 7 the most promising, with 8 as a modest legendary alternative of special meaning to Friends.

George is the only one of us who has both *had* and *been* a parent, and the only one who can feel all the feelings built into those tales from personal experience of both roles, father and son. He'll do the most effective job as teller, we think, so the rest of us have stuck him with the title and the task. Not for nothing is he known as the biggest mouth in Swarthmore.

Field Notes: Sevenday, 15 November 2233 (Alice). Examination of the reproductive organs of the two swamp turkeys shows them to be in every way homologous to those of the folyokh. Specifically, the glandular structures behind the penicles are connected by very thin ducts to the vaginas and thence to the egg chamber; and the penicles themselves appear to be solid tissue without a "urethra" or passageway leading to the outside.

The digestive system, as in the hross and folyokh, is primitive and unspecialized.

The swamp turkey is not, of course, a bird, or even birdlike. It's narrow membranous "wings"—the modified second pair of limbs—can never have been an adaptation for flight. Perhaps the animal, which is semiaquatic, rows itself with them; unlike the amphibious hrossa's, its feet are not webbed. Our whimsical name for it stems from the combination of the winglike structures, the roundness of its body, and a long "neck," a snorkel arrangement with sensory organs (eyes, nares) at the tip. The heart/brain is in the dorsal anterior thorax, as with the other two species investigated. And like those species it is naked—that is, lacking in any skin covering such as fur or feathers or scales, but with a layer of fatty insulation under the tegument.

Item: recent dissection of some swillets has proved more productive, now that I have some idea of what to look for. They are like the higher forms generally, though they have neither legs nor external genitalia. They do possess the testicular-vaginal (TV) duct.

Item: a conversation with HrukhKeeb produced the information that a great quantity of wild vegetable food is gathered and eaten by the hrossa all through the summer gardening season, and that the garden produce is saved and stored almost entirely for winter use (all three crop plants are good keepers). Also, that meat makes up a much larger proportion of the diet in winter than it does during the rest of the year, since that's the season most large animals choose to make their sacrifice. *Very sensible:* their young are reared, their vegetable food supply is sharply diminished; this practice increases the amount of food available and at the same time reduces the number of mouths that must be fed. Meat will of course keep fresh longer in the cooler weather. I'm inclined to believe this because it feels true.

Field Notes: Eightday, 16 November 2233, Evening (Katy). Geronimo!

Field Notes: Firstday, 17 November 2233 (George). While everybody else prepares for the next two days of meetings I'm charged to complete this account.

On Sevenday afternoon I went for a long walk by myself and ran over the four chosen stories in my mind until I'd settled on versions of each that I thought would "play well" to the intended audience. (*Lear* was the hardest—all those daughters and sons-in-law!) I also tried to *feel* my way through all of them, so the relevant emotions would flow easily into the rhythms of narrative. I was looking forward to the storytelling, which seemed an excellent means of pleasing the hrossa and doing our research some good at the same time, and wanted to make sure that the plot line of each tale was colorful, simple, and clear.

That evening I led off with Abraham and Isaac, one sentence after another, with Danny translating, for the whole village assembled in the open. At this particular juncture in my own life it isn't at all hard for me to empathize with Abraham's dilemma, especially as Danny was right here doing the translating (and having feelings of his own about the story). On the whole, I think the experimental *procedure* was about as successful as it could be. The breeders were no problem.

How did the audience react? Well, with uneasiness. Certainly they remained less blandly detached from Abraham's trials than from Adam's. As a matter of fact we gradually realized that they found the story *obscene*, to the extent they were able to take it seriously. The hrossa have to suppose that the protagonist we call God is like, if not identical to, The One That Loves Life—Danny was more or less forced to say as much, since the alternative would be to call him Tanka Wakan, a name that refers too specifically to Pennterra, the planet itself. That The One That Loves Life could ever, under any conceivable circumstances, test a parent by pretending to require of him that he kill his own child—the idea simply embarrassed them. They felt terribly sorry for us, for the barbarousness of human nature: sort of "They're better off in quarantine, poor things, it's for their own good." Even KliUrrh, who's more used to us barbarians than most, was perturbed by the story, though he understood that it represented not Quakers but the tradition of the larger culture that produced us and that we've separated ourselves from.

The hrossa had heard equally offensive tales from us before, I'm sure, but probably never before told in such a way that they couldn't miss the message—a backhanded compliment to my skill as raconteur/emoter, I guess. We were all shaken by the reaction, and Bob and Alice were inclined to drop the experiment right there. But Katy suggested we tell another "to take the bad taste away" in effect. So we did "Hansel and Gretel" in a speeded-up watered-down version, emphasizing the food shortages that forced the woodcutter to abandon his children in the forest and their mutual joy at being reunited.

By now most of them have heard from KwikhKai that animals in our world have many offspring, and that young ones as well as old are killed and eaten, which is probably why they accepted the child-abandonment business as horrific but plausible. (One adult said, "*Two* children in a hungry time?" and before I could reply another said, "Any time, and often more than two.") I soft-pedaled my own feelings of parental grief and in general tried to tell the story less effectively. At the end I explained that actually all human parents, not just Quakers, commonly would starve themselves rather than let their children go hungry, that the story expresses not our customary practice but the secret fears of children that they will be abandoned. (I didn't broach the topic of stepmothers, *that* can of worms!)

Then when I'd finished, Bob impulsively asked: "What happens among the People when there's not enough food?" But of course the minute he said it we all knew what the answer would be: first the elders offer themselves, then if necessary any adult whose child may have attained breeding age. And in such cases they don't feed the ground. They feed the children. Another taboo made nothing of by hross practice. (In fact Danny told me afterward that one of the breeders, genuinely puzzled, had asked him why the woodcutter didn't eat Hansel and Gretel himself, instead of leaving them where the witch would eat them, since he hadn't *wanted* to feed the witch!)

By this point we had learned that the Old Testament God horrifies the hrossa but cannibalism doesn't, and that hross children don't need to hear stories like "Hansel and Gretel." I had also discovered how much I dislike the role of storyteller when the stories only confirm the audience's belief in the subpersonal nature of the teller and his kind.

But in for a penny, in for a pound. I agreed to one more day of it if the hrossa were willing, and they were. (Apart from hunting and village upkeep there's not a whole lot for them to do in winter—good reason for the timing of the rut. I don't mean they're bored, just amenable to suggestions.)

So we all packed onto the beach again—I brought my chair down this time—and we told them "The Prodigal Son."

Now, it so happens that I am myself the older of two sons, and that I've always felt that, for an older son himself, Jesus was irritatingly softhearted (and -headed) about irresponsible younger children. See also his responses to Mary and Martha—you just *know* which of those two was the elder and which the younger. I'm also annoyed by those fairy tales in which the handsome and charming third son succeeds after the first and second sons have made prize chumps of themselves. The translator, being an "only," doesn't vibrate to the pangs of sibling rivalry himself, but the sense of personal grievance I put into the telling required no translation.

And this time we got the results we wanted. Right from the start my audience listened intently. They were really interested in the actions of the Prodigal and in his chastened return and warm welcome—as we'd hoped—but to our surprise they found the older son's anger and resentment, toward both his father and his brother, even more riveting. Partly this was the way I threw myself into the telling, but it wasn't only that. There was the sort of perfectly motionless silence among them that means you've got everybody's undivided attention. And a virtual *groundswell* of emotional response, matching pitch with my emotions—a very heady experience to address an audience whose feelings you can not only infer but feel intensely! So I finished strong, still indignant for the dutiful son, though able to sympathize with the father's joy and relief as well; and then, after a minute or so of shifting and stirring among the listeners, KliUrrh got up and replied to our story with one of his own, in Hross.

We'd been taping ourselves so we got the whole thing. Danny and Katy are doing a transcription now; I'm going to take a break and a walk with Alice and finish writing this up after supper.

By the way, Danny speaks the hross language now with what seems like stunning fluency to me. He was already pretty good when we came, and our weeks up here have improved him amazingly. Katy and I are getting so we understand more than we used to, but uttering those stops and plosives in sequence is permanently out of the question for us. Danny has certainly justified his weeks of being let out of school.

Transcription of KliUrrh's Story

Long ago, when the world was younger, there were not enough living things in it. There were enough of some kinds, but not of others. So Tanka Wakan caused the plants and animals he wanted more of to make more than one child.

He did this to the hrossa. When the world was younger, we were not so many as we are now. Tanka Wakan fixed it so that every hross remained a breeder until he had given birth to two or three children, instead of just one. The One That Loves Life had told him how to do this. The adults helped the breeders care for all these children. They were traveling in those days, not living in houses and villages as we do. They had to fill up the world.

It was a hard life in some ways but Tanka Wakan gave them many kinds of wild food [listed], and the hrossa liked to move around, sometimes walking and sometimes swimming, and see the different places. And they liked it that there were so many children to cherish and so many breeders to make the autumn delightful. They were happy.

One certain hross, his name is not remembered any longer, had two children. In the time I am speaking of this hross was an early elder and his two children had both become breeders. The older had a child of his own. Now, as the hrossa moved about, one or another of the elders would see a lake or a river and say: "This place feels/looks/seems [good] for me." Then they and their children and children's children would stop traveling, weave houses for themselves beside the water and learn how to live well in that place. And always the lines-of-descent would keep together.

One day in autumn this elder was traveling with his friends and descendants through a fair country when he came to the lake that was [good] for him. "Here we stay," he said to his children and grandchild. "This one is ours." Two other friends felt the same;

the rest of the group prepared to move on without them, to seek/happen upon their own proper places, out there in the world.

The elder's first offspring looked upon the lake and thought it very beautiful. He thought how his child would swim and play there, and how he and his sibling would build holding pens and put the swillets in, and how he would walk into the water in the spring so that the baby in his [chest] could be born.

But the second offspring looked without liking/recognition at the lake. "This place is not [good] for me," he said. "So I will go on with these others."

The elder was astonished/horrified. Everyone understood that the second child felt no rightness for himself in the lake; but neither was there a feeling of rightness in him about remaining with his parent, and that seemed incomprehensible to them all. But so it was.

His parent said in dread: "If you go on, I may never see you or copulate with you again. Your [brother] may never see you or copulate with you again. We will never know your children or what becomes of you. I will not be able to feed you when I die." For in the years of the marches, the elders always offered themselves to their own offspring when their time to die was come.

The one who wanted to go on said: "But how can I live in the wrong place? If I stay here, I will spoil it for you and for my [brother]."

His parent said: "[Empathically] you will spoil it for us if you go." But in spite of this the younger offspring went on when the others did.

The older child set about building a house for himself and his family. He wove swiftly and well, and the lodge was soon complete. He made the swillet pens and stocked them. He planned where the garden would be. Other houses went up, and the village took shape. His child thrived in the new place. When spring came his baby was born, an excellent swimmer.

Yet none of this gave his parent joy, and a day came when a snow cloud covered the heart of the elder's first offspring entirely, and he came to his parent and said: "Am I not your child as well? You could be taking pleasure in me, and in this place, and in the children; yet always and always you must be thinking of him."

His parent roused himself and answered in pain: "I see now that it is best for the People each to have one child only. I know I am wrong with you, but I cannot change myself at all. Perhaps one day your firstborn that is now but a youngster will be a dutiful [son], and the infant there on your back will break your heart; and if that happens you will not ask me why I think of him, and not of you.''

Then the first offspring felt how there was no help for his parent or himself. He felt how they both were caught in a web of grievous wrongness and disharmony, and his [brother] also. He went sorrowing into the lake and swam out a long way. And deep in the water of the lake he opened himself to Tanka Wakan and said: "Wrongness runs through all our life, and if we cannot mend it, then how can we live any longer?''

—AND THAT, to *our* amazement, was the end of the story! When we realized KliUrrh wasn't going to say anything more, Bob got up again and asked him what happened after that. Did the second child come back? And of course I knew what KliUrrh would say: *We don't know.* More than that, though, they don't *wonder.* The point of the myth—we can call this one a myth, surely—is not what was done about the mess, but that a mess existed. Whether the elder eventually cheered up and took an interest in his grandchildren, or whether the second, or prodigal, child had a change of heart and came back, or was driven back by famine in the far country he'd traveled to (like the original Prodigal), or the whole family despaired and committed suicide, *nothing* can ever change or mitigate the fact that these feelings once occurred and disrupted the harmoniousness of life for that time.

And now we know that any such disruption is one thing the hrossa do fear and dread. We've seen nothing like that in our years on Pennterra, but it *has* happened or this story wouldn't have the power to move the audience as it did.

We retired to have lunch and hash it all over. The next scheduled event was *Lear*, this afternoon. I slipped out briefly to see KliUrrh before we all reassembled on the beach for the final act; I'd been a bit uneasy about telling *Lear*, lest it prove too strong for the stomachs of an audience already unnaturally stirred up by this morning's adventures. (Funny how we keep using human metaphors for beings who are, for instance, never nauseated.) But KliUrrh said not to worry, and as it turned out the mad king and his evil (older, naturally) daughters were simply too *monstrous* to upset the hrossa, who listened to the story calmly and seemed to enjoy it. (We tend to forget, too, how much of the play's power is in the poetry, not the preposterously grounded plot.)

Our group thought that was that and were about to go. Danny was tired out from translating in two directions for so long. But before we could leave, old PaahOokh, the latest elder in the village, got up and said: "I am going to tell them 'Tanka Wakan's Mistake.' That is the one they want." And the whole packed crowd, even the breeders, got very still.

The DisCorder had run out halfway through the story of *Lear*, so we didn't get it on tape, which is a great pity; but we rushed back here afterward and taped a paraphrase of it from joint memory. PaahOokh told the tale in English, luckily—the hrossa could evidently follow it well enough just from the emotional pattern PaahOokh produced as he spoke, because even those who've learned no English at all were raptly attentive. They must have heard it often before.

The story goes like this:

Tanka Wakan's Mistake

A long time ago, Tanka Wakan made a mistake. There was a wrong hross who did not die in infancy. The name his parent gave him was KaaKlah. No one knows why he lived, he should have died. Time passed, and he became a breeder and conceived a child, and when the child was hatched he too proved to be a wrong one. But the child died.

KaaKlah was still a breeder then, and the next autumn he conceived again and bore another child. This one lived for a while, but this child too was wrong and he died as well. By then KaaKlah had ceased to be a breeder and knew he would never have another child. [At this point KliUrrh and SwikhKarrh were observed to push up close on either side to SwiAakh, the childless adult member of their household. Interesting; KliUrrh told me once that the hrossa do not touch one another physically because they have no need for physical comforting.]

When the second child died, KaaKlah's grief was unendurable to him. He could not resign himself. He was a very large Person and strong; his legs were like flokh trees. The youth of his life had not been pleasant, since the other People in his village were not able to be easy in his presence and were always making him know how they pitied him, but without liking. It was not their fault. He did not blame them, but his insides were full of disharmony.

On the day his parent offered himself to feed the ground, KaaKlah swam out into the deep river beside his village and, hardly knowing what he did, cried aloud to Tanka Wakan: "Shall I die now also? My parent that was covered by cloud since he bore me has ended his life already, because of me. My two babies are dead. Henceforth I am cut off from the People and from you; neither before me nor behind me am I connected anywhere. My wrongness is the reason for it. Why then was I let to live? It would have been better for me and for KliOokh my parent if you had ended me as my own hatchlings were ended; for nothing can come of wrongness but wrongness."

He listened then; but Tanka Wakan gave nothing back.

Then KaaKlah cried out again, for his heart was bursting. He cried to Tanka Wakan with all his voice and with all his feeling. He said: "Then I will die. But first I will hurt you!"

Then leaving his village, where the substance was of his parent and his two children, he began to travel through the world; and wherever he went he pulled up plants and crushed the seeds, and killed young animals who had not yet replicated. He did this without prayer or copulation, and whenever he could. The wrongness and grief in him made it possible. Finally he killed a Person, and then another, and yet another. Some he ate. Some he cut without killing. No one knew what to do about it.

At last one day he knew within himself that a new kind of harmony had been wrought by all this destruction. He said, "Now wrongness is matched to wrongness, and there is an end." Then KaaKlah died, and fed the strange ground where he found himself that day. No one knows where that place is. He was then an adult, not even old. [End.]

Addendum (George). I remember KliUrrh saying something to me last summer, to the effect that there were stories of hrossa who had been at odds with Tanka Wakan. The moral of the tale might come to this: Redemption is almost never required on Pennterra, but if ever it should be required it is unavailable at any price. Or perhaps the moral is only, or mainly: If you have a "wrong" baby, don't grieve too much when he dies; there are fates worse than death.

A painful tale. Yet perversely I find I'm glad we haven't invaded Paradise after all.

I wonder: what exactly do the hrossa mean by *wrong*?

Meeting for Concerns: Summary of Minutes (Bob).
Seconday, 18 November 2233

Alice and I have been drafted to take this task in turns. I'm clerk for today's session.

After chores this morning, those of us who hadn't had baths last night took them. We put on the last of our clean clothes. The bedding was arranged so three of us could sit comfortably on one of the sleeping platforms (George sat in his chair), and the stove was stoked and a big supply of wood brought in. When everything had been ordered, we took our places—all but Danny, who is excused from this meeting—and had a longer silence than usual for morning meeting up here. We were then as ready as we could make ourselves to work out an agenda for the discussion, keeping in mind its goal of becoming clear about what we've actually learned so far at Lake-Between-Falls and what we still need to find out. This meeting was called, both so we could summarize and organize our findings to report them back to Swarthmore, and so we can get on better with the project when we get back up here.

Working out the agenda took the rest of the morning. Ultimately we agreed on 12 topics or questions of central concern:

I. To what extent are the hrossa representative of animal life on Pennterra?

II. Sex:
   A. What is the biological purpose of the "Excessive" sexual energy of the hrossa during breeding season?
   B. What is the purpose of their symbolic copulation with food animals during the hunt?

III. Self-fertilization:
   A. Does it happen?
   B. If so, does it happen
      1. everywhere on Pennterra?
      2. every*when*? under all circumstances? (implications for speciation)
      3. among plants and animals both?

IV. The single-child rule: does it apply
   A. to all animal life on Pennterra?
   B. to all plant life?
   C. under all circumstances of time and place?

V. What is the role of empathy
   A. in hunting?

B. otherwise (big topic)?
VI. From all the above, can we generate any hypotheses
       about the biological principles or directives that apply
       to Pennterra (analogous to natural selection on Earth)?
(Queries derived from the storytelling:)
VII. "How the World Got Started"
       A. Can we account for its accuracy?
       B. What about the planet they call ??Kreeb??
VIII. "The Prodigal Hross"
       A. How is this tale relevant to IV (above)?
IX. "The Wrong Hross"
       A. What do they mean by *wrong* in this sense and
            context?
       B. What's their attitude toward the idea that Tanka
            Wakan can "make a mistake"?
       C. What meaning can we read from this myth?
X. Additional points worth discussing:
       A. What are the theological implications of The One
            That Loves Life and Tanka Wakan as described in
            all the stories?
       B. Why swim out into the lake or river in order to
            address Tanka Wakan?
       C. What do the hrossa
            1. value?
            2. fear?
XI. What do we tell them at Swarthmore about our sexual
      activities up here?
XII. What have we learned about the danger to the Sixers?

We then broke for lunch. Meeting reconvened at 1:30.

Minute for Question I. Alice pointed out that dissections of the folyokh, swamp turkeys, and swillets all reveal physiological similarities to the hross reproductive and digestive systems, and none diverged in significant ways, but that four species is still only four species. All hypotheses will therefore necessarily be preceded by *If . . . then*. We can't safely extrapolate from the hrossa, but we can of course hypothesize if we bear the if-then clause in mind. All agreed.

Minute for Question II: Sex. George cited his conversation with KliUrrh, in which KliUrrh said to him that the breeders' sexual energy *is* productive—of pleasure—and his own thought that (for instance) producing millions of frogs' eggs to make a few mature frogs is wasteful too, from the point of view of the individual frog that lays them. A hross "lays" only one egg, in the all-but-certain knowledge that that one *will* produce a mature hross. Katy asked Alice if it's proper in any sense to speak of community pleasure as the "purpose" of sex; Alice replied that sexual energy in the village here certainly has a very high community-bonding value, perhaps as a kind of spin-off of its original function. She said further that the heavy fruit production of the garden plants strikes her, intuitively, as "excessive" in the very same sense as hross breeder sexuality: several orders of magnitude beyond expectation, extremely costly to the individual plants, and without any apparent reproductive payoff, since the seed is "vouchsafed" (GQ) before the fruits are made. We discussed this for quite some time without getting anywhere much, and finally agreed to table the subject in hopes of understanding it better after we've been here longer and learned more.

The purpose, or meaning, of the symbolic copulation between hross "hunters" (only they're really gathering then too, aren't they?) and the folyokh and swamp turkeys remains mysterious. I spoke about the propitiation rituals common among Amerindian hunters going out for deer, bear, or caribou; I feel there's a similarity there, though exactly what it might be escapes me. I agreed to think further about this.

Minute for Question III: Self-fertilization. Insufficient data. Alice is positive that even if it does take place now, it has to be a relatively recent turn of evolutionary events. Otherwise there could theoretically be as many species as individuals here. George suggested that life on Pennterra may go through periods of cross-fertilization and periods of self-fertilization in response to varying external pressures. Katy mentioned that the paramecium (unicellular terrestrial organism) does something like that—divides by fission for a time, then copulates (conjugates) with another paramecium, with which it exchanges nuclear material. She added that external conditions plainly do vary here, citing the "Prodigal Hross" myth and the dread of disturbance and instability pouring off the hrossa while they were listening to it.

I said it may be many years before we can get this one answered; but Alice said the Sixers will have an answer fast enough. We all felt shocked at the idea of killing a breeder of any species. Hross fundamentals must be rubbing off on us. (No data available as yet on plant reproduction.)

Minute for Question IV: The single-child rule. Katy suggests that Pennterran organisms may produce one offspring during stable periods, but in periods of environmental crisis they may be able to reproduce themselves several times and build up depleted populations or colonize empty territory that way. This is based partly on intuition, mostly on the myth of "The Prodigal Hross." An environmental crisis would be very bad weather, earthquake, flood, volcanic activity, large-scale forest fire, collision with an asteroid; it could also be a change of climate. Anything causing a massive die-off. (Epidemics would apply if they occur on Pennterra, but we have no evidence that they do.)

Alice commented that she's been entertaining a similar hunch about the self-fertilization question, wondering if the hrossa (for example) mightn't be self-fertile during stable periods but not during unstable ones, to encourage new combinations of genes (?) and new adaptive traits. I said we appear to have landed here in a period that is stable locally. Katy remarked that she only hopes our arrival, and/or the arrival of the Sixers, doesn't turn out to be an environmental catastrophe.

George made the point that we've all put in countless hours weeding sweet corn—we know from our own experience that the one native weed that invades the cornfields acts precisely like weeds do at home, moving onto bare ground as fast as we can pull them out and competing with the corn for space and nutrients. (For the first time we all suddenly realized what we'd been doing—killing baby plants before their seeds had formed.) Surely the one-child rule can't apply in the case of those weeds? There are just too many of them.

This observation caused some excitement. After discussion, Alice offered the hypothesis that the one particular weed we fight all summer might only perceive the existence of open space and be "deaf" and "blind" to the corn plants—not realize the corn is *there* and already in rightful possession of the space. She pointed out that apart from the willows along the river, that one weed is close to being the only native plant we ever encounter in significant numbers within the settlement. After having our attention drawn to this, we all realized it was true. Alice complained that we ought to have had the sense to look more closely at those plants instead of just grubbing them up and composting them, but that's spilt milk at this stage.

Katy cautioned that the case is still unclear—the behavior of the weeds *could* tend to confirm the multiple-offspring-in-unstable-conditions hypothesis; on the other hand, it could just mean that some plants make one seed while others make many. Nothing will clarify the question but a great deal of close observation, and that will have to wait for summer at least. George said we ought to try to discover why no other native plants invade our crops. Are they more sensitive—aware the corn is there? endowed with an instinctive aversion to our alien organisms, as we've always thought? extinct within the settlement? working on some different principle?

We agreed to end our deliberations for the day at this point. The meeting concluded with silence.

> Respectfully submitted,
> Robert Wellwood
> Clerk *pro tem*

Meeting for Concerns: Summary of Minutes (Alice).
Thirday, 19 November 2233

All present but Danny. We began with silence.

Minute for Question V. After lengthy discussion we are generally agreed that we can reach no firm conclusions about the role of empathy in hross society. We do have some observations, which in themselves lead nowhere definite. They are these:

1. We (and all hrossa) are without resistance to breeder sexual feeling, which is broadcast at immensely high volume, analogous to other, sensory, signals of sexual readiness: pheromones, a buck's roar during the rut, a male tropicbird's mating display, a cricket's chirp.
2. Sending HUNGER may attract "prey" species to the hunters. The various Pennterran species appear to be empathically audible to one another, if not to us.
3. An empathic exchange of some sort between hunter and hunted (Bob: "gatherer" and "gathered") takes place before the administering of the *coup de grace*. The elder

PaahOokh may have been referring to this as *prayer* (see p.208). There's no telling what the hrossa have picked up from us about prayer over the years. We feel sure this is important but do not know how to interpret it.

4. We have no information about the physical seat, or organ, of the empathic sending, or the means—whether electrical, chemical, or otherwise—whereby they are sent. Nor do we know how *we* receive them.

The sense of this meeting is that we must add greatly to our store of knowledge before attempting even to form a hypothesis about the phenomenon. Bob noted that he has a theory about the role of empathy on Pennterra, but would reserve it for discussion of the next question.

Minute for Question VI: Are we now able to address the subject first raised last summer by Tony Comfort: What are the biological principles, or directives, by which the Pennterran ecosystem operates?

Katy said again that she is now positive natural selection is not the mechanism of evolution here. However, creatures living on a world that changes must themselves be capable of change. Unless The One That Loves Life performed an elaborate Special Creation on Pennterra, the native life forms have been diverging from one another for a *very* long time now, perhaps several times as long as life on Earth has been at it.

I agreed with this and asserted that our hypotheses regarding Questions II and IV are relevant here. A long, unhurried evolutionary history, punctuated by periods of microenvironmental stability (no change) and shorter periods of instability (relatively rapid change), seems most probable for this planet as for our own.

At this point Bob announced that he was now ready to unveil his theory. He had prepared a statement to be read into the minutes, and here it is:

Altruistic Perpetuation: Principles

1. Every organism on Pennterra, small and large, plant and animal, is sensitive to the ecological *balance* of the whole (micro) environment (?) where it finds itself, like a hive

of honeybees is to the health of the hive, or a nest of termites or ants to their own nest.

2. Chemical pheromones emitted by the queen bee pass information along to the workers, so they can maintain or adjust the balance and harmony of the hive. Here, every organism is a worker, and the role of the queen's pheromones is played by empathy. (The $64 question is, who is the queen?)

3. During stable periods the chief directive works to maintain the status quo. Each organism (a) grows up safe from being eaten; (b) reproduces itself, probably by self-fertilization; and when the replica can survive independently, (c) feeds itself to other organisms.

4. During unstable periods the chief directive works to restore the environment to stability. Each organism:
   a. picks up and transmits the sense of imbalance and disharmony, which is communicated empathically.
   b. is caused by its awareness of imbalance, which affects its hormonal output, to produce either more children or none, whichever tends to correct the imbalance and restore harmony. (Reproduction could be by cross-fertilization during such periods.)
   c. moves to colonize space perceived as empty (out of balance), like the corn weeds (maybe) or the hrossa in "The Prodigal Hross."

5. When stability is restored, reproduction switches back to self-fertilization, with one child, in that area; and migration stops.

Whether or not this scheme proves to describe Pennterran biology accurately, Katy, George, and I were dazzled by the neatness with which it ties loose ends up into a coherent pattern, and by the boldness of the creative leap it took to formulate it. The ensuing discussion was animated and intense. Bob admitted that while he had been working on these ideas since the day of the first hunt, they actually fell into place only last evening when he stayed home to do some laundry while the rest of us were out visiting. A number of implications and oddments remained to be worked out. George brought up the question of the role of *mutation* under this scheme. In the absence of natural selection, during stable periods all viable mutations should survive equally; then in times of crisis there would be a spectrum of varieties, some of which might withstand crisis conditions better than others. This would amount to a limited form of natural selection, but it would lack the element of active inter- and intra-specific *competition*.

Katy introduced the question of what would happen if a natural disaster killed all the breeders and children of a given population of some species. Bob said he could see only two alternatives: either the young adults would turn out to be capable of regressing into fertility, or that population would become extinct and its territory colonized by others of the same species, who would sense the vacancy and move in, producing more progeny in order to right the balance. I volunteered that the "regression" angle might be consistent, at that, with the general hormonal adjustment postulated by Bob's theory.

I also realized, and expressed the opinion, that the theory is in fact sufficiently consistent with the small amount of hard information we do have. According to Bob's idea, a Pennterran organism uses, and is in no way hindered from using, its own physical substance for its own ends until it has reproduced itself and the offspring has become self sufficient. Then it offers that substance to feed others. The four animals we know something about *and* the three hross garden plants all do this, according to what we've been told and as confirmed by Bob's and Danny's eyewitness accounts of the two hunts. I asked once before in these pages how the plant's interests are served by generating all those fruits *after* the seed is set; but if self-interest isn't the operative mechanism, that was the wrong question.

Much as on Earth, there is a cycle: the hross elder feeds the ground; the ground feeds the ground nut; the ground nut feeds the elder's child and grandchild. But on Earth the organism instinctively struggles and competes for its share of things. Here, if Bob's right, the share is instinctively given without a struggle. The byword would be not *competition* but *cooperation*.

George suggested that this would incidentally explain the outward passivity, placidity, and lack of sharpness or inquisitiveness we have always observed in the hrossa.

We discussed the Question throughout a late, hasty lunch, leaving it only when forced to in order to cover the remaining items on today's agenda. We could think of nothing that certainly invalidated Bob's theory, and a multitude of random data that tended to support it. It may be wrong, but it has the elegance that is a hallmark of all true and proven theories, and that an amateur came up with it is an astonishing thing.

Minute for Questions VII-X, derived from the storytelling. Discussion was preceded by silence, which restored calm. Each story was then referred to in turn. With regard to VII, the creation tale, Katy mentioned the possibility that life may exist on another planet of this system, the one called Kreeb in the tale. She wondered whether the amazing accuracy of the tale apart from this might be accounted for in some way by hross empathy. She acknowledged that this seemed farfetched, but thought it might be true all the same, and worth investigating.

Regarding Question IX, "The Wrong Hross," George suggested that KliUrrh ought to be asked directly what he and PaahOokh meant by (1) a "wrong" child and (2) a "mistake" (when made by Tanka Wakan), as this would save time and might illuminate these matters helpfully. The meeting agreed that he should undertake to put the questions to KliUrrh tomorrow if possible.

Regarding Question X, Bob reiterated that in his opinion the hrossa chiefly *fear* disharmony, or more precisely the social consequences of disharmony, and accordingly *value* ecological balance: harmony between themselves and the world. They show no fear of many things that frighten us, including death. Bob admitted frankly that his theory fails to account satisfactorily for this calmness in the face of personal annihilation; possibly the hrossa lack the necessary imagination? George volunteered that KliUrrh had expressed fear of what the Sixers' use of heavy machinery would bring about, but agreed that this could be seen in the larger context of ecological disruption. For that matter, so can discord between parent and child, "the worst trouble we know."

Everyone felt that the larger religious issues raised in Question X should become a major focus of attention when we come back after Thanksgiving. Several of us expressed surprise and chagrin at our general failure even to wonder about hross religion in our all-out pursuit of scientific information. We are, after all, a religious group ourselves, even more than we're an extraordinarily frustrated scientific one. And religious experience is strongly indicated in all these stories. We're unprepared at this point in our work even to speculate much upon the subject, but as soon as we get back we must address ourselves fully

to the query Bob raises in his Principles: we must try to discover
who the queen bee is.

Minute for Question XI. A poser. After some discussion it was
agreed that keeping the issue from surfacing for the best part of
four days might be preferable but would probably not be possible. It was decided that a statement describing the situation of the
breeders and our response to them should be drafted and approved. The statement should then be read out at the meeting for
concerns on Sixday the 22nd. Katy volunteered to have a draft
ready for approval by breakfast time tomorrow. It was further
decided that all open references to Danny's participation in sexual activity should be struck from the Field Notes until after the
field study is completed at Christmas.

Minute for Question XII. Have we learned of any harm that
must necessarily befall the Sixer town? In a word, no. Bob suggested facetiously that every breeder on the Great Continent
might surround the town next autumn and drive the Sixers mad
with lust; but no serious hypotheses were advanced. Yet Kli-
Urrh is unwavering in his certainty. We will have to go on learning a while longer.

George mentioned his chagrin about having often failed to
focus on this crucial matter for days on end. I countered by
expression my view that in such an enterprise as this the indirect
approach yields more fruit in the long run than a direct, all-out
attack.

We concluded with silence, tired but very well pleased with our
two days' work, and generally clear about our various posi-
tions.

Respectfully submitted,
Alice Flower
Clerk *pro tem*

Personal Journal: Sevenday 23 November 2233 (Katy). Strange
to be back home! I do love the R&R aspects of the break, the rich
"benison of hot water" and other creature comforts. At the same
time I'm aware of losses. Already the fine edge of my concentration is dulled; I'm not quite at peak condition for the field
work anymore. I think of Lake-Between-Falls, and it seems an
almost wholly dreamlike place, a different reality, remote and
compartmentalized. I'm anxious to get back, anxious in an-

other sense that something will happen to prevent our going back—I really don't see how I'd *stand* it if that happened!!

I came home in the second lot, with Bob and Alice. We had high winds on Fifday so the lake crossing was rough and the flight bumpy, but we arrived without mishap and made a bee-line for the bathhouse, which was blissful beyond description—we've been cold for weeks without thinking much about it, and grubbier than usual without thinking much about that either, sponge-bathing sketchily every couple of days or so with a proper tub bath maybe once a week. I'd stopped by the domicile just long enough to dump off my laundry and stuff and collect a change of good clothes to put on after bathing—hadn't spoken more than a brief greeting to anybody—so it wasn't till I got to the dining hall for the big dinner, and bumped smack into George engrossed in conversation with Maggie Smithson, that I realized a party of guests from the *Down Plus Six* encampment was in Swarthmore.

Now, this is odd. I reacted instantly as if to a dangerous enemy; my impulse was to rush up and grab George, shouting, *Don't say anything!* We were all set to make a complete report (well—almost complete) to the meeting, but we hadn't even thought about how to behave toward the Sixers, what to say, what not to say—we hadn't expected to run into any! I was *furious* at Ike Logan, our gig pilot, for not telling us they'd been invited and giving us a chance to decide on a course of action.

I saw a few more of them scattered around the room in spiffy uniforms, talking with Friends. Byron Whatsis was one. Bob came in, and I grabbed him and hissed, "There's a bunch of Sixers here!" But he only said, "I know, don't worry, it's OK." He'd seen George when he went back to his room from the bathhouse, and George said Billy Purvis had told him and Alice that they were coming. Those three were all dead certain we shouldn't breathe one single word about the Lake-Between-Falls study, but Billy said the meeting had already decided the same thing anyway when they were considering whether to invite some Sixers to the dinner. Bob was laughing at my paranoia, and had put one arm around me, and all of a sudden we were looking at each other and grinning, and probably both blushing—he was anyway—because we were both thinking the same thing, even with no breeders around; I reckon it's a habit we've acquired.

Well, this struck us both as hilarious and got me nicely past my first alarm about the visitors. So then we went on in and found places, and I have to admit that after 11 turkeyless Thanksgivings and Christmases and a month at the village, that dinner alone would have been worth the trip. Danny and George ate with Maggie, Alice with Edith and some other cronies. The Sixers—half a dozen of them or so—were mixed in at different tables all around the hall. Those were the only individual faces I seemed able to see—everybody else was one big welcoming blur.

Afterward I went and said something polite to Maggie and to Byron (who was very buttoned-up and formal), and then Bob and I ducked out and walked down to the river. I just didn't feel up to being mobbed by curious friends as yet, somehow. It was still windy and clear (and *cold*, though the village was colder), with a full moon—a beautiful night. Danny tagged along after us. He said, when pumped, that Maggie seemed "really nice," but his thoughts were elsewhere. We huddled together and watched the river. In a few minutes Danny caught hold of my wrist and pulled my hand down to feel the bump in his pants: "Katy, what am I supposed to *do* about this?" He sounded so mournful I could hardly keep from laughing. I said something like "I guess you'll have to grin and bear it, sweetie, you know I can't help you out down here. The rules are different." Bob said, "I spent four or five years jerking off in bathrooms, kid. So did your dad, I guarantee it. It's the way of the world."

Danny said: "Not *this* world it isn't."

Bob: "Well then, the way of the Delaware Valley. The civilized human way, definitely."

Danny (muttering): "This is the valley of the [unpronounceable]."

Me (briskly): "Oh, come on, Danny, cheer up! Why don't you talk to Jack Wister about it? He'd probably be delighted to have some company; he's been having a solitary adolescence for a couple of years already."

Danny: "*That* geek."

Bob: "Why, what's the matter with Jack Wister?"

Danny (passionately): "He can't *stand* the hrossa, that's what's the matter with him! He used to call 'em the horses, now he calls 'em the *spiders*. Get it? Eight legs, ha ha. He's mad as hops about us not using machinery here. He's got these little tractors and dozers and stuff, see, models, that he brought with him from Earth when he was a little kid. He *loves* those damned models—keeps 'em in a special box and takes them out and fusses with them. He says he could build a tractor *himself*, out of stuff in the dump—he's been studying the computer about it a lot and he knows how. Only his dad won't let him. [Ferociously:] I'm not asking anybody that calls KliUrrh a goddamn *spider* for tips on how to do my adolescence!''

Bob said, ''Good God, I had no idea.''

Danny, his father's son, became contrite at once. ''I shouldn't have told you that about those toy trucks, he really loves them. You won't spread it around, will you?''

I said, ''Of course not. And I apologize for the ignorant suggestion.''

''Anyway,'' said Bob, ''we'll be back up at the village again in a few more days, so you don't have to start coping quite yet.''

We tussled with him and hugged him, but we *did* leave him there, looking cold and out of sorts. I felt a pang: it would have been so easy to solve his immediate problem at no cost to myself. But the web of custom had already settled over me again. And I knew his father wouldn't approve, and thought that quite possibly George was right to feel that human mores must prevail here in the settlement. But the fact remains that Bob and I went off back to the domicile together, and it was obvious from Danny's resentful expression—plain to see in the bright moonlight—that he assumed we were on our way back to bed together too. (As a matter of fact we were both far too stuffed even to consider it; but suppose we hadn't been?)

No wonder the poor kid's disgruntled. Up at the village he's an essential team member, with all the rights and privileges that go with that. Down here, he's just a kid. The rest of us keep the same status now that we're back in Swarthmore; he's the only one that loses his right to sit in council if he likes, feel valuable, and be sexually active just like the rest of us, and he's probably the one who needs it most.

I'm afraid George is going to have his hands full when we terminate the project. Our circumstances are extraordinary; he mustn't expect Danny to act as if they weren't, whatever George-the-Dad would prefer him to think, feel, or do—particularly do.

The all-settlement meeting for concerns to present our findings convened yesterday, after the Sixers went home, and I thought it went very well. George (our team's early elder) read out the Minutes and myth transcripts, but first he read the statement I wrote, about our sexual carryings-on. It did raise eyebrows. But Bob's theory caused such a sensation among the biologists later on that the little stir created by my revelations never amounted to much—though if there hadn't been a general assumption that Danny wasn't involved it might have been a different story.

Alice's nose has been put a bit out of joint. By rights, *she* should have been the one to bring back a provocative theory and gotten fussed over, not some young construction-navvy-cum-Amerindian buff with no advanced scientific training. She's struggling to be a good sport about it but I'm sure it must rankle. Right in meeting Tony Comfort practically went apoplectic from a combination of excitement and sheer howling jealousy and envy of Bob.

Not a little envy on all sides, in fact. Everybody's jealous of our getting to do science, and there are those who wouldn't object to a little recreational orgy-making either. We five (except Alice) got picked for the project because of our special relationships to the hrossa; we weren't *supposed* to come back in triumph one month later with a respectable theory about the way the whole world works. Even though they're delighted to have the theory, they hate not having been in on the work that culminated in it. Nobody's betting on the theory's being true quite yet, but they're happy enough that it's not full of obvious holes.

I feel strangely detached from my friends—Norah, Jeremy, all of them. Yet I *love* being back among Friends en masse. The one absolutely, unequivocally, unambiguously GOOD thing about having had to come back here is the lift of taking part in the whole gathered meeting for worship, 300 strong. Nothing like it, not for us. Behind everything we do, it's the basis and foundation of our life on Pennterra, the sine qua non. (I sound like George.)

But all the same, I'm with Danny—marking time till next Firstday.

Personal Journal: Eightday, 24 November 2233, after breakfast (George). I must attempt to catch this up while I have a chance; we go back up tomorrow and after lunch will be putting in some hours seeing to our provisions and clothes. Danny's gone to watch Andrew Bell train the new sheepdogs. Since we left, the puppies grew up enough that they could start being schooled—no easy task without an experienced older dog for them to imitate, but Andrew's amazingly good with them. Turns out his grandparents had a kennel, lucky for us.

I'm worried about Danny. Again. Since we got back he's been moping around in a very uncharacteristic way. I finally asked him yesterday if something was the matter, and he said, grumpily but quite frankly, "Yeah, sex is. Everybody else gets to do sex down here except me. I just want to get back *up* there." This of course is exactly what I was afraid of, and hearing it set dozens of alarms to clanging in my head, but I remembered KliUrrh's counsel and tried not to panic. "KliUrrh said it would hurt you badly to be sent home, and hurt you a little to be allowed to stay. Maybe it would have been better not to let you come up with us in the first place, if only I'd known it then."

He said, "Oh, it's not your fault, Dad, you know I'd have died if you hadn't let me come. It's just that I feel so rotten and mad, and I'd been feeling so great up at the lake. I never had such a good time in my life before."

"I never did either, but it is a kind of holiday, you know, for all of us. Coming home will probably be hardest on you, for lots of reasons, but that's just how it is, Danny, those are the terms of the contract."

"I know, I already figured it out. But I still *feel* lousy. I really hate to think about coming home at Christmas, if I feel this lousy now."

I rejected the idea of not taking him back with us before it even formed itself as a possibility in my frantic brain. Because it really isn't one; things have gone much too far to be fixed that way now, and besides, the study needs him.

But it *is* worrying. This passage in his life would have been worrying anyway; puberty is enough of a trial under the best of circumstances, let alone without viable peers of either sex around. But our experience at Lake-Between-Falls does complicate things more. I'll have to give some thought to what might compensate him for all the extra grief...maybe he'd like to work with the dogs, or the draft horses they've quickened for a spring parturition—some special assignment that would be interesting, fun, and *important*, that would give him an extra measure and sense of responsibility. Right after the holidays I'll bring it up at a meeting for concerns, even if I have to call one myself.

I'm still not *sure* I was right to go with the team myself, though the constant sense of being where I ought to be, doing what I ought to be doing, has reassured me right along. None of the upsets and quandaries that beset us up there have detracted one scrap from that basic conviction. (I remember thinking a decade or so after college how unhappy and confused I'd been at various specific moments during those four years, yet that I still looked back upon them collectively as the happiest period of my life.) (Till now, till now.)

It helps to find that I fit surprisingly comfortably back into my life in the larger community, and don't really mind the thought of winding up the project in a month's time. The conflict of loyalties seems far less acute. This is not for any reason I can put my finger on, but thank God for it anyway. I suspect it's mainly because, though nothing's been resolved, I've gotten better at negative capability.

The minute Danny and I were out of the gig on Fifday, who should we spy standing there grinning up at us but Maggie Smithson, a welcoming committee of one. I was absolutely delighted to see her (*why?* we parted on rather less than cozy terms) and clumped down in my muddy boots to give her a hug. Then I introduced Danny, who brightly remarked: "Oh! You're the one I yelled to at the bathhouse pool last summer!" ("She was diving in, so I told her not to," he explained.) Maggie seemed both embarrassed and charmed by this coincidence. I was about to ask what she was doing here, all tricked out in her fancy-dress blues, when she volunteered the information that the settlement had *invited* half a dozen Sixers for Thanksgiving dinner, as a gesture of thanksgiving (for the turkey embryos) and also for the Sixers' safe arrival on Pennterra.

I wasn't too sure what I thought about that—Maggie as Maggie is one thing, quite another as a Sixer commander. But there she was, and it was great to see her. We made a date for dinner and excused ourselves to get cleaned up and changed.

When I saw Billy later on, he told me that quite a lot of Friends had felt strongly that we should maintain at least tenuous ties with the Sixers, rather than let them go their own way entirely. They're here, they're human, we might well need one another's help someday, etc. They'd discussed in committee what form such tenuous ties should take, and this dinner invitation is the first result. Billy sees it as a kind of ecumenical move: emphasize our common concerns, not our differences. I'm not so sure. I think the question of what sort of relations to maintain with the Sixers is more important, and more complicated, than anybody here may have realized. I know I feel like that because KliUrrh is still so positive that Tanka Wakan is going to destroy the lot of them. But until we're clear about what it all means, I'm inclined to think we ought to keep separate from their operations altogether. Or draw the line at radio contact, something like that.

Which isn't to say that I didn't thoroughly enjoy the twenty or so hours I spent in Maggie's company. A month of constant sex must have strengthened neural connections that had weakened and withered, and probably it's done me good to put all inhibition aside for a time. Whatever the explanation, there's no doubt that the old spark was rekindled between us and that we made the most of the little while we had. I'd even venture a diffident hypothesis: that lots of jolly unemotional screwing, if it truly IS jolly, far from detracting from the value of "good sex," keeps you in shape physically and psychologically for the top-quality stuff when it happens along.

Danny knew perfectly well what we were up to, which is why he said, "*Everybody* gets to do sex except me." He didn't mind about us, but he did mind that there's nobody here for him.

Let's see—the meeting. It went well, and Bob is now the Infant Savant/Boy Wonder/Holy Innocent of the biologists, who think his theory has plenty going for it even if it turns out to be partly or wholly wrong. I found out from KliUrrh before we left that *wrong* (as in "the baby was wrong") means "unable to live well in the world, in body or in spirit." As for *mistake*, apparently we remembered the phrase incorrectly, or else PaahOokh expressed himself inexactly in English. It wasn't "Tanka Wakan made a mistake," but something more like "A mistake happened to, or on account of, Tanka Wakan." The implication being not that Tanka Wakan blundered, but that he was unable to prevent a blunder from occurring to the hapless hross of the story. The point isn't that TW is imperfect in compassion or understanding, but that there are limits to his power and control—for instance, he can't keep an earthquake or a flood from occurring, any more than we can keep from having hiccups. Can he make them occur? KliUrrh found the question barbaric as well as pointless, and sent a tender wavelet of pity over me. The distinction about mistakes is subtle but it seemed to matter to KliUrrh. (this ¶ will have to be transcribed into the Field Notes, using writers that I sincerely hope will be fixed in time to come back up to the lake with us.)

Maggie tells me they're moving fast in Sixertown, that so many passengers preferred the thought of an uncomfortable winter on Pennterra to a cozy one in orbit that the captain finally decided to throw up a lot of prefab domiciles like ours and move them down. Meanwhile, construction of permanent buildings proceeds apace. There are almost a thousand Sixers, including a lot of families with kids of all ages—who would all be working and playing and going to school with our kids by now, if things had gone according to plan; but we all know how little profit there is in this depressing line of thought.

Anyway the die's cast. They've been using every kind of heavy equipment for earth-moving and construction, to build the town and prepare farmland for a spring planting. One way or another we'll find out now whether the hrossa know what they're talking about, and so will they.

On that subject: after he heard the Minutes, Billy came up with a very good idea. He suggested that we ask the Sixers whether they've detected signs of life on any of the other planets in the EE system. We can't investigate ourselves; the *Woolman* hasn't any fuel to spare. But there's no good reason *they* couldn't burn some in a useful cause, and the crew are probably at loose ends with no passengers to cater to. They may go for it.

Billy said: "Suppose there is life on one other planet, and only one, in the system—suppose the hrossa are right about that, just as they're right enough about how the sun and planets were formed, and right about how many heavenly bodies there are altogether. Well, if they are, I don't know about you all, but I for one am going to start taking them *very* seriously when they say Tanka Wakan won't let the Sixers use machines or live outside this valley and get away with it. I'm going to start telling myself that I don't know how they can *possibly* know things like that, but just to be on the safe side, better put those dozers to bed again for a while yet. And I bet the Sixers'll think the same way."

What *I* bet is they won't believe a thing we tell them unless we can come up with some conclusive proof that they're committing suicide, and I don't think they'll consider finding life on Kreeb (?) as conclusive. With half my mind I feel the future of the Sixers is fixed, that the town will be built and the consequences follow no matter what we do. With the other half I'm as eager as ever to get to the bottom of the mystery and save their necks for them. Or at least save the necks of those who'll let themselves be saved, Maggie's for one.

How much calmer things were—and, oh yes indeed, how much duller—before the Sixers came! No discord amongst ourselves, nothing to think about but work and surviving. I well remember that in those days I was viewed as a calm, imperturbable character, a very steady fellow, when I'm really an awful worrywart who had, for the time being, nothing but the matter of simple survival to worry *about*. No moral conflicts, no complications. Those were the days. Whether or not the arrival of humans initiates a period of instability for Pennterra, the Sixer arrival has certainly brought chaos to Swarthmore and to me.

Also turkey dinners, draft horses, sheepdogs, and Maggie's company. A softer and more stressful life. I welcome it, I do. I don't thing I *trust* it at all, nor do I think well of myself for being seduced by its benefits.

What to do now but huddle inside KliUrrh's four arms, trying to think what's right, and putter around Lake-Between-Falls village for another month, trying my best to learn what's true?

That, and try harder than I ever tried before to be the best father I can be.

The moon's cold fire may burn and burn,
But never that girl at childhood's close
By fleetness, or craft, or courage, learn
To mount the Unicorn; this she knows.
Now all of her hope is memory.
Not for an age will his horn be let
In her lap instead, and she mourns him yet,
And mourning, believes, and can never forget
The lovely, pitiless thing on the sea.
                    —from "Unicorn," by Celia Irving (1973-2038)

1 Sanctuary

The first thing Danny saw, when he'd climbed down out of the lander behind Jack and turned around, was the hovervan parked in the snow—glossy, red, and roomy enough to hold a dozen people. While he and George were being greeted warmly by Maggie, Jack dragged his mother straight over to the van and started explaining the hovercraft principle to her. The pilot, Ike Logan, hauled the boys' duffels out of the cargo hatch, dumped them on the ground, shut down the ladder, and stood blowing on his bare hands waiting for something to happen.

Maggie said, "Suppose we load the bags and get out of the cold, OK?" The boys pitched their things into the van and scrambled inside, kicking the snow off their boots and claiming a window each. George and Jack's mother, Lynn Matthews, climbed in after them, followed by Ike, Maggie, and Sub-Commander Levy and his wife, who were going to be Jack's sponsors.

Nathan Levy settled into the driver's seat, then turned impulsively back toward Ike. "Like to drive?"

"Love to!" In an instant Ike was snuggling happily under the wheel. "My family used to have one of these—smaller and older, but same idea." He started the engine and in a moment lifted the car smoothly into motion along the straight, wide, snow-filled track. "Where to?"

"Down to the intersection, then right, then right again." The car swished along above the packed blank surface, past buildings and large stationary vehicles muffled in sloping drifts, past bundled-up people. It was a bright day, blue and dazzling white. Ike swung right, into a broader thoroughfare, where he passed several parked hovercars and a growling snowplow. "We've been using the air cushion vehicles as much as possible because of the snow cover," said Levy, "but underneath it there are about seven klicks of paved roads we've put in, in and around town."

None of the Quakers found anything to say to this. There were no roads at all in Swarthmore, since there were as yet no vehicles to use on them—only curving paths of dirt or gravel. The coming of horses meant that wagons and buggies would now be built, and that roads to drive them on were certain to follow. They would not be made so straight, however; they would skirt hillocks and hollows, taking the easiest way. These roads of Sixertown had been cut straight through the unevenness of the terrain.

Some brightly dressed youngsters went by in three shiny yellow open cars mounted on skis, laughing and yelling. Danny turned all the way around in his seat to look at them. When he turned back the van was settling to a stop in front of a barnlike structure, obviously a domicile, and Maggie was saying "OK, Quinlans, here we are."

As commander of a section Maggie rated four rooms on the second floor all to herself: a sitting/dining area, a kitchen, and two bedrooms, plus a private toilet and shower. The smaller bedroom that was to be Danny's was covered—walls, floor, and ceiling—in white fabric, and held a ship's bunk, a chair, a table, a bureau, and a computer console. The light came on when he opened the door. Danny could not believe his eyes. He sat down on the bed, overcome, trying to imagine being able to take such luxury for granted every single day.

"Come and have some tea," said Maggie kindly. "You can unpack after the shock's worn off a bit. Do you like tea?"

"I don't know, we ran out of it before I was old enough to want any. I'd like to try some, though."

A quarter of an hour later they were seated around a plain, serviceable table on three sturdy chairs in the hollow cube of blue that was Maggie's all-purpose front room. On the table rested a tray containing a brown ceramic teapot (under a cozy printed with Tenniel's drawing of the Mad Tea Party), a plate of little iced cakes, a silver sugar bowl, and a small silver pitcher of milk. Their cups and saucers were brown like the pot and tinted a delicate blue inside, and the spoons were silver.

"We've got twenty-six kids between twelve and fourteen, who at this point are all being taught together in one class," Maggie was saying as she poured out. Danny gazed at her dumbly, thinking of twenty-six peers. "You may find yourself way ahead of the class average in some subjects and way behind in others. We'll have to see how it goes—but one of the main reasons you're here is to get to know some kids your own age, right? So in another sense the formal instruction may not matter all that much.''

George said, ''Whatever he learns is all to the good, but meeting other kids is the main thing.''

Danny roused himself and looked about him, still in wonder at the splendor of Maggie's domestic arrangements. ''You've got your own kitchen here,'' he marveled. ''Your own stove and fridge and sink and everything.'' Absently he put one of the little cakes in his mouth and stared round at the fabric-clad walls and up at the rough blue ceiling.

Maggie smiled. ''Rudimentary but adequate. I don't always cook for myself, but it's nice to be able to when I like, and on special occasions, like today.'' She showed Danny how to adulterate his tea with sugar and milk and watched the first sips go down. ''Of course we've got nothing to eat yet that's as delicious as what I was fed in Swarthmore last summer. How good a cook are you?''

Danny set his cup down and wrinkled up his nose. ''Fair, but I'm used to helping cook up one huge thing, like a lamb stew or something, so I'm not sure I could do a whole dinner for only two people. I'll learn, though.''

Maggie laughed, surprised. ''Would you really not mind? I was only pulling your leg. No Sixer boy your age would be caught dead in a kitchen.''

Here was another wonder. ''Why not?''

''They don't have to, and they all think cooking's for girls.''

''For girls? You mean *only* girls? Really?'' He glanced at his father, who nodded.

''I ought to have known Quakers would manage that kind of thing better than we have.'' Maggie spoke as if the topic were tiresome. ''But we've got a lot more families here, you know, and I'm convinced that the nuclear family is the perfect breeding ground of division of labor by sex. Our women have to struggle like hell to keep from lapsing into it.''

George said grumpily, ''I'd have thought that on a ship where half the officers are women, those traditions would have died a natural death.''

''Ah, but we don't have *families*, you see! Two-thirds of the male officers—like Nathan Levy, you just met him, Jack's sponsor—do have families, and just about all the settlers do.'' She made a wry face. ''It's stupid of me to be so astonished at how fast those patterns reasserted themselves once the skeleton town was built and the families could move into their own quarters and set up housekeeping."

Danny was still grappling with the concept that boys in Sixertown could refuse to be on a kitchen squad. Now he asked, "What do the guys here *do* then, instead of cooking and stuff?"

"Oh, they'll work till they drop on some special construction or agricultural project, if somebody organizes them. And, ah, they take out the trash and so on. Not that there's a lot of trash yet. After we move to the permanent town they'll mow the grass in summer . . . and when the stock's been birthed and the crops are in we'll probably give them some regular chores."

"Hunh. What about the girls? Will they do all that kind of thing too?"

"Some will, if the boys'll let them. Nobody will expect it, though. The girls will help out more at home."

"I've *read* about this," Danny mused, "only I guess I didn't really take it in. In storybooks, lots of times the boys and girls do different things. And their mothers are always at home, and their fathers have jobs, but I never thought about that. And also, my mother died when I was just a baby, so I never did see people really acting that way."

"Your mother was a chemist," said George gently. "She wouldn't have been one of those traditional mothers."

"You must have been reading some pretty old books," Maggie said. "Family life wasn't too traditional for a lot of people in the years before we left." She drained her cup and sat back, locking her fingers behind her head. "In a few more years, when we've got enough land cleared, our families will be working their own farms with their own stock and equipment. The kids will come to school in town, but otherwise their parents will be in complete charge of what sort of work they do, and I fully expect to see it split along traditional lines."

George leaned toward Danny, forearms on either side of his crumb-strewn plate. "You know, it's not a bad idea at that, your getting a taste of what social arrangements on Earth used to be like, you and Jack." For the first time since the landing genuine interest breached his reserve, and Maggie's eyes flickered toward him. "All *that's* part of what Friends were reacting against when we decided to set up another kind of society in Swarthmore."

"Oh." At the change in his father's voice Danny brightened and sat up.

"The reason we haven't been preaching equality of the sexes at you kids directly is that up to now there've been so few of you. We've just counted on you to copy us, and you have. So far." He looked at Danny hard, a look that meant: There will be more children soon, now that the hrossa understand our biology better, but not in time to help out with *your* problem. Danny nodded alertly; he made the connection, both with George's point and with the underlying message that it wasn't to be spoken of—that nothing about the project at Lake-Between-Falls was to be spoken of in Sixtertown, not even to Maggie.

That was all right; but then of course his father could not resist adding, George-like: "The boys here feeling they'd be diminished by doing what they think of as 'women's work'—that attitude goes *with* the grain of human nature. Ours works against it, like our traditional attitudes toward war, slavery, every sort of superior-inferior approach to human—"

"Ok, Dad, OK," said Danny, grinning. "You can stop right there, I won't let 'em corrupt me, even to get out of kitchen duty. Hey, Katy doesn't like kitchen duty any more than I do, just think what she'd say if we told her she had to do it and we didn't!" He looked at George eagerly and a little tensely, trying to keep the spark of enthusiasm alive.

"She'd be plenty familiar with that point of view. Katy grew up on Earth, remember?" Then he recollected himself and added, "But apart from conventional attitudes like that, I'm sure you're going to find a lot of these kids nice and fun to know."

"They really are nice kids," Maggie volunteered. "Just give yourself a chance to know them a little before making up your mind about them."

"I bet a lot of their parents are telling them the same thing about me and Jack right now," said Danny wisely.

"Should he have different clothes?" George suddenly wondered. "Sometimes, not looking like the other kids can be a problem at the start."

"What about it? Do you want to dress like everybody else, or would you rather wear what you brought with you?"

Danny considered the question. "What does everybody else *wear*?"

"Oh—synthetics, bright colors, padded pants and jackets. It's not so much what they wear as that they'll all be dressed one way and you'll be dressed another."

"Oh, I don't mind that. Maybe I'll just wait and see if I like their clothes better than mine. Is that OK?" He looked down at

himself. "Mine're all brand-new, it would be stupid to just put
'em away." His homespun tweeds, trousers and jacket, were the
several natural grays of Herdwick fleece. In his duffels were a
couple of thick off-white pullovers made from Dorset wool, and
last year's one remaining wearable pair of pants, let out and
cleaned for him by a man called Joe Hickson, a nuclear physi-
cist, in fine defiance of the Sixer view of the sort of labor appropriate to men.

"Good enough, but if you change your mind later on, just let
me know."

"OK, I will. Thanks." As he drained his cup and set it down
a wave of tiredness broke over Danny, and he excused himself
and went into the bathroom, mostly just to be by himself for a
minute. To his surprise the toilet bowl was half-filled with water; he stared into it, perplexed, then stuck his head around the
door again. "Is there *supposed* to be water in the loo?"

"Oh!" Maggie sat up straight. "Those composters in
Swarthmore! Yes, this is a different system. You just pee right
into the water, then step on the pedal."

"OK," said Danny doubtfully. He closed the door, did as instructed, then watched the rush from a tank obviously concealed in the wall sweep the stained water away and replace it
with clear. He went back out. "Where does it go to?"

"The toilet contents? Into a septic tank behind the building,
buried underground."

"So how do you reclaim it from there?"

"We don't reclaim it. When the houses are finished and we
move out of here, we'll let it leach for a while, then fill in the
tanks and forget them."

Danny blinked. In Swarthmore all manure, animal and human, was saved, carefully composted, and spread on the fields.
Every gram of it mattered. Again he glanced involuntarily at his
father, who said, "The Sixers would use sewage for fertilizer too,
if no other sources were available."

Maggie said, "Right, but we had enough of that on shipboard. We'll use animal manures when we've got a reasonable
supply, supplemented with some stuff we're making now, mainly
out of atmospheric nitrogen—you'll hear all about that, Danny,
if you take the agricultural elective."

Danny said "But—" then remembered Maggie's sensible advice about making up his mind too fast and clamped his jaw
shut. He reminded himself that his own people would have been
preceeding the same way, pretty much, if there had been no

hrossa to stop them. They would have wasted resources and gouged straight roads through the living soil, and done in general as the Sixers were doing. Why not, with a whole planet there for the taking? The Quakers had never suggested these practices were wrong in themselves—only that to use machinery against the wishes of the hrossa would be wrong. But all the same he *knew* something had to be faulty about a system that moved in only one direction, instead of cycling back upon itself to its own beginnings.

Already, without realizing it, Danny had jumped to his first conclusion: that machinery saved you a lot of work and time and made you rich enough to waste things.

NOT VERY LONG after his first dinner in Sixertown Danny lay in his new bed, the only thing in Maggie's flat of luxuries that looked and felt familiar. Travel, excitement, and newness had first overwhelmed him, then overstimulated him, then worn him out. His few clothes had been stowed away in drawers and a cupboard, where he thought they must feel even stranger than he did, stowed away into the darkness of his bunk. He could hear his father's voice and Maggie's in the sitting room, speaking quietly: a man's voice and a woman's, sounding the way a father and mother might sound to a child just put to bed. Danny smiled to himself, remembering how George had cheered up at the thought of the object lesson in Sixer social behavior his son was about to receive. Yet funnily enough it had been Sixer social behavior (in a more attractive aspect) that had persuaded George to override both his principles and his deep misgivings and let Danny accept the invitation to live with Maggie for a term and go to school in Sixertown.

Danny thought that invitation had probably saved his life.

The second phase of the Lake-Between-Falls project had been much less productive of new information than the first. Though many more details of Pennterran biology had been found to reinforce Bob Wellwood's theory of "Altruistic Perpetuation," the team's chief interest had become hross religion—and the hrossa seemed unable to *tell* them anything much about their religion. The team had ascertained with certainty what they had always supposed, that the concept called Tanka Wakan occupied its center. Tanka Wakan: the world, a consciousness the hrossa conceived of as less powerful or knowing than a god might be, but more powerful and more knowing than the Quak-

ers were at all prepared to think a planet might be. The One That
Loves Life emerged as a prime mover figure, who had made
Tanka Wakan and instructed him, then gone away—presum-
ably to make more worlds and engender more life elsewhere—
and never come back. And that was still just about all the
Quakers had managed to learn for sure.

The problem wasn't language. The hrossa didn't seem to talk
about anything like doctrinal beliefs in their own language either;
hross religion appeared to be entirely a matter of feeling. These
feelings of theirs about the world communicated a good deal to
the team, but the "content" communicated was the wrong sort
to take them further with the study in the form and manner in
which they had been pursuing it, and now they were in a hurry.
A different approach might have been worked out, but it would
have taken more time than they had left.

To the Quakers, the feelings of the hrossa were readily recog-
nizable as religious, mingling elements of reverence, respect,
gratitude, and so forth, with less familiar ones it was harder to
put English names to. But there was nothing to analyze, nothing
they could come to grips with; all was insubstantial. They had
worked as hard as before, and delighted in being there nearly as
greatly, and had as enjoyable a sexual fling besides—though that
had been tapered off fast toward the end—but they simply didn't
get anywhere much, except to consolidate what had been done
already. It was pretty frustrating.

They learned nothing new about empathy. They had no idea
who the queen was, or if there was a queen, or if the beehive
metaphor, which had seemed such an inspired leap of intuition
at first, had any relevance to Pennterra at all. It was almost as if
the Thanksgiving hiatus had broken both their momentum and
the concentration that precedes insight.

KliUrrh was as kindly as ever when with George. But along
toward Christmas George had announced to the others one evening, "I get the feeling KliUrrh thinks we've done enough, and
it's time we got on about our human business and left the hrossa
to get on with theirs." So they'd packed up when the time came
and returned to the settlement for good, with no plans to come
back till milder weather.

When SwikhKarrh said goodbye to Danny he also said:
"Come up when it's summer and stay awhile then. I don't know
why, but it's important. Most of us are leaving soon anyway to
look for meat higher in the mountains. You should come back
in the summer." And Danny promised to come if he possibly

could, though summer was high farming season in the settlement, and he gave SwikhKarrh the sort of body-length embrace that George and KliUrrh customarily shared now. His friend had not become pregnant, but his first breeding season had altered him, made him seem older and somehow deeper, an impressive Person whose advice carried weight. "I'll work it somehow," Danny had told this new Person.

Recalling the embrace now made Danny's penis get stiff. He turned over on his stomach and groaned quietly. Coming back to the settlement after all that sex and serious work had been as terrible as he had feared. Even the holidays were no fun; somehow he just couldn't get interested in making presents or ornaments or even cookies, as he surely would have had the project been scheduled to continue after First Firstday. Instead, day after day, lethargic and glum, he had dragged himself like a sleepwalker through the routine of winter chores.

Sex bothered him a good deal, but what bothered him more was the sense of being demoted from responsible team member back to child, set to work at dull jobs like seed cleaning and milking, not that the goats were giving much by January—deprived of any hrossa to spend time with, and an opinion that mattered in meeting, and the option of sharing a friendly fuck with anybody he knew. He thought of SwikhKarrh's new dignity in contrast to his own diminishment and fumed. He felt defiant, but cast about only listlessly for avenues through which the defiance could be expressed or exorcised. Never in his life had he been so disgruntled.

One dark, snowy afternoon in early January, when he had hauled a handcart mounded with hay out to the pastured sheep, and in total ignorance of the many farm boys who had traveled that route before him, he fucked an ewe. It was entirely unplanned: there she stood with her head in the manger and he just did it. An outlet for the defiant mood had thus been created; but afterwards he felt not so much disgusted with himself as stupid, for unlike other farm boys in similar straits Danny had had superior sex with human beings first, and the contrast was discouraging.

Not discouraging enough to stop him, of course. He would go out to the pasture angry and defiant and come back angry and depressed—at odds with the settlement and powerless to change his lot. He could not center down. He could scarcely be civil to people.

A day came when he and Katy, assigned to the same maintenance squad, worked side by side all day to tighten the big barn
near the gristmill and repair a couple of the broken paddles in the
mill wheel. All day he replied with a few gruff monosyllables
whenever she spoke to him; and after they were finished, and
Danny had started away to wash up before supper, Katy called
to him to wait. She let the others clear out of the mill, and then
she put down her tool belt and simply wrapped her arms around
him tight, not saying anything.

At first Danny stood like a stick inside the hug, but she didn't
let go and finally he weakened, let his hammers thunk into the
straw and hugged her back. When his chest and throat started
aching he thought to his horror that he was going to cry, and he
burrowed his face between her collar and her neck, squeezed his
eyes shut, held his breath. There was something about Katy's
seeing and reaching through his tough exterior to the misery underneath that made him feel dangerously little and grateful. He
didn't like feeling little, but the sympathy was pure balm.

After a bit Katy pulled back and made him look at her, still
without speaking; instead she kissed him on the mouth in a way
that drove the threat of tears right out of his mind. She rubbed
her cheek against his and kissed him some more. Before long they
were both breathing fast, and then Katy was drawing him back
behind a tall strawstack heaped in a corner of the mill.

Afterwards he did cry, he couldn't help it, it was such a relief
to feel halfway *normal* again. Katy patted him matter-of-factly
and said, "We're going to go see your father, my lad. We can't
go around doing this sort of thing behind his back. I'll tell you
the truth, though, I'm not looking forward to it. I hate fighting
with George almost as much as you do, and is he going to *hate*
having to deal with this right now."

"Fighting would be kind of a relief," said Danny, wiping his
nose on his chaffy sleeve. "We hardly talk to each other these
days."

"Oh, he's worrying himself to death about you, but he just
hasn't screwed himself up to confronting it yet—keeps hoping
you can both tough it out till the colts come to term, so he can get
you a special work assignment in the stables and maybe avoid
having to face up to the sexual issue at all."

"Katy—"

"Your going around so silent and wretched is a constant reproach to him, did you realize that?"

"Katy—"

"Mmm?"

"It really isn't only the sex. It's a lot of things, I don't exactly know what all. The sex just kind of stands for the rest of it."

"Even your dad knows that, dummy. That's why he wants to get you assigned to the stables, given more responsibility. You'd like that, wouldn't you?"

"Sure I would! Why didn't Dad say anything about it? It would have given me something to look forward to."

"Because," said Katy, starting to get up, "he didn't want to get your hopes up till it went through the committee. Lots of us would enjoy working with horses. He'll have to plead your case and let them chew it over along with everybody else's." She held out her hand to him.

"Oh." Danny let her pull him up and started to brush the straw off his clothes. Suddenly he stopped and turned to face her. "Katy, why's Dad so *scared* about me doing sex? I can't figure it out. He makes too big a deal out of it, there's something weird about the way he feels."

Katy gave him a level look. "I don't know, sweetie. I know what you mean. Something from his past, maybe all the way back in his childhood. He probably doesn't know himself why it upsets him so much."

"Bad luck for me, though," said Danny with a trace of his former glumness.

"Worse luck for him," said Katy briskly. "Come on, let's go get it over with! Here, let me get the straw out of your hair, you look like a scarecrow."

But they were spared the particular confrontation after all. When they arrived at the domicile George was pacing up and down waiting for Danny, and there on the table lay the radio printout from the Sixers.

When Danny understood that he and Jack Wister had been invited to Sixertown for the eighteen-week spring school term, he didn't have to think about it at all; he knew instantly that he wanted to go. The message said he would live with Maggie, and Jack with another officer's family. Fine, he'd liked Maggie when he met her at Thanksgiving. But the main thing was to get out of Swarthmore, away from everything and everyone that had defined him before he went on the Lake-Between-Falls expedition and couldn't see to redefine him when he came home changed; and most of all away from his father. Until the message came he hadn't thought there was anyplace *to* go.

George himself was half dead against the idea, half perfectly aware that it would solve several acute problems for them both. On the pro side, seeing Danny so unhappy was a continual misery to him. Sending him off to mingle with boys and girls his own age for a while, in a place whose novelty would necessarily distract and stimulate him, would remove that difficulty. On the con side, KliUrrh had said again and again that the Sixers were in danger, that they would not survive outside the valley, and without being able to confirm this George believed KliUrrh.

Never once in all their discussion had he sounded at all worried that Danny might find life among the Sixers more attractive than life as a Quaker peasant. His agitated early comment to Katy—"This is what comes of dinner invitations and hands across the ocean!"—did express another worry, however. He felt in his bones that the settlement should have nothing at all to do with the Sixers. The Quakers' hard original choice and its arduous consequences couldn't help but be subtly undermined if they did; he was sure of it. Demonstrating that there were no hard feelings on either side was all well and good, but sending Quaker children to live in Sixertown seemed implicitly to affirm the Sixer position, and George objected entirely. Everything considered, he had to be more against than for. All this Danny understood.

A decision that important could not, of course, be taken only by the boys' parents. The meeting had to discuss it, in committee and as a whole, and the sense of the meeting was that with their parents' approval the boys could go to Sixertown. This judgment was given with a certain sanction, or pressure, to the effect that they *should* go, that it would be in the interest of the community for the invitation to be accepted.

It happened that Jack's parents, John Wister and Lynn Matthews, were as divided in their minds as George was in his, though their reasons were different. They took the disaster foretold by the hrossa much less seriously than he did; but Jack was now agitating night and day to be sent where the machines were used and respected, and they were genuinely worried that he might decide not to come home. They and George spent painful hours together, sometimes talking, sometimes in silence. In the end they were all agreed that the boys had better be allowed to go—since both wanted to so much, it seemed no good could come of preventing them—but none of the three were happy about it, and all heartily wished the Sixers had never cast them into such a quandary.

And now they were here.

Before George would give his final consent he had requisitioned a gig, and one calm day between January storms had flown himself and Danny up to the lake. He could not bring himself to agree without KliUrrh's specific assurance that his son would be safe.

They found the village two-thirds empty. Most of the Lake-Between-Falls hrossa were at one of several hunting camps beyond the nearest range of mountains, and SwikhKarrh and all the breeders had gone with the hunters. But the dark dot on the beach that they spotted from half a kilometer away turned out to be KliUrrh, expecting them.

"It will be safe enough," he said, when George had explained why they had come. Shuffling toward Danny, he drew the boy into all his arms. Presently, still holding him, KliUrrh said to George: "That is not a good place, but it may have goodness to give *him*. He needs to go away from you. Ahhhhhh I am sorry for you both; this trouble between you is a trap you cannot get out of for this time. Danny belongs to you, he belongs to us, he belongs to both and neither, but most of all he belongs to himself. Give him room to do what his growth requires. He will be safe enough."

But all the time Danny could feel, within the haven of KliUrrh's embrace, the unquietness of his feelings: whiffs and hints of disaster, the dread of disharmony he and his father both remembered from the telling of "The Prodigal Hross." Serenity and assurance lay deep above it, but the twisting unease wafted up between the cracks.

"KliUrrh—" said George, and could not go on. The hross released Danny gently and went to press his long gray thorax up against George. "Tanka Wakan is not the God of Abraham, my friend. He will not allow the child to be killed in order to try the faith of the parent, I tell you he will not."

"Then when—"

"Soon. It begins soon, for he has taken notice now. But Danny will not be harmed with those others. He is important to Tanka Wakan. How would Tanka Wakan let him be hurt. When the Sixers are destroyed, Danny will not be among them."

Destroyed. Was KliUrrh reacting to the disharmony between Dad and me that day, wondered Danny, or was it about the disharmony that's supposed to be coming when [TuwukhKawan] destroys the Sixers? He didn't know, couldn't guess. The idea of the Sixers being destroyed at all seemed wholly unreal, yet like his father he believed implicitly that when KliUrrh knew a thing, he knew it. Still, how could both be true? Would [Tuwukh-Kawan] maybe "destroy" them in some symbolic way?

Whatever it meant, KliUrrh had told George that Danny wouldn't be there to see it. Danny yawned; he was finally getting sleepy.

With a rush of warmth he thought now again of Katy, arguing and arguing with his father, putting Danny's situation to him in psychological terms that could not be gainsaid, sitting up till all hours with him after John and Lynn had gone home, sleeping with George one night when both were tired out and upset—Danny had woken briefly and smiled to hear the unmistakable noises coming from the big bed—and, in the end, carrying her point.

That wasn't all. In the middle of yesterday afternoon, when nobody was around her domicile, Katy had come out to the earthworm farm to find him and had sneaked him into her room, where for once they had both undressed completely and fucked twice, in close to total silence, by way of celebration and farewell. He wriggled face down against the mattress and thought he would love Katy his whole life. In another couple of minutes he was asleep.

2 A False Start

By the time Maggie got home the next evening it had already grown dark. Danny had drawn the curtains, reconstituted some dinner, and was sitting cross-legged on the floor of his room arranging holos on a shelf. The pleasant, homey smell of cooking filled the flat, and Danny's bedroom, though still bare, now looked as if somebody lived in it. Maggie came and leaned in the doorway, dangling her coat from one shoulder. "I can't tell you how nice it is to open the front door and smell dinner in the oven."

"I hope I did it right—and I hope you're in the mood for chicken gumbo, that's all there seemed to be." He looked hopefully up at her, a holo in his lap and one in his hand.

"We'll get some more supplies in tomorrow, now that there's a reason to be eating at home more. After dinner let's make a list of what you like and what you don't."

"Oh, I like everything...well, not plain foddercake. We lived on that for a whole winter when we first got here, did Dad tell you?"

"He mentioned it." Maggie made a face.

"I was only six, and then seven, but I still remember how I used to hide under my bunk and cry about it, lots of times. I hope I never see another piece of foddercake in my whole life."

"Well, you won't see any in the Sixertown PX." Maggie's glance, drifting around the room, alighted on the console where a stack of text viddies now rested in a spot that had been empty that morning. "How'd it go today? Or wait, let me change and dish up the dinner, then you can tell me while we're eating."

"It went pretty well, I guess," said Danny later above his steaming plate. He frowned at his heaped fork and added, "If I had a chicken and some fresh okra and herbs and stuff, I bet I could make us a really good version of this." He had, by conscious effort, omitted the silence before eating known as Quaker grace.

"I'll bet you could too," said Maggie with respect. "So tell me: which subjects did you sign up for, and what's your impression of our school?"

Maggie had taken Danny and George along that morning and introduced them to a few of the instructors; then Ike had collected George, together with Jack's mother, and driven them off toward the lander. The distractions had gotten George and Danny through their goodbyes with a minimum of fuss, and now that his father was really and truly gone Danny felt able to relax completely for the first time since before Christmas, more than a month, and think of him with simple affection—even with gratitude—if not, as yet, with understanding.

He felt a rush of gratitude also toward Maggie, and smiled at her again, remembering the oddly comforting murmur of her voice and George's in counterpoint the night before, while he was falling asleep. "I'm taking everything except mechanical engineering and math. I already did algebra and I feel like I know enough math for now. Literature I'm *way* behind in—nobody's ever got interested in steering my reading for some reason so I've always just browsed around and read at random, whatever looked good."

"I guess it didn't seem urgent, the way soil chemistry would."

"I guess not. They always let the computer print things up for us, then we'd feed 'em back again when we were done. I didn't really read that much. Rachel Heineman—she's a girl in Swarthmore—she was always the big reader."

"What looks most interesting so far?"

"Well, to me, agriculture and Earth history. I've had lots of that already at home, but it's all been from a special point of view. I think it'll be very interesting to hear a different one." He paused. "Jack's more interested in anything to do with machines."

"How's chemistry?"

"I'm just about even with the class. I think I should have as much chemistry as I can, because I might decide to work in the lab later. Um, how was *your* day? I don't even know what you do."

Maggie was surprised, then touched; it was unusual for anybody to ask her how her day had gone. "I'm a doctor—supervisor of the medical unit, actually. Like you, we were sent out clear of disease organisms, but like you we do get the odd broken bone to set or appendix to remove, and then since the town's been established we've had a fair number of prenatal cases to see."

Danny swallowed and said, "Prenatal?"

"*Pre*, before; *natal*, birth. Pregnant women. Most of my time's spent administering supplies and personnel, though—I don't do much hands-on doctoring anymore. But later on, when we're training the next generation of doctors, I'll be teaching. I'm looking forward to that." She got up to get the pan of gumbo and ladled most of what was left in it onto Danny's polished plate.

"Thanks. Sure you saved enough back for yourself?" He took her word for it and dug in. "I never had teachers before," he remarked between bites, "just the computer. Everybody was always too busy or tired; and also, for a long time Jack and I were the only school-age kids, so we were sort of on our own... somebody would check to be sure we were getting on with it fast enough, and somebody would always make time to explain if we just *couldn't* work something out for ourselves—in my case usually Dad or Katy or Billy—but the computer did most of the teaching."

"So a schoolroom must seem strange for lots of reasons."

"Well, it's *interesting*," said Danny quickly. "I've read some books about kids that were going to school, and now I get to try it for myself."

"But?" Maggie leaned back and smiled at him encouragingly.

Danny shrugged and sighed. "But . . . I'm used to being able to go at my own speed, pretty much, and get up and move around if I'm stuck or bored—without asking—and, you know, I'd go for a swim or pick a bushel of tomatoes or something and then get back to work. And also, I'm used to working by myself."

When he didn't elaborate on this last point Maggie prompted gently, "Did you get a chance to meet any of the other kids today?"

Danny picked up his fork and drew circles in the gravy on his plate. "Not really meet, but I was in classes with them all day, and I sort of *watched* them . . . Maggie, I don't know if I can explain how weird it is to see so many other kids who're the same age *I* am. I've never met *anybody* who was my age in my whole life before! It's just—it brought home to me like nothing else ever has how really strange it is for us to *be* here. At all."

Maggie got up to clear the table. As she reached for Danny's plate, on impulse she put her hand on the back of his head and rubbed it inexpertly, not sure how a caress from her would be welcomed but moved to make some sign of sympathy. "That'll wear off, you'll get used to it. I wouldn't worry."

But Danny, used to caresses, quite un-self-consciously put up his hand and pressed Maggie's hand and wrist against his head, saying, "Oh, I know, I'm not. It'll be OK."

"Anything you need?" she asked later. They had had some dessert and made a shopping list together; now he was heading for his room to do a little homework. "Is the viewer like the one you use at home?"

"Pretty much. A little fancier. No, I'm fine—oh, unless you've got some scrap paper, or a slate."

It took Maggie a few minutes to find some sheets of coarse paper in the bottom of a drawer. Danny had clipped in a viddy and found his place by the time she brought them to his room, and stepping inside to hand them to him brought her in view of the holos he had been setting out earlier. She made a noise of surprise and appreciation. "I'd love to have you show these to me sometime, if you wouldn't mind."

Danny's face brightened. "We can look at them now if you like: it won't take a minute. Here, sit down right here on the bed." He shut off the machine, swept the pictures into a stack, and came to sit beside Maggie, passing her one holo at a time to hold while he described the occasion of its being made.

The first showed a summer day, bright and evidently hot. A younger, even slimmer Danny in a skimpy white dhoti, very brown, with hair bleached nearly white, stood with lifted arms at the apex of a fifteen-person pyramid. The others who made up the living structure were also deeply suntanned and lightly clad, and everyone was grinning broadly. There was George at one end of the bottom tier of five men planted on all fours, hands and knees wide apart, in the middle of a grassy area that Danny identified as the settlement commons, where the tents had been. "This was taken the day after the wheat harvest a few years back. We always have a big picnic to celebrate getting the cereal stores in, with races and stunts and stuff. This was my first year of being the top of the pyramid—I got big enough just as Jack got too big! (There he is, in the second tier, see? Right by Katy.) Dad's at the end because of his back. I was point man last summer too, but next year it'll be somebody else's turn, a girl called Rachel, the one I said was a big reader, and I'll be down in the second tier."

"You all look mighty happy," said Maggie, a trifle wistfully.

"Oh, you can't imagine what a load off our minds it is when the grain's safe in the barns for another year," said Danny, not aware of how elderly he sounded. "Now *this* one was taken at a shearing contest. I won't be old enough to be in that for another year or so—I know how to shear, but I'm not strong enough yet to hold the dratted sheep! They struggle and kick something fearful, they don't like it—well, who would? I don't blame them. But I always loved this holo of Katy and Dad—*and* the sheep!—and I took it myself." The camera had caught the two human subjects leaning shoulder to shoulder on a partition, next to what appeared to be the bare floor of a barn. In the foreground a bending man whose face could not be seen had removed half the fleece from a Herdwick ewe, which gazed directly up into the lens from the wooly folds, wearing such a comical expression of disdain and forebearance that Maggie laughed aloud. The shearer's tunic or shirt was sweated dark under the arms; his bunched back muscles could be seen beneath it, and the muscles of his left arm that clamped the ewe backwards against him.

The picture had immense vitality, and its composition and lighting were excellent—mostly by chance or instinct, since Danny had been taught nothing about such matters. The absorbed faces in the background, so much together and so entirely at ease, contributed an undefinable extra value to the shot. "Danny, this picture's superb! No wonder you're proud of it. Now tell me about Katy—I met her and liked her last summer, you know. Has she become a kind of unofficial stepmother to you over the years?"

This was a quite creditable job on Maggie's part of sounding as if her interest was casual, on the boy's account alone; but, as George might have told her, Danny was uncannily sensitive to voice tones set to deceive. Also he had not forgotten the Thanksgiving visit, and he was aware that Maggie and his father had slept together in Maggie's bedroom the previous night. The clear look of perfect comprehension he gave her now was the first she would receive from him, though by no means the last.

"Oh, no," he said, very kindly. "Not a stepmother. A friend— our best friend, along with Billy. Katy's wonderful to us. We all love each other and Dad and Katy do sex together sometimes. But they don't want to be married to each other, they're *friends*." He selected another holo from the stack. "Dad took this," he said, handing it to Maggie. "At Lake-Between-Falls, right on the lakeshore."

In the picture it was early summer. The long mountain ridge, thickly covered with flokh trees in their new blue-green foliage, filled the background, and part of a domed hross lodge could be seen at the left edge. George must have waded into the lake to get the shot, or stood or sat in a boat, for a band of water and wet disturbed sand bordered the bottom edge of the scene. Danny was leaning with his bare back and rump against a hross who stood half in and half out of the water, a large lidded basket clamped in its arms. The figure of the boy described a sideways curve, so that his head was against the hross's head and one arm rested across its...withers? Their shapes at first suggested a child with a very large dog or a midget pony, but that impression was superficial and quickly lost. Both were wet and shiny from the lake, and Danny's hair was plastered to his scalp.

The pose evoked pleasure, grace, and the physical ease of the two creatures with one another—this last a quality it shared with the holo of Katy and George. Danny's skin was not so dark here nor his wet hair so pale as in the harvest picture; both appeared to be the same shade of light gold, warm against the blue-gray hide of the hross. "This is [SwikhKarrh], the closest thing I've ever had to a 'peer' on Pennterra so far. He's [KliUrrh's]—son, you'd say. His child. That basket is full of [swillets]; they're a kind of eel-shaped animal the hrossa like to eat . . ."

But Maggie, discomfiture forgotten, said when she spoke only, "Danny, this is a portrait of a beautiful boy."

He looked up at her, startled. "It is? But I was so skinny! I thought I was just starting to look better *now*."

Maggie shook her head. "You look just fine now, but people can be beautiful and skinny both, especially children."

Danny laughed then, surprised and pleased. "Well, thanks. Actually, you probably can't see it, Friends mostly can't either, but [SwikhKarrh] is a really, really beautiful hross."

Maggie peered closely at the holo and shivered, a sharp spasm. "You're right there, I can't. I disgraced myself last summer when Lieutenant Powell and I went to meet with the hross elders—did you hear about it?"

Danny hesitated. "Well—only that you didn't want to unite with them in meeting for worship. I remember you weren't there, and then Dad told me later you hadn't wanted to come."

"I was afraid to! I told myself it wouldn't do any good, or prove anything either way, and maybe that was true, but it's also true that I was just plain scared of the hrossa—of the—the melding, the empathy. It made me feel—I don't know how to tell you. *Creepy*. Invaded. I loathed the whole idea so much I let Byron take it all upon himself, out of sheer cowardice. I felt terrible about that afterwards, I can tell you."

Danny listened thoughtfully to this. When Maggie stopped, "It's a shame," he said sadly. He saw nothing unusual in Maggie's confiding this to him; he was used to being taken into the confidence of grown-ups and used to having his responses taken seriously. "A few Friends have that reaction too. It's called, uh—"

"Xenophobia."

"Xenophobia. It's really too bad, because the hrossa are better than the best *people* you ever knew, and the empathy, that just lets you get closer to what you want to get close to anyhow. I *love* it," said Danny passionately. "I love going up to the lake. The happiest I ever am is with [KliUrrh] and [SwikhKarrh], and Dad's just the same as me."

"There are drugs that have that effect too." Maggie glanced down at the holo and sighed. "I didn't mean that snidely—but it does seem almost as if some people are made so they can respond to what the hrossa are, what they offer, and some are made to be repelled."

"But why would that be?"

"Search me. Maybe chemical pheromones, something like that...but it's strange that I should be among the repelled ones, because I love the planet itself almost as if just *being* here were a sort of drug high. I've loved it from the very first day."

Danny regarded her gravely. "We feel that way about Pennterra too, Dad and I do, and most of the rest of us in Swarthmore. What I feel about the hrossa, that's exactly the same feeling, only, like, amplified. So maybe you can understand what I was trying to say. About them."

"Maybe I can." Maggie glanced at her watch. "Should we talk about the others some other time? It's getting pretty late."

"Well, there's just these two left, and they're really the same picture." He handed both holos to Maggie side by side, felt her sudden intake of breath, and turned to watch her face. "You knew my mother, didn't you." It was not a question.

One picture showed Susan Siljan in a blue dress, seated, smiling down upon the naked three- or four-month-old baby in her lap, the crown of his head toward the camera, his feet against her midriff, both of his hands in both of hers. In the other, obviously taken on the same occasion, Susan was standing beside a George with a less lined face and a darker, though no fuller, thatch of hair. He was wearing a woven yellow shirt with short full sleeves and cradling the baby close in one arm; the other was around Susan, whose own arms were clasped about his waist. The two beamed joyously down upon the infant Danny, who seemed to be gazing from his father's arm across into his mother's eyes. His expression, in contrast with those of his parents, was sober.

Sober herself, Maggie said, "I didn't really know her. I did meet her a couple of times, but that was quite a few years before you were born." The holos were ikons of Danny's and he was pleased to see that Maggie handled them respectfully. "She looks terribly happy about *you*, doesn't she? They waited a long time for a baby. She must have been just overjoyed when you finally came."

This time Danny did not react to anything he might have sensed beneath Maggie's words. He said, "I guess she was, but if she'd never had me she wouldn't have died."

At Maggie's shocked look he explained, "See, I was coming with the cord around my neck, and when the midwife pushed me back inside she tore an artery, and my mother lost a lot of blood. So she had to have transfusions, and there was something in the blood they gave her or maybe in the injector—some virus, that one that disrupts nerve cells? She died a couple of months after these were taken." He lifted his gaze to Maggie's. "I know it wasn't my fault, I understand that. I just wish it hadn't happened."

"I'd never heard how she died," said Maggie awkwardly.

"Dad came on the *Woolman* because of it." He gathered the holos up and stacked them again slowly. "It's been hard on him and hard on me, that she wasn't ever there. Course, I've been really lucky that Dad's like he is. Most people couldn't have done anywhere near that good a job being a father *and* a mother to a little kid; that's what Katy says. It's just that there's this whole thing in Dad's and my life that's always been *missing*." Danny got up from the bed and started to set the holos up on the shelf again. "Katy says go ahead and feel angry about that, it's a big gyp and I have a perfect right to be mad."

"Katy's a smart lady." Maggie sounded tired; the evening had made unexpected emotional demands on both of them. "When *were* you born, Danny, by the way? When's your birthday?"

"It was last week, January 25. I was thirteen." He smiled ironically. "Officially a teenager."

"You seem older." Maggie hoisted herself up and moved toward the door. "You look a bit older than thirteen too, I'd say— taller, more filled out."

"It only started happening a few months back. Dad says I'm having a growth spurt and not to let me eat you out of house and home." They shared a smile at George's expense. "And if I seem older, it's probably because I've only ever had grown-ups and hrossa to talk to, up to now. Well, and *little* kids."

"It'll be interesting to see whether *our* kids your age seem like 'little kids' too."

"I was thinking that after five years on a starship, when you don't know what'll happen to you at the end of the trip, the people in my class might seem old for their age too. I was too little to realize what was going on."

"It's a point," said Maggie, "but they seem pretty normal to me."

THE SCHOOL DAY was six hours long. Danny had never done that much daily sitting at a stretch in his life, and for weeks he was badly troubled by physical restlessness. His chances to mingle freely with his classmates were limited by the rigid structure of the teaching day; but for the better part of six years his was the only new face they had ever seen, and at the beginning the younger Sixers' curiosity about him was intense. George had worried quite unnecessarily about his eccentric clothing, whose only effect upon the other students was to make Danny seem more exotic and therefore more interesting. This was just as well, since the gaudy colors and slick synthetic feel of the fabrics they wore struck him as sleazy and clownish, and he discovered no wish in himself, either then or later, to imitate their dress.

Throughout the first week, both boys and girls crowded around Danny at the lunch breaks and after school, firing questions—"What do Quakers believe in?" "Is it really true that you don't use machines over there?" "How come?" "What are the natives like?" "What do you think of our town here?" "Hey, don't you wish you could stay in Sixertown?"—few of which he was able to answer truthfully, or carefully, or at all, in a couple of phrases. But the crowds were friendly, if loud and pushy, and he kept his head and on the whole made an agreeable first impression.

The impression the Sixers were making on him was more complicated. He found their loudness jarring and their readiness to quarrel and shove among themselves unnerving—people in Swarthmore *never* squabbled like that—and he would tend, for instance, to flinch when people bawled questions at him from only a couple of feet away. Here was where his having missed out on an ordinary rough-and-tumble boyhood was most evident. For a good while it was also impossible for him to separate individuals out from the gaudy, noisy, aggressive flocks of his schoolmates.

His biggest handicap, with the boys especially, was a certain seriousness or literalness that lent itself poorly to the badinage, clowning, horseplay, and "dirty talk" that constituted their ordinary forms of interacting; while Danny was far from humorless himself, his sense of humor had been formed along very different lines. And though he possessed a range of sexual experience surpassing the wildest dreams of the boys in his and higher forms, had they but known it, they could readily see that their coarser speech made him uncomfortable. In truth he was something of the prig they thought him. A son of George Quinlan's would have had a hard time being anything else, unless he were an out-and-out hellion.

Yet despite his handicap Danny was better equipped to make his way in this place than many other youngsters might have been. He was an attractive boy, well made and self-possessed, with an open countenance and a nice smile, and he was not at all backward or shy. With no experience of nonconformity within a larger society, he had yet been familiar as long as he could remember with Quaker tales and traditions, and was not upset to find himself the one odd member of a group. Indeed he had very often been the only child his age in a group of adults or almost the only human in a group of hrossa.

When his novelty value had worn off somewhat and he was just beginning to be able to tell people apart and learn their names, something happened to divert him from the natural course he might otherwise have taken. There was a gym of sorts in the building, where boys from the different forms would meet and play pickup basketball games after school, and toward the end of his first week several of the boys from his own form invited Danny to join them there.

Danny had never played basketball in his life or seen it played, not even on a viddy, but he was agile and strong, able to throw accurately, and heartily tired of sitting still all day, and he caught on fast. But he possessed neither talent nor experience that could help him function really well as one of a group of aggressive competitors acting in concert against another group. His role as youngest team member at the harvest relay races certainly hadn't taught him how. Though he enjoyed the skills involved in shooting baskets, and darting the ball around the floor during practice, he found the actual games—or rather the wrangling, yelling, cursing, crowding, and fouling of them—disagreeable, even a little scary; a harsher sport, soccer or football, would have put him off completely. He understood that all this was part of a ritual none of the others took that seriously, but after a few weeks he admitted to himself that he wasn't really having much fun and stopped going to the gym after school.

This decision was made easier because of a need to put another aspect of the school athletic scene behind him: the ritual sexual joking in the showers. He had watched this joking, at first, with the liveliest interest. Wasn't it just the sort of thing his father wanted him to know about—this bragging and hooting and putting each other down without malice, that got the huge sexual tensions they all felt out in the open? He never reached the stage of joining in the gibes and insults himself—nobody flicked a towel or a remark at him—yet the atmosphere included him all the same, and he was easy with it here as he could not be with its analogs on the basketball court or the schoolyard, for here the sexuality was open and frank, not masquerading.

He liked that; and, had things been different, time and greater familiarity would have taken care of the uncertainties on both sides. Already the other boys had been forced to modify their first view of him because of the several occasions when, back in the shower alcove where the splashing water would cover any sounds they made and clean up the evidence, he had joined in willingly with a group of guys who were masturbating together. It was very exciting for him, that first time or two, to watch the other boys' faces get redder and redder and more and more dopey-looking above their pumping fists, the whole group of them so entirely without pretense it felt a little bit like being back among the breeders at the lake. Watching them made *him* come harder and quicker. He found it wonderfully reassuring to know, not just theoretically but for certain, that other people really did what he did and went about it in pretty much the same way.

But then in a while he discovered that afterwards he felt too much like he used to feel after fucking sheep—stupid, slightly depressed. It baffled him: how were these later sessions in the showers different from the earlier ones? Once, on his way home in the gathering dusk, he was drawn into a circle-jerk behind the school building with four of the guys from the gym. No good whatever came of that: the cold, the faint light, the furtiveness and hurry, all gave a chill impersonality to their encounter which the actual touching did almost nothing to reduce. It was in fact much *gloomier* than the ewes; Danny disliked thinking of it later, almost in the same way he disliked remembering the foddercake winter.

As more days passed, he gradually began to understand that he had somewhat misread what the boys were doing together back in the showers. For one thing the element of rivalry was much more important and more serious than he'd realized. For another there was so much *defiance* in the boys—as much as there had been in him during the period of his visits to the pasture. Danny experienced these group antics as variously enjoyable, exciting, dreary, or dumb. But he didn't view any of them, not even the dismal circle-jerk, as dirty or wrong in a moral sense; and gradually he was made to see that most of the other boys did. Sexual pressures might drive them to defy the belief, for now, but it made their playfulness fundamentally unlike that of the hross breeders.

Once recognized, this insight disturbed Danny as much as the first group masturbation had reassured him. The other boys were, when you got down to it, an awful lot like his father. Danny had not come to Sixertown to resume that conflict where he and George had left it off in Swarthmore, yet that (he now said to himself resentfully) was the only reason he had been allowed to come: *Dad was counting on my "peers" to make a regular guy out of me!* He *couldn't do it, so he just turned the job over to them!* This was not very reasonable or just—George had been nothing if not forthright on this subject—but for the moment Danny didn't care; things looked different to him now, he was getting worried about himself. Perhaps he too had expected that he would be "regularized" in some indefinite way by mixing with people his own age. But he was still an innocent.

Ironically, it was this absence of guilt (misinterpreted as an absence of prudishness) that had gained him ground with the basketball clique. Their revised opinion stayed revised, even after he stopped playing, but at no time did any of those boys undertake to make a friend of Danny. Most were not very interested in *particular* friendships, being at a stage of development where they felt most comfortable as part of a boisterous collective, a gang. Danny could have all of them or none, that was how it was; and he knew after a while that friends all lumped together wasn't what he needed.

Maggie had made a friend of him, and he of her. But he was very experienced at having friends that were adults. He wanted one his own age—one, for starters. Maybe (he thought in a moment of relative calm) I just haven't looked in any of the right places yet.

Only some of the boys stayed after school for basketball. None of the girls did. Where did everybody else go? Not to do chores, that was for sure; Danny could hardly believe how little was expected of the young people in the way of contributions to their community. He supposed they must do some work in their own homes, like the "shopping," housekeeping, and handiwork he did for Maggie, but after he stopped playing basketball that used up hardly any of his after-homework time.

All the "work" of the community seemed to take place at a distance from the daily life of the domicile town. The noise of construction, for instance, was constant and unpleasant but distant. People drove back and forth between Sixertown and the site of the permanent town over several miles of paved highway that followed the coast. The two visitors had been given a tour of the site a few days after their arrival, but Danny retained of that experience only an impression of deep square holes of raw earth in the muddy snow, thick walls half-raised, a grid of straight snowy streets, and a fleet of enormous yellow and green metal machines, none of which he had any idea of the purpose of, though Jack had seemed transfixed by everything he'd seen and had asked a million intelligent-sounding questions.

It occurred to Danny on the third post-basketball afternoon that he couldn't remember having laid eyes on Jack in weeks; and now, with nothing better to do, he looked up Commander Levy's address on a map of Sixertown and walked over there. Mrs. Levy answered his knock, and gave him a cup of cocoa in her warm kitchen with her two little girls, along with the information that Jack was now spending all his afternoons in the school machine shop—which would explain why Danny hadn't caught a glimpse of him; he never went near the place himself. "I had been hungry all the years, my noon had come to dine," said Mrs. Levy, explaining that these lines from a famous nineteenth-century American poem described Jack's situation to a T.

Danny bantered skillfully with the children for a few minutes, then thanked Mrs. Levy for the cocoa, pulled his sheepskin coat and boots back on, and trudged off through the fading winter day. The snow was gone but the weather continued cold and dreary—though milder at that than it had been at the higher altitudes of Swarthmore when he had spoken by radio with George the previous Sevenday—no, Saturday, he corrected himself. Seven days in the week. In Swarthmore Saturday might be Fourday or Seconday or anything; he'd lost track. A dense cloud cover had stalled over the Delaware Valley for so long that the batteries in one of the greenhouses went dead, and temperatures had dipped so low inside as a result that supplemental heat had had to be patched in from the bathhouse generator, meaning no baths for anybody for four days. It happened every winter, usually more than once. Danny wasn't sorry to have missed it.

Where were the greenhouses in Sixertown? He hadn't been shown any, yet there were always fresh lettuces and tomatoes and carrots and so on in the PX. Things like that, growing vegetables, why did they always take place where nobody in Sixertown had to notice if they didn't care to? And who tended the plants? The subject had not come up in his agriculture class, not yet; the teacher, a pleasant black woman called Sextus, who was bald, had focused thus far on the growing of certain field crops, chiefly

corn and soybeans, in the immense outlying fields that had been
made ready nearer the permanent site the previous fall.

Danny found the course very interesting. He also enjoyed it
because Dr. Sextus often asked him to describe to the class how
the Quakers handled problems like planting, harvesting, and
ensuring soil fertility and tilth, without machinery. She drew
practical contrasts between the labor-intensive practices of the
Quakers and the mechanized ones that were to be employed on
Sixertown's new farmland, but was obviously really fascinated
and impressed with what Swarthmore had achieved the hard way,
and also with Danny's practical knowledge of how their system
worked. For his part he was looking forward to seeing the Sixer
methods applied as spring came on, and thought he might discover, then, in the losses and gains these would measure against
Swarthmore's, a reason for the hross restrictions.

Danny turned in at the school. Shouts and the pounding of
feet and basketballs came through the doors of the gym; but he
went on by, following his ears to another noisy room at the far
end of the building, a room he entered now for the first time ever.

At once he knew the real reason why he hadn't "seen" Jack for
so long: the pants and jacket of Sixer motley the other boy was
wearing would have camouflaged him from any distance at all.
Together with several more students Jack was working on
something under the guidance of an instructor, a husky young
man in blue uniform trousers and a thick red pullover.

This instructor was the first to become aware of the intruder.
He threw a switch, and the torturous shrieking abruptly stopped.
"Hello, you're Danny Quinlan aren't you? Were you looking for
Jack here?"

Jack swung round, but Danny spoke first to the man he now
recognized. "Oh, hello! I saw you at Swarthmore, didn't I? Your
name's Byron—ah—"

"Powell. That's right. We saw each other across the room last
summer in meeting, and I spent the best part of that day with
your dad." He put out his hand, and Danny shook it in an unpracticed way; people in Swarthmore didn't shake hands. "Welcome to Sixertown. Making out OK?"

"Yes, fine, thanks. I just thought I'd come by and say hi to
Jack. Mrs. Levy told me he'd be here." He stumbled just per-
ceptibly over the "Mrs." The Quakers, by revived tradition, used
no titles at all among themselves.

"Come see what we're making," Jack said. He sounded rather
pleased than otherwise to see Danny.

Danny, stepping over to the workbench, beheld a contraption bolted together out of scrap metal and junk, a blocky thing with parts sticking out. He looked at Jack, mystified. "What is it?"

"It's a model of an internal combustion engine," said Jack, "or it will be in a couple more weeks. It's a *working* model, it's actually going to run!"

At the look on Jack's face as he said this, Danny had a flash of insight: *That's how they all kept saying I looked up at the lake, when we first got up there!* "Gosh," he said, doing his best on such short notice to sound interested and impressed. "But I thought—didn't they used to run on gasoline?"

"This one's going to burn ethanol," said Jack, with so much gloating joy in his voice that Danny's heart gave a painful squeeze, and he understood all at once that what had made him dislike Jack in the past had not altogether been Jack's fault. Since the holidays he had learned a thing or two about how it feels to be at cross-purposes with the world you have to live in.

"Could you make a model railroad with an alcohol-burning engine?" he wondered, and now there was no need to fake an interest.

"Sure. Not just a model, either—a real miniature railroad! But first we're going to finish this, and maybe build a little car for it to run." The look Jack now directed toward Danny was by far the friendliest he had ever given him. "How's it going for you? These guys are Dave Adler and Randy Jarman, by the way."

The boys said hi and shook hands with Danny, who decided to treat Jack's question as rhetorical. "Go ahead with what you're doing, I'll just stay and watch a little while if I won't be in the way."

So Jack had made some friends. Danny watched them bend again possessively above the model and envied Jack. As the awful racket resumed, he became aware of Byron's gaze upon him and wondered fleetingly if there was something he wanted to say; but the screeching was terrific, driving all else out of mind. He steeled himself to endure it for five minutes, out of respect for his newfound insight into Jack, before slipping away, and watched in total incomprehension the manipulations of the older boys—reminded in a funny way of Alice probing about in the folyokh intestines, absorbed to the point of entrancement—as he marked off the time.

Then upon the very point of his release the door swung inward and a boy from his own form, called Joel Adler, came into the shop. Byron's attention flickered toward him, but this time he merely raised a hand in greeting without switching off the sound. The boy waved back as he crossed to the engine-builder Jack had called Dave Adler and yelled above the racket, "You were supposed to be home by five, cabbage-brain!"

The blank look Dave turned upon him changed abruptly to one of horror; he yelled "I gotta go!" to Byron and his two friends, snatched up his coat, and crashed out of the room, already running. The younger boy, Joel, obviously Dave's brother, arched his eyebrows and grinned, shrugging expressively, at the others. His regard lingered on Danny in an interested way, and as he moved back toward the door Danny waved at Byron too, and they went out together. Jack didn't look up.

All Danny knew about Joel Adler was that he didn't come to the gym after school, and that he didn't have much to say in any class except literature, where he was the star of the third form. It didn't occur to him to wonder what Joel might know, or suppose, about himself. They eyed one another with frank curiosity.

Joel spoke first: "Did you stay after for basketball?"

Did that mean Joel knew where Danny had been spending his afternoons? "Nope. I did for a while, but I quit."

Joel seemed pleased. "How come?"

Danny hesitated. "Oh—I liked some of it, but there were parts I didn't like much. After a while."

"What were the ones you didn't like? If you don't mind my asking."

"I don't *mind*," said Danny carefully, "but I'd rather not say. Well, for one thing—a lot of those guys want to win real bad." He jerked his head toward the door he and Joel were passing. The shouting and running noises behind it had stopped; he knew what that would mean and deliberately blanked out the steamy picture that tried to form in his head.

"If you don't want to win *pretty* bad," said Joel, "you don't play very well." He glanced sidelong at Danny.

"I guess not." They walked the few steps to the outer door in silence, and Danny pushed it open. "Why didn't you ever come out?"

"I'd rather not say," said Joel, and cackled at his own wit. After a second Danny laughed too. "Not yet anyway," Joel amended.

They came out onto the street. It was quite dark; Danny flipped up the hood of his coat. "Which way do you go?"

"The other way from Maggie's. But hey... could you come home with me tomorrow after school? I mean if you haven't got any other plans. We could, you know, work out or look at viddies or something." We could get acquainted, was what he plainly meant.

"Oh—" Danny froze in the freezing street "—that would be great! I'd really like to! I'll ask Maggie, but I know it'll be OK," he added in what he meant to be a less gushing sort of voice.

"Well—see you tomorrow, then."

"Yeah, see you. Thanks." Embarrassed by his own gladness, Danny turned right and walked, then sprinted, home through the dark straight streets to Maggie's domicile.

3 Family Feelings

Already it was far too late for Danny ever to become, in any sense at all, a regular guy. KliUrrh had understood this; so had SwikhKarrh. Katy suspected the truth but hoped she was wrong. Danny himself did not yet clearly know it; still less did his father. But Danny did now know, at once, in that way he sometimes had of filling up with certainty as a vessel fills with clear water, that he had made a false start in Sixertown, and that what Joel had just offered him amounted to a chance to get back on his true course and accomplish what he had set out to accomplish here.

When he told her, Maggie seemed pleased. "Oh, that's a really nice family—Joel Adler's father, Ben, is one of the most long-suffering people I've ever known. He's in charge of the dairy herd, maybe being with cows makes you patient. He and Becky—that's his wife—have two other children besides Joel, an older boy and a girl about nine or ten. I always think of them as a kind of ideal family, the sort I wish I could have grown up in."

"What was your family like? I'm interested in families." Danny was chopping greens for a salad while Maggie made a sauce for the broiled fish they were having for dinner, adding pinches and dollops as she went. From time to time she picked up a glass of sherry and sipped from it.

"Oh, well-meaning. Poorly off. My father owned a small newspaper that just about supported us with nothing much left over. I was the oldest by a long way—I was born when my parents were still very young, and my father was hardly around at all till I was three or so—he got work in the tin mines till they played out and was saving every cent to buy the paper. My mother and I lived with her family while he was off mining." She took the sauce off the heat and tasted it, frowned, sprinkled in some greenish herbs, then put it back on the burner. "I think his having missed out on so much of my early childhood made him kind of inhibited with me. Maybe he felt more affection than he showed. But he worried constantly about money, and he had a terrible temper when he was young, and some way or other he started to feel that the lack of warmth between us was *my* fault."

"How could it be your fault? You were just a little kid."

"Oh, my father had no insight whatever into how a little kid feels, poor man. It never entered his head to wonder what it must have been like for me, at three, to have this large irritable stranger move into the house and claim the lion's share of my mother's attention, that I was used to having mostly to myself, and start barking orders at me and spanking me for not instantly doing everything he said. My mother let it slip once that for years after he came home, practically the only thing they ever fought about was how hard he was on me."

Danny, cutting small tomatoes neatly into quarters, listened raptly to this tale. "Well, did it get better? How'd you feel about each other later on?"

"Feel?" Maggie stirred and tasted, head bent above the saucepan. "Well, I can't remember *ever* feeling that he loved me, if that's what you mean. And I know that for years and years he bitterly resented my not loving him." Maggie glanced at Danny, all attention, now silently peeling a cucumber. "As a matter of fact, while I don't have any memory of loving him, I'm not quite ready to swear I *never* did, and I'll tell you why. This is kind of an awful story, actually. Sure you want to hear it?"

Danny nodded, slit the cuke along its length, and began to slice it with a practiced wrist action. "Fire away."

"Well, when I was five, I developed a big cavity in one of my molars. There hadn't been any money for regular dental checkups, but my parents must have decided that this ought to be seen to; anyway, they made an appointment, and Dad took me himself. We didn't have a car, and there weren't any trams, so we walked, the two of us. Our house must have been about two klicks from the dentist's office. The way I remember this, it happened at night, and I don't know whether it was summer or winter but I think winter.

"Well, we got there, and the dentist sat me up in the big chair and told me to open my mouth. Dad was out in the waiting room. I saw these big shiny things, that were forceps, coming at me, but I remember deciding to open up anyway—I was an incredibly *obedient* child, God knows what I was always getting spanked for—and one-two-three in went the forceps and out came the tooth."

Danny winced and made a face. He had stopped cutting up vegetables; Maggie had stopped adding things to the sauce, which she went on moving the spoon through automatically. "What I remember all these years later isn't the pain but the *shock*. He hadn't used an anesthetic or warned me what to expect, and naturally blood spurted everywhere, the tooth had great long roots on it. What with one thing and another I must have been badly frightened."

"What did your father *do*?"

"Well, the next thing I remember is walking home in the dark with Dad, but feeling quite alone—I have a sense of walking on his left side and him going along next to me, very big and tall, not holding my hand or anything. And I was sobbing, convulsively, the way a kid'll do after they've been crying very hard, you know? Not *still* crying, but . . . and suddenly," Maggie's voice veered into bleakness, "he grabbed me and paddled me, right there on the street."

Danny gasped. "He *spanked* you? But why, what for?"

"As a matter of fact," said Maggie, "I think I can tell you exactly: for crying, in the first place, but really for something else. But do you know, Danny, for years and years I repressed this little trauma, I had no conscious memory of it at all! And when I did suddenly remember it again, thirty years later, I thought I must surely be wrong, he couldn't have done anything so cruel, he wasn't a monster! So I asked my mother about it."

"What'd she *say*?"

Maggie flashed him a gratified smile. "You're a terrific listener, you know that? Well, she didn't remember anything about a spanking, but she did clearly remember my coming in with blood all over—all over my dress, and my face—and washing me off, and rocking me till I stopped crying."

Tears actually stood in Danny's eyes. He threw down his paring knife and hugged Maggie hard. "Oh, I'm glad, I'm glad she did that!"

A little self-consciously Maggie hugged him back. "*I'd* probably be the monster by now, if she hadn't. That time and others—there were lots of others, this was just the worst one, the only one I know I needed to repress. But let me tell you why I think it happened."

Danny let go of her, stepped back and wiped his nose on his sleeve. Maggie said, "My mother told me she remembered Dad being absolutely furious *at the dentist*, when we came in that night."

Danny's face lit with quick comprehension. "Ah ha! And he couldn't spank the dentist, so—"

"Exactly. I think now that those sobs must have seemed like a reproach to him every step of the way home, and at a certain point it just became unendurable. Mind you, this is all second-guessing. We never discussed it. But I've asked myself, would I have been so hurt—broken-hearted, really—if I hadn't loved him a little, or at least trusted him, before that happened?"

"But you never did afterward?"

She shook her head. "Yet, you know, he mellowed a lot in later years, after he came to feel less angry at the world. My brother and sister, who were much younger than I—though they aren't anymore, how funny to think of that!—they never used to want to hear anything about how he'd treated me when I was little. He'd been such a different kind of father to them, you see." She turned off the heat under the saucepan and lit the grill. "You shouldn't take having a father like yours for granted, Danny, whatever his faults."

"Any more than *you* take him for granted." Maggie turned her head quickly to find his grave, clear look fixed upon her and smiled. "But your mother was nice to you, wasn't she?"

"Very nice, when I was small. Later on it got complicated, the way things are complicated now for you and George. But she saw me through the early thin times. Is that salad ready to go? These will be done in a couple of minutes."

Danny scraped and scooped his choppings into an aluminum bowl and clanked it down on the table. "And you never tried to work it out with your Dad later on, after he mellowed." He picked up two large forks and began tossing the salad in an abstracted way.

Maggie didn't reply at once; she was turning the fillets. Then she sighed. "No, I never did. What would have been the point? He didn't beat me or violate me, not literally. He had no idea in the world that the kinds of things he did do, ordinary punishments from his perspective, could damage a child for life. And suppose I'd been able to convince him that they had, what could he have said? 'I'm sorry?' When that sort of damage is done, it's *done*; being sorry doesn't change a thing. Actually, he *was* sorry, he knew he'd been a lousy father to me, though not how destructive a one."

"I guess you're right, only it seems like such a waste."

"Sometimes, Danny, you have to accept that it's just not possible for family problems to be fixed. I dearly love to see a family like Joel's in action; it restores my sense of the possible." She stared into the flames and sighed. "Anyway, it wasn't all bad. We had some of the same interests. He made sure I got to college. He was a good model of a responsible citizen."

The fish was done. She slid their golden oval shapes onto the warmed plates, spooned boiled potatoes onto each plate, then picked one up with a pot holder in either hand. "Bring the sauce, will you?" she said to Danny, then saw that he was standing rigid, staring at her. "What's the matter?"

"I was thinking about Dad—"

"What about him?"

"—and you. Dad and you. I was thinking, now I *really* understand why you like to be around him."

DANNY SAT in his literature class the next day, listening to Joel. The form was studying a poem called, "Unicorn," by a twenty-first century American poet named Celia Irving. Irving had claimed that "Unicorn" was an exercise in imitating the style of an earlier minor poet with the peculiar name of Vachel Lindsay; and Joel, with his usual relish and volubility, was explaining to the class where the elements of Lindsay's style cropped up in Irving's poem. Danny thought to himself that both poems had nice rhythms, but they didn't appeal to him much otherwise—one seemed too grand, the other too gushing. Still, by paying close attention, he could follow what Joel was saying fairly well.

"Unicorn" was about a girl "at childhood's close"; that was why the teacher had chosen it for study—everyone in the class was the right age to relate to it. In the poem this girl is walking along the beach under a full moon, thinking about how much she

dreads growing up. Suddenly she sees a unicorn out on the sea.
Then and there she leaps to the conclusion that if she can get onto
his back she'll be allowed to stay a child forever. Danny couldn't
see why this would follow, or for that matter what the girl had
against growing up, anyway; but he did grasp that the unicorn
was supposed to be a symbol of childhood, and "magical," and
that the dreamlike and supernatural elements of the situation
resembled those in the poems by Lindsay they had read. He listened to Joel and watched the screen at his desk, frowning with
concentration:

> What made it happen? The surf broke free,
> The moon burned liquid; out on the sea,
> Gathered of light and spray, was born
> A dream-thing bearing a single horn
> Of light, and she knew him: the Unicorn.
>
> Fidgeting, dancing on air and foam
> He poised there, checked in a fury of speed,
> Moon-colored, tide-colored, mercury, chrome.
> The pride of his neck was a god's indeed—
> The dark wind tangled his mane and tail—
> Oh, he seemed Life then, and Joy, and Grace,
> Kept for the instant, but flexed to race,
> His forelegs trampling the sea in place,
> Tendons of cable, feet like a flail!
>
> "I ran and shouted and sobbed for breath
> While the waves strove whitely against the shire,
> *Wait for me, wait*—while they raged toward death
> And stuck at the gale with a fuming roar;
> And the flint moon melted to ivory,
> And my ears went thick with the bump of blood,
> For still in that simmering light he stood.
> His shoulders and flanks gone snowcloud-hued
> He stood like an ice-beast, looking at me . . ."

Next to this, on the left side of the screen, was a long poem of
Lindsay's, "The Ghosts of the Buffaloes." Joel would say things
like "The metrical base is iambic, but every other kind of foot
gets stuck in too, especially anapests," and punch the keys so that
certain words, first in Lindsay's poem and then in Irving's,
would leap into bolder type.

"Anapests sound like galloping," said Joel.

Danny knew what flails and cables were, but what was flint, exactly? What was ivory? Were they minerals, or maybe colors? He had seen viddies of buffaloes; as for unicorns, they were supposed to look like a kind of little horse with one horn sticking forward from its forehead. Now Joel was saying, "Both poets pile up images of power and motion and, uh, awesomeness—like, the buffaloes 'Snuffing the lightning that crashed from on high,' and 'Coughing forth steam from their leather-wrapped lungs,' and the unicorn 'checked in a fury of speed,' and 'trampling the sea in place, Tendons of cable—'" On both sides of the screen the words hiccupped and stood forth more boldly as Joel pronounced them.

And suddenly Danny, concentrating hard to follow this, was visited by a flash of enlightenment. All at once he really saw that the imagination that had evoked these "royal old buffaloes" that "burned to dim meteors, lost in the deep," was kindred to the one whose unicorn "flowed, and spun, and leapt for the light, And nothing was left on the sea but night." He felt elated and slightly stunned; it was a brand-new sort of empathy.

"Thank you, Joel, for the usual first-rate job," Mr. Glesen said. "I don't think that leaves us in any doubt about Irving's appropriations from Lindsay. But we're still left with the riddle of why any poet should want to dress up in some other poet's style. 'Unicorn' is actually far more lush and florid in its language than the rest of Irving's work—more romantic, more excessive in every way. Any ideas about why she would choose, this one time, to speak in an older poet's voice?"

"Well, she says it's an exercise, doesn't she?" said a boy called Peter Hopkins, who was always fouling people on the basketball court, in a bored voice. "Maybe that's what it is, period. Maybe she just wanted to see if she could bring it off."

"Well, maybe," said Mr. Glesen, but his tone said *no*. "Any other possibilities? Or should we take her at her word and be done with it?"

"We should unless there's a good reason not to," Peter complained.

"I agree. *Are* there any good reasons not to, that occur to any of you?"

"Yes!" blurted a girl called Caddie Birtwistle, a skinny nondescript sort of kid with stringy, dirty-blonde hair. Her seat was behind Danny's; he craned around to look at her. "I don't think it's an exercise at all. I think this was written in Lindsay's style because Lindsay had a special meaning for Irving that was connected to the subject of the poem."

Mr. Glesen bounced on the balls of his feet, looking alert and interested; Caddie rarely opened her mouth in his class.

"Go on," he encouraged her. "You might be on to something."

Being the focus of attention made Caddie's pale face go blotchy. She gulped a loud, nervous breath. "Well, I know Irving doesn't normally write like this. I read some of her other poems from the same period and I thought they were hard to understand, I didn't really like them. This one's different, like you said, but I don't think it sounds like—like she doesn't *care* about it."

"You mean, if it were just an exercise you'd expect her to sound—what, insincere? Detached? Cool?"

"Yeah, and she doesn't. To me it sounds like she's, maybe, copying the kind of poetry she liked when *she* was the age of the girl. 'Cause I think she's writing about herself."

"Well, it's a theory." But Mr. Glesen nearly cooed with approval, and everyone in the room knew Caddie must be on the right track. "What makes you think so? Can you say?"

Caddie scrunched down in her seat. "I'm not sure; it's just a hunch."

"All right. Any *hunches* about what Lindsay could have meant to her, then?"

"I think," Caddie gulped desperately, "that his poems made her feel like there was some way to escape."

"Escape? From what—from growing up?"

"Not from growing up. From whatever it was that made her not *want* to grow up."

"So your idea is that she wrote in Lindsay's manner in an attempt to recapture the magical feeling it once gave her, that escape was possible—is that it?"

"Yes, that's it," said Caddie with relief.

"But the girl in the poem *doesn't* escape," Joel now burst out; he had been following the exchange intently. "She doesn't catch the unicorn. Look, look how it goes on:

> The surf seethed toward her. She wailed and fell;
> *I've lost him—lost—I'm lost* like a knell
> Tolled in her head till she flailed the sand,
> Answered and lost. On the empty strand

The emptier ocean broke and broke,
And the froth said: *Lossst.* And the child awoke
To colorless breakers, a gritty beach,
The dream forever beyond her reach."

Joel read this expressively; Danny shivered, obscurely moved.
"So where's the escape?" Joel asked in a reasonable way. "She
says she's lost, and the sea says so too, so why do you think the
poet's saying she *isn't*?"

Caddie looked flustered but stubborn. "I know what it says,
but that's not how it *feels*."

"She's right," Danny heard himself blurt, to his own mild astonishment. Now everyone craned around to look at *him*; he had
never spoken up in this class before. "She's right," he said again,
"because Celia Irving was *grown up* when she wrote this poem!
She's remembering how it felt to be twelve or thirteen or whatever, but at the same time she's having the feelings of a grown-up
about herself as a kid. See, it's two sets of feelings, overlaid.
One, the kid's, says she's lost—there's no escape. The other..."
he faltered; he had lost the thread.

"The other, the adult's," said Mr. Glesen, "says that poetry
is itself a kind of magical escape from despair. Maybe we could
sum it up like this: a child can't escape growing up, but a child
who feels these feelings has them to make a poem out of when
she's grown—and all creative work is a form of affirmation, one
kind of escape from the grim side of life."

Caddie and Danny nodded happily in unison. Joel said, "I get
it. And a kid who *doesn't* have these feelings, who isn't so unhappy and scared, also *won't* have them to make a poem out of
later."

"And that's the silver lining to that particular cloud," Mr.
Glesen concluded, beaming upon all three of them. "As a matter of fact we know some things about Celia Irving's life that bear
out your reading rather well, Caddie. Her relationship with her
father was quite difficult; she felt later that it left her ill-prepared
for adulthood, and her later history tends to confirm that. Read
the last section aloud for us, would you?" And in a guarded
near-monotone Caddie read:

"The moon's cold fire may burn and burn,
But never that girl at childhood's close
By fleetness, or craft, or courage, learn

To mount the Unicorn; this she knows.
Now all of her hope is memory.
Not for an age will his horn be let
In her lap instead, and she mourns him yet,
And mourning, believes, and can never forget
The lovely, pitiless thing on the sea.''

"That's a bit cryptic," said Mr. Glesen. He cleared his throat. "Traditionally, in myth, the girl doesn't chase after the unicorn—the unicorn comes to the girl and lays his horn in her lap. It's a sexual image, of course." There were a few snickers from the class and he glared at the snickerers. "Symbolically, by reversing the roles, this girl is trying to forestall her own sexual development—everyone sees that, I trust, even you nitwits in the back of the room."

"Only the unicorn won't let her," said Joel.

"The unicorn obeys the world's rules. The world plays rough with rule-breakers, even in myth. Or especially in myth, perhaps I should say."

"Why call it an exercise then, if it wasn't one?" asked Peter Hopkins in a sulky way. He was one of those who had laughed.

"Why, I suppose it was an exercise too in a way. Irving does use these devices lifted from Lindsay. The point is that that's not all it was, or is. This kind of poetry was completely out of fashion in 2014, when 'Unicorn' was written; Lindsay himself had been all but forgotten by then. Calling it an exercise would have given her an excuse—or maybe she just wanted to throw people off the track. Maybe it was embarrassing, or painful, to own up publicly that at your age she'd been this sort of upset and frightened person—maybe she didn't like people knowing the things she'd longed for and been afraid of in those days."

"No wonder," Peter muttered. Mr. Glesen threw a piece of chalk at him.

JOEL LIVED on the other side of Sixertown, the inland side, from Maggie and Danny. The Adler flat was a good deal less lavishly appointed than Maggie's. Only the floors were carpeted, not the walls or the ceiling, and the kitchen lacked a washer-upper. But there were three bedrooms and a second lavatory besides the big bathroom for the five of them; it was a family flat. Danny had expected to like Joel's mother after what Maggie had said, and he did like her. She seemed a pleasant person, down-to-earth and good-natured, and happy to meet him, though his entry with Joel disrupted what she had been doing and part of her attention remained upon her task of sorting and folding clean laundry, underwear and socks, into the many piles of different sizes and shapes crammed onto the dining-ell table. A plastic crate heaped with unsorted outerwear stood beside her on the floor. She was wearing a faded green jumpsuit and a pink cardigan, and her short black hair was crinkly. Dave looked a lot like his mother. Danny gave particular attention to this person, younger than Maggie, who was the mother of three children including a son his own age; he attended when they spoke to each other. Here was a commonplace mystery outside of his own experience.

"I picked up some cookies for you and Danny," she was saying. "They're in the bread box. I meant to bake you some myself this afternoon, but I forgot I was supposed to have a conference with Heather's teacher, so I just stopped at the PX on the way home. They're not too bad, I tried one."

"Oh. Thanks," said Joel, none too graciously.

"But take your things and put them away first, please, I need the space. Five people wear a lot of socks," she said disarmingly to Danny.

He smiled back at her. "Do all the different families do their own washing here?"

"The families do, yes. Don't you and Maggie have a laundry room over there in officers' country?"

"I don't think so. She takes the stuff away and brings it home clean. I guess I never thought about it. Back home, laundry's one of the regular work squad assignments. People drop their clothes off dirty at the laundry and pick them up later—like what Maggie's been doing with ours."

"Do they beat the stuff on a rock?" asked Joel, coming out of his room and crossing to the kitchen.

His mother glared at him but Danny laughed. "Nope, the laundry and bathhouse and kitchen all have electrical power. The farming's what's labor intensive. When it comes to cooking and cleaning we're as civilized as you."

"Your manners aren't all they might be, for such a very civilized person," said Mrs. Adler severely to her son.

"He knows I didn't mean it like that," said Joel, unperturbed. "Milk or cocoa?"

Danny had learned to be fondest of tea, but he didn't like to ask when it hadn't been offered. "Milk, I guess."

Joel bustled about, putting glasses and plates on a tray. "Where's Dave? In the machine shop or still in Dutch?"

"Both, sequentially," said his mother. "Machine shop till four, then penance four to six. He was supposed to help distribute the *Home Town News* yesterday," she explained, "but he got wrapped up in that engine they're building and forgot. He's working off a sentence in the calf incubators, two hours every day for a week, helping his father." The *Home Town News* was a community tabloid, published weekly on infinitely recycled paper stock. Somebody had interviewed Danny for it right after he came to Sixertown. The article had misquoted him four times and given his age as fifteen.

"Well, then we can be in my room," said Joel and led the way bearing the tray. There was no table; he put the tray down on the floor between the two bunks. There were no chairs either. Joel indicated one of the beds. "Have a seat. I can sit on Dave's bed as long as he's not around." He handed Danny a glass of milk and a plate. "So what do you think of it all by now? You've been here what, a month?"

"Five weeks tomorrow." Danny leaned over, took a cookie from the tray, and put it on his plate.

"Long enough to have some opinions. Are you glad you came? I know Jack says *he* is, but you're not much like him, are you?"

"Well." Danny bit into the cookie. It was, as Becky had said, "not too bad." He swallowed. "Sure I'm glad I came. I've learned a lot about how people who aren't Quakers think and decide and do things—that's been really interesting. I like living with Maggie." He stopped and thought, wanting to be careful. Joel bent down and felt for another cookie, watching his face. "Jack likes machines and I'm not that interested in them—that's a difference."

"He doesn't like the hrossa," said Joel firmly.

"Did he tell you that? What'd he say about the hrossa?" A sharp pang of missing SwikhKarrh pierced Danny's middle, his first honest pang of homesickness.

"Oh, just about not being allowed to use tractors and that. You know." Joel's tone was exactly like Maggie's, asking if Katy was a sort of stepmother to Danny, pretending not to care. "He said *you* spent a lot of time with them, at their town, and he said you speak their language."

Danny wished Jack would mind his own business. "My best friend's a hross breeder," he said and waited to see where the fake-offhand tone would lead.

Joel sat up straight on his brother's bed and squeezed his arms against his sides. "We haven't had *anything* to do with the hrossa over here. What are they like? What's it like to be around them? I'd really like to know."

Danny gave Joel one of his limpid looks. "Is that why you invited me over today—because Jack told you I know a lot about the hrossa?"

Joel was a little embarrassed but not very. "That's not the only reason, but yeah, it was a big part of it, I admit."

"Heck, why didn't you say so in the first place? I don't mind, I *like* talking about the hrossa. I'm glad somebody's interested! Maggie's not."

"And also," said Joel, "I'm interested in Quakers, sort of. If you feel like explaining to me why the Quakers ditched the mission, I'll tell you—are you interested in what being Jewish is like, for example?"

Danny laughed. "I already know a whole lot about being Jewish—we've got tons of Jews in Swarthmore! Every year we celebrate Christmas *and* Hanukkah. Quakers don't have to be *Christians* anymore! *You* could be a Quaker, easy as I could be a Sixer."

"You think it'd be easy for you to be a Sixer? Hunh. I don't."

Danny filed that in storage to think about later. He drained his glass and set it back on the tray, then leaned back comfortably on Joel's bed. "What do you want to know about the hrossa?"

"Everything!" Joel's eyes glittered. "Every single thing! Like, tell about the first time you ever saw one and what you thought of him."

"OK," said Danny. "Well, there I was, walking along the beach one night, thinking all these gloomy thoughts, and all of a sudden I saw this funny-looking silvery thing out on the water, prancing around in the moonlight on these tendons of cable—" and ducked Dave's pillow as Joel slung it with a delighted whoop at his head.

DANNY'S LIFE NOW CHANGED completely. Most days he and Joel went somewhere together after school—to one of their homes, or down to the beach, or upstream along the creek. Joel was interested in Quaker ways and listened closely to Danny's expla-

nation of why Swarthmore had done what it had done, but his
craving for information about the hrossa turned out to be bot-
tomless. Within a week his sister Heather was able to complain
to Danny that Joel was driving her nuts, going around the house
hissing and gurgling like a maniac—Danny had taped some simple hross phrases and words for him to practice, and he did
practice them, constantly. The complaint was lodged at the dinner that was to be Danny's first of many meals with Joel's family. "You mean I'm 'Gibbering and yipping with hollow-skull
clacks'?" said Joel and nearly fell out of his chair laughing.

"It's from 'The Ghosts of the Buffaloes,' by Vachel Lindsay," Danny explained. "We were reading it in school."

"I see. Very witty," said Joel's father. Everyone else groaned.

Joel finally sobered up enough to say, "I *have* to practice,
Gorse Bush. Hross words are hard for humans to say! I have to
exercise my mouth muscles."

"It *would* be nice if you could exercise them silently, or in a
low whisper." His father smiled apologetically at Danny. "I'm
afraid he's driving us all nuts, happy though I am to see him applying himself to a useful project."

"Say that one that sounds like flibbertigibbet," commanded
Heather. She was nine, homely and smart, with hair even redder than Bob Wellwood's.

Danny stared at her. "That sounds like—*oh*, you mean
[>>>>>>>>]."

Joel's parents and siblings all looked at each other and said
Ohhhhhhh and *Ahhhhhhh*. "So *that's* what it's supposed to
sound like," Becky marveled. "Well, well. Is Joel ever going to
be able to say it like that, do you think?"

"Sure, if he keeps on exercising his mouth muscles."

Joel said "Ha!" Everyone else groaned again.

"What does it mean? That flibbertigibbet thing, what's it
mean in English?"

"Left little arm," said Danny.

Heather scrunched up her face. "Say 'left big arm.'" He said
it.

ANOTHER EVENING when Danny had stayed to supper, Byron
Powell came home with Dave, and they announced that the engine was finished and they were ready to start building a car to
go around it. "I never in my life saw anybody as happy as Jack

is," said Dave. "He's like a little kid that got every single thing he wanted for Christmas."

Byron agreed. "He's so excited it kind of hurts to watch him." He looked at Danny across the table, crowded now with plates and bowls and a soya roast on a platter. "It's going to be hard as hell on him when he goes home. He doesn't want to repair washing machines and stoves, that kind of thing, or even service the landers and whirligigs, and he sure doesn't want to drive a team. He's not very interested in building windmills either. That kid's a born machinist. What are they going to do with a guy like him over in Swarthmore?"

There was more frustration than challenge in this, but a slight tension descended upon the table. Danny said frankly, "They'll give him the best work assignments they can, but I know what you mean. It's tough on Jack, it's always been tough on him. To tell the truth I've been wondering whether he'll go home at all."

"He says so," Dave put in.

"Yeah, I offered to try to work out a way for him to stay on permanently, but he says no, he has to go back."

Danny was surprised, and said so. "Course, his parents are back there. And he *is* a Friend. But I wouldn't have thought his mind would be that made up already."

"*You* weren't thinking of staying by any chance?"

Again Danny was surprised—to find he could imagine living out his life among these people, or at least among the ones in this room, plus Maggie. He hadn't expected to feel this as even a remote possibility and glanced at Joel, aware of why it had become one. "No," he said, "but I'm not ready to go home yet for a while. I like it here, I'm having a good time." Becky Adler winked at him; Heather said "Good!" loudly.

"But you miss the hrossa," Joel protested.

"We don't see that much of them in winter though anyway."

"I kind of miss them myself," said Byron surprisingly. He laughed, self-conscious. "I know that seems like a weird thing to say, but they had one hell of an impact on me last summer— bowled me over, and then stuck in my head afterward. That meeting . . . I keep catching myself wishing I could meet up with them again some time."

Danny said in great earnest, "Joel's coming up to the lake with me next summer. Would you want to come with us?"

"That's *if* there's a diplomatic shuttle next summer, and *if* there's any room aboard for nonessential personnel," Ben Adler cautioned. "Trips between Swarthmore and Sixertown aren't

exactly cheap. I don't want you guys getting your hopes up too
high.''

''Yeah, I know, we won't, but if it works out I'm sure you'd
be welcome to come back for a visit. Really.'' And you could see
Katy again, he would have added, had not his weeks away from
chronic Friendly bluntness taught him something about the uses
and purposes of tact.

By this time, the middle of March, Danny had become a kind
of unofficial Adler, an honorary member of the family. As far
as they were concerned he could have spent even more time with
them, but Maggie was ''family'' too, and he felt bad enough
about leaving her alone so much as it was. Maggie insisted she
didn't mind a bit—that she could appreciate the attractions of
family life as well as anybody alive, and was especially happy that
this particular family and Danny had taken to each other as they
had. And sometimes she joined them. But Danny knew she
missed him if he stayed away too often, and he did honestly enjoy her company. It was only that just now he was hooked on the
pleasures of feeling like part of a family—a nuclear family, with
parents and siblings—after a lifetime of being squeezed between
George on the one hand and, on the other, the whole tight-knit
community of Friends.

In this context of family life his sexual pressures had become
less difficult to cope with. Danny had other things to think
about, lots of other things. He masturbated more without
minding so much, usually in the shower at home, as Joel had let
drop that he and Dave usually did. Dave had a girlfriend, but
they weren't sleeping together, said Joel; the girl didn't want to
yet. He said that he himself was interested in girls generally,
looking at them and thinking about them and so on, but not in
any particular girl at the moment. In fact, Joel thought a lot of
the third-form girls were morons (which is what he thought of
most of the third-form boys). He wished there were more of
both, a bigger pool to choose companions from.

The first, slantwise, conversation they'd had about sex, Danny
was in difficulties right away. He'd promised not to discuss the
field study, but just about all his ideas about sex had as their
starting point those two months up at the lake. It turned out that
Joel had heard about the goings-on in the showers after basketball and frankly said *he* thought stuff like that was tacky and
crude and that he couldn't see why Danny had ever played along
with it, now that he knew him better. It was impossible for

Danny to explain himself without reference to his time up at the hross village.

This was a genuine conflict of loyalties and values. Danny gave away nothing on that first occasion. But later, when he felt more sure of Joel, he brought the subject up himself, made the other boy swear not to tell anybody else, then described the effect of the hross breeders in season on the other hrossa and on the humans. He was careful to say nothing else about hross reproduction and was vague about when and how long the Quakers had lived in the village.

A topic that included both hrossa and sex made Joel's eyes shine with anticipation, but it was as well for their friendship that Danny had waited. The new knowledge disturbed the comfortable pattern of their days for long enough for a cold flower of panic to bloom in the pit of Danny's stomach. What if Joel judged him now as his own father judged him? What if Joel broke his promise and told his parents? Would they shun him if they knew? Would they tell Maggie? For several afternoons Danny trudged home by himself, waiting for Joel to work it out, not knowing what else to do.

Then came a day when Joel arrived at Maggie's flat a few minutes behind Danny and stood in the doorway in his yellow pants and padded green jacket to announce that he had finished thinking. "Sorry it took so long. Want to walk out to the fields? They're turning the ryegrass under today."

Weak with relief, Danny put his coat back on and clattered along the balcony and down the stairs beside Joel. "Should we try to hitch a ride?"

"No, I want to talk." Having said this, he walked along in silence for so many minutes that Danny began to dread what he would say. "OK," Joel began at last, "you stuck your neck out, telling me about all that, and the reason I didn't handle it too well is, I could understand a guy getting into something with a bunch of other guys better than I could understand him doing something with his own father. The more I kept thinking about that, the more it made me sick."

Danny looked at him out of a strained face. "I know. My Dad feels sick when he thinks about it too, he thinks people are supposed to feel sick about stuff like that."

"Yeah, so how come you don't? That's what I couldn't figure out. I went over and over it, I just about went crazy. My mom thought I *was* sick, then Heather told her we'd had a fight so that I had this big fight with Heather . . . but anyway, I finally figured something out. I figured out that you feel like you do about it because you belong with the hrossa, you're really one of them—you feel like *they* do. See? Isn't that right? If you really were a hross, you'd be perfectly normal!''

"You mean—like, when you think about [KliUrrh] and [SwikhKarrh] doing sex together, it doesn't bother you?''

"Unh-unh, not at all, because the hrossa have different rules. I thought, Danny's a hross inside, so why should I mind it about him if I don't mind it about them?''

Danny could think of nothing to say. Was he a hross inside?

"It doesn't bother me at all about you and your dad if I think of you as a hross. Only if I think of you as a person. See what I mean?'' And when Danny still did not reply, "In fact, it's kind of neat having the one and only human hross for a friend.''

Danny went cold. He burst out, "You wouldn't think it was so neat if it was you! And anyway, I don't know if you're right, and I hope you're not!''

Joel was taken aback; he had expected Danny to be glad. "Listen, I didn't mean I think you're some kind of a *freak*, it was just so good to get it straightened out . . . and anyhow, I kind of assumed you saw it like that too.''

"Well, I didn't, and I don't want to,'' said Danny stiffly. "I'm sick and tired of being the *one and only* everything all the time.''

"Listen—'' said Joel again, and he stopped walking so that Danny stalked past him and had to turn around, "—what I've been *thinking* is, what if there could be *two* of 'em?''

"Two—?'' As the implications sank in, Danny's fury abated and his voice dropped a couple of decibels. "Two freaks? Come on—I thought you said the whole thing made you sick.''

Joel grinned weakly. "Heck, maybe I'd get over that—or, like, rise above it, like your dad.''

"Yeah. Temporarily.'' They began to walk ahead. After a minute Danny said, "I don't know if people should try to do what they basically hate, and I sure don't know why anybody *would*.''

"So maybe I don't hate it all that basically—''

Danny whirled upon him. "Well let me tell you, my dad does, he really *hates* it—it just scares him shitless. He only put up with it while [KliUrrh] was right there to help. According to my dad, what we all felt up at the village, that wasn't *us*, it was just the breeders' feelings being felt *by* us. He thinks it's not human to feel those feelings except when the breeders are around.''

"Yeah, but don't *you* feel them—just you, all by yourself, without any breeders?"

"I—"

"Like I said—the human hross!"

Danny stopped dead in his tracks; he thought he might faint, right there in the road. "I'm going back, Joel, I've got to think. I'm all mixed up." The thing he suddenly, sharply longed for, a thing not available in Sixertown, was meeting for worship. He did not think he had ever been so frightened in his life.

Joel stopped too. "Hey, don't be mad," he pleaded. "I didn't mean anything bad by it, honest!"

"I'm not mad, I just need to be by myself. See you tomorrow, OK?" Without waiting for an answer he turned and started hiking rapidly back along the road toward the domicile town.

"OK," Joel's forlorn voice came after him. He took a few more steps and heard Joel call, more cheerfully, "[See you tomorrow!]" in awkward Hross.

4   *Off Chasing Unicorns*

If Joel was right about Danny's being a human hross, then everything would make sense. But that didn't *make* him right. As with Bob Wellwood's "Altruistic Perpetuation" theory, a persuasively argued case didn't therefore have to be a true one. Danny was intuitive, but he had a logical mind. Hurrying back along the road he reviewed his situation.

Joel had meant that *sexually* speaking Danny was a hross. He must seem human enough, otherwise. Joel had also said once that it would not be easy for Danny to become a Sixer, but Quakers were as human as Sixers and apart from sex Danny knew he was a perfectly ordinary Quaker. Sex was the problem. Think about sex, then.

He considered first (and thrust aside) the larking in the shower room, a mistake based on mistaken assumptions—hross assumptions. Weren't they? He thought about it. They were.

Next he faced resolutely up to the fact that for weeks he'd been feeling sexual impulses toward both Maggie and Joel. Swarth-

more as much as Sixertown had given him to understand that he
must make no overtures toward either of these friends, despite
his certainty that Maggie at least was aware of him too in that
way, and that that was why she always wore a wrap of some sort
to and from the bathroom and closed her door when she was
dressing. In Swarthmore, with its communal bathhouse, nudity
was more casually dealt with; living in Maggie's home Danny had
learned to cover himself, but it was a courtesy and no inclination of his own. To deny a mutual sexual attraction was basically anti-hross and anti-Danny.

Despite these erotic undercurrents, even in Sixertown it was
acceptable for him to hug and kiss Maggie—but never Joel. Sixer
males of all ages appeared to be much less demonstrative toward one another than Quaker males were. Boys didn't touch
boys at all, other than in ritualized ways disguised as rough-
housing, competition, or scrupulously impersonal adolescent
sex-play. Here Danny saw that he mixed hross and Quaker values together confusingly. Wanting to hug Joel wasn't a hross
thing; as a rule the hrossa only clasped each other with their arms
when they were copulating, if then. On the other hand, liking the
idea of "copulating" with Joel was certainly hross.

In fact, when you got right down to it, he had to admit that the
idea of sexual contact with any member of Joel's family (except
maybe Dave, with whom he had never felt wholly at ease) held a
definite appeal. Not that he felt *particularly* attracted to any of
them; but friendship and liking as a general basis for sexual exchange did deeply attract him. It was a hross attitude, he could
see that. Nothing as strong or specific as love operated to inten-
sify the occasional carnal twinges he felt on account of Ben,
Becky, Heather—or sure, even Jack Wister, so happy nowadays
that he was very nice to Danny whenever they met. There *was*
love in his impulses to touch Joel and Maggie in nonerotic ways,
however. The former thing was obviously hross, the latter just as
obviously Quaker.

By now Danny was breathing hard and almost running. He
looked blindly out upon the bay, inland toward the beginnings
of the town, down at the paved road rolling under his boots, but
in none of these directions was there anything to divert his mind
from the conclusions toward which these thoughts were leading.

He tried hard to imagine having a girlfriend like Dave's, one
girl, who would be—as long as she *was* his girlfriend—the focus
of all his sexual and most of his emotional energy. The idea had
no reality whatever: he couldn't see the point of an exclusive

sexual bond at all. His own fantasies usually focussed on Katy—on her generosity and sense of fun, embellished by memories especially of his last day in Swarthmore when she had smuggled him into her room. He loved her, he desired her also; but he could discover in himself no wish to possess her entirely. As far as Danny could tell he wasn't at all "in love with" Katy, the way Dave was with Amanda, or Maggie with George.

Just to cover all the bases he tried to imagine Joel as the focus of all his sexual feelings (in case he might be gay). The results were the same. No more than Katy did Joel seem to Danny to be what the guys at school called "sexy."

Sexy—there was the problem in a nutshell! The guys were always talking about how sexy Margie Blackwood or Pat Griffith was, and the word had registered on his mind. But never on his senses; to desire any person because she had Margie Blackwood's beauty or Pat Griffith's slinky way of moving seemed not to lie in the range of Danny's responses. On the other hand, he thought he could probably enjoy going to bed with just about anybody he *liked*, if he or she had Katy's relaxed, good-humored approach to the business. But he would have to like her or him. He didn't much like either Margie or Pat.

Joel, now, didn't think that way. He looked girls up and down, appraisingly; *he* knew what "sexy" meant. Nor did George think that way—so far as you could tell *what* George really thought, down underneath all the anxiety and complicatedness. You could speculate that his father might not actually *do* anything unless he liked a person, but that beauty and a slinky walk would affect him, would turn him on. Danny wasn't too sure about Katy. But his own view of it all couldn't be called either a Quaker view or a Sixer view.

It was, however, precisely the view of the Lake-Between-Falls hrossa.

So Joel... might be right.

Despite the chilly wind off the bay, Danny's face felt hot. He had seen nothing wrong with the hross approach to sex before and he saw nothing wrong with it now, for them; but what was *he* to do with it, all by himself? Joel's offer to become the second human hross, brave and sincerely intended as it might be, was hard to take seriously. Even if Joel meant it—and could overcome his revulsion, spurred by the prospect of getting closer to the hrossa by becoming more like Danny—you would need a *lot* of human hrossa, a whole community; nonexclusiveness was the very essence of hross sexuality. They had no couples, and the only single hross Danny had ever heard of was the "wrong" one in old PaahOokh's story.

He had reached the foot of the domicile staircase, and now began to struggle upward. It was borne in upon him now, with immense finality, that living in Sixertown for these few months could not make him "normal" as he and his father had both hoped; that it could change nothing really because, however successfully he might be socialized in other ways—however well he learned to behave as expected—his sexuality was *formed* now, so that what he wanted was not to become like everyone else but for everyone else to become just like him. And he absolutely knew that that could never, never happen.

Then his troubles with George, like Maggie's conflict with her very different father, could have no resolution, ever. Ever! He would have to conform without changing inwardly, just as Jack had always had to do. His future in Swarthmore seemed unendingly bleak and lonely; for Danny was not supposing for an instant that the question of his sexual identity might someday come to seem less important, either to himself or to his father, than it did at that moment.

The future seemed a wasteland—and then, miraculously, did not. At the top of the staircase Danny stood looking out to sea; and as he hung there, in contemplation of unendingness without and within, there came a shift of stresses inside him—a settling and a lightening—and he felt himself become able to accept the situation. *Something happened to me up at the lake last fall. KliUrrh knew, and it was OK with him. Then let it be OK with me.*

Again he longed intensely for the solace of meeting for worship.

("*Quaker* hross," he would say to Joel the next morning outside the school building.

"What?"

"Not human, Quaker. I figured out that you were almost right, except you should have said the one and only *Quaker* hross."

Joel would look then as if all the lights had just been switched back on inside him. "So the position of only *human* hross is still available? [Good.]"

"[Good]," Danny would say, correcting his accent.)

When the light had almost gone even off the water he walked to Maggie's door and put his key in the lock, then stooped to pluck the *Home Town News* off the mat. This wasn't the usual delivery day ... he turned it over, a flimsy, thin edition, and read the banner headline: EXTRA! LIFE DISCOVERED ON EE4!

THE CONVERSATION at dinner dragged and stalled. Danny finally asked Maggie if she had something on her mind and got an apologetic smile. "Sorry, I'm lousy company tonight. Problems at work."

It was a Friday evening, and Joel and Danny had been friends again for more than a week. Danny felt just fine. He clicked effortlessly into sympathetic-listener mode. "Want to talk, or would you rather not? I don't mind either way."

"It's no secret, under the circs." She put down her fork and propped up her chin with her hand in a weary way. "We've been having what almost amounts to an epidemic of miscarriages and spontaneous abortions. A few would be understandable, but there've been a couple *dozen* in the last ten days or so, women in perfectly sound condition, fetuses at every stage of development from six weeks to eight months. Nothing wrong with most of them as far as we can see. The few in the last trimester really count as premature births, we can save those, but the point is that all of a sudden something's making pregnant women lose their babies, and we have no idea what the cause is, none at all! If it keeps up, every pregnancy begun since we made landfall will have ended short of term." She glanced at Danny, struck by a thought: "You folks never had any of that kind of trouble over at Swarthmore, did you?"

"I don't think so. I'm not positive I'd *know*, if it happened right after we got here, but there've been, um ... eight kids born since we came, and they're all fine. Nobody ever mentioned any trouble that I remember."

Maggie frowned. "Only eight? That's not very many—though I suppose you wouldn't have wanted babies while your future here was still so much in doubt."

"Partly that, and partly that the hrossa are pretty strict about how many of us there can be."

"Hmm." Maggie massaged her cheek reflectively. "Danny, I believe I'll come along with you tomorrow if I may, when you put your call through to George. It's worth asking whether Swarthmore can shed any light on this—just on the off-chance."

Danny turned his chair sideways to face Maggie, trying to think whether it would be all right to say what was in his mind.

He came to a decision. "You know about them finding life on EE4? I'm not changing the subject."

"Lichens and on down. I haven't followed the details."

"And you know why the ship went looking for more life in the system?"

"Mostly because it gave the crew something useful to do while we were getting things organized down here, wasn't it? Or wait— was there something about a tip from the Quakers? I don't remember, quite honestly."

"There *was* a tip from us, but we got it from the hrossa." Maggie frowned, but Danny pushed on anyway. "Billy Purvis said once that if the hrossa turned out to be right about that— that there was life on *one* of the other planets and no others, when there's no possible scientific way they could know—then he'd be ready to take everything else they said pretty seriously too."

He let Maggie make the connection herself, which she instantly did. "You're not saying that this problem could be a warning of worse to come, are you?"

"Well, yeah."

Maggie looked as if she could hardly believe Danny had said anything so dumb, which made him squirm; but he added, "I bet you anything you like that's what Dad's going to say, unless we had a lot of miscarriages too, and I really don't think we did. The hrossa always said we would die outside the valley—well, maybe what they meant was, the Delaware Valley is the only place where humans on Pennterra can have *babies*!"

Maggie stood up abruptly and began to gather up dishes. "There's some perfectly ordinary explanation for this, Danny. We haven't found it yet, but we haven't been looking very long; don't you think it's a little early in the day to be taking that mumbo jumbo of the hrossa's seriously, just because they happened to guess right about EE4?" Maggie said these things with energy; she was put out.

The flash of anger was mostly frustration about the babies she had not known how to save, Danny understood that. All the same he was stung. For his sake he thought she might have kept a more open mind.

But no more than Maggie did he want an open row. "Mumbo Jumbo will hoodoo you," he said, making a joke of it.

Maggie froze, a saucepan in one hand, its lid in the other. "How's that?"

"It's a poem by Vachel Lindsay:

Mumbo-Jumbo, God of the Congo,
And all of the other
Gods of the Congo,
Mumbo-Jumbo will hoo-doo you."

She laughed and relaxed. "Better not let Annie Sextus hear
you quoting that old thing." They cleaned up the kitchen together amicably enough but there was tension between them, and
for the first time Danny felt somewhat estranged from Maggie,
from her work and her world. He went to his room as soon as the
washer-upper had started to whirr; and Maggie, who often suggested a game or a viddy in the evenings, sat bent over her own
computer and hardly glanced up when he told her good-night.

Next morning he woke early. Sunlight streamed in when he de-
opaqued the window panels; spring was coming fast now. The
air, when he pushed the window open, felt chilly but delicious,
and Danny hastily pulled on his cast-off clothing of the day before. In the kitchen he drank a glass of milk and nipped two
bread rolls out of the box, then let himself carefully out the door.
He padded in his socks along the balcony and sat down at the top
of the stairs to put on his boots. Sitting on the top step, he
gnawed on one of the rolls and stared out upon the beautiful
morning, considering where to go: along the beach? up the
creek? The tide was out, and the blue-gray sand presented a firm
surface for walking. Could he wake Joel up somehow without
disturbing the whole family? No, he thought regretfully, not a
chance; if he shied pebbles at Joel's window Dave would wake
up too. He would walk west up the beach toward the permanent
town...no! he would walk *away* from the town, into the un-
cleared territory. That would be more of an adventure.

Swallowing the last of the second roll, Danny went down the
stairs—quietly, where another boy would have clattered down,
heedless of the sleepers in the building behind—and turned right
at the street beyond, which led directly down to the shore. He felt
wonderful. The little woundedness of the night before healed up
without fuss in the clear sunlight and bright water of the day.

Twice before in his life, on salt-finding expeditions, he had
traveled down alongside the Delaware of the estuary. But living
within perpetual sight and scent of the bay and its shifting moods
and vistas had taught him something really new about Pennterra. Ignorance of Earth saved Danny from missing the shore
birds and gulls that would have thronged an earthly beach, or the

crabs and mollusks that would have littered the sand. The tide
had left some dead kelplike stuff around and some empty
shells—that was all. He had seen plenty of native shore life at the
mouth of the Delaware, but here the presence of the Sixers had
driven it away, just as native life had been (mostly) driven out of
Swarthmore.

Danny didn't mind. Wind, water, sun, sky, and the smell of
salt in the air were good enough for him.

The sun's warmth felt delicious in the shelter of the domicile,
but the breeze off the sea had chilly teeth in it, and Danny began to walk faster and then to jog eastward between the town and
the low line of surf. He passed domiciles and outbuildings and
the lander pad, picking up speed as well as he could in his sturdy
winter boots, and soon began to put the town behind him.
Around a curve in the shoreline, a mixed forest of trees and
shrubs appeared like a low, solid wall beyond the scraped grayish earth left by giant machines. As he totted nearer, he made out
that a tall mesh fence, four or five meters high by the look of it,
had been erected between the township and the trees. Now, what
could that be for? What was it meant to keep out, or in?

It wouldn't keep him in at any rate, not a low tide. By squish-
ing out where the sand was too wet for easy running he could get
around it easily. He slowed and angled out toward the water,
seeing as he did so what the sun's glare on wet sand had prevented him from seeing, or at least from noticing, till now: a set
of fresh tracks parallel to his own. They were small tracks,
smaller than his, and they led around the fence. Somebody else
with the same impulse had been up even earlier than he had.

For a hopeful moment Danny thought the tracks might be
Joel's; but Joel's feet were bigger, not smaller, than his. Well,
unless the other person meant to make a day of it, he was bound
to find out who it was pretty soon—the fence meant they would
both have to come back before the way around it got cut off by
the tide, which might already be turning. From now on he decided to pay closer attention to the tides. Making a day of it
would be fun. Today after lunch he had to call his father—he had
to tell him about being a Quaker hross. Some other time, though,
he and Joel could plan ahead, pack sandwiches and flasks and
stay out a long time.

Danny glanced up as he edged past the end post. As he'd
thought, the fence was at least four meters high; all these weeks,
without realizing it, he had been living in a compound. At the
last minute he decided not to touch the post. The earlier walker

had also made a wide turn around it, and gotten his feet wet in the process. Danny struck back toward firmer sand, now following the other set of tracks with conscious interest.

Beyond that obstacle he slowed to a walk and got his breath back. Sometimes he walked backwards to rest his eyes from the glare. After half an hour the trail of tracks angled up toward the woods above the beach, and Danny struggled through the soft sand to follow them. Owing to the shape of the shoreline he was now well out of sight of Sixertown. The trees here were of a different generic type from the tall flokh forests that covered the mountains north of Swarthmore—smaller and scrubbier, multiple tough level, with fleshy, stiff, spatulate leaves each already about the length of his thumb. Danny paused to stroke these leaves gently and touch the tough stems with his fingertips. The unfamiliar trees made him happy, and his spirits, oppressed somewhat by the mesh fence, rose again. The leaves of one sort of tree smelled especially good to him, almost edible; he found that despite his makeshift breakfast he was hungry.

He strained momentarily to pick up some sign of his mysterious kindred spirit but could hear nothing except the wind and, between gusts, the distant hissing of the surf. The trail of footprints led among the trees. Danny decided to follow them. He was not a practiced tracker and on dry sandy ground would probably lose the trail; on the other hand how far ahead of him could his quarry be?

Not far at all. Fifty cautious steps farther into the scrubby forest brought Danny in sight of the person he sought.

It was a girl. There could be no question on that score, because she had taken all her clothes off and folded them into a tidy pile beside her—a skinny, pale, plucked chicken of a girl, lying on a ragged blanket in a protected, sunny hollow among the trees, eyes closed against the light that drenched her, hanks of colorless chicken-feather hair at her crotch and all over her head. She had nipples like a boy's, with no breasts worth mentioning behind them, and her bones poked out under her skin. The girl was Caddie Birtwistle.

The sight of her startled a noise out of Danny: was she alive? One second later he desperately regretted that little exclamation, for Caddie's mouth and eyes flew open together, and out of her flew a scream of terror so pure it nearly frightened him out of his wits.

Anybody might carry on some if discovered in such a state. But Caddie behaved as if seeing Danny seeing her had unhinged

her mind: she twisted into fetal position on the blanket, arms
protecting her head, and screamed again and again, the screams
gradually becoming mixed with sobs and chokings. Danny's
scalp prickled as his first fright turned to horrified dismay. He
tried talking to the girl, and—when this proved unproductive—
thought that perhaps the best thing would be just to go away. But
there was something so really *demented* about the sounds and
contortions Caddie was making that he was afraid to leave her.
Finally in desperation he squatted down and shook her by the
shoulder, shouting "Hey, stop it, shut up! Stop screaming! Nobody's going to hurt you!"

Caddie's reaction was to assault Danny with a pitiful frenzy of
weak blows and scratches—weak, but unlooked for; a few of
them connected. Before he knew it *(Some Quaker!)* he had nearly
thrown a punch at her. Instead he did the only other thing he
could think of: used his greater strength and size to hold Caddie
down so she couldn't kick him and wrapped his arms around her
to pin her own thin arms against her thin body so she couldn't
scratch. She struggled a little, feebly, but trussed up like that
there wasn't much she could do, and in a minute, sobbing helplessly, she gave up. "Please don't, please don't, please," she
sobbed.

"Please don't *what*?" Danny panted. "What the hell do you
think I'm about to do—rape you or something?"

Caddie didn't answer but she stopped saying "Please don't,"
which seemed a hopeful sign. Danny relaxed, slightly, his strait-
jacket grip upon her. "Listen," he said, "I'm sorry I scared you.
I didn't know you were *here*. I was following your tracks for
fun—I didn't know whose they were." He waited and then said,
"Am I getting through or not?"

"Yeah."

"So can I let go of you now, without getting clawed to rib-
bons?"

"Yeah."

"OK," he said. "I'm going to turn you loose, then I'm going
to sit down with my back to you while you get dressed. All
right?"

"Right."

Danny let her up and seated himself cross-legged on the warm
sandy soil. Behind him he heard the small sounds of Caddie
scuttling into her carefully folded clothes. Then things got quiet.
After a bit Danny said, "Can I turn around now?" and something fell on his head like a ton of bricks.

WHEN HE CAME to the sun was half an hour higher, he had a lump on the back of his head the size of a pullet egg and hair stiff with dried blood, and Caddie was nowhere in sight.

He felt awful, incredulous also at the wacky turn of events. Caddie Birtwistle! That little white mouse of a girl! What the devil was it all about? How the devil had that skinned rabbit, that plucked chicken, managed to hit him hard enough to knock him out? She'd used a rock—he saw it on the sand behind him—an eggplant-sized lump with one wicked corner. A person like Caddie would have to be out of her mind with fear to bash somebody on the head with a pointed rock! Such behavior in *anybody* was fairly unthinkable to a boy of Danny's background and training, but doubly so in Caddie. He couldn't conceive of a motive that would cause a kid like Caddie to inflict a violent injury on another person purposely. He had nearly poked her in the jaw himself, but that was just a reflex—not the same thing at all. His cheek burned where she had scraped it with her nails; what if she'd been packing a knife?

Feeling sickish and confused, Danny struggled up and made his way out of the trees and back down onto the beach. There he saw with dismay that the small waves were breaking much nearer the trees than before; if he didn't hurry he would be trapped on this side of the fence till afternoon, with nothing to eat or drink and nothing to do but nurse his headache. He hadn't thought to leave a note for Maggie, he'd expected to be back for a more official breakfast in a couple of hours. At first she might assume that his feelings were still hurt and that he'd gone off on his own in order not to bump into her; but if it got to be time to call George in Swarthmore and he still hadn't turned up, she would begin to worry.

Danny hated to be the cause of worry. He felt no anxiety on his own account—the beautiful weather would certainly hold, and he could live without lunch for one day—but Danny was not a boy who found himself in situations of this kind as a rule, and he was furious at Caddie for dumping him into this one.

He wondered a little what could be wrong with her—for clearly something serious must be—but mostly he just fumed and rehearsed what he would say to her when he got back.

The tide poured up the beach. A couple minutes of head-punishing walking were enough to convince Danny that he wasn't going to make it. He stopped then and tried to think what to do. He was beginning to be thirsty; even in the streaming shore breeze the sun now felt very warm. He had passed no creeks on his way out from town, but on the off-chance that there might be one a bit farther in that direction he turned and walked effortfully through the dry sand, shading his eyes with his hand, trying to sight the gully of a streambed. The glare, a knife in the eyes, made his head hurt unbearably. During the ten or fifteen minutes he walked along looking for a break in the shoreline, Danny felt worse physically than he could remember ever having felt in his life before, and began to wonder if Caddie might have concussed him.

Finally he stopped again. To put so much painful effort into trying to find something that might be miles away seemed stupid and pointless. More sensible to walk back as far as he could toward Sixertown, get out of the dehydrating wind, and wait for the tide to retreat. He had only the vaguest notion how much time must pass before he would be able to wade around the fence—three or four hours, something like that? Then another thought struck him: if the fence was electrified, the charge might carry through water as long as mesh or posts were still submerged. He wouldn't be able to risk wading. He held his head and groaned.

Danny wasn't wearing a watch, but it looked like 10:00 or so by the sun. Really thirsty now, he floundered along at the edge of the trees, back in the direction he had come from.

Halfway back to the barrier he sat down to rest just inside the scrubby forest. For a while he slumped on the ground with his forehead on his drawn-up knees and his eyes shut. Then the powerful scent of the fat stiff leaves, swinging in the wind within reach of his hand, caught his interest. Thick as they were, there must be some moisture inside. He broke off a leaf and bent it in the middle till it split, then sucked on the pulp, which was just damp enough to be refreshing and had a pleasant flavor. He broke off another, peeled back the brittle skin, and stripped off a piece of pulp with his teeth. Meaning only to suck the water out, he discovered shortly that he had chewed and swallowed the pulp as well; he was ravenous. The worst the stuff might do, act upon him like a laxative, seemed a reasonable price to pay for even the slightest relief of his thirst.

By the time he had consumed a dozen leaves his rest had done him good. He got up and plodded off again toward the fence, trying not to look at the water which, even with the sun behind him, was painful to his eyes. So he heard the little craft before he saw it, yellow and round as an egg yolk on the blue water, though its tiny motor made the merest mosquito buzz beneath the wind.

The boat had come close before he noticed it in a lull between gusts. It was heading straight toward him.

Danny stopped then and waited to be rescued, letting himself fill with relief and tiredness and gratitude, but when he saw who his rescuer was the gratitude was doused by anger.

"Hurry up and get in," said Caddie. "I have to get the boat back before anybody finds out I took it."

"You're crazy if you think I'm going anywhere with you! I'll wait for the tide."

Caddie said frantically, "I haven't got time to argue! All right, I'm sorry if that's what you want me to say, but just get in! If they catch me with this boat I'm gonna get killed."

Danny still wanted to refuse. But the wish was childish, it was more important to get back in time to make his call. He gritted his teeth. "Oh, the hell with it." *And the hell with you.* He pulled off boots and socks and lobbed them into the boat, rolled up his pants, and helped her push off; then he settled into the bottom while she started the little motor and steered them out into deeper water. In a few minutes they passed the fence. Very soon after that Caddie cut back toward shore again. She cut the motor and jumped out, pulling the boat up onto the sand before Danny could move to help. He threw all their shoes and socks and Caddie's backpack onto the beach and climbed out. "What are we stopping here for? Why not go all the way back to town?"

"I told you, I'll be murdered if they find out I took this boat out." She went on working feverishly to deflate the little craft, panting as much with anxiety, evidently, as with the labor. Danny put on his boots, then stood and watched, knowing too little about these inflatable lifeboats to be any help. Gradually it dawned upon him that Caddie was really scared stiff about something, not much less scared than she had been of him, and that she had really run some sort of risk (or thought she had) in order to pick him up. He began to feel more puzzled than furious. Nothing about the morning's events made any sense to him, but Caddie's several terrors made the least of all.

Very soon, working with practiced movements, she got the boat compressed into a packet the size of a loaf of bread and was cramming it, still gritty with adhering sand, into its backpack. After it went the disassembled motor, the rudder folded like a fan, and two oars with telescoping shafts. When everything had been stowed Caddie knotted the top shut, pulled on her own socks and shoes, shrugged into the pack, and—completely ignoring Danny—headed off at a very fast walk in the direction of town.

This was more than he was prepared to take. He trotted to catch up with her, wincing at the effect on his throbbing head. "Listen up, you," he said, and pain harshened his voice. "I'm going to tell Maggie every single thing that happened unless *you* tell *me* what the hell's going *on* here. I mean it, Caddie, I want to know. This whole thing is *crazy*."

Caddie bent her head and walked faster, gasping. Danny thought she wasn't going to answer, and when she finally did he had to strain to hear. "I can't talk about it. I can't tell anybody."

"You should have thought of that before you clobbered me."

This time she didn't answer at all; she was crying again, her jaw clenched, her sobs indistinguishable from her gasping for breath. They were coming into the town; the first outbuildings lay just ahead.

"Caddie," he panted, "I promise I won't say anything for a day. But meet me at three this afternoon, at school. In the library. Be there. If you don't come, by this time tomorrow Maggie's going to know."

He could not keep up the pace any longer; he had to let her get away. Though he no longer felt really sick, his head was thumping like the jungle drums in Lindsay's poem: BOOMlay, BOOMlay, BOOMlay, BOOM. He went slowly toward his own domicile, getting his breath back, thinking what to say to Maggie if she were home before him.

But to Danny's immense relief the flat was empty. A note on the table read: *In the lab all morning, home for lunch ca. 12:30.* The clock on the stove said 11:38.

The first thing he did was drink a liter of water, standing at the kitchen sink. Next he went back outside and shook his boots and socks over the balcony railings to get out the sand. Then he took some headache tablets he found in the bathroom and spent twenty minutes in the shower. After that he sprayed his scratched cheek with antiseptic and combed his thick wet hair over the tender lump on his scalp. By the time Maggie came in he had heated up some leftover soup, made some cheese and lettuce sandwiches, and devised a vague version of his morning that would account for the visible wounds without committing him to an outright lie. He didn't enjoy lying to Maggie, even by implication, but he didn't want to worry her and he meant to keep his promise to Caddie.

But Maggie, who had spent the morning failing to make any progress on the problem of the miscarriage epidemic, was not in a mood to fuss over a few scratches. She apologized for last night's "rudeness" in a way that sounded perfunctory and preoccupied, but Danny was happy enough to dispose of that topic anyway. He had a new preoccupation of his own.

After lunch the two of them walked together to the radio station on the ground floor of one of the admin buildings. The tower in back of the building looked just like the radio tower at Swarthmore's station, from which its one monthly message, obsessively repeated, was beamed toward Earth: *Don't come! Don't come!* The Sixers had not, as the Quakers once feared they might, tried to interfere with Swarthmore's transmissions. They simply sent their own, and month after month the conflicting messages on their different frequencies streamed forth toward the sun called Sol by both groups of settlers: *Come at once / Don't come / Come at once . . .* Danny could picture a troubled listener on Earth, switching back and forth between stations, trying to decide which set of instructions to obey.

The technician, as he did every second Saturday, raised Swarthmore for Danny and put him on the line. He never left the room on these occasions. Before today Danny hadn't minded; this time, though, he had something personal to say to his father, and now here was Maggie listening too.

Planting absorbed George entirely these days, as it had absorbed him each April since the Quakers' first on Pennterra. In Sixertown there would always be space left over in life for other things at this season; in Swarthmore, never. Danny had to hear which crops were in, how many lambs and kids had been born, how the sheepdogs were coming along, and what the weather was doing—the complete farm report. He had always taken a lively interest in the farm report, he was even interested in it today, but he was glad when his father began to run out of steam and got around to asking how things were going for him: how were Joel and his family? what had Joel and Danny been up to?

From the first, Danny's accounts of Joel had been pure balm to George's anxiety. He could tell, reading between the lines, that after a slow start Danny's conditioning had gotten underway at last, that he was finally beginning to learn from one normal human adolescent something about how to be another. And George had seemed delighted to agree that Joel should come to Swarthmore for a visit next summer and spend some time at the lake with Danny. But now there was something Danny wanted his father to know about Joel, and about himself.

When he had talked about ordinary matters for a little while, he leaned toward the microphone and, speaking slowly and clearly, said: "Dad, I have something important to tell you. Joel says he thinks I'm [A Quaker hross]." He spoke the Hross words distinctly for the benefit of his father's inexpert ears, using the hrossa's pronunciation of *Quaker* and their own name for themselves, a word meaning "(one of the) People." Behind his back he could feel Maggie and the technician come to attention.

There was a short silence, filled with faintly crackling static. "Say again," said George.

"Joel thinks I'm [a Quaker hross]." He waited. "Did you get it?"

"I got it. That's what I thought you said. Can you explain?"

"[I told him of the breeders. Only the breeders. He will say nothing.]"

George sighed heavily. "I presume you had a good reason."

"I really did."

"All right, Danny. I understand." There was another, somewhat longer, silence. "What's *your* opinion about this—the same as his?"

"Yeah, I think so. I think he's right." Danny's back muscles tensed; he held his breath.

George said slowly, "Katy's been telling me all along it might be something like that, if I understand you right. She's been working on me, trying to get me used to the idea in case it turned out to be true. Danny, I'm sorry about last winter, I know it must have been awfully hard on you. I'll say right now that *whatever* you are is OK by me. We'll work it out somehow or other."

"Dad," said Danny, relief spreading along his limbs like heat, "whatever *you* are is OK by *me*, too. Nobody can help how they are, I've sort of been finding that out."

"So have I, I suppose. With Katy's help." George blew his nose while Danny wiped his on his sleeve, thinking *What a soppy pair we are!* His father spoke again. "About what Joel said—"

"Yeah?"

"Do you *mind*?"

"I did when I first realized it, but not anymore. Just like Joel—he's saying now that *he* wants to be—" Danny shot his two eavesdroppers a wicked grin over his shoulder "—[a human hross. Again: a *human* hross. Human.]"

George laughed faintly. "Not too put off, then?"

"He was at first, but not so much now." Danny laughed too, reading his father's mind: *I send a Quaker hross among humans to be humanized, and damned if he doesn't hross-ize himself a convert instead!*

"How long is it now till you come home? All of a sudden I miss you like the dickens, it seems like we've been apart for years and years."

"Less than two months now. I miss you too." He realized how true this finally was. "Dad, Maggie's here; she wants to ask you something. I'm putting her on, OK?" He got up to let Maggie settle into his chair (shooting him a sharp look as she did so) and turned his clear gaze on the radio tech. "It wasn't anything secret, just something private between my dad and me."

The tech shrugged. "None of my business, kid."

Danny smiled without answering. Both of them knew that this was less than strictly true. He walked over to the window beyond which waited the still-splendid day, feeling as if a sackful of boulders he'd been forced to carry for months had just fallen into the bay.

5   Danny's Education

Maggie and Danny left the station at the same time, passing Jack on his way in to place his own long-distance call home. They left at the same time, but they were not exactly together. Maggie stalked along incommunicada, sobered by what George had told her, aggravated also by the suggestion Danny had guessed he would make, that the Sixers might well be wise to consider the epidemic of miscarriages in the light of a warning. George had offered to take the matter up with KliUrrh as soon as he could get away for a day; but Maggie had said with some asperity not to bother, and Danny, seeing that her mind was fiercely closed against the idea that the town was being warned, made up his own mind not to bring the matter up again. She'd said the hrossa gave her the willies, hadn't she? It was a pity; but Danny's thoughts were veering back to the morning's adventure, and the glow of happiness created by his father's acceptance formed a backdrop now both to Maggie and her troubles and to the mystery of Caddie, and changed the meaning of both. Everything seemed at once more cheery and less portentous. He walked beside Maggie in the sparkling day, light as a helium balloon, his headache a mere whisper.

When she turned left, Danny went straight on toward the school. As he passed the PX he met Joel coming out with a bulky load of supplies. "Where were you all morning?" Joel complained. "I came by but there wasn't anybody home. What'd you do to your face?"

"It's a long story. Listen, there's something I have to do right now, but where are you going to be later on?"

"That's what I came over to tell you—Dad decided the weather was right to birth the calves today! I was out at the barn all morning and I'm going out again as soon as I get home with this stuff. We thought you might like to help. Can this thing you have to do wait, or can you get through pretty soon? They're really cute. He's got Dave and me rubbing them down and setting up bottles in a rack and stuff."

Danny had let out a sort of squawk. Instead of enduring frustration, thirst, fury, bewilderment, and the worst headache of his life, he might have been having a terrific time caring for the newborn calves with Joel—and it still wasn't over, he still had to meet Caddie and hear what she had to say! Was it truly necessary to meet her? With great regret he decided that it was; but he swore now not to hang around waiting if she was late, and not to waste much more time on Caddie's craziness than he already had if she did show up.

Joel had been watching his face with lively interest. Danny pulled himself together. "I don't think it'll take all that long, so I should be able to get out there pretty soon. Maggie'll be in the lab all evening. She said I should mooch dinner with you if I could, so I won't have to get back, if it's OK with your mom."

"Oh, it'll be fine by her, she's so glad we're not having a fight anymore."

"Great!"

"So I'll tell her to count you in for dinner." Joel hoisted his bags of groceries. "Hurry up! See you later!"

"I will. Thanks!" He started to walk on, then turned back. "Hey, Joel, do you know Caddie Birtwistle very well?"

Oho! said Joel's crafty face. He shifted the bag to his other hip. "Nope. She never had that much to do with the other kids, even on the ship. Mom and Dad think her father's a jerk. He's some kind of building genius—that's why they took him on the *Skeezix*—only his wife, Caddie's mom, didn't want to come. He *made* her. He treats her bad, everybody thinks he's a bully, and he's really mean to Caddie—I remember Mom said one time, no wonder she's so mousy and shy. That day in school when she talked about the unicorn poem, remember? Well, I *never* heard her talk that much before. In fact I remember thinking, you'd expect somebody like that couldn't *wait* to grow up, so she could get away from her dad." He peered at Danny alertly. "How come you're so interested in Caddie Birtwistle all of a sudden? No, no, don't tell me: you'd rather not say."

Danny laughed and bopped Joel on the shoulder. "I rather *would* say, but I can't! Anyway, I'll get through as quick as I can and meet you at the barn. I wish I could come right now!"

Joel went off, clutching his burden in both arms, and Danny strode on briskly toward the school. If Caddie didn't show, he could be at the barn in forty-five minutes, giving a calf straight out of the incubator its first rubdown and bottle of formula. He had helped at lambing time for years but had never even seen a calf, not a fully developed one, though he had watched these developing for the past month in the artificial uteri Ben Adler was in charge of. He had also never seen any sort of fetus birthed from a machine—he couldn't remember the first generation of lambs. Right now in Swarthmore, Belgian foals in large-mammal uteri on loan from the Sixers were coming to term. By leaving he had lost his chance of being assigned to work with them, and this thought caused him a momentary pang of regret.

Maybe the Quakers would run their own dairy herd someday, after the horses were trained and working. Horses would make it feasible to grow a lot more hay... but cows would mean another barn or three, besides the new one the horses had now made necessary, to house themselves and their own winter feed. What materials could be found or devised or recaptured to build them out of, and where could they be sited? A dairy herd would require tremendously expanded pasturage, too, lots more clearing of native vegetation, lots more killing of unreplicated plants on the land along the river downstream from the settlement. Would all the planning and work, and especially guilt, be worth it? Swarthmore would need to chew these questions over for a long time before embarking on a development that ambitious and demanding.

For the first time in three months Danny wondered what sorts of projects Alice had spent the winter dreaming up, against the

time when the native plants would have broken dormancy or
begun to sprout. Alice's work was, of course, a taboo topic as far
as radio conversations went, so George would not have been able
to tell him anything about it even had Danny been bursting with
curiosity, instead of totally indifferent all this time...

His mind hummed busily, trying and discarding various sites
for the barns and pastures of the possible future; peopling both
with cows; picturing Alice bent over and delving greedily into the
weeds and willows with all the resources of her own lab behind
her now. He walked through half of Sixertown and saw only
Swarthmore all the way. He was at the school before he knew it.

Returned with a jolt to the here and now, Danny stared about
him at the straight streets and trued buildings and remembered
the ominous fence, and he thought: *Oh, I'm a Quaker hross, all
right. That's just exactly what I am, as much hross as Quaker
and as much Quaker as hross. That's what I am!* How much
easier it was to accept, once he knew it was true and could no
longer hope it might not be. *Some of these Sixers are my people,* he thought, *but this place couldn't ever be my place.* It was
all perfectly clear. And he wondered whether Jack, who belonged in Sixertown in a way he couldn't possibly belong here
himself, still felt determined to go home.

It was almost three o'clock when he entered the empty library, on the first glorious day of the first spring after the Sixers' landfall. With some minutes to wait, Danny looked up Celia
Irving's poem and read it through again. When he'd finished he
switched off the screen and did something else he hadn't done in
months: he sought to center down. Even a little earlier he might
have had more difficulty finding the center; but today, filled with
self-knowledge and the sense of his father's acceptance, he settled more readily into that familiar state than at any time since
the research team had returned for the holidays from Lake-
Between-Falls. Something had straightened out inside him.

*Suppose I'd kept on trying to center down through all these
months in Sixertown,* he wondered, *would the thing have
straightened out sooner?* He knew that Friends had traditionally sought clarity in chaotic personal and public circumstances
by keeping centered, but his own life had formerly held so little
personal chaos that he had not known how to proceed, and these
months had been spent among Strangers, who could not advise
him. Still, he might have tried. His long cool drink before lunch
had relieved him no more than this—except that this morning he
had *known* how thirsty he was.

The door bumped. Danny's eyes popped open.

Caddie stood with her back to the door, looking so scrawny and scared that he felt doubly sorry she had come. He stood up. Caddie said tonelessly, "You can fuck me anytime you want if you just won't tell."

The bizarre offer told Danny once and for all that something was badly wrong with this girl, and that whatever it was was more than he could possibly fix by himself. He felt more relieved on his own account than sorry for Caddie, and not too ashamed to admit it. A problem that was too much for him couldn't be his responsibility, though he might have to take responsibility for deciding whether to go to somebody else with it. But he didn't *like* Caddie. He no longer felt any need to make her explain herself, either; he wanted to convince her not to be afraid of him, and then he wanted her to go away.

"Look," said Danny carefully, "I don't understand why you were so scared of me this morning, but I think we should just forget about what happened—at least, I will if you will. And you don't have to worry that I'll ever tell people about it, or about your special place, or ever bother you there again, either. I promise I won't, OK?"

Caddie stared at him. At least half a minute went by. "I'm sorry it was you," she said unexpectedly. "I thought you were nicer than most of them."

He blinked at the weird idea of Caddie's having an opinion of him, any opinion. "Is that why you came back for me?"

She shook her head. "No, it was because I was afraid you'd try to swim for it and the fence might be turned on, and you'd get killed and it would be my fault."

So that fence was as lethal as it looked. Somebody should have warned him! Actually, though a very strong swimmer, Danny had not even considered braving that frigid water as an alternative to waiting out the tide. He said, "Well—so if I promise not to tell, can we just forget about it? I'm not mad anymore."

She shrugged in a hopeless way, as if without the element of blackmail his telling were inevitable. "I'll do whatever you want. If they find out at home that you—that somebody saw me—you know, like that—then I might just as well be dead."

"I don't *want* you to do anything! Anyway, it wasn't *your* fault I saw you!" That flat, dead voice gave Danny the creeps; the sense of something being badly amiss weighed down upon him again.

"Then you'll tell, I know you will."

"Jesus!" What should he do about the wretched girl? "Look—does your dad beat you up? Is that why you're so scared of him? Because if it is—" Belatedly he realized that he could not recall seeing bruises on her skin that morning; it was the sort of thing he would certainly have noticed. She shot him a trapped look, slantwise and away, and shook her head. And abruptly the events of the morning and what Joel had told him snapped together—pieces of an ugly puzzle—and Danny knew what it probably was that Caddie's father did.

In the first blast of shock he thought helplessly of his own father, of the grotesque contrast the two men made. The issue, technically, was the same in each case: a father and a child, with sex between them. Yet here was Frank Birtwistle, a monster; and there was George. Danny thought of his own father's moral anguish, his grief, his struggling to do what was right, even the self-sacrifice in what he had said today. The memory of George's struggles with himself squeezed Danny's chest tight, squeezed tears into his eyes, he had to blink them back; and Caddie, who could have no inkling as to the cause, saw this and was finally reassured.

So for the space of an odd little interval the two of them stood facing one another, eyes locked, a viewscreen and half the room between them, the secret grief of the one oddly mirrored in the new comprehensions of the other.

"I have to get back," Caddie said, and the moment shattered. "Do you really promise you won't tell? About my dad?"

But now Danny shook his head violently. "There's got to be somebody we can talk to."

"Oh no!" Caddie cried in fright. "It wouldn't do any good, he'll never admit it in a million years! He said if I ever told he'd make me sorry I was ever born."

Danny refused to listen to this; he was thinking. "Does your mother know?"

Caddie said nervously, "I think she—sort of knows and sort of doesn't. He's pretty rough on her. It would, like, make things worse if she had to face up to it . . . but I don't see how she could *not* know, really."

"Think she'd back you up if you told?"

"I *can't* tell, why don't you see that?" Caddie sounded ready to cry. "She wouldn't back me up; she's too scared of him. I—I really have to go." She felt behind her for the door handle. "Don't talk about telling anymore," she pleaded. "I know you're trying to help and I'm really, really sorry I hurt you, but you don't know what he's like. He really will kill me, I'm not kidding. I *know*."

Danny shook his head again, hard. "I'll think of the right person, but we have to tell. Don't you want it to stop?"

Without answering Caddie slipped through the door. He heard her running down the corridor, and the bang as she left the building.

Danny sat down; his head whirled and his headache had revived, a tom-tom pulse that would get worse unless he took another tablet soon. He knew—now, at last—what his father had been afraid of at Lake-Between-Falls. Now he understood what could really happen to a child whose father...Danny got up and bolted from the library.

Had he been home in Swarthmore he would have gone straight to Katy with this problem (supposing such a problem thinkable in Swarthmore). Not just because she was a sensible and flexible person, but because she was also a psychologist by training, and this was clearly something for an expert to take charge of. And Danny was desperately eager now to turn the business over to some adult. Jack's sponsor, Nathan Levy—he was a psychiatrist; mightn't he be the right one? Jack ought to know by this time what kind of person Nathan Levy was; Danny could ask him.

First, though, he would have to find him. Where would Jack have gone today, after he got through talking with his folks? Danny checked out the machine shop first, but like the library it stood empty and silent today. He could go to the Levys', as he had done once before, and ask whether anybody there knew where he could find Jack.

For lack of a better plan he left the school and headed out that way; but partway to their domicile he changed his mind and turned into the road he and Joel had walked along the week before, the road leading out of town toward the new buildings and their outlying fields, pastures, and barns, including the dairy barn where the calves were being birthed—the past half hour had driven the calves right out of his mind. Yesterday a crew had started out there with the immense planters that could sow acres in a single day. Jack would be watching, maybe helping, but surely involved in some way, like practically every other kid in town, at least every other boy. The Sixers had spent five years on their ship; where else would they be on this beautiful day? Pretty nearly the whole town must have gone out to watch the planting. Apart from Maggie and her staff the place felt deserted.

Danny walked fast, hoping for a ride, but the road remained empty and he had to cover the whole distance on foot. He looked longingly toward the dairy barn as he went by the lane leading to it, but kept going—following the deep grumble of the planters, which carried far over the flat coastal plain.

There were a lot of people standing around in the sunshine in their shirtsleeves watching the great machines ply back and forth, ponderous but rather majestic, over the broken ground: three to loosen the plowed soil, followed by three more to sow and cover the seed. Each machine could be set to do all three tasks at once, but this way was faster—more rows could be planted by two machines that divided the labor than if each did everything. They had studied about it in agronomy class, just before Dr. Sextus had stopped teaching them and started organizing things for this first growing season.

His first sight of the planters doing the work they were designed to do made Danny stop and gape. Spring planting was a subject he knew plenty about. He knew how long it took the Quakers to plow and sow one of their little fields, according to how many Quakers put in how many hours at the work, and had known—theoretically—how many worker-hours one tractor-hour could replace; but watching the theory applied was another thing altogether. Despite his headache and the urgency of his mission, Danny stood and stared. It was plain to him that by evening six people would have completed a job that would have taken the entire Swarthmore community a couple of weeks to do. By following the instructions of the hrossa the Quakers had knowingly accepted a sacrifice he had never been able to appreciate till this moment; nor had he ever understood why the hrossa had required this sacrifice of them. He did not question the decision to submit to it, but the scene before him forcibly rekindled his need to understand what it was the hrossa so hated about machines.

Presently Danny remembered his purpose and began asking people he recognized if any of them had seen Jack. It didn't take long to find him, along with Byron Powell and some other sixth-formers, including a girl Danny had never noticed before. They were watching the nearest planter turn at the end of the field and gesturing and talking together. Jack had changed into his Quaker clothes, which were wet and muddy to the knee. He greeted Danny in a friendly manner and willingly stepped aside with him. "I drove a planter!" he announced right away. "Not to harrow, but from the fuel tank, back there, down the road and back into the field. They had to refuel, so Byron drove to the barn while the regular driver took a break, then he let me bring it back out!"

"Did you like it?"

Jack laughed happily and gave Danny a pitying look. His eyes shone. "Heck, even you have to admit it's pretty terrific when six guys and six planters can get all this much done in a day! Think about what's going on back home right this minute—seven or eight squads are dragging plows around on the west bank, another three or four are broadcasting peas and beans, everybody in the settlement's covered with mud and dog-tired—and look at these people here!" He made a broad gesture toward the clumps of townspeople in holiday attitudes, the picnic hampers set alongside the road, the excited children. "And you and I'd be just as dirty and tired as everybody else, if we were there instead of here—not standing around relaxing and having this conversation."

It was perfectly true, everything he said. Still—"Yeah, but right now the kitchen squad's cooking up a huge dinner for everybody, don't forget that. All these people had to bring their own stuff." Then he conceded, "I admit I can't think of anything else right now that's better than this, when it comes to planting."

Jack's eyes unfocused, seeing the dining hall and the workers seated shoulder to shoulder at the long tables, tired but powerfully bonded by their labors, falling upon heaped plates of food; and he said, "And I admit that's a real good point."

"I was looking for you. I wanted to ask you about something," said Danny now, eager to get off this subject and onto what was preoccupying *him*. "About Nathan Levy."

"What about him?"

"Would you say he's the sort of guy you could tell a secret to, or, um, a bad personal problem you didn't want anybody else to know about?"

Jack looked at Danny more sharply and raised his eyebrows, but said only "I think he's a great guy—quiet, you know, but the kind that sees all the sides of a question. He's been really, really nice to me, they both have. *I'd* trust him with private stuff. I already did, actually." He studied his muddy shins.

Danny could easily imagine the kind of private stuff Jack might have needed to discuss with a sympathetic listener. "So you wouldn't think he'd mind if *I* talked to him about something?"

"Oh no, I'm sure he wouldn't, he's always helping people that've got problems. He's a shrink, that's basically his job. Sure, go ahead and ask. He's right over there, see? With the kids."

"OK, I will then. Thanks. Hey Jack—" Danny said on impulse "do you—I was wondering—do you miss meeting at all?"

Jack looked surprised and a little embarrassed. "Funny you should bring it up. I just started to, just lately."

"Did you? Well, in that case, would you want us to try meeting together? The thing is," said Danny, ducking his head, "I haven't been keeping centered here, and I want to try to get back into that now, and it just seemed like it might be easier with two of us. If you were interested."

Jack appeared to deliberate, slightly warm in the face; it was odd how much discussing this common practice of their former lives appeared to discomfit them both. "I guess so, sure. But how come—I mean I never figured *you'd* have any problem staying centered." He looked quite gratified. "I mean I thought *I* might, but if even little Mr. Perfect can't—I mean, you're the *last* person I'd have expected—"

"'Little Mr. *Perfect*'?" said Danny, appalled.

Jack laughed, rather too loudly. "Sorry, I didn't mean that like it sounded—well I *did*, but just from habit, I don't really feel like that anymore." But when Danny simply gawked at him, not sharing the joke, Jack shoved his hands into the pockets of his Quaker pants and twisted aside. "Well, dammit, you were always so damned *good*! You always did everything right, every goddamned thing! It used to just drive me nuts! Not only did you cozy right up to the hrossa—not only did you learn their fucking *language*, which nobody else in Swarthmore could learn— you even got to go on that field trip, that every scientist in the settlement was drooling to be chosen for! Jesus, how'd you expect me to feel?"

Danny was dumbfounded. "You sound like you hated me!" He had never suspected a thing.

"If you want to know the truth, I guess I sort of did. Sometimes." Jack made a face. "I knew it was childish, I used to tell myself that, plenty of times. I *knew* I'd have been having a hard time even without Everybody's Favorite Kid around to show me up, and I would have, too, so forget it. That's all over now. I shouldn't have said anything. It's not *your* fault I was born with this mechanical thing."

"But it wasn't yours either! And I was making it worse for you, and too dumb to know it—I'm the one that should be sorry." Suddenly Danny felt exhausted, surfeited with enlightenment. His father, then Caddie, now Jack: he seemed to have spent the whole day saying "I'm sorry," or "It wasn't your fault," or both, to people he used to be angry with. He thought that if he couldn't escape soon to the dairy barn he would collapse right where he stood. What a day! More than anything now he wanted to get rid of the burden of his knowledge about Caddie and her father.

"So shall we meet tomorrow morning?" Jack asked; he wanted this scene to end too.

"Fine," said Danny. "At the usual time?" The usual meeting hour was Firstday morning at 11:00. Neither of the boys had any idea whether the next day was Firstday or not. They had both long since lost track of the eight-day Quaker week, but at any rate it would be Sunday in Sixertown.

With that arranged, Jack went back to his friends and Danny went over to speak to Nathan Levy; and by 5:30 he was finally safe among the calves with Ben and Joel, with a headache pill inside him. Dr. Levy had been great—had listened carefully, asked sharp questions, then said Danny had behaved exactly right and not to worry about it anymore—he would take it from there and something would be done right away.

Danny believed him. He didn't want to think any more about Caddie—or Jack, or even George, and least of all about himself. Enough was enough for one day.

A week later Caddie quietly moved in with a family Danny hadn't met, called Tillotson, a middle-aged couple with a baby that had been born on board ship. No scandal broke; Sixertown could not afford one. Frank Birtwistle continued to direct building operations and to bully his rabbity wife; he did not discuss Caddie's move with anyone, but then he had never discussed her at all. The Tillotsons talked a good deal about how wonderful Caddie was with the baby and how useful around the flat—with both of them working so much of the time they didn't see how they had ever managed without her. Beginning right away, Nathan saw Caddie professionally twice every week. At school there were no quick changes in her, but now she smiled at Danny whenever their paths crossed, anywhere in town.

April wore on without subjecting the only Quaker hross to any more wrenching or painfully enlightening surprises. Danny and Joel, thick as thieves, fed the calves and pastured them in the hardy alfalfa sown the previous September, Danny chattering in Hross, Joel getting better all the time at understanding and marginally better at pronouncing the difficult words himself; already he was far more functional in Hross than George or Katy. In return Joel made up a very good rainy-day reading list for Danny; someone had finally taken an interest in his literary education. Together they explored beyond the fence, into the scrubby forest. Along with other youngsters they requisitioned the little backpackable lifeboats Caddie had rescued Danny with, and paddled around the bay in calm weather, or down the bumpy, stony creek. Cricket and baseball teams were organized by enthusiasts, who coached the boys and handful of interested girls in these games that could not be learned aboard the *Down Plus Six*. School dragged along. Danny and Jack both discovered that meeting together made them like one another better. The sun shone, the newly planted crops sprouted, and the Sixer children tore around delirious with the pleasures of the first spring any of them had experienced, or all but the oldest could even properly remember.

At first the pleasures of this spring were equally intense for Danny. At home he would have been working hard through all of April and May and most of June; the Sixer kids weren't given much work to do at all, unless you counted things like feeding the bumptious greedy calves as "work," when it was actually not only fun but entirely voluntary. Danny enjoyed his vacation from the rounds of labor and made the most of it, knowing that next spring would be business as usual for him.

But life was not quite perfect, and gradually grew less and less so. The miscarriages continued, in perverse counterpoint to the burgeoning crops and leafing trees, until no pregnant women were left in Sixertown at all. Failure to find either cause or cure made Maggie quietly, grimly frantic; there were no more evening games or viddies, and Danny spent more and more time with the Adlers in their flat. Nor were humans the only ones afflicted. The hens and then the turkeys began to lay infertile eggs; the doe rabbits reabsorbed their young.

When the cause of the epidemic was discovered, Maggie's frame of mind did not much improve. Her lab succeeded at last in isolating an inorganic compound, sometimes but not always present in the creek water, which acted as both contraceptive and abortifacient on the Sixertown women and livestock; but specialists had tested that water thoroughly over a period of weeks before locating the temporary town where it was, and they swore there had been no such stuff in the creek the previous fall. By late summer the Sixers would begin moving into the new town, whose water would be supplied by a small river that emptied into the bay. So far, this river showed no traces of the lethal compound; meantime the drinking water from the creek could be treated to remove it; but the matter was both infuriating and disturbing.

George, who heard about it from Danny, said again that it seemed to him the abortifacient was acting exactly like the antibodies an organism might make to fight infection. Where had it come from, if not from the planet's own "immune system" in some metaphorical sense?—a hypothesis Maggie still refused absolutely to entertain. But neither could she seriously suggest that the Stone Age hrossa were cooking the stuff up secretly and dumping an intermittent supply of it into the creek. There were in any case no hrossa within many kilometers of Sixertown so far as anybody knew, and the aerial and beach patrols *would* know—that was what they were for.

Something else caused Danny to ponder the hross's warning anew. As spring advanced and the farming activity intensified, he gradually became aware that the land was in distress. The fields *looked* healthy enough; the crops were growing beautifully, powered by the various NPK mixtures produced in the Sixers' fertilizer "factory"; but when Danny would walk across the calf pasture and through a gate into the tilled acreage, the ground beneath his feet felt wrong. Nobody else seemed to notice, and he couldn't account for the feeling. But stuck like a leech at the root of his pleasure and growing every day was an unquiet conviction: *something's not right here*. And he could not help beginning again to wonder, half-consciously, wholly reluctantly, whether the destruction KliUrrh had predicted might after all be not symbolic but actual.

And yet when he looked around him his worries seemed preposterous. Here were the wheatfields and cornfields, vast by Swarthmore's standards, the many thousands of little plants sturdy, healthy, and visibly taller every day. Here were the nearly completed single-family houses in the streets of the new town that would not be called Sixertown when it was finished but either Home Town or something dignified and grand: Plymouth, Washington, that kind of name. Here were all these people going about their activities, people like the five Adlers and Maggie and Byron and Dr. Sextus and Nathan Levy's family. It was impossible to imagine them all being destroyed.

By day it was impossible; at night Danny lay in his bunk and fretted, and when he fell asleep he dreamed unhappy dreams. He was not uneasy on his own account, since KliUrrh had said he would not be around when the lightning struck and he believed KliUrrh. He was merely uneasy. He didn't speak of this to Joel; still less would he have said anything to Maggie. But May came, and the feeling grew harder and harder to ignore.

One afternoon, as he was coming back alone from helping in the calf barn, Danny met Jack on his way in from the fields, also on foot and alone, and they fell into step together. "How's it going?" Danny asked—cautiously, for the older boy looked rumpled and out of sorts.

"Oh, I dunno. OK." Jack slouched along a few more paces, then blurted, "Does it feel to you like there's something wrong out here?"

"You too?" They stopped and stared at each other. Danny's relief at hearing his secret fears spoken aloud was so great he had to stop himself from hugging Jack. "I thought it was my imagination. I *hoped* it was."

"That's what I thought." Jack worked his shoulders to ease the stiffness there. "But this week I've been running the cultivator in the corn, tilling in fertilizer, and every day after about half an hour I just start to feel *bad*. Every fucking day! *I* can't figure out what's the matter, I love that cultivator; it's a beautiful machine. But it's like I'm *allergic* to the damn thing, or the work or something—"

"Maybe to the fertilizer?"

"Naaaah. I thought of that. I checked it out at the clinic, and I'm not."

Danny said, "We did some cultivating in agronomy, the third form did."

"What did *you* think?"

"It's like you said before, great to get through the work so fast and fantastic to think how you'd never have to worry about starving anymore, but..."

"Yeah. Nobody here is ever gonna have to go hungry. *But*."

"But—I felt the whole time like I was connected to the cultivator and not to the field or the corn."

Jack looked back down the road to the field where he had been working, hands stuck in his back pockets. "That twenty-row cultivator's a beauty," he insisted again, half-angrily, "but the damn thing makes such a commotion you can't think straight after a while. I keep catching myself thinking, it's too big, it's too heavy, it compacts the soil, the corn can hardly get its breath. You smell the fumes so strong you can't smell the dirt."

"I wouldn't have thought *you* cared all that much about smelling the dirt."

"Yeah, like I wouldn't have thought *you* couldn't center down any old time you liked!" For the first time Jack grinned. They started walking again; the grin faded. "To tell you the truth, *I* didn't think I did either—it's not like I ever *liked* farming. This is a funny place, there's a lot of things I didn't know I cared about that I found out I do. Don't get me wrong, now—" he glanced quickly at Danny "—I still think we should be using machinery at home, but lately I've been thinking—and Byron's been helping me—I've been thinking, we could build some really *little*, light farm machinery, tillers for instance, that would run on solar batteries or wind-charged batteries and be a lot quieter even than a whirligig... because there's no reason we can't design a tiller that wouldn't put much more of a barrier between you and the land than a hoe does, but would save us one hell of a lot of work and time. If I just knew a little more about it I bet I could build something even the hrossa would have to approve of, and Byron says—"

Danny thrust an oar into this stream of words: "Made out of what?"

"Pieces of what we've got in the dump, for now, and later on—didn't your dad's survey show there were minerals in the valley? Well, why couldn't we mine some of 'em? Just a little at a time, using hand tools, like they did in the old days on Earth. Iron, mainly. Maybe tin. And we'd build a forge—we wouldn't *need* much, so we could be real slow and careful. We wouldn't blast. Byron says he might come over this summer for a while, take a look at the fields and help me design some things and *then*, maybe, take it up with the hrossa."

"Wow, you've been thinking about this a *lot*!"

"Yeah, I have. So what d'you think the hrossa would say? If we had little, battery-operated machines, not the ones we were using when they first showed up in Swarthmore, or like these here—heck, three hundred people don't *need* twenty-row cultivators and moldboard plows!"

Danny tried to picture demonstrating the uses of a mechanical plow to KliUrrh. "Weeeeell...it might be worth a try at that, if you made them *really* small and *really* quiet, because *I* was just thinking, the hrossa don't object to the windmills or the generators. Matter of fact, now that I think about it, they might actually like little machines better than the idea of using draft horses—you know, living things, animals—to do our work for us.''

"Hey! I never thought of that angle!" Now Jack really grinned. "Boy, that would be great! I could really look forward to going home, for once in my life I'd have something to contribute that I felt good about."

Danny took this in with all its implications and hoped for everybody's sake that KliUrrh and the others would approve of small, quiet machines. "I've been wondering if you were gonna go home at all," he ventured now.

"They said I could stay," said Jack simply. "Before I came I told myself if I ever got out of Swarthmore I'd never come back again; but it's weird. I hadn't been here a week before I started seeing things different. My parents, for instance, and what Friends are, compared to these people, and all that. I know I'll probably feel cramped back there, but I always knew I'd want to go when the time came. And I do."

"Even if the hrossa say no about the little machines?"

"Yeah, I think so. Even then, at least for now."

To himself Danny said, *The one and only Quaker Sixer,* and smiled at Jack with enormous liking.

LESS THAN A MONTH now remained of the boys' sojourn in Sixertown. On the second Saturday in May Danny struggled through a downpour to the radio station to make his final phone call home. He concentrated hard all the way on his and Joel's plans for the afternoon, so as to hold at bay the undertone of dread, now a constant of his life, like a slight ringing in the ears. "Hi, Dad," he said, very glad this day to hear his father's voice. "Is the weather as lousy over there as it is here?"

George skipped the preliminaries. "Would it be possible for us to speak privately for a few minutes?"

Danny blinked with surprise. He turned to the tech, who hesitated, shrugged, then got up and went outside. When Danny could see him through the window he said, "OK, we're alone. What's up?"

"They'll be recording this anyway, but it can't be helped. There's something we thought you'd better know now, so you'll have time to be getting used to it before we come to get you."

Danny had been feeling fairly anxious already, and now his heart began to thump. "What's the matter? Did something bad happen?"

"I don't honestly know whether or not to call it bad. Danny, Katy's going to have a baby. It's a boy, due at the end of October." He paused to let this bombshell strike home. "She should have been infertile, but obviously something went awry... and it seems there's only one person who could possibly be the father."

Danny left the station more than half in shock. He walked blindly about in the rain—first through town at random, then out toward the beach. Katy had decided she definitely wanted to have this baby; he would be a father. A father! To be somebody's father at thirteen was—crazy, it was unimaginable! He thought, *It must have happened the day before I left, when she came hunting for me at the earthworm farm and brought me back to her room.* It was his favorite memory of Katy, the stock plot of his favorite fantasy about her; to think of this now made him walk faster over the wet sand, parallel to the colorless water, awash in confusion.

Some time later and some distance down the beach he came to himself enough to remember that Joel would be waiting for him; they were supposed to study for the chemistry exam together. But he couldn't possibly study chemistry, he couldn't sit still for a minute right now! What he needed was to wear himself out a little; and then, when he felt less unreal and his head was clearer, he needed to tell somebody—maybe some grown-up, Maggie or Nathan Levy, somebody who could be trusted not to spread it around and not to be too horrified. This person could not be Joel, and a moment's reflection explained the instinctive certainty. Joel had already had as much of Danny's weirdness as he could handle for one season, he wouldn't be able to swallow this too, not so soon after all that other stuff.

He ought to have told Joel he wasn't coming, but to head back now seemed an insupportable effort; he was halfway to the fence, and the tide would be turning soon. And he longed to be in the forest. Deciding this once to be irresponsible, Danny pushed on into the wind that plastered his red Sixer rain parka against him and was beginning to soak into his pants. He hoped Joel would forgive him—after he knew, if not before.

Danny had almost reached the fence when he spotted a figure in yellow being blown toward him—Caddie, returning from her secret place among the trees—and realized that here was exactly one Sixer he could certainly tell.

6 Crisis

On Monday morning Danny was in chemistry class, hunched over an exam he had hardly studied for at all, when the door opened and two big midshipmen in black slickers clumped into the test-taking hush. Dr. Garvey looked up in annoyance. "Sorry to bust in like this, professor," said one, "But there's a bunch of those hurrossa down at the beach, saying they want to talk to the Quaker kid."

As if he had been waiting for this to happen for weeks without knowing it, Danny was out of his seat and halfway to the door before the crewman had finished speaking, and Joel was right behind him.

"Where do you think *you're* going?" Dr. Garvey complained. "Nobody's asking to see you. Sit down there and finish that exam."

"Sorry, I've got to go too," Joel said firmly. "I'll have to do it later."

The class was growing restive. "Go on then, if you're going, and let the rest of us get on with it," he said crossly, and the boys burst through the door, pelted down the hall and out of the building into the rainy day.

A hoverjeep sat in the street outside. "I dunno," one of the middies grumbled as they caught up. "We were only supposed to get this one kid, nobody else."

"If you don't take me with you," said Joel, still firmly, "I'll run all the way to the beach and get there a couple of minutes after you do anyway, so what's the difference?"

Rain had spangled his black hair and was already beginning to darken his cobalt blue shoulders as he stood and faced them. The men shrugged at each other. "Ah, what the hell. Hop in." One of them got into the jeep and started the engine; the second stalked round to the other door but stopped with one foot still on the ground: "Hold it, here comes another one."

This was Caddie, tearing out the door with three rain parkas flapping like red, green, and yellow wings behind her. The boys made room in the back and she scrambled in next to Joel, out of breath and elated by her own boldness. Joel, who'd heard something from Danny about Saturday afternoon in the woods, slipped his friend a covert grin; but Danny sat gripping the back of the seat in front of him and stared straight ahead as the jeep lifted, zigzagged through the pattern of streets to the edge of town, then made a beeline over the broken ground toward the beach.

And there at the edge of the water, hovered round by a small group of humans, were three hrossa, and one was an elder. Even before the jeep had settled, Danny's door was open. He hit the soft sand running, staggered, recovered, and ran on; he had never seen this elder before in his life, but he dodged through the clot of slicker-clad humans and flew straight into his arms.

Awkwardly but willingly the elder gathered the stranger in. Danny pressed himself hard against the smooth gray hide, warm beneath wetness, and let the world go away—let the hross's concern and kindliness flow freely through him and drown the undertone of dread which had dogged him waking and sleeping for many weeks. He had grown used to the dread, and used to ignoring it, as old people learn to ignore their familiar aches and twinges, but now that it was gone he realized how completely dread had filled up the background of his life. He wanted to stay right where he was forever.

["Clearly this place has made you wrong,"] said the old hross calmly after a time, ["but that will pass."] His speech was so precisely like that of the western mountain hrossa Danny knew that the voices of his friends seemed to sound in this stranger's voice. He pressed closer. ["There is a message for you from KliUrrh of Lake-Between-Falls village. Are you ready to hear it?"]

Danny moaned but allowed the interval of no-thought to end. ["If it comes from KliUrrh, yes, I'm ready."] But he remained where he was.

["KliUrrh tells you that TuwukhKawan's mind is turned against this place now. If you stay with these humans he will hurt you when he hurts them. You should go away from here at once, and the other Quaker breeder must go with you."]

Danny relaxed his grip to look up at the elder. ["KliUrrh told me himself that when the trouble came I would not be here!"]

The elder conveyed serenity and assent. ["You must leave now so you will not be. Your parent will speak with you tonight—this KliUrrh has already called to him, out of the distance."]

That meant the village had united with other villages to reach the Quakers, probably during the main weekly meeting for worship. Getting several villages coordinated for a sending was difficult, and would be done only for a matter of serious urgency.

The danger must be imminent, and must have taken even Kli-Urrh by surprise. Then they would have to go. ["What's your name?"] he asked the hross. ["I want to tell KliUrrh who it was that brought his thoughts to me."]

["I am KahEemh. And you are called DanhIh, as I know."]

["KahEemh."] Danny laid his head back against the elder's no-neck neck and tightened his arms. ["Can you tell me now how TuwukhKawan will hurt these humans? KliUrrh has said many times that he did not know how it would be done."]

["We know that his attention has turned here, only that,"] said KahEemh, and saying this his inner serenity harshened and darkened. ["The land hereabouts is wrong. These humans watching us are all unaware of the wrongness, except for one only, who wonders and is troubled. All of them should leave, but I see that they will not do it."]

Danny asked eagerly, ["Which is the one that wonders?"] Had Joel been worrying too all this time?

["He,"] said the elder, and Danny followed the goggle eyes' line of sight to Byron Powell, at the very edge of the knot of Sixer onlookers. ["You know TuwukhKawan, therefore, you feel this wrongness in him. That one does not, yet he feels something. It is strange."]

["That man,"] said Danny, meeting Byron's intense gaze for a moment, ["spoke with three of the People once, and once he heard a sending."]

["That will be why,"] said KahEemh comfortably. ["And who is this other man that understands some part of what we say?"]

Danny turned within the four-barred cage of arms, then pulled free of it. Nearest to him of all the humans stood Joel, his ears almost flapping with the effort of trying to follow the conversation. Danny reached and drew him by the wrist up to the elder, saying ["This is my friend."]

The other two messengers, both adults, had been resting on the beach, letting their senior member handle things; now these rose and approached, flanking the boys, and the quick ripple of the Sixers' concern passed through them to strike Danny. "It's OK," he called over his shoulder; then to the three: ["His name is Joel."]

["Why does he love us like this, so loud? He has never seen even one of us before,"] the younger of the two adults inquired.

Joel, white with excitement and drenched to the skin—neither he nor Danny had put on the parkas Caddie brought for them—held himself straight and said, quite creditably considering, ["It's because I always feel that you are good."]

At this KahEemh stepped toward Joel and, in a series of deliberate movements, collected him into the frontal embrace he had only just learned from Danny how to do; and looking past the wet black human head beside his, he said, ["When you leave, you must bring this one away with you."] The hross's pleasure seeped into Danny, and in the alien embrace Joel gasped and gulped.

["The humans want us to go now,"] the older adult remarked in a moment; and sure enough a lean woman separated herself from the group and came toward them. "Sorry to interrupt, boys, but it's time we knew what's going on here. I'm Maria Esposito, Danny—First Officer of the *Down Plus Six*."

He had heard Maggie speak of this person. "They're saying the danger is here now, and Jack and I should go home. I guess you know what they mean by 'the danger.'"

"I heard about it." Maria looked at the tableau of hross elder and wet Sixer boy and frowned. "Joel," she said sharply, "break it up now. If the message has been delivered, then I think it's time these—visitors were pushing off, unless they have another purpose in coming here."

At once KahEemh said to Danny, ["We will go away now, as this person wishes. Perhaps you and I will meet in a better place one day."] Gently he released Joel, and turned, and the three hrossa walked together out into the water and began to swim, bobbing through the breakers, then striking south and east. In the salt water they did not sound, but swam with their heads well out, making good time nevertheless. The sadness and kindliness of their presence faded as they grew smaller and more blurred by the falling rain. Then a far curve of the bay cut them off, and it was done.

Beside Danny a radiant Joel was gabbling to anyone who would listen, "I could *understand* them, I really could follow it pretty well! Did you see how they talk with the tops of their heads so you can't watch their whaddyacallums move, well, I always thought that would make it a lot harder to get what they were saying but you can *feel* so much it doesn't matter!" And to Danny, "I'm gonna go talk to my mom and dad *right now*."

"Wait a minute, hold everything," Maria interrupted. "I need a report before you go anywhere, please, and I need it from both of you."

All the others crowded in closer: Byron, three ship's officers, the two midshipmen incongruous with sidearms who had been patrolling the beach when the hrossa arrived, and Caddie. To this audience Danny said: "My father will be coming to pick up Jack and me right away—tonight or tomorrow I think, anyway he's supposed to radio in tonight. They don't know what the danger is either, but the elder, KahEemh, he says the land is sick. It is sick." Danny said, and fired his clear look at Maria, expressionless in her shiny slicker. "KahEemh says all of you should leave, but that he doesn't think you will. And he wants Joel to go with us. And that's all he said."

"Is that a fair account?" Maria asked Joel.

He nodded. "I didn't get it all, but I picked up the feelings— couldn't you *feel* them worrying about you?"

The others eyed one another. Maria said, "OK, that's enough for now. You kids go home and get some dry clothes on. I'm going to report to the captain. If we need to get hold of you again before tonight, Danny, will you be at Maggie's place packing?"

"Well, for a while, but I haven't got that much to pack and I have to tell Jack about it."

"Better stick close to home all the same, so we can find you fast if we want you." Without waiting for him to agree, Maria started up toward the car, waving the crewmen to follow. But Byron stayed, and Caddie came up now and gave the boys their rain parkas.

"I'm gonna go talk to Dad," Joel repeated as he struggled into his. "Hey, how come you didn't tell *me* the land was sick? What's the matter with it?"

Caddie said, "I want to come too."

For the first time that day both boys really looked at Caddie. After a lame moment Danny said, "To Swarthmore?" She nodded. "To stay, you mean? Are you sure?"

"Sure I'm sure. The Tillotsons don't really need me. I want to come."

"Why?" Byron put in from the sidelines, and at the same instant Joel asked, "What *for*?"

Caddie looked stubborn. "I just do."

Joel snorted, breaking the awkward silence: "She thinks the hrossa are *unicorns*, that's why she wants to come—'The something something things on the sea,' remember? 'Tendons of cable—'"

Caddie turned pink. "I do not! Don't be a dope."

A gust of wind blew the rain sideways and Danny shuddered; he was freezing. Byron, still standing by, now took charge. "You guys go home now and change, like Maria said. If we were on Earth you'd catch some bug or other for sure. I'll find Jack for you, Danny, and tell him to get ready."

Danny dragged his parka on, shaking almost too hard to find the sleeve holes, and asked through the chattering teeth, "How did *you* find out the hrossa were here?"

Byron looked out across the lead-colored water. "I was driving back to school from the farm—I'm supposed to be teaching a shop class"—he checked his watch—"right now. I was way across town when they came ashore, but I knew what it was the minute I felt it—but by the time I got down here the patrol had already called admin, so I never got a chance to talk to them myself."

"I think you should come with us too," said Danny.

Byron looked grim. "To Swarthmore? I want to, I won't lie to you. Getting permission's another matter."

"Come anyway," said Joel stoutly; *he* meant to go with Danny with or without permission.

"You know Danny's father's not going to take *you* out of here without your parents' say-so, don't you?" He gave Danny's shivering form a gentle shove. "Go home and hit the showers, kid. We've all got things to see to; we can talk later. You go on home too, Caddie. Don't worry, we won't forget about you."

Joel started to run backward up the beach. "*I'm* coming if I have to *stow away*," he yelled.

Separately they all headed up to the street above the beach, striking it at the four points nearest their different destinations; and once on the pavement Danny went fast. He got home in three minutes flat, pounded up the stairs, and dropped the parka and his sodden shoes outside on the balcony. He extracted the key with difficulty from his deep wet pocket and let himself in, then stood just inside the door, shaking violently, while he stripped off the rest of his drenched clothing. His breath hissed in and out between his clicking teeth.

He had peeled his socks off and was kicking off his pants when the bathroom door opened and Maggie's head, its wet hair rubbed into a brown-gray rat's nest, poked through the crack. "Danny! I thought I heard the door—why aren't you in school? You're sopping wet, you must be frozen."

"I am," he chattered. Maggie's head disappeared; in a moment she came out in her dressing gown, with a big dry towel—

and at that instant Danny experienced a vivid flashback: the memory of the morning, nearly a year before, when he had stood on the bank of the dammed crook in a plastic poncho and seen Maggie step out of the bathhouse on the opposite bank and dive into the pond, and had called to her through the driving rain, "You're not supposed to *dive* in!"

Thinking of that day, he felt old. At the same time he felt more like that boy on the bluff than he'd felt in weeks and weeks and weeks. He was all of a piece again now; the old hross had restored him to himself. Even about Katy and her baby he felt calm. The clammy shirt came loose over his head; he pulled his face from it and said, "I'm going home. Tonight or tomorrow, not next month. Some hrossa were here . . . I've got to go now."

"Hrossa? *Here?*"

"Yes." He dropped the shirt; and then, in his oldness and wholeness and Quaker hrossness, pulled off his underpants and dropped them too, then scooped up the whole pile and heaved it out onto the balcony and closed the door. He took the towel from Maggie's hand and began to rub down hard, to warm himself; and Maggie stood by, not talking and not leaving.

HALF OF SIXTERTOWN seemed crowded into the blue cube of Maggie's sitting room. Since there weren't enough chairs or sofa seats to go around, those with young bones had lined up on the floor along one carpeted wall. Back in Danny's room his duffels lay like split sausages on the bed, hastily stuffed with everything he had brought in or acquired in the town except the clothes that had been whisked from the balcony to the laundry for speedy treatment; when those were fitted in somehow he would be packed. He sat crosslegged on the floor with Jack, Joel, and Caddie. In seats above the level of the floor were Maggie, Ben and Becky Adler, Byron Powell, Maria Esposito, June Tillotson, and a bony man a little older than Byron, named Gerald McWhirter, whom Maria had brought with her to the gathering. The room was crammed with people and nervous tension.

Maggie had handed round cups of tea and other drinks, but the occasion did not feel much like a social one. It was already late afternoon, and a number of important decisions had to be taken before this day had ended. No one knew whether contact with Swarthmore was to come from the settlement via satellite, as usual, or from a lander en route to pick up Danny and Jack, or at all; Sixertown had been unable to raise Swarthmore, during the satellite's one o'clock orbit, to confirm the hrossa's message. They had nothing to go on but the information that had been passed to Danny by KahEemh, and few of those present put much store in that. A radio operator was standing by to establish contact at the next pass, around six. If he succeeded the people in Maggie's flat would be the first to know. Meanwhile there was plenty for them to discuss.

Under other circumstances a visit from three hrossa would by this time have created a clamor of general interest in the town. But the weather had kept them from being noticed, and the fact that the visitors had stayed so briefly, and never left the beach, and had therefore been seen by very few people, had helped keep the lid on the news. Of course the entire third form knew about it, so by evening there would be plenty of curious inquiries; but for now the eleven people most concerned with the visit could get down to their business undisturbed.

These people wanted close to eleven different things, which made the conference hard to run. As ranking officer Maria assumed charge of it—of running it, that is; for in a real sense the central figure was Danny. Of all those present in the blue room, he was the calmest. The deep contact with the hross seemed to shield him; he did not feel pressured by what the others wanted. "They said it to us when we got here, and they said it to you—to you and you," he was saying, bobbing his head toward Maggie on one side of the room and Byron on the other. "It's the very same message. Humans on Pennterra have to, one, live in the Delaware Valley, two, not use machinery, and three, keep their numbers the same, or they'll be destroyed."

"Except that now they're saying it's actually under way—that the destruction is in progress *now*?"

"That's right."

"They said, 'The land is sick.'"

"Yes. Well, [KehEemh] really used a word that means more like 'wrong.'"

"And when you reported that to me this morning, you said 'It is sick.' What did you mean by that?"

"I meant that when I'm out in the fields I *feel* like something's wrong, I feel bad. Jack does too."

"Is that right?" Maria made a quarter turn to look at Jack, who nodded. "What can you tell us about it? What do you mean, 'feel bad'?"

"It's just like Danny says. We've both done a lot of farm work at home, and I never felt that kind of thing coming up at me out of the ground—like when you can't decide whether you're sick or not, or like you had all your clothes on backward." He wriggled in his place. "I was bothered by it most when I was running the cultivator."

Maria pounced on this. "In other words, when you were using heavy machinery to farm—is that what you're saying?"

Jack looked surprised. "Maybe I am."

"Don't tell me you hadn't considered that." Maria didn't bother to hide her disbelief.

"But I didn't," said Jack surprised still more. "I *like* machines. I don't like farming without them, I think it's stupid. Do you mean," Jack started to get red, "you think we're *pretending* we feel something, to try and make you believe the hrossa were right?"

"I don't think anything yet," said Maria, unperturbed. "Did either of you mention these impressions of something being wrong to anyone else?"

Jack said, "I only mentioned it to Danny. I nearly told Dave and Byron a couple of times, but I didn't think they'd believe me—I thought they'd just figure there was something wrong with *me*."

Maria raised one eyebrow. "Why tell Danny, then? Why wouldn't he have the same reaction?" Unless you two are in cahoots, was what her tone implied; and Danny saw Jack look down and wait before answering, fighting to keep his temper.

"Even if Danny did think I was crazy," Jack said quietly when he looked up again, "he'd be nice about it and try to help. And also I remember thinking, if there is something wrong, not with me but in the fields, maybe he'll feel it too. He senses stuff. People tell him things they don't tell anybody else." He sent Danny a private grin that said, *Boy did I used to hate you for that!*

Maria now switched her attention back to the paragon. "You didn't mention your qualms to anybody either, I take it?" Danny shook his head. "Because you thought no one would believe you?" He nodded. "Not even Maggie?"

"Don't blame Danny for that," Maggie interposed. "He's been trying to tell me for months that our sterility problem might be linked with the hross warning, and I've slapped him down every time he said so, so it's not too likely he'd run to me about it if he thought there was something wrong out there."

Maria looked hard at Maggie from under her black eyebrows. "Are you saying you think now there may be a link?"

"No," said Maggie curtly. Danny, watching Joel's face, knew he was wondering again why *he* had heard nothing about these sick fields. Danny felt a pang; but Joel had represented hours and hours of escape from an otherwise chronic anxiety, and telling would have ruined that—there would then have been no way at all to get free of it.

"I wish one of you had mentioned it to me," Byron now offered.

Maria's head snapped around. "What's that? Are you saying *you* picked something up, Lieutenant?"

"That's right. I did—and thought it was all in my head. I've been feeling something, off and on, ever since the crops went in, and I'll tell you right now I'm mighty relieved to hear I'm not the only one."

McWhirter now stirred and spoke. "I don't think *I'd* be relieved, in your shoes." He turned and addressed Maria: "So the, ah, susceptible people seem to be these Quaker boys, and a guy who was knocked off his feet by the meeting with the natives last summer, and nobody else, am I right?" He glanced around the room. "Maggie, you were exposed to the hrossa. Any problems?"

"I haven't felt anything like Byron and the kids are describing, no. However, you ought to bear two facts in mind. One, I haven't gone near the fields all spring, and two, I've been working on a very disquieting and absorbing medical problem. I doubt very much if you can draw any useful inferences from me."

"I do, all the same," said McWhirter, and Maggie gave him an intensely irritated glare. On the present issue they were substantially in agreement, but as usual they rubbed each other the wrong way.

Ordinarily Maggie didn't find Maria quite so exasperating. However, it was plain to everyone that Maggie thought the first officer's inquisitor's manner toward the boys offensive. "Danny, you didn't mention Maggie's problem to the hrossa this morning, did you?" Maria was asking now; and Danny watched Maggie glower and shift her position in her chair at the insinuating tone. Jack minded it too, and had to keep struggling not to get rattled or flare up. Funny, Danny thought, that he didn't mind more himself; but Maggie's own indignation made him feel warm, after the many weeks of relative coolness between them.

Finally Maria settled back, folded her arms, and stared into the middle distance. "OK. Then as far as I can make out, there's still no hard and no significant soft evidence of problems here in town, other than the sterility problem, at this time. Anybody disagree?"

"I do," said Byron, "but I guess I'm not considered a credible witness."

"Not without somebody else to back you up," Maria agreed bluntly. "Somebody who's never been anywhere near the natives at all. On the other hand, we shouldn't rule out the possibility that other people have been picking up signals and keeping quiet about it for the same reason you all did. We can put out a bulletin on that, and I think for the sake of completeness we ought to."

"There's another thing that should be pointed out," said McWhirter. "The fact that we've been keeping ourselves to ourselves could very well be the only reason we *don't* have more problems. If we hadn't steered clear of the natives we might all be getting bellyaches every time we drove out past a wheatfield."

Maria nodded. "I'd agree with that. Point noted."

Everyone at the meeting now understood the lines of contention. *Either* there was a real danger, which contact with the hrossa enabled Danny, Jack, and Byron to perceive; or these three had been deluded through contact with the hrossa into perceiving a problem where none existed. The evidence was exactly the same in either case; how you interpreted it depended on who you were. There was no way to adjudicate the question without more evidence of a different sort, and Maria didn't waste time trying. She stretched and glanced at her watch. "Now then, the next thing is the question of the kids who want to go back with Jack and Danny. Supposing the Quakers agree to take them, what do you parents and guardians say about it?"

June Tillotson said simply, "Caddie can go if she's positive it's what she wants."

McWhirter said, "I'm not a parent or a guardian, but I do have the interests of the colony's future at heart and I just want to say I think it would be a big, maybe a tragic, mistake to let any of our kids go over to Swarthmore."

Ben Adler uncrossed his long legs and sat forward. "I appreciate that, Jerry, though I feel I know Danny well enough to doubt the justice of what you imply. Now Becky and I don't object to a visit in principle. But the timing's hardly the best—if Joel and Caddie skip their exams, they'll have to be given a whole new set when they come back, which is a lot to ask their teachers to do. Why not stick to the original plan—pay Danny a visit later on in the summer?''

"I told you, he said *now*," Joel insisted.

Maria cocked an eyebrow. "So you're just planning to take off and leave your family to weather the storm without you, is that it?"

Joel's face crumpled. Ben interrupted, sternly for such a mild-mannered man: "Cut it out, Maria, that's the wrong tactic to use on this boy." Maggie flounced in her seat and beamed at Ben, but Maria didn't so much as blink.

Joel said, furious, "But they *won't* come with me, they don't think the hrossa know anything! If I get through OK, then maybe I can come back later on and—and help somehow—"

"Sounds like they've convinced you trouble's on the way." Maria succeeded in lacing this with so much irony that every adult in the room except McWhirter was put out.

"All I'm *really* convinced of," said Joel with unexpected dignity, gazing at the blue floor, "is that KahEemh wants to keep me safe. And so I want to let him, by doing what he says." McWhirter snorted; Joel's parents exchanged a worried look with Maggie.

"I just don't know, Joel," said Becky. "We're being rushed to decide something that might be really important, and *we* want to keep you safe too, don't forget. I'm sure you'll be in excellent hands"—she smiled nervously at Danny—"but there's something about the whole situation I don't like."

"Mom, I just have to go," said Joel in an agonized way. His mother shook her head, perplexed.

"Wouldn't we do well to wait and see what the Quakers say?" Maggie suggested.

"We'll have to, of course, but it can't hurt to spell the issues out beforehand and see where we stand." Maria looked at June and at the Adlers. "It doesn't seem to have occurred to any of you that the captain may have something to say too about letting the kids go. I'm not sure this is something the three of you will be allowed to decide entirely by yourselves. As for you, Byron—you've applied for leave to go with them—I'd definitely not count on it. As Jerry's reminded us, these matters do have import for the whole community."

McWhirter nodded his strong approval of this speech, but "You don't need to sound so smug about it," Becky said a little hotly. The idea that she and Ben wouldn't be allowed to make a decision about Joel on their own—without consulting the admin people—had not, in fact, occurred to her.

"It was the same with us," said Danny. "Dad and Jack's parents had the final say, but before that the meeting debated it for hours."

"Days," said Jack. Maria's eyebrows went up.

At that moment they all heard someone running up the steps, and by the time Maggie got to the door the radio tech had already pounded on it several times. "We got through," he panted, and then, "I have to get back, there's nobody on duty." He rushed away. The room was suddenly bustling with people donning rain gear and finding umbrellas.

"Are we *all* going?" Maria inquired, clearly hoping some of them would say no; but when nobody did she said, "I brought a van, I can take all the adults anyway, but the kids will have to hoof it."

"Not Danny," Maggie objected. "He's first on the line to George, he shouldn't be all out of breath." So Danny piled in the very back with Byron, June Tillotson, and Maggie, and sat on Byron's lap, and they covered the three short blocks to the station in a crammed, strained silence.

The three runners arrived in a panting pack just as the overloaded van settled in front of the station. "Don't anybody faint if all this is news to Swarthmore," McWhirter said; but Danny felt Byron's arm tighten around him in a little quasi-hug of reassurance as he moved to crawl out.

When the whole mob had crowded into the little control room, Danny sat down before the speaker and said, "Dad?"

"I assume this call means the hrossa have managed to contact you," was the first thing George said. A stir went through the group, for the biggest uncertainty had now been settled. "I came in a few minutes ago to put a call through to you and found your man at that end trying to get our attention over here. Nobody was on the radio after lunch today—I'd have been here, or sent somebody, but I didn't expect the hrossa to get to you so fast." George was speaking rapidly and sounded harried. "I meant to make an in-flight call tonight, but we've got some problems, Danny. The big lander's in the shop, and Joe and Gus took the little one up yesterday morning before the sending, to make an orbit correction, and that means I can't come and get you tonight, unless they get the malfunction fixed in the next couple of hours. The damn thing would pick today."

"When can Joe and Gus get back from the *Woolman*?"

"Tomorrow night or Fourday morning—not soon enough; we want you guys out of there pronto. Is anybody in authority there with you?"

Maria pushed forward and leaned toward the speaker. "Maria Esposito here, Dr. Quinlan. I'm the first officer. You're about to request a lander and pilot to convey the boys to Swarthmore, am I right?"

"Yes—if you deck the request all over with apologies, chagrin, frustration, and abjectness at our inability to explain what the fuss is all about."

Maria smiled briefly. "I don't have authority to release a lander myself, I'll have to consult with Captain Harrison. He's expecting a report as soon as we establish contact, so I can get you an answer fast. Will you stand by?"

"Indeed I will. And thanks a million."

"While we're working on that one," said Maria, "here's something for you people to be thinking over. Two of our own kids would like to come back with your two. If we decide to let them come, would you be able and willing to take them in for—shall we say, a visit of indefinite length?"

There was a little silence. "Commander, we'd gladly take any or all of you in for a visit of indefinite length, if you'd only come."

"I'll have a word with the captain, then," she said. She yielded the speaker to Danny again and worked her way back through the crowd to the door. "Jerry, better come with me."

"Is Maggie in the station?" asked George.

"Yep. Shall I put her on?"

"Just tell her that if the Sixers bring you home, I do *most particularly* urge her to come along too, even if it's only just for the ride. And the rest of Joel's family—I'm assuming Joel's one of the two kids. And Danny—if they can't let us have a lander, and we can't get this glorified bucket of bolts repaired in time to fetch you in the morning, you and Jack start walking. Start tomorrow, as soon as you've checked in with us by the eight o'clock satellite. Head west along the shoreline, it's fairly easy walking for fifty klicks or so by the look of the aerial photos we took when we brought you over. We'll locate you and pick you up in a day or two at the most; but the main thing is for you to get the hell *out* of there, even if it's still pouring. Bundle up good and pack some supplies. We'll come back for your other things in a while."

"OK," said Danny. "When do you think all this is finally going to make some sense? I sure am tired of telling people something awful's going to happen but I don't know what."

"You and me both, but if it's going on already, as the hrossa claim, then *what* it is ought to be clear pretty soon. Anything new on that stuff in the creek water, by the way?"

"No. I didn't think to ask the hrossa, and anyway if I *had* thought to I wouldn't have, because I would have known Maggie wouldn't want me to say anything about it to them. Dad, how did [KliUrrh] get through to those hrossa that came here? There's no village around here, they must have had to come a pretty long way. How'd they get the message, and how'd they know to ask for me by name?"

"Sequential sendings? The same message we got, passed along from village to village? Your guess is as good as mine."

A presence appeared at Danny's shoulder. "George, this is Maggie. How could a telepathic message be passed that far, that many times, without the risk of its content being changed? Remember that old game, 'Telephone'?"

"Hi, Maggie! Not analogous. 'Telephone' messages have cognitive content, they rely on accurate hearing; a hross sending is just shaped feelings, plus the odd single word or image. The same rules wouldn't apply. Are you coming with Danny? Please do!"

"Not if I have to walk." At this sign of weakening Danny bounced a little in his chair.

Now the conversation took a general turn. Joel's parents came up to introduce themselves and cautiously discuss the matter of Joel's visiting Swarthmore, though declining on their own account. George emphasized how happy the settlement would be to have Joel; he did not waste breath pushing the safety factor, though it was implicit in his saying several times that if Ben and Becky should change their minds and decide to come anyway they would be very welcome. Then Lynn Wister arrived at the station in Swarthmore and spoke with Jack while George went to check on the progress of the lander repair crew; but no progress had as yet been made.

Finally Maria reappeared, and with her instead of McWhirter was the captain himself. He was a middle-aged man with a strong face and iron-gray hair. Danny had never seen him before. For some reason he was in full uniform, and made a trim and formal appearance among the group of mussed, slicker-clad interested parties. He approached the speaker and settled smoothly into the chair Danny vacated for him. "Dr. Quinlan, this is Captain Harrison speaking. I'm going to ask you myself if you Quakers are fully as ignorant as you claim to be about the nature of the danger these indigenes think we are facing." Even his voice came straight from central casting.

"You know everything we know about it, and most of what we speculate. There's no hard evidence, but many of us—not all—feel we have excellent reason to trust the hrossa when they are as certain about something as they are about this. That's absolutely all I can tell you."

The captain nodded once, crisply. "All right. I'm going to put out a bulletin this evening. All our people will be informed of what you've told us and given the chance to leave. We'll put all our landers to work ferrying people over to you tomorrow if anybody wants to go. Frankly, I don't think any will, but the offer will be made. And in any case we'll send your boys home in the morning."

"We're extremely grateful to you," said George, and Jack's mother also thanked the captain, their relief sounding clearly through the speaker.

"I want to say that I do appreciate your concern for us over there, and your willingness to take us in," the captain added. "You folks have had reason and opportunity to form a judgment of the natives' credibility, I know. Some of our people are still talking thought control, but I admit now that we may have erred on the side of caution where these creatures are concerned."

"I'm very much afraid," George said soberly, "that your error at this time is not to be cautious enough. If you were to *order* the town evacuated, and it turns out we were wrong, you only lose a little time and look a little silly; if *you're* wrong I think it'll be worse than that."

"Well, we don't see eye to eye here, but we won't force choices on one another either. Your boys will go off in the morning—and let's keep in touch, shall we?"

THE CAPTAIN'S all-points bulletin appeared that evening in the form of a special edition of the *Home Town News*: a single sheet describing the visit of the hrossa and listing points for and against evacuating. It also contained an offer of transportation to Swarthmore, without penalty or prejudice, for anyone who felt the hrossa's warning should be taken seriously in light of the facts, i.e., definite contamination of the water supply and hints of what might be construed as trouble in the croplands. There was also an appeal for anyone who had felt ill or upset when in and about the planted acreages to come forward.

The bulletin's presentation was fair, but nothing in it came as news to the Sixers by the time it had been distributed, and the appeal produced only a few mothers' reports of young children who had seemed fretful at the farm (and everywhere else they were taken, very likely). People who had chosen voluntarily to spend five years on a colony ship took little notice of mere rumors and hints of danger. They knew all about actual danger, and had long since come to terms with fear.

So the group that climbed aboard the single lander on Tuesday morning consisted only of Danny and Jack, Joel and Caddie, Maggie, and Byron, who would pilot them. He was to fly Maggie and Joel back in a few days' time, and it was a measure of his standing with the officers that none of them, even Mc-Whirter, doubted he would do this. Caddie could come back with them too, if she changed her mind. A promise had been extracted from Joel that he would return without fail, unless overwhelmingly persuaded by developments that it would be wrong to do so. His parents had in fact been on the verge of deciding that one of them should go with him after all; but several calves were having digestive difficulties—hairballs were suspected, which might require surgery—and they had still been discussing the question when Heather contrived to fall off the second-story balcony of the domicile while tightrope-walking the railing and break her arm.

Ben and Becky, and Heather in her cast, had come to see Joel and Danny off, and none of the three even pretended to be happy about it. The Tillotsons had brought the baby; Caddie held him and couldn't stop crying, though she still insisted she wanted to go. Maggie looked grim—wanting to see George too much to turn down this chance, but badly hating to give the appearance of fleeing from danger. Byron's face too was sober. Only Joel, Danny, and Jack, of all the travelers and seers-off, appeared happy at all.

Danny said to himself, as he waved to Joel's family through the port, that despite everything he clearly did not believe even now that disaster was really about to strike the people of Sixertown. If he believed it, then wouldn't the prospect of leaving these loved three to their fate fill him with grief? Instead he was filled with exhilaration.

Byron closed and sealed the hatch, and the people on the ground moved back behind the shields as he started the engines and prepared the lander for vertical takeoff. In the seconds before they broke through the clouds, Danny looked as hard as he could to catch and keep this last broad view of the place that for the past four months had been his home. The view his window gave him took in a graphpaper scrap of the town, the tainted creek kinking down to the long line of coast, the new town straddling its small river up along the bay, the green expanse of troubled fields, and then the vast grayish sea. He looked down upon it all much as Maggie and Byron had looked upon Swarthmore a year before, and told himself that everything he saw might have vanished into rubble before the lander was to return, but still he could not believe it. He felt affection and gratitude toward the double town for what it had taught him, but also exhaustion at the manifold contradictions of his life there, and was glad clear through to be leaving now.

For a long time after takeoff each passenger sat silent, absorbed in his or her own thoughts. Joel, his escape effected, now seemed gripped by reaction; plainly he didn't feel like talking and Danny left him alone. Caddie soon stopped crying but stared out of her own port, though for an hour or more there was nothing to see but blue sky above a rumpled floor of sunlit cloud. Jack sat up front with Byron, and Maggie was reading.

Left without willing companionship, Danny settled back in his seat and began to daydream about how it would be when he brought Joel to the village to meet KliUrrh and SwikhKarrh—an enjoyable fantasy that presently faded or merged into serious thoughts about Katy and her baby. Joel would have to be told about that now, everyone else in Swarthmore must know already. He himself would have to finish taking in the reality of it. How great it would be to see Katy again, though—still the one human in the world who knew him best and accepted the peculiar mix of things he was with the fewest reservations. If he *had* to be the father of somebody's baby right now, he could at least be glad the baby was hers. He could feel a small lift, even, at the thought that Katy *wanted* this baby that she and he had made between them—

The lander coughed and bumped, coughed and bumped, snapping the passengers out of their private reveries into a common tension. Byron's hands had become very busy at the controls, but nothing they did seemed to have any effect on the hiccuping motion of the lander. A long minute went by, then another; then the lander stopped bucking and began to lose altitude.

Byron swore, "One of the engines has cut right out. Hang on, everybody, I'll have to take her down."

7   *In the Wilderness*

An hour later a group of scared-looking people stood or sat or lay on the littered ground, listening to Byron explain why their vehicle had been crippled in the crash landing. Below the clouds, unbroken forest stretched in every direction. After searching to the limits of his single engine's remaining range for an open place, Byron had been forced to bring them down into the trees, and something called a booster tube had caught in the branches and snapped off. Repairing the engine itself would be a breeze, but the ship would not be able to take off. They were stranded.

Byron had done his best, kept the lander's nose up and the power pack undamaged. An interior steel panel, jolted loose by the first hard impact, had given Joel a deep cut above one eye and a hard thwack on the opposite knee, which was already badly bruised and swollen. But his were the only injuries more serious than a bad scare, and Maggie had promptly bandaged the cut, popped a bag of ice from the galley onto the knee, made a pallet for Joel on the ground, and promised him he would be all right in a couple of days. It might have been a great deal worse.

Still, there was no denying that they were in trouble. Danny, shaken and frightened as anyone, saw nevertheless that Maggie and Byron—while trying to make the four kids feel reassured—were shaken up and very worried themselves, and far from certain how this episode would end. Byron also felt terrible about having dumped the lander and damaged it. Danny's own first impulse was to cast about for the presence of hrossa within sending range of the crash site, but he could pick up no trace of them. Had there been a hross village anywhere nearby, its members might sooner or later become aware that humans and destroyed vegetation now existed where neither belonged and decide to investigate; but Swarthmore must be their best hope of immediate rescue.

"We can't be more than four hundred klicks from Swarthmore at most," Byron said, "and we might be quite a lot closer— I don't know just how far we crippled along before we came down—but even four hundred klicks is within whirligig range, barely. Now, I doubt anybody in a gig could see us from the air unless they flew directly overhead, we're pretty well hidden under the trees in spite of these ones here that we brought down with us. *But*—" he stressed the word "—they know our flight plan in Sixertown, so the Quakers will know right where to start looking."

The kids were silent, taking this in.

"Now then," Byron said, trying hard to sound brisk and competent, "I think the first thing for me to do is to get that engine working again, because we want to be able to charge it up good and fast. Jack, you can give me a hand with that. We haven't got the power to bounce a signal off the satellite, even if I knew when and where to find it, but we'll want to keep somebody on the radio right through the daylight hours, once people have had a chance to start searching for us."

"And I," said Maggie, "am going to reconnoiter our supplies. The galley didn't get fitted out for this excursion, worse luck, we left in too big a hurry, but there's a fairish stock of dehydrated staples. We won't starve yet awhile. Water's a *bit* of a problem, though—there's some, but not a lot. I noticed the tank hadn't been topped off when I was cleaning up Joel's cut."

"Water shouldn't be a problem," said Danny brightly. "You're never very far from water on Pennterra. Why don't Caddie and I go see if we can find some?"

"No," said Maggie quickly, and her own pose of brisk efficiency cracked for a second. "Let's not get separated just yet. If you should get beyond earshot in this wilderness we might never find you."

Uneasily they looked about them. The local forest consisted chiefly of a kind of tree Danny could not recall having seen before, one with a tall, thick, smooth, beechlike bole. Its spindly branches, set high on the trunk, supported huge umbrella-shaped leaves that screened out so much of the light that now at broad midday they stood in semi-twilight.

In this the woods resembled a jungle, but in no other way. Like other forms of Pennterran vegetation the trees did not attempt to crowd or jostle one another. Their crowns were regularly shaped and the ground beneath them was quite clear, almost parklike, though at the bases of some large trees Danny noted (and understood) the presence of a single suckerlike sapling, springing up from the roots like this season's blackberry cane beside the second-year cane it will replace; and where this occurred the foliage above the sapling was thinner. Elsewhere the leaves of each tree touched those of its neighbors, and the canopy spread out laterally, nearly unbroken, five or six meters above the ground.

Owing to the openness and lack of undergrowth they could see through the dim forest of trunks for a fair distance. But in all directions it looked the same, and from the air they had all seen that it seemed to stretch out forever from the point of their crash. Getting lost would be extremely easy, that was obvious.

When the silence threatened to stretch out as far as the forest, Caddie spoke up pluckily: "We'll blaze a trail. We won't get lost. Come on, Maggie—it'll give us something to do while the rest of you are working."

Maggie could be seen to acknowledge to herself that keeping all the mobile kids busy was a good idea. "Well, if you're very careful...does any of us have a pocket knife? There must be some kind of knife or cleaver in the galley you could use."

"We mustn't cut the trees," said Danny firmly. "We can use something else to blaze a trail, like white paint—I guess there probably isn't any paint aboard, though."

"I wouldn't risk bread crumbs if I were you, Hansel," said Jack, and they smiled in a strained way at this feeble attempt at humor. "What about a can of oil and a stick?"

Byron vetoed that. "Oil wouldn't show up well enough; it's too dark down under here. Why don't you want to cut the trees, Danny?"

Instead of answering Danny said, "Hey, I've got it—hold on a second." He climbed, with difficulty, back into the lander, which was canted on one side with the trunks and crowns of two trees crumpled beneath it, and reappeared shortly carrying his thick white pullover and a butcher knife. "We can unravel this and tie pieces of yarn around the trunks, it's too small for me now anyway." He tossed the sweater down to Caddie, dropped the knife carefully, and climbed back down; then he retrieved the knife and sawed at the sweater's waistband until a length of kinked-up yarn could be pulled free. "See? We can cut off pieces as we go." With a regretful glance at Joel, lying on the ground with his one visible eye closed, he said gallantly to Caddie,

"Come on, you unravel and I'll tie," and to Maggie, "We won't go far, don't worry."

The land at the site of the crash looked almost equally flat in every direction, but Danny picked the one with the closest resemblance to a slope and set off. Walking in the open forest was easy despite the gloom. After fifty meters or so, with the lander still in plain view, Danny ran the loose end of yarn around a fat trunk, tied it, and sawed it off.

"We're gonna use sweaters up fast at this rate," said Caddie as she measured out nearly a meter of yarn; and in fact the method had drawbacks as applied to these trees, with their thick boles, very high branches, and smooth bark where no scrap of wool could be securely snagged. They moved on down the slight incline, stopped, Caddie unraveled and Danny tied off, and now they could no longer see the lander. In this way they worked along, keeping every woolen blaze on a line of sight from the next. They were as thrifty as possible with the yarn, but after a slow hour the sweater had vanished and they had not found water.

Danny went back to the lander for a second sweater, a gray one, and now their luck improved. Half the back and both sleeves were still left of it when their progress brought them over the lip of a shallow valley with a tiny streamlet at the bottom. It was not much more than a trickle, and hauling water that distance for very long would be no joke, but having thought one important problem through to a solution made them all feel more confident. Though rescue could be expected in a day or two, it was good not to have to conserve water too grimly in case the gigs from Swarthmore should be delayed.

Bedding down in the tilted lander proved impossible. Instead, as the day waned, Byron pried loose and tossed down the cushions from the seats, and they made beds for themselves under the propped-up lander's belly. Nobody slept well, but Joel had the worst night despite the sedative Maggie had given him, and by morning was in so much pain that she suspected the flying panel must have fractured his patella. He needed attention and treatment, but there was little she could do for him except keep him quiet and dose him with headache pills. Toward morning it rained, enough to put several centimeters of water in the bottoms of the bowls and pans Maggie had set out and to thoroughly dampen the jackets and dressing gowns most of the stranded travelers were using for bedclothes (for only two blankets had been found in the lander's locker, and Joel got both of

those). They began the day stiff and bedraggled yet in fairly
cheerful spirits; for by now the search would surely have been
mounted, and they all had high hopes of spending the next night
dry and safe in Swarthmore.

But that day, and the next, and the next, their hopes were disappointed. Five days after the accident they had still failed to
raise anyone on the radio. Dead wood had been collected and
dried, and a signal fire laid and covered with a plastic sheet,
ready to torch at the first wispy sound of a whirligig motor, but
not once had one been heard.

While outside in the world it rained and rained, inside the
lander the water tank went dry. The rainwater catchments were
poured in and used for dishwater. They all walked down to the
creek to wash—Caddie and Jack had dammed up a little pool for
the purpose—and carried back just enough water in small con-
tainers to reconstitute each day's meals.

These got smaller, then much smaller. At dinner on the fifth
day Maggie announced that in a few more days the cupboard
would be bare.

"We're going to have to do something," Byron admitted to the
circle of pinched faces. "I won't try to fool you kids, we're in a
tight spot here. I don't know why nobody's managed to find us
yet, but it's time we stopped just moping around waiting—some
of us better try to walk out of here before we run right out of
food."

"Somebody's got to stay with the lander and man the radio,"
said Maggie, "and somebody's got to look after Joel. Byron and
I agree that it makes sense for me to be that somebody, and for
him to try to lead some of the rest of you out of these woods."

"Danny's father told him and Jack to start walking along the
shore if we couldn't bring them home, so Maggie and I figure the
best plan is for me, and whoever comes with me, to try to get out
to the coast. Visibility's no problem there, at least, and Maggie
thinks they'll likely be looking for us there."

Danny nodded. "Dad would think like that. He'd remember
what he said and expect me to remember."

Jack frowned. "How're we gonna know where the coast *is*?
You can't even see the sun from under here, with all this overcast, let alone the stars. I can't tell north from east from anywhere, can you?"

"That's a problem," Byron said frankly. "The lander compass works on the battery, and even if it didn't it would be too
heavy to pack along. I know we were bearing almost due west,

about eighty kilometers inland and parallel to the coast, when we lost the engine. But after that I was hunting a clear place to put down, without reference to my bearing. But we weren't in view of the ocean when we broke through the cloud cover, I'd bet anything on that, so we must have come pretty far."

Danny listened to Byron with mounting surprise. "*That's* west." He pointed toward the little stream. "That's north, and Swarthmore's over *there* someplace, on the other side of the foothills. Can't you guys really tell?"

"You mean you really can? You're positive?"

Danny nodded. "I thought everybody could."

"Well, OK, I've heard of people being electromagnetically sensitive. I believe you. Well, great—then we've got a walking compass, and that's one big problem solved. But still, we can't tromp along through a forest and over a mountain range on a compass bearing; we need to keep near to water, and we need a passable road through whatever kind of vegetation and terrain we run into—it can't all be this easy to get through. Now, my idea is that we follow our creek till it comes to a bigger creek, and follow that one till it comes to another, and so on. I'm *almost* certain there's no catchment basin anywhere around here, and we're definitely the right side of wherever the watershed is—we can't have gimped *that* far inland—so this land here has to drain into the ocean. We follow streams, eventually we come out there. It won't be the shortest way by a long shot, but it'll be the surest, and there's a good chance it's even the fastest."

Joel spoke from his pallet. "That makes sense to me. On a direct bearing you can't choose your route, you'd be having to cross streams all the time and bushwhack through scrub and stuff." *Bushwhack* and *scrub* were words from novels he had enjoyed, and he used them with a trace of relish even now.

"Right enough—though we'll be crossing streams in any case, I guess. But here's another thing: it would be harder for anybody to find us, if Maggie does make contact with a rescue party. Walking that far won't be easy," said Byron, very serious now. "And it'll get harder real fast, because the food we've got left just isn't going to stretch over the whole distance, unless I'm mighty wrong about how far we have to go. We're none of us properly dressed or properly equipped for that sort of trek, especially if we get a lot of this weather." He looked around at them. "All right, who's coming with me? Besides Danny, since we'll need a compass."

"I am," said Jack.

"Me too," said Caddie.

The others stared at her; it was like the day the hrossa came, when she had announced that she wanted to come to Swarthmore. "Won't you hold the others up if you go?" Maggie asked. "I don't mean to put you down, honey, but they may have hundreds of kilometers to cover and they'll be moving as fast as they can. They won't be able to wait for you."

"She'll be OK," Danny said impulsively, "if all she has to do is walk, not carry a lot of weight or anything." Caddie flashed him a glittering look of gratitude, though she did not smile, and Danny felt ashamed; he hadn't wanted her to come to Swarthmore and he didn't want her to come now, though he'd been glad enough to talk to her about Katy and the baby.

Byron looked narrowly at them both, then nodded and smiled at Caddie. "OK, you come with us," he said. "I reckon you're tougher than you look."

"OK then." Maggie got up. "I'll get started packing up the food and things you'll want. You're going to sleep cold on the road, I'm afraid, but my guess is you'll all probably be too tired to care."

They spent that evening scouring the forest floor for deadfall wood and bringing back container after container of water until the lander tank was full. While the three youngsters toiled away at these chores, Byron worked to clear dirt and flammable materials well away from the exhaust, then started the engines and ran them to charge the battery. When everything was ready for their departure, Danny crawled under the lander and spent some time with Joel. A week of pain and enforced invalidism had wrought a startling change on a boy of even Joel's mercurial and lively temperament; he lay and looked up at Danny with an expression of passive elderliness under the black tangle of curls. Both boys knew they might never see each other again. "I feel so damn useless," Joel said fretfully. "I sure wish I was coming with you."

"[I wish that too.] But somebody would have to stay here with Maggie anyway—and if any hrossa show up here, somebody ought to be able to talk to them. You won't be useless if that happens."

"Then I sure hope it does. [I hope it happens,]" he repeated, his pops and clicks of Hross so comical-sounding in their weakness that they both had to laugh, though two tears squeezed from the outer corners of Joel's eyes and slid sideways down his temples.

THEY STARTED AT FIRST LIGHT. It was so hard for Danny to say goodbye to Maggie and Joel when the moment came that he almost wanted to change his mind and stay behind; but he had to march out anyway with the others, over the now well-marked track to the dammed pool in the streamlet, then left in the direction of its flow. Danny had brought the other half of the second sacrificed sweater and the galley knife. Whenever two streams merged, so that a person backtracking would have to choose between one branch and another, he planned to tie a length of sweater wool to a tree beside the branch they had descended. This was their insurance; they would be able to return to the lander.

Jack carried all their share of the food in a makeshift backpack. The blankets and two plastic sheets in a rolled bundle were lashed across Byron's shoulder, and Caddie was packing a cooking pot and some spoons. In Danny's own pack were a few spare items of clothing for everyone, jackets and socks and toothbrushes. They badly needed a length of rope, but there had been no rope at all in the lander.

The going was much easier here than in the coastal forest of close-growing mixed scrub, or in the flokh forests in the mountains northeast of Swarthmore, where KliUrrh's village was. The impression of graciousness, of a parklike plantation of smooth straight trees, was sustained throughout their first day of travel. Each tree stood in its own space, its crown symmetrical, its outer leaves brushing those of its near neighbors except for the trees that were rearing a sapling. Here and there a healthy full-grown tree still stood joined at the base with its dead parent, or towered above a fallen trunk now punky with rot. Occasionally these fallen logs impeded the travelers' progress, but the ground was virtually free of undergrowth and covered with a soft duff, inches deep, that made walking a sensuous pleasure. Had the four humans been less hungry and less anxious they would have enjoyed their journey, for the forest was beautiful in its own way, as well as spacious and grand.

In the treetops they repeatedly caught glimpses of some kind of small winged animal. The animals were hard to see, but what could be glimpsed of their behavior suggested some combination of bird, flying squirrel, and monkey. A few sighted near the camp in the first day or two after the crash had quickly withdrawn; now the four looked upward as they walked to watch the small dark shapes wing or clamber from branch to branch, uttering no sound. They stopped to watch as one monkeybird at the edge of an open space pulled a large leaf toward itself with little limbs and chomped its way along the edge like a caterpillar.

Alien wildlife of any kind was interesting to them all, for only Danny had ever seen much of it, and he was as happy as the rest to be distracted from his empty stomach. "On Earth, in the old days," Byron told them, peering up at the monkeybirds, "there'd be dozens of species of birds in a wet forest like this one, in spring, all yelling their heads off—and squirrels and possums and raccoons and frogs and snakes and I don't know what all. And lots of different kinds of trees, too, all sizes, plus prickerbushes, weeds, vines—you wouldn't see all the animals but you'd sure see more than one kind, and dozens of kinds of plants and trees. I wonder what makes this planet tick, I can't figure it. This is practically a monoculture we've got here. The only place you'd come close to that on Earth would be in the northern conifer forests, where the climate's extreme. I'm talking about the old days, you understand—*I* never saw all this stuff I'm talking about."

Danny did not respond to this speech, and Jack looked at him, then looked away. They knew nothing of Earth, and more of "what makes this planet tick" than they felt free to tell Byron.

In the first hour the little stream had run into another and that one into still another, larger creek, whose water ran nearly level with the banks at times while at others the land rose several meters on both sides above the channel; but always the walking was easy. They made good time that day and bivouacked the first night beside the stream, now some six meters wide, though still very shallow. Byron built a little fire of kindling, just large enough to boil their meager ration of stew. All of them ate from the cooking pot, spoonful by scrupulous spoonful, careful to see that each got exactly as much as the others. They rinsed the pot, already polished inside by scraping fingers, and scoured the blackened outside with sand till it was free of stickiness if not of blackness. In the last light they spread the ground sheet over a fluffed-up bed of duff picked smooth of sticks, and snuggled between the blankets, all together, well pleased with their first day's effort.

Sometime in the night Byron awoke to the sound of rain pattering on the leaves high above them and spread the second plastic sheet across the sardined kids and himself; but in the morning scarcely a droplet lay upon it, so gentle had the shower been and so heavy the protective canopy of foliage.

The second day was like the first, except that they followed the gradually broadening and deepening creek from morning till evening without encountering a larger stream. Danny had tied a big, eye-catching piece of sweater to a tree at the point where the second little creek had met this larger one, and soon they could all see how necessary that had been, for small creeks now fed this one continually and they could never have picked theirs out from the rest. All the tributary streams on the near bank, of course, had to be crossed; and as the main stream cut more deeply into the land, these crossings took more time and consumed more energy. But still they made fair headway, and camped that night as well with a sense of solid accomplishment. Morale was good; nobody whined or complained. But they were hungrier now—hungry enough to be kept awake by gnawing emptiness had they been less worn out by the long day of scrambling down and up.

Danny, no whit less hungry and tired than the others, lay awake with aching legs between Caddie and Jack for a few minutes that second night and thought with dull wonder how things like being a sexual oddity, and being the father of Katy's baby—matters whose import had so recently colored all the world—now meant less than nothing to him, compared with the plain matter of survival. If he lived through this he intended to celebrate his life on any terms whatever; and he imagined that Jack, and his father, and even Caddie, would all say the very same thing if he asked them. Lying there on the cold ground he vowed to himself that he would hang on tight to this altered perspective of what was truly important, if he came through, and not slip back into blowing things up in his mind till they seemed to matter more, or at least differently, than they really did.

Where was his father? Nothing could have prevented George from getting to him by now if something hadn't gone badly wrong—maybe Byron had logged his flight plan incorrectly, maybe both the whirligigs were down...maybe, he thought—and the thought froze his heart—maybe Sixertown has really been destroyed, and nobody knows where we are.

Just as the expedition was getting under way the next morning, a heavy, foliage-penetrating rain commenced and they had to stop and put on rain parkas, and Byron had to rewrap the blankets in the plastic sheets, before moving out along the boiling creek. The rain was cold and heavy and it lasted all day long. Toward midday the wind blew up. They slogged along miserably in their soaked, mud-plastered footgear, slipping down the banks of tributary streams, wading through the muddy water, wishing again and again as they struggled to climb the far side of each one for the rope they didn't have; and now for the first time Caddie began to lag behind. Abused by water and rough wear, her light shoes had begun to come apart, and she was stumbling with exhaustion. When Byron called an early halt there was no dry place to make their camp, nor any dry wood, though they had all picked up a few suitable sticks of wet wood toward the end of the day's march. Everyone voted to go to bed hungry and at once, in the hope of better weather in the morning. Unless the rain stopped, keeping a fire alight would take more effort than even Byron felt able to make.

Sometime during that long day of misery, unnoticed in the poor visibility and the grim single-mindedness of moving forward, the character of the forest had begun to change; and that wet night there was no bed of duff dry or wet to fluff up for a mattress. While the youngsters stood in a huddled stupor, Byron cast about till he found a piece of higher ground where the runoff drained to either side; and there they slept, with one blanket spread beneath them for some poor insulation over the ground cloth. As Maggie had foretold, they were now too exhausted to care and were all asleep in seconds, jammed against one another—clothes, parkas, muddy shoes, and all. They even brought the bundle of firewood in with them.

The rain had stopped pelting on the plastic oversheet when they awoke, but it was a sorry group that groaned and rose stiffly to face the new day. And the forest about them was dripping. They limped around, saying little, trying to scrape together enough tinder to get a fire going that would burn wet wood if it was good and dead. It took a long time, and Byron had to use two sheets of his precious supply of paper, but eventually they had a blaze and could stand near it to watch the soup bubble in the pot while their blankets and wet clothing reeked and steamed. Byron stuck a few last sticks under the pot and stirred. "Almost ready. Thank God this godforsaken planet decided to build its life-forms out of carbon, that's all I can say. *And* thank God we left all our viruses behind when we came here—if we were doing this on Earth we'd all have colds by now, or worse."

There was a near quarrel when it developed that the three males could eat the thin soup hotter than Caddie could, so that she held them all back, cooling her spoonfuls one by one. Byron stopped it: "We're all worn out, and tired, hungry people get crabby. Let's try not to snipe at each other, OK? We're all doing our best here. Much better to eat slowly now anyway—make it last. You'll feel less hungry later if you do." Caddie looked at none of them while he was speaking, and tears ran down her cheeks, though she made no sound. Her shoes were ruined; both tops had come unsealed from the soles in front. It was obvious that in that condition she would not be able to walk fast or far.

They finished eating in silence, but afterward Jack and Danny worked off their small remorse by wrapping Caddie's feet, shoes and all, in straps of torn cloth and tying them up with lengths of the unraveled sweater, while Byron cleaned up the pot and spoons and broke camp by himself. When they were done Caddie could walk, wade, and even scramble without losing her shoes, though she resembled a private in George Washington's Continental Army. This day, they all moved like old people— slow and creaky. Danny's clothes hung on him; Byron, once a beefy fellow, was downright gaunt; and Caddie, who had already been skinny, crouched by the creek like a bundle of sticks. Looking at her Danny thought helplessly, *It was wrong to say she'd hold up. She can't. She hasn't. She's going to get left behind, and it'll be my fault.*

"Danny, which way is the creek heading now—still eastward?" Byron asked when they were ready to move out.

He tried to think. "It goes everywhere except west, so I guess so. We're east of where we started out, but I don't know if we're any closer to the coast or not."

"The trees here are different. Any idea whether that means our elevation's lower or higher now? I'd like to think we were lower— there aren't any coastal cliffs along this stretch that I know of."

Danny looked around him without much interest at the trees, whose branches emerged from green trunks at a level about even with Byron's chest. Though these grew in the same orderly fashion as the larger trees they stood much closer together, and instead of leaflike foliage the branches bore a thick felting of bluish mosslike stuff. It was a great relief to be able to see the sky again, but it looked like they might soon have to walk bent over or even crawl; pushing through those branches looked impossible. Slowly he shook his head. "I can't tell. I just never saw trees like this before, not in the mountains and not along the lower Delaware."

Byron sighed. "If I could have kept the lander in the air just a little bit longer we could have come down in these things, and maybe not broken the fucking booster tube. Oh well."

He poked his head through the blanket loop and led them off downstream. The overlap zone between the big umbrella trees and the small moss trees was narrow, and they had passed through most of it in the rain the previous day. In a short while they had left the last of the former behind and were forcing a difficult passage through the latter—an exhausting business. Branches snagged their bundles and hair, poked into their eyes, streaked them blue with moss. Byron soon called a halt. "This is no good, we'll have to wade. Now you see the point of following streams instead of striking overland." The kids looked dubiously at the creek, high and opaque with runoff now, and doubly treacherous to the walker because pitted with sinkholes and pools. Byron read their faces and tried to jolly them on: "We'll all probably fall in a few times, but hey! at least we'll make some progress! Better than putting our eyes out anyway, right? Now—can all of you swim?" When they all nodded, he sidled straight down the bank and stepped with a grimace into the water, shoes and all. "Cold! But clear sailing, so let's go."

"What about our shoes?" Jack asked. "Won't they get wrecked?"

"We'll tie 'em on if they do, like Caddie's. Shoes on, no cuts. But you and Danny are in good shape with those Quaker boots of yours. Anyway, look at the bright side—no more climbing up and down the banks every time we meet a feeder stream!"

During a rest stop, while they huddled together shivering on a gravel bar against one bank, the sun came out for the first time since the beginning of their journey and shone full upon them through the open channel above the creek. Though Jack was wet clear through—his boot sole had slipped on a rock, and only a full-length belly-flop and a twisted knee had kept the food he was carrying dry—the sudden warmth deeply comforted them all. They lay back groaning with relief, put the packs under their heads, basked and grew drowsy; and Byron allowed the break to draw out beyond the usual limit, believing they all would be the better for the rest.

The sun's appearance brought with it an orderly cloud of "insects," small winged creatures that fluttered like butterflies or dragonflies above the surface of the water. Such creatures were never seen in either settlement, but Danny said sleepily, "Those are the first familiar things I've seen. There are lots of those up at the hross village in summer—they ride around on the hrossa on sunny days, when they come up out of the lake."

"Maybe they're hross sweat bees," said Byron.

"What's a sweat bee?"

"Oh, just a little bee that used to light on people's skin and drink the—"

"Oh look!" cried Caddie, as several of the pretty things cruised slowly across the bar where they were resting, bobbled and hovered above them, and then came delicately, hesitantly down to alight upon Jack's soggy clothing and bare arms. "Gosh, aren't they beautiful." Each fly was big as a hand, with four jointed legs and a neckless, one-piece body and head of smooth black. The single pair of wings, pale blue and deep turquoise, swept slowly forward and backward. The knob of the head would have been disproportionately big on a terrestrial insect of similar size, such as a large moth, a cecropia or a luna; they could almost read an expression on the tiny faces. There were two huge eyes, and a pair of down-pointing projections on the abdomen. The wings never ceased to beat, but the flies perched quietly, evidently basking in the sun like the weary humans. Jack held perfectly still.

"What makes you so special?" said Danny.

"Maybe I smell better than you guys," said Jack, "or maybe—hey! Hey! *Ow!*" He sat up and batted frantically at the insects, which fluttered away in confused swirl except for one he had crushed against his trouser leg.

"Don't—stop it—don't hurt them! Jesus, you *killed* him!" Danny yelled, horrified.

"Tell 'em not to *bite* me, then!" Jack yelled back, pulling up his damp pantleg. "Look at that!" On his bare calf, where one of the flies had perched, were two clear punctures and two thin trickles of blood.

They all stared uncomprehendingly at the little wounds. Danny picked up the broken body of the butterfly Jack had killed and touched the two points on its abdomen; they left a tiny blood-stain on his fingertip. He looked up and met Jack's eyes. "I didn't mean to kill it, it was a reflex," said Jack. Like Danny, he had had time to take in the fact that a form of native life had inflicted unprovoked harm on a human being.

"The butterfly must have made a mistake," said Danny, still looking at Jack.

"Not butterfly," Caddie said in a thin voice. "Dragonfly."

Byron examined the two little fang marks. As yet there was no swelling. "Does it hurt?"

"Not much. It hurt plenty when he chomped me, boy, just like a bee sting."

"Itch?"

"Unh-unh. Not yet."

"Tell me if it starts to, or if you start to feel strange." Byron took the dead fly out of Danny's hand, wrapped it carefully in his handkerchief, and tucked it into the pocket of his shirt. "We'd better get moving, gang. If you see any butterflies—"

"Dragonflies," said Jack and Caddie together.

"—dragonflies, shoo first and ask questions later, but don't swat to kill if you can help it."

Though the blue things fluttered all about them, making them duck nervously at first, they were not bothered again and gradually stopped thinking about the dragonflies at all. The day faired up and turned milder. Direct sunlight on the surface of the water made their footing still more difficult to find, but no one wished it away, and no one fell in.

By early afternoon the vegetation on the banks had begun to change character once more as the soil grew stonier. The moss trees spaced themselves farther apart, and occasional tall foliage plants like giant crotons appeared here and there between them. Gratefully they crawled up the bank, wrung out their pants and socks as best they could, and began to walk again on the relatively open ground.

Hunger and exhaustion from the long day's wading dragged at the travelers, however, and they made poorer and poorer progress as the afternoon wore on. By teatime Danny was shambling along in a fog that allowed no room or energy for thought. His mind was filled with the maddening memory of foddercake—and with an exquisite appreciation of the difference between having nothing to eat but as much foddercake as you wanted, and nothing to eat at all. Crossing the tributary creeks was easier here, in that the banks were not so muddy and were studded with stones for handholds and footholds. But the energy it took to climb them was fearful, and after scaling one particularly steep bank they stood gasping and swaying at the top, all of them—even Byron—near collapse. "We'll cross the next one, then we'll stop," he promised; and they had just begun to straggle on when Jack, who was last in line, gave a grunt of surprise, and they looked up to see a little gray animal scuttle straight toward them out of the thick heart of a giant croton.

Danny's first thought—that this was a second native-species attack—was so long in coming, and he so sluggish in response to it, that the animal had approached within a meter or two of the humans and paused to gaze up into each face with what seemed fearless confidence before Danny felt the pang of his own fear, and by that time it seemed irrelevant. The group drifted to a halt and stared blankly at the animal, almost beyond curiosity. It looked to be about rabbit-size and moved rapidly on six very short legs; it was tailless, and its smooth skin was the pale gray of dirty snow. Two little forelimbs, the forewardmost pair of legs, were held clamped against its thorax.

Having made eye contact with each of the travelers, the animal suddenly reared back on its hind end, exposing a whitish belly. Between the second and third pair of limbs they could see a swollen region bearing three little nipples arranged in a triangle; and at this sight—moved by an impulse he did not pause to analyze—Danny fell heavily upon his knees and fumbled at his pants.

Holding its reared-back position, the animal danced forward on four legs, right in between the boy's thighs, and delicately pressed the three little protrusions against the proffered tip of Danny's penis.

As if a current had been closed, at the instant of contact Danny gasped and swayed, swept by strong feelings not his own. He understood, at once, everything about this little animal's life: its pleasure in water creatures and croton leaves, its matings and pregnancy, its grown baby, its burrowing and bathing along this stretch of the creek, and—overwhelmingly—its total interconnectedness with each branch, blade, stem, dragonfly, rock, and trickle of water in the world. It was appalling—unendurable—to be forced to feel all that and be so weak; it felt to Danny as if his brain had been blasted to pieces by understanding.

But he knew his part as well, and that speed was essential. "Somebody give me a rock," he managed to say. "Quick!" He stretched his free hand behind him blindly and felt a heavy object be placed in it—just in time; the peak moment of the conjunction came almost at once, and in the midst of it he brought the rock down with all his small remaining strength, at that awkward angle, upon the creature's thorax, right above the place where he knew the organ that was both heart and brain to be.

The next thing he knew, water was being dribbled in his face. He came around, coughing, to see his three companions staring down at him, and attempting to fasten his clothes together and sit up, but found himself without any strength at all. Byron helped him into a sitting position and supported him. "Here, drink this. Are you OK? What in thunderation was that all about?"

Danny's head spun, and he slumped against Byron's bony shoulder. "Is it dead?" He saw that it was. "That's how the hrossa hunt. I went on a couple of hunts, and I saw it, but I never—never did it before. They, the hrossa, they just walk along sending hunger, hunger, and after a while an animal comes up to them . . . and they make a sexual link with it. And then they kill it."

Somehow Byron found the energy to be interested. "They *hypnotize* it to make it come?"

Danny shook his head in feeble impatience. "No. That's not it." But he didn't feel up to trying to explain further—or, for that matter, deciding what he should and shouldn't tell, if such things were still important any more. He wanted them to let him sleep, just sleep . . . no: he wanted to *eat the little animal!* That was precisely what he wanted. That was why it had come to him, and that was the point, the only point, of killing it.

"What are *we* supposed to do with the thing?" Jack was saying. "*We* can't eat it. I wish to hell we could." He sounded about a hundred years old.

"It must have thought we could." Caddie gazed wanly at the little corpse. "We sure were sending hunger, hunger, hunger."

Danny reached inward for the ghost of his remaining strength. "I'm *going* to eat some of it, if you guys could please bring me a piece."

Nobody argued, or even commented. Jack pulled the knife out of Danny's belt and began to skin the little carcass, fumbling a bit. "Could you find a couple of sticks, Cad? We can spit a chunk of this."

"No fire," said Danny. "Raw."

Minutes later he said, "It's good. This is really *good*. You guys better all try some."

THEY MADE CAMP in that place, since Danny could not go any farther, and each of them, even Caddie, ate a little of the animal's raw flesh. An hour later first Byron and then Caddie made a hasty trip into the crotons, as painless but emphatic diarrhea emptied them of the morsels of alien meat; but by sunset an astonishing thing seemed clear. Not only had Danny and Jack not been forced into the bushes, but both felt very much as if they had recently eaten something more or less like a square meal.

Jack, who like the others had swallowed only a skeptical mouthful or two of the stuff, now cut a few more pieces from the carcass; and when Byron filled the pot and started water to boil for that evening's stew, it was to cook up just enough to feed himself and Caddie—for somehow, against all previous beliefs about the realities of life on Pennterra, the little animal had fed the Quaker boys.

"But how come you have to eat it *raw*?" Caddie complained. "It's *awful*."

"We just do. It's not so bad."

It was hard for any of them, tired as they were, to take in the implications of what had happened. Jack shook his head in a baffled way. "After the fit you threw when I killed that dragonfly, I couldn't believe you were going to whack *this* thing with the rock—and I couldn't *believe* what you were doing with it before that—and then I remembered about the field report, but it was all still—I couldn't make it make sense. But now," he stretched out before what was left of the minimal fire they had made, "I'll believe anything you like. I didn't ever expect to feel this good again." The reference to the field report went unremarked by Byron, and by Danny as well.

Three times during the next four days an animal sacrificed itself to feed the famished travelers. Danny did not require himself to talk about the moment just before the killing blow. He sniffed about in the vegetation, and whenever he found a kind of foliage that smelled appealing he would collect a few leaves to vary his and Jack's new diet of raw meat. All these things seemed to agree with them, and everything nourished them; and though they never got quite enough to eat, they were soon much better off than Caddie or Byron. But all the lander food could now be saved to feed the other two, and the psychological boost to all four carried them through many difficult miles of wading, walking, and climbing. Danny hunted up a sturdy length of dead tree and made himself a killing club, like a policeman's baton, which he hung around his shoulders on a thong of yarn. The fine weather held; sometimes they were even hot.

But finally, on the fourth day, the lander food gave out. Caddie and Byron traveled for nine hours on their sketchy breakfast, but progress was poor, for Caddie was by now in very bad shape. It was obvious to them all when they bivouacked that evening that because the two boys were able after a fashion to live off the land, they would have to leave their companions sheltered beside the water and go on alone.

The vegetation at this point was low enough to give them a view, and the land to southward, though somewhat rolling, revealed no mountain ranges or formidable high country. Unless Danny's sense of direction had played them false at the beginning, their course from the lander—like the lander's course from Sixertown—had run roughly parallel to the coast, and they had covered perhaps 150 kilometers, perhaps 200, of actual distance, though a good deal less than that as the monkeybird or dragonfly might measure it.

The creek, though still refusing to swing appreciably southward, had become wider and much deeper; it seemed probable that it would either empty soon into a south-flowing river or become a river itself and bend south finally to empty into the ocean. If the boys saw a good-sized hill on their left, they might climb to the top and try to see the ocean; and if they could actually see it they might make a judgement about leaving the creek to head overland, depending on the look of the terrain they would have to cross in order to reach the sea.

The next morning, the ninth of their journey and the fourteenth since the crash, the party split up and the boys set off alone. Jack had rolled and lashed one of the plastic sheets and one blanket across his shoulder, and Danny carried his killing club, the galley knife, and his and Jack's rain parkas and oddments of extra clothing. This parting was stranger than any of the others, for this time they all knew that unless help arrived within days, Byron probably and Caddie certainly would die. None of them knew how long a person could survive without food if he had plenty of water to drink, but the condition of the two Sixers was grave enough. They had all come a long way on very little food, but even had they been feeding well the journey would have overtaxed them all. The boys had the advantage of the others, having eaten better of late, but they too were emaciated and very footsore. The knowledge that the survival of everyone else depended on what speed they could muster, which might not be good enough, and on luck, which lay outside their control, was an added burden.

Caddie lay huddled in the remaining blanket with her eyes closed, and did not open them or respond when they said goodbye to her. Byron hugged both boys, tears glittering in his eyes. With his two-week stubble, brilliant eyes, starved face, and tattered garments, Byron looked slightly mad; but Caddie looked like a corpse.

The creek had really grown into a small river already, much too deep to wade in. Jack and Danny turned away, Jack in the lead, and began to force a slow passage along the bank, now lined with the same kind of yellow willow tree as those that lined the banks of the Delaware in Swarthmore. The ground cover sprang up behind them harmlessly, but the low woody growth snapped back when pushed and released, and Danny had to walk several meters behind Jack in order to avoid being continually lashed by branches. They turned once to wave. When they turned again, the camp was no longer in sight.

There was no energy to spare for conversation. In the early afternoon Jack broke a silence of some hours to say, "We need a boat. This is too blame slow."

Danny stood still and looked about him. "Where do we get a boat from?"

Jack pointed. "There." A whole willow tree, washed out of the bank by high water, had grounded on a sandbar on the other side of the creek. "It wouldn't carry us if we tried to sit on top of it, but I bet we could hang on to it and ride the current."

They stood, considering the problem. Suddenly—at the same instant—both heard the sound they had been listening for, waking and sleeping, all through the past two weeks; the distant buzz of a whirligig. Desperately they scanned the clear, open sky. The sound was very faint, and died before they could spot the source of it, but both were certain of what they had heard. Ordinarily the whirligigs never flew south from the settlement; it could only mean that people were still out searching for them.

Danny and Jack had been walking for so many days now that much of the time the walking had come to have no felt purpose beyond itself. Belief in the reality of a world and a life outside the Pennterran wilderness, outside of being cold, wet, hungry, and too weary and footsore to take another step, was impossible to sustain for long. But the sound of the whirligig made it real again; and without any more discussion Danny and Jack slid down the banks into the water. They waded across, chest-deep in the cold current, holding their irreplaceable bundles over their heads, and wedged and lashed them securely into the branches of the uprooted tree; then they dragged and shoved it off the sandbar into the middle of the creek and held on as the current took hold of it and swept it, stem-first, off downstream.

As soon as it was properly afloat the willow rolled in the water, plunging the bedding and extra clothing under. Jack yelped in dismay, but Danny said, "Don't worry—it's tied on good and tight, we won't lose anything. Anyway, it's worth getting things wet if we make time."

By experimenting a bit they discovered how much of their weight the crown of the willow would bear, and lay finally half out of the water, clinging to branches above their heads. In this position they were riding backwards, but attempts to make the tree proceed downstream with its top foremost were unavailing and they had to make do with a watchful over-the-shoulder glance every minute or so. The stream was much too cold for comfort, but at least the sun lay warm on their heads and shoulders and the current was brisk. Several times they had to shove the tree off when it snagged or grounded, but the channel was deep enough to be clear of most of what fell in, and it was wonderful to make speed while conserving energy. And every meter gained brought them closer to where the whirligig had been, and might be again.

Late in the afternoon the sky clouded over, and shortly the boys began to look out for a place to moor their tree for the night and partially dry their blanket and clothes. As a craft the tree was ludicrously unwieldy, and several suitable spots went past before they were able to kick it out of the central channel. But eventually they spotted a place in time and dragged the willow up out of the water by its branches, far enough to feel it would still be there in the morning. The rush of adrenaline evoked by the sound of the gig motor had long since worn off. They had not eaten since morning, and their legs ached with cold. Moving stiffly, they fumbled at the tree, trying to turn it enough to reach the blanket and jackets tied beneath without letting it slip back into the stream. The blanket bundle they got hold of, finally, but the pack of socks and jackets was gone.

"Scraped off, one of those times we went aground," said Danny, desolate. He shivered.

"Come on, give me a hand with this." Jack stuck two corners of the sodden blanket into his hands. "We're gonna need it tonight. Where's dinner, by the way? If we don't *walk* along being hungry, do the animals not know we're here or what?"

"You tell me," said Danny, still trying to adjust to the loss of the burden he had borne so far. And in fact they were not fed that night, and had to be content with a few leaves, a fire, and the still-damp blanket stippled with spark-holes. They slept, in violent discomfort, inside an envelope made of the blanket spread on the ground sheet and folded over, blanket innermost; but while they were breaking camp and preparing to go on the next morning, an orange animal the size of a muskrat crawled up the bank and reared back upon itself to expose its erected penicles; so Pennterra did not allow them to go too hungry after all.

The sky was still overcast, threatening rain. Danny looked at the now-considerable stream with dread as he chewed the flesh of the creature he had linked with and then clubbed to death. He had only fainted that once, but every time the same totality of interconnectedness with the creature's life and world affected him with terrible force, and yesterday in the water he had felt twinges and rumors of that same connectedness tugging at the edges of his mind. In other circumstances the sensations would have been moving and uplifting; in his present weakened state it was all he could do to endure them. He felt wrenched about, buffeted, violated almost, by the selfhood of other creatures.

For lots of reasons he did not want to enter the water again at all. But there was no help for it, for the current bore them along much faster than they could walk, and speed was all-important now—to their own survival, but even more to Caddie's and Byron's, and beyond them to the survival of Joel and Maggie, whose supplies must have run out even before their own did. With dull amazement Danny realized that he had not thought of Joel and Maggie for days.

Jack piled the picked bones of his half of the carcass neatly on the ground, as Danny had taught him, then washed his hands, laced up his boots, and floundered down the bank into the stream with the rolled bundle of bedding. Danny cleaned his knife on a leaf and stuck it into his belt. He hung the killing club across his shoulder like a quiver. Then there was no more help for it, and he followed Jack down the bank. Together they pushed the tree into the current and clung to it again, and again the current swept them away.

After a very long time Danny stopped shuddering, because the cold had numbed him. He hung on mindlessly to the thick lower branches of the tree and was borne backward into the unknown. It was as much as he could do; at first he hardly ever roused himself to look downstream along the trunk for obstructions or improbable waterfalls, and finally he never did. The sense of minds and voices in the water tugged at his own mind distressingly. He closed his eyes and suffered them, and the cold.

When he opened his eyes again, much later, he still saw only the shaggy heap of the tree before him, the willows in two yellow lines—farther apart now—along the banks they were passing between, and the whitish sky of filtered light. What was it that jarred him out of stupor and made him look about—had the

whirligig come again? He made a terrible effort and turned, un-
cramped one hand and shifted his hold. He could then see Jack
on the other side of the trunk, and Jack was craning his neck to
peer ahead, so Danny did the same.

Directly before them, above the roots of the tree, the willow-
lined banks disappeared; he saw wide water and then, in a
straight line across the far view, another willow-lined shore. He
tried to shake off the murmurous undercurrent of voices in his
head, and blinked and squinted to clear his vision: had they
fetched up in a lake after all? If so, unless hrossa had a village
here, their luck was very cruel. But his mind felt as nerveless as
his body and he contemplated the possibility of final failure
numbly, from a long way away.

Jack said, "I think we're coming into a river. Listen, doesn't
it sound different? We should try to get to shore and look
around."

But while Danny strained his ears, strained to see, the tree
swept them out between the tall banks into deeper, wider water;
and as they passed into the river and were seized by its more
powerful current, it was as though the subliminal tuggings upon
his attention were at once immensely amplified, so that what had
seemed like snatches of hummed music or speech swelled into
something more like a chorale. In shock, in joy, Danny gasped
and choked and almost let go of the tree. He let out a croaking
shout. "The Delaware—Jack, it's the Delaware! We're back, we
made it! We're almost home!"

FROM KATY KENDRY'S PERSONAL JOURNAL:
THIRDAY, 19 JUNE 2234

I was having my lie-down after lunch yesterday, stupefied but not asleep, when suddenly the triangle began to let out a clamor like a firehouse alarm Back Home, and I was up and running before my wits caught up with my feet. The first thing I saw was Bob Wellwood out in front of the kitchen, beating the hell out of the alarm, and the second was Gus Johnson running for the whirlipad. Just as I came across the footbridge George burst out of the radio station. He saw me, waved, started to run to meet me. We collided by the rabbit hutches, and George, white as a sheet, gasped out, "Ike found them—they're alive!" I thought he was going to collapse, I nearly did myself, but by that time a lot of people were tearing out of the kitchen and laundry and in from the fields, and George managed to stand there holding himself together somehow, telling everyone over and over that the boys were all right, while Bob kept on making the triangle clang until there was nobody left who hadn't turned out.

Shock takes us funny. I'd swear I was more overjoyed, or that the joy had more emotional *immediacy*, when George told me Danny was safe than when we discovered after five years of suspense that Pennterra was all we had hardly dared hope it be.

I heard a gig start to warm up. More people kept arriving all the time, and things got very noisy and confused. Gus took off and headed down the river. In all that tumult and shouting I didn't get all the details, but in general this seems to be what happened:

Every day since the lander was lost, Gus or Ike has taken a gig downriver to the ocean and flown eastward along the shore as far as was safe, because of George's persuasion that the kids would get out to the coast if they could. Then they'd bring the spent gig back for recharging and fly the other one inland, searching a different area each day for a sign of the lander or the whisper of a radio signal. They'd found nothing anywhere near the route Byron logged before he left Sixertown, and until yesterday neither we nor the searchers from that end had turned up the ghost of a clue. With so much time gone by already we'd all just about lost hope of finding them, dead or alive.

A few days ago George went up to consult with KliUrrh and came back distraught. KliUrrh had told him that Tanka Wakan would not let Danny die if he were alive on the ground, but no more than George could he say whether Danny might have died in a lander crash—there are no hross villages in that stretch of terrain because there are no really big lakes or rivers between the Delaware and Sixertown. KliUrrh, understandably enough, had never thought of a *mechanical* failure. Seeing that he was distraught himself completely broke George's spirit; nothing but faith in KliUrrh's assurances had kept him going that long.

It broke my spirit too, I may as well admit now, with all appropriate chagrin and dismay. Ever since they were lost I've dwelt in a fog of anxiety and spiritual myopia—could take no interest in anything (including keeping this record current) and no comfort in meeting, though George did derive strength from meeting, I think (as did Lynn and John) until he went up to see KliUrrh. But that ended that; and as for me, I ceased to function at all. A disgraceful performance; I'm not a bit proud of it. But we all have our limits, and that was mine.

Anyway: Ike was about fifty km below the settlement and flying fairly high so as to scan as much of the country to eastward as possible. His attention was on that, and not on the river itself, but his eye was caught by a dead tree that seemed to be floating *across* the current and he went lower to have a look. Right away he spotted the boys holding on to the tree—their heads, and their arms waving. They'd been using it as a lifebuoy to come down a big creek that empties into the Delaware just above that point, and had been trying to kick it in to shore when he overflew them.

Ike dropped the ladder, but neither of them had enough strength left to climb up. Seeing how it was, Ike waited till they'd both let go of the tree and grabbed onto the ladder, and then he towed them to shore. There was no place for him to put the gig down, so once they were on dry land he hauled the ladder up again and dropped the sling, and Jack went up in that. Ike intended to pick up Danny too, but as soon as he came aboard the gig Jack said he and Danny had worked it out between them that they'd better save space for one of the Sixer kids, a girl they'd left in very bad condition two days before, who would have to be brought up in a stretcher. Jack said he would direct Ike to where the girl was, and that Danny preferred to wait for the next ferry.

It was at this point that Ike called in, and Bob rushed across from the station and started ringing the alarm fit to raise the dead.

Less than an hour later we heard the gig coming back. Everyone in Swarthmore was at the pad to see it set down. Jack crawled down off the saddle just *shining* with happiness, despite being wet and filthy and bedraggled and thin as a rail. He and Lynn and John rushed together and stood there holding each other and crying as if their hearts would break (I seem to be falling back upon cliché after cliché this morning, but maybe moments like these are what clichés are for), and the whole settlement witnessed it and snuffled right along with them. It was a community affair, no question. We had shared the anguish, and we were clear about our right to share the joy, and we did.

Meanwhile Bob had hurried up to help Ike offload the stretcher and the girl, wrapped in a blanket, unconscious and only just alive. They took her straight to the infirmary, which is where Jack went too as soon as he and his parents could bear to let each other go. They wouldn't let him walk another step. He rode over in a cart, his father pulling while his mother walked alongside holding his hand, and I never saw three happier people in my life.

Gus had taken off in the other gig, which was about three-quarters charged, just minutes after Ike radioed in to give his position. He picked up Danny, and they flew on up the creek to drop off some blankets and food for Byron—Ike had already collected the stretcher case by the time they got there—and then Gus worked his way toward the crash site, intending to pick up Maggie and/or the injured boy who was with her there. They had quite a time finding the site—Danny was trying to navigate by landmarks he couldn't see from the air—but finally Gus picked up a signal and they homed on that. But by this time the gig was very low on power, so all he could do was drop more food, along with a note to Maggie to get the boy ready to be lifted out, and make a beeline for home.

The other gig had been fully charged overnight, and that left Ike with just enough juice to go after those two and come straight

back. Poor old Byron would have had to spend another night on
his own in the woods with only soup, sandwiches, and several
fresh blankets to comfort him, but the lander from Sixertown
(with a gig on board) arrived in time for Gus to give their pilot
the position. So we got them all.

We'd been waiting at the pad for a couple of hours before we
heard the noise that was Gus bringing Danny home. I'd been
keeping an eye on George, because the shock of having his despair overturned had *not* worn off and I felt glad that Jack's
prior arrival had given us both a chance for a kind of emotional
dress rehearsal; but here came the real thing, and George was
shaking like a leaf. The gig settled; the door opened; out came
Danny, transmogrified into a stranger; a tall, emaciated, hol-
low-eyed, ravaged and battered-looking version of himself. He
dismounted like a stiff old man, as if every movement were
painful, and climbed down very slowly to the ground, blink-
ing…a very weird moment, one I'll never forget. He was just as
filthy and soggy as Jack had been, but there were *differences*.
George started to go to him; nobody else made a movement or a
sound, though the crowd had cheered and called to Jack. But
Danny seemed too fragile to bear it somehow.

He stood there with his hand against the whirligig, bracing
himself, looking around in that befuddled way—and then he saw
George. And then there was a blur, and they were clamped together. An unnerving sight, not *at all* like Jack with John and
Lynn. There was something truly awful about the way those two
grappled and strained at one another. The Wisters' utter joy had
been easy for the rest of us to witness and share, but what George
and Danny were doing had the feel of something intensely private, and the crowd sensed it and after a minute, very quietly,
started to break up and drift away.

I didn't go. I told myself I'd better not, that George looked too
close to a nervous collapse that Danny was in no shape to deal
with alone (or vice versa?); but the truth is that wild mastodons
could not have budged me.

So I watched, while that terrible tension mounted and
mounted between them till even I could hardly endure it; but then
luckily they both managed to start crying, and after that straining, hysterical note began to moderate into something less difficult and less agonized, and their strangleholds on one another
began to ease up, and I relaxed too. It occurs to me only now that
there may well have been a sexual dimension to the agony and
something climactic to the release. I didn't cry myself, not then

(though I seem to be crying rather a lot as I write this now); nor did I entertain sappy melodramatic thoughts like *Here is the father of my child restored to us from the dead*. But I have lived through no bigger event than that one, though I was not a protagonist but only a witness to it all.

We've got all six of them in the infirmary now, hooked up to IVs, though Danny and Jack will probably be released later today. Maggie, and probably Byron, will be kept in a while longer but there's nothing wrong with either of them that some rest and proper feeding won't cure eventually. Joel Adler, the boy hurt in the crash, has a fractured kneecap. The girl, Caddie Birtwistle, is comatose and not expected to pull through. Joel's parents are here, also the girl's guardian, June Something.

We gather that Jack and Danny came through their ordeal so well partly by eating the native plants and animals. Nobody but Alice can work up too much interest in this just at present, but if it's true it'll be—as we used to say—a whole new ball game.

There ought to be plenty of time to find out.

Danny has come back to us changed. It's more than the misery he's been put through these past weeks or the physical beating he's taken; the difference is fundamental. I know that, though I can't yet tell just what it is I sense about him; we'll have to let him recover before he's quizzed or scrutinized for such information, even by me. But: when I finally got my turn to speak to him—just before Bob got back with the trundle and carted him away—he gave me a long, tight hug (during which dirt and tears from his face got transferred to mine) and then laid his hand flat on my tummy and said, first thing: "How's the baby, is he OK? I hope all this fuss isn't too bad for him," and smiled beatifically, as if he thought "the baby" were the greatest thing in the world. The boy who left us last January could not have handled himself like that.

All things considered, and despite my misgivings about the element of *extremeness* in his relationship with George, it does seem to bode well.

I must get myself off to work now, but wanted to set down these impressions before they could fade. One of these days, or years, I'm sure I'll be glad to have made a contemporary record.

FROM GEORGE QUINLAN'S PERSONAL JOURNAL:
SIXDAY, 30 AUGUST 2234

We flew Danny and Joel up to the lake yesterday afternoon and left them there for a week of R&R. It was a wrench; even now I can hardly bear to let my son out of my sight. But nobody begrudges the boys this vacation smack in the middle of harvest-home, least of all me. Joel's cast came off only a week ago. He's still pretty stiff, and lots of swimming will do him more good than anything. As for Danny, not only has he been carrying his full share of field work for the past month; he's put up with weeks and weeks of being stuck full of needles and tubes with admirable patience (as has Jack Wister) in the interests of scientific inquiry and the future of the human race on Pennterra. He's earned a break.

Byron rode up in the fourth saddle. He asked particularly to come, saying he wanted to speak with KliUrrh. He didn't tell me what they talked about, and I didn't ask, but I'm sure it's to do with the small-machine experiments under way this week at the Sixer site in the lower valley, where Jack will be spending *his* equally well-earned week off. Joel sailed himself across to the village; Danny and I, of course, meant to swim; but I assumed Byron would ride over with Joel in the boat. Not a bit of it: he plunged right in and swam along with us. He and I sailed back together in a silence far more companionable than I'd have expected, and I found myself liking the guy for his own sake at last, and not just for helping bring the kids out safely or helping Danny cope with the death of that poor sad little girl.

Danny knows that if Caddie had stayed with the lander she would probably have been all right, and if he hadn't spoken up for her the adults might have decided to make her stay. That would be a hard thing for anybody to live with, and was a pure torment to Danny for a while; but Byron kept telling him, very patiently, over and over till he more or less believed it, that *none* of them knew the odds—that it might have been the walkers who were saved and the stayers who died, if their luck had run another way, and that he, Byron, had had the final say and had decided to let her come.

It's the pathos of Caddie's death that hurts Danny most, the lost chance to make a happier life for herself with us, after all her unhappiness at home. But neither Byron nor I nor anyone can help him see that in a different light, because her lost chance truly is pathetic. And we are all pained and saddened as well to think that our first death on the new world should be the death of a child.

I've been charged by the meeting to compose an account of the events of the spring and summer, and given a day off to do it in, but I'm going to put a fuller account of matters both public and personal into this record and decide afterward which parts to excerpt for public consumption. I haven't been writing much in here; why let the meeting underwrite my own records of events, if they get what they want in the end?

The thing they want most, naturally, is an account of the Disaster—a narrative "lay" account to supplement the technical reports still being filed by Alice and Tony, and by Maggie and her lab staff. Undoubtedly somebody over there will have been putting a report like this together too, but the meeting wants us to have our own, and I quite agree that it's an excellent idea.

Chronologically then:

Sometime early in the spring—I don't recall exactly when, but we'd just started to plant, so probably the first week of April or thereabouts—Maggie Smithson got on the radio and told me that the Sixers were being plagued by a mysterious epidemic of spontaneous abortions. She wanted to know whether we had experienced anything of the kind; I told her we hadn't and suggested that she might do well to consider the problem in the light of a warning from the hrossa. Maggie was very hostile to the suggestion, as she was to any idea of asking the hrossa for information—so much so as to make me suspect that her resistance might be more emotional than scientific. I knew that the encounter with the hross elders last summer had upset her profoundly. She advanced plausible reasons for excluding them from council, but those mightn't have been the real reasons. So I thought at the time, and so Katy thought when we talked it over.

Many of us in Swarthmore were passionately interested in Sixertown's problem, since any difficulties experienced there, which we had avoided, might be a clue as to what was going to happen. The Sixers, however, took no more heed than Maggie had of the warning, and viewed the problem as pointing to itself alone, rather than beyond itself. They were very concerned and exercised, but not afraid.

We bided our time. Weeks of persistent effort on the parts of Maggie and her people resulted finally in the isolation of a complex inorganic compound, found in the creek that supplied the temporary town with water for drinking and other purposes. By the time she succeeded in identifying this compound (see Alice's report for its chemical and physical properties) there wasn't a pregnant woman left in the town, and some of the animals had also begun to be affected. Once the compound had been identified it was a simple enough matter to rig a filtering system for the water intended for human and livestock consumption. The system worked fine. The abortifacient is a big molecule, a straight shaft curled at one end like a buttonhook; and that, alas, is what they began to call the stuff. On purified water the hens started laying fertile eggs again almost at once, and by early June a few Sixer women had become pregnant. There could then be no real doubt that the culprit was buttonhook, that it came from the creek, and that it could be eliminated by a bothersome but essentially simple filtering procedure.

Now, this was all very well, but questions remained: where had the stuff come from in the first place? Why had it appeared in the Sixertown creek but not in our own creeks or in the Delaware? There was as yet no sign of it in the river on both sides of which the permanent town was being built, but neither had there been any sign of it in the creek before the temporary town had been put there. Identifying the compound had been so difficult at first partly because it was sometimes, but not always, present in the water; but they continued to monitor the creek, taking hourly samples and so on, and by June 1 the samples all had plenty of buttonhook in them and they were having to clean the filters every day.

Since the Sixers were still not looking out for signs of larger trouble brewing, this problem continued to be a vexing rather than a portentous one from their point of view. But from ours—that is, the half or so of Swarthmore that took the hrossa seriously—it seemed ominous indeed, and in due course I observed to Maggie that the abortifacient bore a remarkable likeness to the antibodies, or perhaps the phagocytes, that an organism produces to deal with a local infection. But her resistance was stronger than ever, and so there was nothing for it but to continue the watch from afar and wait for the situation to develop or resolve itself one way or another.

On the first of June the waiting ended. On that day, during regular Firstday meeting for worship, we received a sending from Lake-Between-Falls village linked with three other villages, to the effect that Danny and Jack should be pulled out of Sixertown forthwith because it would be too dangerous for them to stay longer. A party of three hrossa from a village somewhere northeast of Sixertown also set off for the town that day, arriving on June 2, to warn Danny personally of the risk to himself and Jack of remaining any longer. The following day the boys left; but the

Sixer lander they were traveling in developed engine trouble and was forced to make a crash landing in a heavily forested area well inland of the normal flyway between the two settlements.

The weeks following the lander's disappearance were entirely given over to intensive searching both by us and by the Sixers. Little investigation of the buttonhook problem was carried on by anybody during that period, not least because the chief researcher, Maggie Smithson, was among those lost in the Pennterran wilds. Certainly we were all made aware that the *only* disaster that seemed to have befallen Sixertown, after the boys left it, was the crash itself—and that that, ironically enough, had been the direct result of our insisting on getting our kids *out* of danger.

I should refer in passing, at least, to the fact that my confidence in KliUrrh's wisdom had been desperately shaken by the crash of the lander—by the fact that he had not foreseen the possibility of Danny's being hurt through the mechanical failure of a machine. In retrospect I can't explain how I could have held KliUrrh accountable for not thinking of that, since I hadn't thought of it myself despite having far more reason to; but at the time I could only see that he had promised Danny would be all right if I let him go, and I blamed him for the crash precisely as if he were God. I must have been quite literally out of my mind, beside myself with worry and grief, to fall into such a quagmire of irrationality. The meeting was unable to support me, by itself, through the near-certainty that I'd lost Danny *and* that KliUrrh had betrayed my faith in him. I'm not as tough as Job, not by a long shot. Nor am I the true-blue Quaker I fondly believed I was. If I'd been right about both those things, instead of wrong about both, I doubt I'd be here now.

But as I was saying: during much of June the energies of both communities were, first, absorbed in the search, and then engaged in cheering on the recovery of the five survivors. Both towns also had to come to terms with the trauma of Caddie Birtwistle's death. All this coincided with a period of peak agricultural activity, and we were well into July before rumors of further trouble in Sixertown reached us here.

Maggie and Byron had flown home on July 2. A week or so thereafter I got a message asking me to return a call from Maggie by the 2000 satellite (that's Sixertime). When I got through, she asked what seemed a peculiar question: How were our *bees* faring? Were the hives all right?

I'm allergic to bee venom and not involved in honey production, so I couldn't tell her anything then and there, except that I'd not heard about any difficulties. I promised to check and call her back; and I did, the following day.

When I reported that all our hives appeared to be bustling and healthy Maggie fell silent, then burst out with the news that all the Sixertown hives—*all* of them!—were ailing or dying outright. Several dozen hives had been quickened in very early spring and fed on sugar water and then red clover when that bloomed, and had seemed well established by the time the field crops dependent on bees for fertilization were coming into flower; but within a week or so of that time it was obvious that something must be badly amiss. The individual bees seemed healthy enough but there were far too few of them—the workers weren't being replaced.

Each hive had started out with about 20,000 adult bees and had grown to 50,000 or so by the middle of June. As the food supply increased in the field, the hives should have rapidly built up strength from there. But instead, after a few weeks the numbers appeared to be dropping sharply. When the beekeepers opened the hives they found sheet after sheet of brood comb full of unhatched eggs—and *no* grubs, none at all! And every egg in every hive laid after the first generation of field bees had got seriously down to work in the clover, and after honey made from clover nectar was fed to the queens, was infertile.

The hives had been supplied with filtered water, but there was of course no way to prevent the bees from drinking in the fields. Maggie had been surprised enough to discover that the same compound had been able to cause sterility in species as diverse as humans, rabbits, and chickens; the thought that it could also cause sterility in insects flabbergasted her, and in fact she was extremely skeptical that all this sterility *could* be traced to a common source. She took fluid samples from the rabbits and chickens that had been kept on unfiltered water as a control, and some samples from moribund bees, and set up a rigorous comparative study to see whether buttonhook molecules were actually present in all three.

By the time she got conclusive results it was late July. By then, in desperation, the whole town had turned out and was hand-pollinating acres and acres of potatoes, soybeans, and safflower. It must have been quite a sight. I'm sure they thanked their stars that cereal crops are fertilized by the wind. Several more new hives had been quickened, and these they put into the garden plots. Honeybees work themselves to death in a few weeks but they managed to time the quickenings to coincide with the peak blossomtime of the bean, tomato, and pepper varieties that ripen all at once, in the hope of saving as much garden produce as possible. The varieties that flower over a longer season would have to be written off, or else the town would have to fall back on hand-pollinating throughout the rest of the growing season—not a pleasant prospect.

Maggie's study had identified *three* varieties of the same sterilizing compound, what might be termed galliform, lepine, and apine buttonhook; and the day she saw those three molecules for herself was the day she finally had to consider that the hross warning might indeed be relevant to the buttonhook enigma.

Around the same time, the first woman to conceive in the second round of pregnancies miscarried. She had *not* been drinking unfiltered water. She had, however—like everyone else—been eating lettuce, spinach, radishes, and onions from the gardens—all of which were found to contain the basic form of buttonhook. Tests revealed human buttonhook, a fourth variety, in her blood, urine, saliva, lymph, and tears.

Soil samples from the gardens and fields were found to contain basic buttonhook—lots of it.

By this time the Sixers were frantic. Maggie says she was not even surprised when they discovered that none but the very earliest-flowering plants had set fruit, that all those wide acres of field crops so laboriously hand-pollinated were barren. It wasn't that they'd done the job badly, either, because the oats, wheat, rye, barley, field corn, and sweet corn had all also failed completely to head up. The individual plants were vigorous, grew beautifully, budded and bloomed at the proper time—but that was the end of it. The foliage and root crops did very well but produced no seed when they bolted or bloomed. Maggie, her staff, and a battery of botanists did extensive testing of pollen, ovaries, and leaf tissue—and everything they looked at was full of buttonhook—everything! Under lab conditions, as in the field, they could *not* get a pollen grain to fertilize an ovum; the two halves of the chromosomes would not fuse, though each appeared to be undamaged.

The rabbits and poultry reverted to sterility. The tank fish failed to spawn. The earthworms produced no eggs. Three more women had miscarriages. The larger stock had been on pasture all summer; nobody supposed they could be bred successfully in the fall. Apart from the early clover there was going to be no seed to speak of from the first season, no new generations of animals or bees—or people. The only decent harvest will be of tubers and roots: sugar beets, carrots, onions, turnips, sweet and white potatoes. The hay did well, luckily.

Every individual organism, be it human or parsnip, can apparently live out its own life in a state of perfect health and vigor over there, supposing it can nourish itself; what it cannot do is reproduce—*nothing* that reproduces sexually can do so in the presence of buttonhook! Though we don't know yet why not, I expect an answer will be found pretty soon; but whether a remedy will be found soon, or ever, I very much doubt.

So that is Tanka Wakan's "destruction"; and a thorough and decisive job he's made of it too.

In the final days it began to emerge that the individual organism was also to be deprived of the ability to *go through the motions* of reproducing. Various Sixers began to admit to each other that their sex drive had dropped to zero. Then somebody noticed that the roosters had stopped mounting the hens. Somebody else put a buck rabbit in with a doe: nothing. The Sixer women have continued to ovulate (and to menstruate), just as the Sixer tomato plants have continued to form and open blossoms, but desire has gone the way of fertility.

That did it. A week ago, on August 22, Captain Harrison formally requested that his people be granted permission to relocate the town on the lower Delaware River, beginning immediately. The next morning the meeting sent me up to see the hross elders, and when I returned we radioed the Sixers and told them they would be more than welcome.

That diplomatic mission was my first visit to the village in over a month, so there was a lot to tell KliUrrh. By the time I finished—we were sitting on the beach, I'd brought along an inflatable cushion—he was giving out deep waves of what I think I'd have to call aesthetic appreciation and pleasure. He said: "It is perfect, Friend George, don't you agree? To disrupt between the parent and the child…it is exactly the way." I hadn't thought of the sterility in those terms, but once he'd reminded me, in effect, that Pennterra is a world where all of life turns upon the sacredness, or at least primacy, of the parent-offspring bond and its succession, it did indeed seem to be a perfectly appropriate sort of "destruction," beside which an earthquake or a plague of vermin would have looked crude. What we don't know now, but may know someday, is why they had to be destroyed; but the method of destruction has Tanka Wakan's tracks all over it, and that clinches *that* connection for me. As for why he did it: for my part I suspect that Tanka Wakan is a Luddite and knows a bad lot when he see one—or a rival power. There will be no monster disc harrows or backhoes in the lower valley.

ON JUNE 19, the day after Danny's return, I had flown up to the lake to say that he was safe and well—and also to apologize to KliUrrh for my inexpressible folly. Never having fallen out with him before, I didn't know what sort of reception to expect. But he was merely relieved to see I had come to my senses, and really overjoyed at my news. In fact the whole village was rapturous, and cavorted around like the breeding season had come.

When things had settled down some I asked KliUrrh to walk up the beach with me, as there was something I wanted to ask him. That morning Danny had described to me how he had "hunted" and killed native animals in the hross manner, and how he and Jack had evidently been able to digest the meat, or digest it partially—well enough at least to make a crucial difference to their getting out alive. I asked KliUrrh if he had known they would be able to do this—if that was what he'd meant when he told me that if Danny were alive on the ground, Tanka Wakan would not let him die.

KliUrrh replied that this was like the question of the Sixer's destruction. He knew Tanka Wakan would destroy them; he knew Danny would be kept safe; but no *means* were specified in these convictions. But he was as unsurprised, and nearly as pleased, to learn how Tanka Wakan had preserved Danny's life as he was to learn a week ago how the Sixers had been stopped cold.

Yesterday I was able to tell him that Alice thinks she may have found a particle that produces an enzyme-like substance in the human gut, and which she thinks may be activated by hormones in some way to begin producing the enzyme at the onset of puberty. It's hard as yet to draw firm conclusions. Obviously, Jack and Danny are so far the only Friends to have gone through puberty here, *and* the only ones able to utilize the native life-forms as food. But there are too many variables: they're also the only Friends who've lived more than a few weeks outside the valley, been stressed by near-starvation, made a journey on foot across the planet's surface, etc., etc. Certainly nobody who arrived here *after* the onset of puberty can digest the leaves Alice keeps mak-

ing us eat, and neither can the children. But the Shippen twins are
shooting up fast, so in a year of two we'll see.

Alice doesn't care one way or the other about the aesthetics of
it all, but if she should happen to be on the right track then the
human child would become both a breeder and an adopted
member of the planetary ecology at the same time, and that's
aesthetically pleasing to *me*. (And to KliUrrh.) Anyway, she's
found something in all our alimentary tracts, as well as in water
and soil samples throughout the settlement, which she thinks
may be the relevant stuff. No cutesy name for it as yet—Tanka
Wakan defend us from another "buttonhook"!—because she's
still a long way from sure, but she thinks the indications are
strong.

KliUrrh was much less interested in *how* the thing is done than
in the fact that it's done at all—he is no scientist!—but he certainly does not doubt that if Tanka Wakan were pleased with us,
and wished to, he could devise a means of bringing us more fully
into the family: of *pennterraforming* us, as Katy insists on calling it. I asked him whether he thinks the Sixer kids might be
adopted too. He said they certainly might if their community
learns how to live appropriately here. If TW can tailor varieties
of buttonhook to suit the biochemistries of species ranging from
pollen-making plants to human beings, he can do what he likes
with us, I expect. For kids as old as Joel was when he landed it's
probably too late, though—bad luck for poor Joel, who'd *love*
to be pennterraformed.

Then KliUrrh added—offhandedly, as if I were as aware of this
as he—that it's hardly likely the Sixers will have more children
now.

Until he said that I'd assumed that the infertility was a revers-
ible condition, that once the Sixers had submitted to the house
rules they'd be good as new in a little while. Weren't there several new pregnancies after the creek water began to be filtered?
KliUrrh agreed that it might be so. Yet the reason the hrossa had
been so urgent about getting Danny and Jack away from Sixertown was the danger of their being permanently damaged—ren-
dered sterile and sexually numb, as it now appears—had they
stayed any longer in that toxic place. We were watching the kids
play in the lake, and KliUrrh expressed his satisfaction that old
KahEemh had helped to get Joel away as well, because (he said)
now Joel can sport with the breeders, come autumn, just as
Danny will.

The implications for the Sixers if KliUrrh is correct are dire, but I didn't want to dampen the celebratory atmosphere by pursuing the thought just then. The air above the shallows near the shore was full of those beautiful blue flies that light on the hrossa when they're wet, and I remembered then that Jack had been "bitten" by one on the march and that Byron had showed me the dead fly, which he'd kept. I'd forgotten to tell KliUrrh about the incident, and did so then.

And I dampened the atmosphere after all. When I described how Jack had instinctively slapped the guilty fly and killed it, KliUrrh instantly became sad, saying he hoped such incidents would be few, though some were probably inevitable during the period of transition. I made some remark about this being the only instance thus far of a Pennterran creature inflicting harm on a human. To my surprise KliUrrh demurred. The fly, he said, does no harm. It takes a very little blood, as a hross might collect a few leaves from a plant—not nearly enough to hurt the donor. But surely, I rejoined, the pain itself is harmful?

After some time and confusion it finally emerged that "pain" in Hross—the word, the concept—refers exclusively to emotional or mental distress. What a Pennterran organism feels if pinned by a falling tree is not called *pain*, though pain may follow after it realizes the extent of the damage—that it may be crippled or unable to survive the accident. But only the consequences are painful, not the blow.

I could scarcely believe that in all these years we had failed to discover such an essential difference. Surely one or another of us must have stubbed a toe or had a headache or gotten sunburned in KliUrrh's presence before now! But apparently he just hadn't realized that our experience of emotional pain differs in kind from our experience of physical pain; both sorts appear to have the same empathic value. I hit my hand against a rock to test the hypothesis. He said the feeling of distress came through indistinguishable from minor distress about anything else—say, that Danny was getting too much sun. We were mutually nonplussed.

When the dragonflies extract a little blood from a hross, they cause the hross no pain whatever, and there's no itching or bleeding afterward. The fly that bit Jack would not have known it was hurting him until after it had bitten him; it recognized him as a source of nourishment, sensed his benevolent attitude toward it, and acted accordingly. It must have bitten Jack instead of Danny for some reason, perhaps because Jack had fallen in the creek where they were wading and was wet all over. Since Jack can eat a native creature, it's fitting that a native creature can now eat some of him. Though it might choose not to: KliUrrh asked if Jack had been bitten again and I said no. The "pain" message got through, then, before the fly died for its innocent mistake—got through, that is, to the other flies. Or maybe they bite only benevolent donors, which Jack had ceased to be.

It must be that the empathic capacity does the self-protective job of pain. And there's physical *feeling*, after all; a hross would know if his foot was in the fire. What stuns me, what I marvel at, is the realization that the creatures of this world are able to confront their deaths quite free of BOTH elements that make death so difficult, for us and for all earthly life: pain, and the fear that is mental anguish. Few of us make it all the way through our deaths without first grappling with one or (usually) both of those in the process, and would it were not so.

THE SIXERS WILL DISMANTLE the domiciles and transport them by lander to the valley, just as they were transported down from the ship. The new town will be established at the juncture of the Delaware and Lost Boys Creek—a better site than ours, truth to tell. The river's tidal almost up to there, but the creek has more water in it than the river does at Swarthmore. And the Delaware is navigable from that point to the coast—handy for salt-getting.

Their permanent town, now all but finished, though still nameless, will have to be abandoned. They'll try to salvage the materials bit by bit, over time. Alice badly wants to set up a station at the site of the double towns, it's such a perfect chance to find out how plants and animals colonize a disturbed area, without doing any additional ecological damage ourselves. She has an idea that fertile seeds may lose their bitterness and so be eaten and excreted under those specific circumstances, making distribution faster—a benevolence, as it were, on the part of the seeds. There won't be another chance as good as this to find out, but I doubt the meeting will give permission all the same—too expensive to keep a station supplied at that distance, even if the hrossa were to decide it wasn't a slight but significant violation of the genius loci.

The two communities are to keep apart for the time being and wait and see about the future. (But note: Bob Wellwood was electrified to hear that the Sixers' Section Chief of Food Processing is a beautiful young, female, full-blooded Sioux Indian named Elizabeth Two Clouds!) Already the Sixers' radio signals to Earth have been altered, and now that our two voices are in accord it must be true beyond question or hope that no more humans will be coming here, and no New World be built in our own image. That's both a relief and a deep grief, but the main thing is that it's *finished*, so I needn't be torn two ways about it anymore.

Nor about Danny, not now. I can regard him in the full knowledge that he's no longer entirely human—or is human with something distinctively alien added to the mix—and yet feel at peace. I'm sure I'm not the first to learn that there's nothing like nearly losing a child to make a parent content with him as he is, and not as the parent would have him be. Not merely resigned, as I had already become, but honestly content.

It's also a fact that the more hross elements he internalizes, the more unique importance I acquire in his life; thus am I compensated for my loss.

I'm aware that since getting his strength back he's been sexually active with various friends in the settlement: Katy certainly, perhaps Joel, Maggie a time or two (?)—and yes, also with me. I've ceased to resist that as well, though I'll never be comfortable with it—with the idea of it; I'm comfortable enough with the doing. Danny has a much deeper understanding of my earlier resistance now, because of Caddie. But he is now a sexual creature in a sense I can never become or wish to become, responsive at that level in a dozen directions at once but incapable (as I now believe) of "falling in love" with one woman and forging the unique exclusive bond of a good marriage—a marriage like mine with his mother, or the sort I might have made with Maggie. (Or might still?) I do mind on his account; he doesn't seem to mind on his own. How much of my minding about Danny, I wonder, has been envy all along? Though his sense of connectedness with Katy's baby is very strong, I'm certain he's not in love with Katy. But Byron is, I think, and if he converts and settles with us, as seems likely, something like a "real" marriage may come of that. We are none of us as quick to dismiss Byron as we were a year ago.

But I'm rambling and gossiping, and it's time I wound this up.

We have to suppose now that Danny and Jack may prove to be the first of a new kind of human, no longer confined to this valley but able to move freely about the surface of the world because the world has told them, in effect: *You're one of us now.*

If that's so, then the pennterraformed kids will have to develop their own place in the planetary ecology. Danny represents an extreme degree of single-generation adaptation relative to Jack, owing to his having come under the influence of the hrossa—he is already not only biologically but culturally tailored to fit the situation here. The other kids certainly needn't go as far as Danny has, but from now on it'll be an option.

Joel, for instance, will have chosen the cultural route even if the full biological one turns out not to be available to him—that is, if he never is able to put flokh leaves into his salads. Joel's views on sex and marriage haven't settled out yet, but he's certainly been influenced by Danny's views already, and a dose of the breeding season at Lake-Between-Falls is bound to affect him. I hope against hope that more of the Sixer kids than Joel will grow up able to have kids of their own, for the human gene pool's sake and for the sake of Sixer community morale over the long haul; but only time will tell.

Despite the hardships we are certain to undergo, the failure of our mission which is now absolute, the trauma which the Sixers must endure and the immense labor they face now in starting over to create a new settlement by unfamiliar and hateful means—despite all that, I feel pretty optimistic about our presence and our future here. God knows why! At least we all know enough now to know our limits.

This morning as we stood together by the lake and watched the boys playing in the water with SwikhKarrh—three handsome lively breeders from our three communities of mutually unconfiding sapients—KliUrrh said to me, "Only think if the Earth had had the power and the wisdom to say to your parents' parents: *You may not do this. If you do this, you will die.*"

If only our parents' parents had known how to pray without ceasing, as these hrossa do. It's a thought I've had before; but there's no going back from that fouling of our own nest. And we won't be allowed to foul KliUrrh's—so I believe, though I write this knowing full well that human nature must always be trying to have the upper hand, even of Tanka Wakan.